SALERNO

Also by Eric Morris

Corregidor: The End of the Line
The Russian Navy: Myth and Reality
Blockade: Berlin and the Cold War

SALERNO

A military fiasco

ERIC MORRIS

STEIN AND DAY/Publishers/New York

FIRST STEIN AND DAY PAPERBACK EDITION 1984
Salerno was first published in hardcover
by Stein and Day/*Publishers* in 1983.

Copyright © 1983 by Eric Morris
All rights reserved, Stein and Day, Incorporated
Designed by Louis Ditizio
Printed in the United States of America
STEIN AND DAY/*Publishers*
Scarborough House
Briarcliff Manor, N.Y. 10510
ISBN 0-8128-8105-2

To the Men Who Fought at Salerno

ACKNOWLEDGMENTS

I owe a personal debt of gratitude to so many people who have helped in writing this account. First to the veterans, British and American, who fought at Salerno. It was not possible to include all their stories in the book, but there are so many who shared their experiences of the battle with me. They invited me into their homes, and for all their kindness and hospitality, my heartfelt thanks. Where their memory grew hazy over the details of events that happened forty years ago, many veterans sent me articles and newspaper clippings that were written nearer the time, with permission to use at my discretion. In the United States the 36th and 45th divisions' associations were especially cooperative and forthcoming in my researches and interviews. They welcomed me to their reunions and gave me every assistance. I am proud to be an honorary member of their associations. I am especially grateful to the Fort Worth "trio" of Bob Wallace, Bill Jary, and Bert Carlton, and in Oklahoma City to Bob Armstrong and Pendleton Woods. Vince Lockhart in El Paso has been a mine of information on the historical details of the "T" Patchers.

In the United Kingdom many of the regiments and corps represented at Salerno have been most responsive to my requests for advice and assistance. I am especially indebted to the Royal Regiment of Fusiliers, the Mediterranean Landing Craft Association, the Royal Engineers, and to the Commando Association for allowing me to advertise my research in their journals.

Michael Howard, Regius Professor of Modern History at Oxford, served as a lieutenant in the Coldstream Guards at Salerno. He has given me invaluable help and allowed me to use a number of documents and papers, including the journal that was kept by Lieutenant Leeke of the Grenadier Guards.

Lionel Daiches, prosecuting counsel; William Murgatroyd, defense counsel; and Allan Patient, a producer at the BBC, were of considerable assistance in my researches into the episode of the Salerno Mutiny.

John Hunt, librarian, and his staff at the Central Library, Royal Military Academy, patiently met all my requests for books and documents. My own colleagues in the Department of War Studies and International Affairs were always on hand with help and advice, especially David Chandler, John Keegan, Richard Holmes, John Pimlott, and Keith Simpson.

Dr. John J. Slonaker, chief of the Historical Reference Section, U.S. Army Military History Institute at Carlisle Barracks, has been most helpful as always in my research.

Mrs. Dorothy Fox transcribed the hundreds of hours of tapes and typed a manuscript from my handwriting, which continues to be almost illegible. David Carl of Camberley Travel Agents Ltd. arranged my flights and handled with cool efficiency and calm the frantic last-minute changes caused by the air traffic controllers' dispute.

My publishers, Sol Stein and Patricia Day in Briarcliff Manor, New York, and Jim Cochrane of Hutchinson in London, have given me inspiration and support throughout the project. Patricia Day's careful editing has once again improved my manuscript beyond measure.

Last but by no means least, my wife, Pamela, and my family have shown patience and sympathy and given all their encouragement in the writing of the book.

E.M.

CONTENTS

LIST OF ILLUSTRATIONS

LIST OF MAPS

FOREWORD

The Isole Eolie O Lipari are a group of volcanic islands that lie in the Tyrrhenian Sea, some thirty miles off the northern coast of Sicily. In Greek mythology they were the home of Aeolus, King of the Winds; hence their alternative name of the Aeolian Islands. In September 1943 they were the rendezvous for the Allied invasion force heading for Salerno.

The sea was mirror calm and the weather perfect on September 7 as the first convoys gathered. There were Americans and British, Free Poles and Royal Dutch ships, too, in that huge armada of seven hundred ships of all shapes and sizes. The vast majority, especially the landing craft and attack transports, had sailed from ports in North Africa. All of these ships had been at sea long enough for the soldiers and sailors to paint the appropriate divisional emblems on the bows. Cheers and jeers echoed across the water as the Black Cat and Oak of Sherwood, Texas "T," or the Oklahoma Indian hove into sight. There were some convoys of freighters that had brought their cargos of war materiel direct from ports on the Eastern Seaboard of the United States and from Britain. These ships and their escorts bore the scars of a long and dangerous sea voyage with new salt-encrusted upper works and rust-streaked hulls.

At first all was confusion, but eventually the convoys were arranged into their new order, and the long, majestic columns set course directly for Salerno. The sailors and passengers gazed in wonder at such a picture of military might. The lines of ships stretched from horizon to horizon. Their invasion of Europe and the great adventure had begun.

The spectacular island of Stromboli, most northerly in the Lipari chain, passed by to starboard, and the ships headed into the Tyrrhenian Sea. Around them the destroyers and sloops creamed the waters into crazy patterns as they shepherded their flocks from the threat of U-boat and Luftwaffe. Just above the horizon wary Luftwaffe Junker 88 reconnaissance aircraft shadowed the convoys despite the efforts of the carrierborne Royal Navy Seafires to see them off. The old Mediterranean hands knew the pattern of events by heart; after the reconnaissance planes the Luftwaffe would appear in force. Soon the air above would fill to the banshee wail of the Stukas; anti-aircraft guns quartered the sky in anticipation. Word had also been relayed from Allied headquarters in North Africa that the picket submarine H.M.S. *Shakespeare* had torpedoed a U-boat off Capri, and there were known to be more in the area.

The decks of the transports and landing craft swarmed with soldiers. There were 30,000 of them from the four assault divisions and the special forces. Stripped to the waist, they clambered into rigging, onto deckhouses, superstructure, and lifeboats—indeed, anywhere to find a space in the fresh air and away from the fetid smells of the crowded accommodations below. Some wrote home, a last letter before the landings; many checked their weapons and attended final briefings. The majority just lazed around until it was time to stand in line for the next meal. They played cards, threw dice, and watched the smudged shadows that were the mountain fastness of Calabria where, so their officers had told them, General Montgomery's veteran British Eighth Army was already battling its way northward, having crossed from Messina a few days earlier. What they did not know was that that army had already run into trouble; the mountains and the Germans had slowed their rate of advance to a crawl. Those mountains should by now have been in Allied hands, but they weren't; and it was the enemy who monitored the sedate progress of the convoys up the coast of Italy and probably breathed a sigh of relief as the armada passed by.

The naval veterans had the timing wrong in their predictions because it wasn't until the late afternoon of Wednesday, September 8, that the Luftwaffe made its first serious attempt to contest the passage of the convoys. The once clear blue skies became pockmarked with bursting shells while Royal Navy Seafires flying the Combat Air Patrols (CAP) from the escorting carriers, oblivious of their own flak, tore into the attacking bombers. The soldiers grabbed their helmets and found what cover they could as the first shrapnel fell about their ears. Hulls vibrated to the bursting bombs, and a landing craft burned.

There was something very wrong. The Americans in the army had been told their operation was to be a surprise attack. How come the Luftwaffe seemed to know?

Just by the island of Capri the first ships in the Northern or British Attack Force, oblivious to their foe, turned in toward the shore. The Southern Task Force, carrying the American divisions, kept Point Licosia, the southern extremity of Salerno Bay, off their starboard bow and likewise headed toward the beaches. Flotillas of minesweepers moved ahead to clear the waters of Salerno Bay.

Why did the Allies choose Salerno? It all began perhaps with Operation Husky in July 1943 and the landings in Sicily. At that time the Allies were of one mind, and the objective was clear; for the conquest of Sicily marked the logical culmination of the campaigns fought in North Africa. Once Sicily had been secured, the sea routes through the Mediterranean were guaranteed, and the Allies could move resources eastward to support the Soviets via the Persian Gulf and Iran, as well as to fight the Japanese in Asia. Where next? This was the dilemma that filled the agendas of innumerable conferences throughout the summer of that year. The British and Americans could not agree. The former favored a maritime strategy and turned their attentions to the opportunities presented in Italy and the Balkans and perhaps even to enticing the Turks to declare war on the Axis. The British found the idea of moving against the Balkans particularly attractive. A campaign there would deny the Germans vital raw materials, menace Axis lines of communication to the Russian Front, demoralize Hitler's eastern allies, and encourage insurrection in Greece as well as in Yugoslavia. Washington was not impressed. The Americans were convinced of one thing, however: No new campaign should eat into those resources already earmarked for the second front, in northwestern Europe, or undermine a vigorous pursuit of the war in the Far East. The Americans were anxious to close down the northern shores of the Mediterranean as an active theater of operations. It was a military cul-de-sac. In the "ledger" of grand strategy the liabilities far outweighed the assets.

While the debate, often acrimonious, waged, the campaign in Sicily spluttered to its inevitable conclusion, and the Allies' opportunities for bold action were lost. Confusing the issues were the top-heavy and politically tortuous command structure in the Mediterranean theater and the presence of powerful personalities and prima donna generals. If those factors weren't enough, the Italians put out peace feelers in July, and the clandestine negotiations that followed provided an air of uncertainty and unreality to the military planners.

The Soviets too were demanding that the Anglo-Americans honor the Soviet sacrifice in blood and territory by making a greater contribution to the war effort, land on the mainland of Europe, and tie down the German divisions in the west.

With the resources available in what remained of the "campaign season" for amphibious warfare, Italy was the only theater that presented the opportunity to reconcile the demands of all the protagonists, East and West. The Anglo-Americans could land on the European mainland and prevent the Wehrmacht from being moved to the Eastern Front; and if the Americans ran the show the British couldn't run away with the campaign and use those resources that were already dedicated for the second front. The result was a compromise; it was called Salerno.

The Fifth Army, which started out as an American Army, was given the task of landing at Salerno. It had been in existence only since January, and its headquarters was the first to be established outside the United States. Salerno was to be the Fifth Army's first experience in combat. Previously the headquarters of the Fifth Army had been responsible for the backwaters of war; it had control over the North African population outside the immediate battle area. Its only operational role had been to use its I Armored Corps in Morocco, under General Patton, to guard against any attempt by Fascist Spain to attack the Allies from its African colonies.

Once the North African campaign had been concluded, the Fifth Army became an immense training organization. Under its direction a host of establishments and bases were created to prepare all the Allied formations who came into the theater for the invasion of Europe.

The army was commanded by Lt. Gen. Mark Wayne Clark, a graduate of West Point, whose previous combat experience was spread over a few short weeks in World War I. Clark was a squad leader until wounded in 1918. After 1940 Clark's rise to high command had, like that of his close friend Eisenhower, been meteoric. Clark had served on the staff of Lt. Gen. Lesley J. McNair during the mobilization of the army in 1940-41 and had risen in rank with the expanding forces. Clark came overseas first as a corps commander and then as deputy commander-in-chief of the forces that took part in the North African landings. Clark hankered for command; Eisenhower gave him the Fifth Army upon its creation. Clark then pestered his chief for action, for Clark was a man of action. He had landed in a "cloak and dagger" mission prior to the North African landings to negotiate with the Vichy French. Now that he had a command of his own, it could not remain a backwater rear-area duty; it had to be combat.

From the outset General Clark was convinced that this was to be a "young man's war." He was just 46 years of age, and he attempted to build a staff and subordinate command around him of like-minded men. The Fifth Army's chief of staff was Alfred Gruenther, at 43 years America's youngest major general and already known as the "brain of the army" because of his dazzling performance as a student at the various staff and war colleges. Gruenther fulfilled his potential, for after the war he followed in Eisenhower's footsteps as the Supreme Allied Commander Europe (SACEUR) in the North Atlantic Alliance.

Under command and immediately available for the landings Clark had two army corps—one British and the other American. Despite the fact that both speak the same language, the history and traditions of the formations are vastly different; neither do they share a common structure or organization. Some readers will be very familiar with the British regimental system or the American concept of the combat teams and need no further explanation. For other readers, however, I suspect that the arms and formations of the forces that live on the other side of the Atlantic is something new and perhaps even confusing. You will find in the Appendices an account of the structure and organization of all the major units, Allied and German, that fought at Salerno, together with some historical notes where appropriate.

Let me now present the fighting formations and introduce the British to you first, not because of my nationality, or that I teach at the Royal Military Academy, but because they were intended to have the major role in the battle, and there were more of them at Salerno.

The British X Corps contained two divisions. These were the 46th and 56th Infantry divisions. Both were fairly new to war, having been blooded in North Africa in different but equally unpleasant and bitter battles. The veteran 7th Armored Division, the original "desert rats" who had fought their way through the Western Desert from El Alamein, was available as the follow-up troops once the infantry had secured the beachhead. There were also some special forces—marine and army commandos from Britain and three battalions of United States rangers.

The American VI Corps had the 36th U.S. Infantry Division as its main spearhead or assault force. The 36th was one of the first National Guard divisions to be mobilized; it was tired of training and anxious to get on with the war. Their commander, Maj. Gen. Fred Walker, had nursed the division through all the traumas of early training, and although there had been many changes, over half of the men still came from Texas. Walker had been mortally offended when his division was passed over and other troops selected for the Allied landings in Sicily.

In support of the 36th at Salerno was the 45th Infantry Division, the Thunderbirds from Oklahoma. They had fought in Sicily under Patton, where some believed they had taken the dictates of "Blood and Guts" too much to heart. The Panzer Division Hermann Göring accused the Thunderbirds of shooting prisoners. This elite force of panzers was regrouping just north of Naples and anxious to square accounts with the Americans. The VI Corps had two other American divisions earmarked to land at Salerno once the beachhead had been secured. These were the 3rd Infantry and the 34th Infantry.

Commanding the VI Corps was a man in whom Mark Clark had little faith or confidence. Maj. Gen. Ernest J. Dawley had impressed Generals McNair and Marshall as a vigorous and aggressive officer, and McNair and Marshall were Clark's patrons. Dawley was a graduate of West Point, he had fought in the 1916 campaign in Mexico, and later he was a staff officer with Marshall in France. Dawley was now fifty-seven years of age and did not fit into Mark Clark's exacting requirements for the young man's war; Clark was convinced that Dawley was too old to cope with the stress of high command in combat for the first time. In addition, Dawley was a gunner by profession and so had little experience of the sort of war the infantry would have to fight.

The U.S. 82nd Airborne Division was also made available under the direct command and control of Mark Clark to use as he saw fit.

Italy from Rome southward was controlled by Field Marshal Kesselring, and the German Tenth Army garrisoned the mountain fastness of Calabria alongside their Italian allies. The Tenth Army was a new army. Hitler had sanctioned its existence on August 8, 1943, and its headquarters became operational just two weeks later. The Army commander was a *Generaloberst* (colonel general), one Heinrich Gottfried Von Vietinghoff Gennant Scheel, to give his full name. Unlike his American opponents, Von Vietinghoff had plenty of combat experience. He had commanded a Panzer division in Poland, served in the Balkans, and commanded a corps on the Russian Front. Before moving to Italy, Von Vietinghoff commanded an army of occupation in France.

An Italian coastal fortress division had the responsibility for defending Salerno Bay, but hovering in the same area was the Wehrmacht's 16th Panzer Division. The division had fought on the Russian Front until it was destroyed at Stalingrad. The new 16th Panzer Division was raised in France in March 1943 from those who had survived Stalingrad (the lucky ones who had been injured in battle and evacuated), veterans from other formations, and new draftees.

After the successful Allied invasion of Sicily the Germans drew up two sets of contingency plans. The first assumed that Italy would capitulate before the Allies invaded. In this instance the Germans were to disarm the Italians and withdraw immediately toward Rome. The second plan had as its premise an Allied invasion while the Italians were still Germany's cobelligerent. In this case the Germans would, with Italian support, repel the landings and retreat toward Rome.

At this stage of the war it was still Hitler's custom to grant an audience with his senior officers before they assumed a high command appointment. Von Vietinghoff discussed the operational plans for southern Italy when he met with Hitler on August 17. What was not discussed, because the Germans had not allowed for such a contingency, was a plan of action should the two events—an Allied invasion and an Italian capitulation—occur simultaneously. It happened at Salerno.

The Battleground

Some of the British divisions who fought the Italian campaign from beginning to end finished the war in Austria as forces of occupation. The 46th Infantry was such a division, and before it disbanded some thoughtful officer commissioned a history of their part in the war. Published in 1946, it provides a description of the battleground at Salerno that could have been written only by someone who was there:

> The Sele plain, which lay south of Salerno and was the selected place for the landings, stretched down to a twenty-three mile long sandy beach, cut up by the broad gravel channels of evenly spaced rivers and streams. Especially to the south, the plain was criss-crossed with irrigation canals and dykes. Moving inland—its greatest depth was sixteen miles—the ground rose in a

series of cultivated terraces mounting step-like to the circle of hills. It was an open countryside, except where thick orchards and olive groves provided a low screen of greenness, and from the hills the whole plain could be seen spread out to view against the blue sea. To the north bare brown hills closed down on the coast behind the flourishing seaside town of Salerno. Through this barrier of hills two steep-sided corridors led north towards Naples, the western corridor from Vietri, a little town jammed between rocky hills and the sea, through Cava, and the second itself to Sanseverino. For three miles south of Salerno there was only a narrow strip of flat, wooded country between the sea and the hills, and then the plain broadened out at the straggling town of Pontecagnano. Beyond Vietri the mountainous Sorrento peninsula jutted out to the west with its fringe of terraces and small resorts along the twisting coast road.

PART ONE

The Plan:

Naples in Five Days

"Why," Churchill asked, "crawl up the leg like a harvest bug from the ankle upwards? Let us strike at the knee."

—Churchill to Brook, July 1943
(Bryant, *Turn of the Tide*, p. 671)

Chapter I

It Was Called Operation Avalanche

Blue Salernian Bay with its sickle of white sand.
—Longfellow

For the Allies at Salerno only the weather was favorable.

Afterward they remembered those first hours as a tranquil and serene September night. But then, there is nothing as quiet as a battlefield before the battle. There was a brilliant moon with hardly a breath of wind or a ripple on the water in the bay. The landing craft, attack transports, and their attendant escorts, some seven hundred ships in all, had been gathering in the Tyrrhenian Sea since the early afternoon.

In the late evening the Northern Attack Group had begun its run into Salerno Bay. The force passed close by Capri and the peninsula of Sorrento on their port bow. It wasn't lost on the troops that if they could see Capri, then the enemy garrisons could see them. What chance now for the surprise landing that their army commander, General Mark Clark, had promised in their briefings in North Africa?

The three battalions of U.S. Rangers looked long and hard at Sorrento, for this was where they were to land in just a few hours. As night fell they could see the twinkling lights of Positano and the flares low on the water that were used by the fishermen from Amalfi. Casting a lurid red glow over the hills that towered behind the bay was impatient Vesuvius.

H.M.S. *Shakespeare* was the beacon submarine for the Southern or American Attack Force. From the Oerlikon platform behind the conning tower, Lt. Peter Matterson, R.E., watched through his binoculars as the big transports eased into their release points some twelve miles offshore. The submarine was positioned seven miles out, just on the seaward edge of the minefield that guarded Salerno Bay.

OPERATION

ANCHE

The engines gulped down great draughts of cool night air. The submarine had spent the daylight hours of the last week sitting on the sea bottom, waiting for the assault convoys.

Matterson was awaiting the arrival of the 36th Infantry Division. Their convoy, escorted by the six-inch cruisers U.S.S. *Savannah* and U.S.S. *Philadelphia* and attendant destroyers, had sailed from Oran and Algiers in North Africa on September 5. Their destination was supposed to be a closely guarded secret, but the Allies "sign-posted" their route all the way to Salerno. Allied security had been very poor in North Africa. Towns such as Avellino, Battipaglia, and Agropoli, all near to Salerno, were mentioned by name on an administrative order that was widely circulated among the Allied staffs from Casablanca to Alexandria. Those cities of North Africa, with their teeming cosmopolitan population, were rampant breeding grounds for espionage. While still in port it became something of a guessing game with the Northern Task Force (perhaps the *N* standing for Naples) and the Southern Task Force (*S* for Salerno)! It no longer became a guessing game when officers down to platoon and squad level were issued with 1:50,000 scale maps where the word *Salerno* had been cut out or obliterated. To preserve secrecy, none of the briefings for the troops was to take place until the ships were at sea, but the skippers of landing craft that were already in Sicily were briefed on shore and the word was soon around.

The Americans sailed in 13 U.S. Navy attack transports and six British. The latter included the new Boxer class LSTs, which were custom-built landing ships; they had the funnel and superstructure to starboard to give a clear tank deck. Displacing some 6,000 tons, they could carry 20 Sherman tanks, their crews, and a couple of hundred infantry. Other Americans traveled in what were then called LSIs. These Landing Ships Infantry were specially converted channel packets originally belonging to the Dutch and Belgian railways. Britain had requisitioned them in 1940 after the fall of the Low Countries.

The 36th United States Infantry was a Texas National Guard division that had been mobilized and inducted into federal service in 1940. It was commanded by Maj. Gen. Fred Walker, a regular officer who had commanded a battalion in France during World War I. Walker came from Ohio but he knew his Texans, for he had been with the division from mobilization through the long years of training until it was now ready for battle. During this time the division had changed. It was much bigger than in the old days in Texas and had over time shed many of its National Guardsmen and received draftees as replacements from almost every state in the Union. Now in 1943 as it readied for battle perhaps only half of the men were the original National Guard, but that was more than enough to ensure that the fighting qualities of the Lone Star State remained.

General Walker was a thoroughly professional, tough, no-nonsense soldier, yet he deliberately chose to have his two sons with him in the division. One commanded a battalion and later was a close adviser on his staff, while the youngest was his aide or personal assistant.

The division, known as the "T" Patchers because of their emblem with its "T for Texas," had never been in action before. A senior British officer, veteran of the desert, had described them as "keen but green," and that just about summed them up. To these Texans would go the honor of being the first Americans to set foot on mainland Europe in this war, a formidable mission for such raw troops. To land on a hostile and defended shore is the most difficult thing one can ask of any army.

It had not been easy for Walker to obtain this honor for his division. Although he was supremely confident that it was ready for combat, his one fear was that the men's morale would suffer if they didn't see action soon; others were genuinely not convinced that he was right. Confusing the issue were those officers who were anxious to see the honor of being the first Americans on the European mainland in World War II bestowed on their own formations.

Walker had to peddle his cause through the corridors of power in Eisenhower's headquarters in Algiers while Texas congressmen and senators played their part in Washington. The National Guard might well have been federalized, but local and state politics could still extend their influence into battlefields far from home.

General Clark would have preferred to use a more experienced outfit, but this would have been possible only if he took a division out of the line in Sicily. Clark's immediate superiors—British General Alexander as the army group commander and Eisenhower as the theater commander—left the choice to him. He had seen the 36th Infantry train and was convinced they were ready for battle; so he finally agreed that the Texans should lead the American Army into mainland Europe.

There were other and more serious problems to plague Fifth Army Headquarters during the final run-up to the landings.

Throughout much of July and into August various alternative landings in Italy had been entirely or partially planned. It did not help to have the forces that had been earmarked for the operation dispersed along the ports of North Africa. In addition, planning had started late because the first priority had been the operation to put Montgomery's Eighth Army with its British, Canadian, and Indian divisions ashore on the Italian mainland across the Strait of Messina.

Mark Clark had his headquarters at Mostaganem, which is near Oran; the VI Corps and the American divisions were nearby. However, Eisenhower and theater headquarters were in Algiers, some 300 miles east, while the British divisions were in Bizerte, Tunis, and Tripoli. It is over 1,000 miles from Oran to Tripoli. General Alexander was with his advance or tactical headquarters in Sicily, and Admiral Cunningham was in Malta.

The main problem the staff could not solve was determining the number of landing craft and assault shipping available for the operation. The Mediterranean was full of landing craft, but some were en route to the Far East and others were waiting for a refit after their voyage to the theater. Some of the LSTs had sailed all the way from the West Coast of the United States via the Panama Canal to the Mediterranean, their hastily trained emergency commissioned officers and seamen learning the rudiments of navigation and ship control on the way to war. There were landing craft still awaiting repair to their battle damage suffered in Sicily, and other boats were detailed to take Montgomery's Eighth Army across the Strait of Messina. There were even more assault craft of all shapes and sizes under orders to return to England to prepare for D Day and the landings in France, still nine months away. Nobody could tell Mark Clark or his harassed officers how many landing craft he could use for Operation Avalanche.

An additional problem was that many of the warships and support craft, together with some of the air squadrons, were based in Sicily and in need of rest and refit before they could face the rigors of yet another campaign.

Operational planning for Avalanche was even more hectic, dispersed, and exasperating than for previous amphibious operations. The plan itself was simple enough. The "toe" of Italy was too narrow to allow two armies to fight side by side, and communications through the mountains were too primitive to support more than one logistical supply operation. So once Montgomery had kicked in the door and secured his beachhead, he was to advance northward at all possible speed. Clark's army was to "leapfrog" behind the German and Italian front lines, land on a suitable beach, and link up with the British. The armies would then advance north on Rome. There were a number of beaches that the Fifth Army could use, and Clark ordered every choice examined thoroughly. This further stretched the resources of the staff.

It was not until August 19 that Salerno was accorded first priority, and still the problems kept coming. Many of the staff officers were new to the game, and their inexperience showed. They made seemingly impossible demands on the combat units. The divisional commanders in particular had to fight hard to achieve their minimum requirements. General Walker described the stupidity of some of the higher staff officers as appalling in the demands they placed on his men. He had also to be on the alert to keep some of his own unit commanders from hogging more space on the ships than was allotted them. By the time the Fifth Army had submitted the plans to General Alexander for his approval and thence to General Eisenhower, it was August 30. Final approval had still to be sought, and it was only ten days to the landings.

Even then ships were loaded and reloaded as priorities were changed and new problems were recognized. In the midst of all this Walker received orders from the Fifth Army to modify all the insignia on the vehicles and guns by painting a white circle around the white star. It was a War Department directive from Washington and could not be challenged. Nevertheless, Walker was not alone in regarding the order for such a change at this particular time as little more than bureaucratic harassment.

On August 24 H.M.S. *Shakespeare* sailed from Algiers. Her captain, Lieutenant Commander Ainslie, R.N., was no stranger to "cloak and dagger" missions. In late October 1942 he had taken Mark Clark, then a one-star general and Eisenhower's deputy, to North Africa. Clark's mission was to persuade the Vichy French to cooperate with the Torch landings. Now less than a year later, Ainslie and his submarine were once again working for Mark Clark, only on this occasion they were to make sure that all would be well for his army to land in Italy.

The mission was to land members of COPP No. 5 on the enemy shore. Combined Operations Preliminary Reconnaissance and Pilotage Party (COPP) were elite teams of Naval, Army, and Royal Marine officers whose task was to reconnoiter a beach, its shoreline, and the immediate hinterland. Ramming 1,000 tons and more of assault ship onto a beach was a hazardous business and could be undertaken only with the help of the latest, most complete, and most detailed information. Most charts of coastal waters contained only scant information to the low-water mark, while the ordnance survey maps of the land were devoid of contours below the high-water mark. The task of a COPP team was to fill in the gaps. They operated in two-man teams usually in a canoe launched from a submarine, though some were also trained as frogmen.

This was the second mission that COPP 5 had conducted on the Italian mainland. Earlier in August they had been sent to examine the beaches in the Gulf of Goia, at the very toe of Italy. For a while this had been considered as a possible site for the main Allied landings. The team had had barely enough time to unpack from this mission before they were ordered to return to Italy.

At the last minute, Intelligence experts at Army headquarters had identified a white smear on the aerial photographs taken of the southern portions of Salerno Bay. Previously this was thought to be a blemish, but it was then recognized as a sandbar, approximately 4 miles long and about 200 yards offshore, right in the middle of the American sector. The big LSTs needed 11 feet of water under their keel. In 9 feet of water, they could ram and gouge a way through the sand, but in less than that the ships would simply run aground.

The submarine had taken five days to reach Salerno Bay. They had squeezed through a tiny gap at the southern end of the minefield, near Licosa Point. That night, August 30, *Shakespeare* had surfaced off the mouth of the Sele and launched the canoes.

At this time, when amphibious operations were still in their infancy, the equipment used by a COPP team was rudimentary. Their canoes, sort of two-man kayaks, carried survey equipment, containers for soil samples, simple survey tools, and a car battery. The latter was used to power a signal light if the team was acting as a beacon for a raiding party. There were also the crews' personal weapons, usually Sten submachine guns. The waterproof compass was an ordinary one, encased in a French letter. A couple of enamel mugs for bailing completed the stores. With so much equipment and two men to carry, the canoes were low in the water, and so they would attach buoyancy "sausages" to give a little more stability. However, these could not be fastened and inflated until the canoes had been maneuvered out of the 30-inch-wide forward torpedo hatch on the submarine. Even then, the worst moment was still to come. It was no easy thing to launch the canoe and then scramble on board from the wet and slippery saddle tank of the submarine.

The whole business had to be undertaken in darkness and with a minimum of time and fuss, for no submarine commander relishes being surfaced in shallow water and close to an enemy shore.

Invariably the COPP teams began their missions soaked to the skin. The Navy had invented a special outfit called the CD Gomman rubber swimsuit, a sort of forerunner of the wet suit. However, it was clumsy and very uncomfortable. Peter Matterson found that he sweated so much inside he was just as wet as if he had gone into the water naked. Like most people in "cloak and dagger" outfits, he had affected his own style of dress. For Matterson this was a kapok one-piece yachting suit, which could be purchased from Gieves Ltd. (London tailors who had served the needs of the British officer corps for generations), rope-soled shoes, a revolver belt, underwater writing tablet, and a waterproof watch. Like most commandos, he carried a bowie knife. Though he had had all the courses in hand-to-hand combat, such a weapon really was there just to make one feel important. Matterson knew that in his work, if it came to a tussle with a knife, he was in deep trouble.

Matterson was in the first team away. It was his expertise in watermanship and survey, the skills of an engineer officer, that had taken him into a COPP team. The other man in the canoe was Lieutenant R. M. Stanbury, a regular naval officer and commander of COPP 5. Their first task was to check the depth of water over the sandbar by using a weighted line. One large lead weight and two small ones, which meant that there were 12 feet of water. They tried in a couple of other places, and the answer was the same. Even the heaviest landing ships could negotiate the sandbar with water to spare. From there they moved closer inshore. The two men searched for underwater obstacles, and took regular depth soundings right up to the water's edge. The draught of a landing craft was, of course, dependent on its weight and thus displacement. Planners needed to know precisely where each type of craft would beach, especially in the nearly tideless Mediterranean.

Once they had completed their mission, the two men paddled silently out to sea. Now came the hardest part of all: to find the submarine before dawn and the enemy found them.

This is always a tense moment. The submarine crew is anxious as always to help brave men such as these, but they too feel vulnerable and exposed, surfaced in shallow coastal water.

On this occasion, the rendezvous point was found without difficulty. Stanbury's sharp eyes had spotted the black mass of the conning tower against the lighter sea. Willing hands reached down and hauled the by now exhausted pair over the treacherously greasy saddle tanks while others pulled the canoe onto the foredeck.

Once everything had been secured below, the submarine headed out through the gap in the minefield and submerged into deeper water.

The team's information was vital, and the staff had thought long and hard for a foolproof means by which this could be relayed to headquarters. The landings had to take place by September 9, when the moon was full.

There was not enough time for *Shakespeare* to return to any of the Allied bases. Submerged, she traveled at less than half the walking speed of an average man!

Perhaps she could meet with a seaplane! But in a part of the world where the Luftwaffe still ruled supreme, that was too risky. The Allied high command finally decided that *Shakespeare* should sail well clear of the Italian mainland, surface, and send a simple coded message as part of a plain language signal. The code had been devised by Stanbury.

Shakespeare sent an additional message. Mark Clark's headquarters was told that the minefields in Salerno Bay were far more extensive than the Allies had first believed. This meant that fresh orders and timetables had to be prepared and circulated. The minesweepers would now have to go in earlier to clear a passage while the assault shipping would have to release their landing craft much farther out to sea, beyond the minefields.

When this had been accomplished, *Shakespeare* reversed course and returned to Salerno Bay. A second mission was launched on the next night to reconnoiter the British beaches. These were beyond the Sele Estuary and in the northern part of Salerno Bay. On this occasion a couple of SBS officers, newcomers to COPP 5, were used. They replaced Lt. Duggie Kent, R.N., a veteran of this game and an early member of the COPP teams. Gunn was one of the best navigators in the business, but his ears had gone and they had taken him out of submarines. The new men's navigation was very poor, and they missed the rendezvous. It was only at the very last moment and just before first light that the submarine found them, some three miles off course. Had the enemy found them instead, the whole operation would have been jeopardized.

Once the second set of information had been radioed to base, *Shakespeare* settled on the bottom of the Mediterranean to await the arrival of the invasion convoys. The submarine would surface only when the Allied forces arrived off Salerno, for COPP 5 had a second and even more vital role to perform. The Americans intended to land four battalions in the first wave on four separate beaches. With sea room a prerequisite for safe ship handling, the emphasis for the emergency war-trained navigators was on keeping clear of land rather than approaching beaches. Just in the same way that a ship's master would use the skills of a local pilot to take his ship in and out of a port, so the four members of the COPP team would navigate the leading waves onto their correct beaches.

Shakespeare spent the days resting in some two hundred feet of water. Matterson, who suffered from claustrophobia in any case, didn't find the waiting any easier when the first lieutenant told him that at that depth there was a total weight impinging on the pressure hull of some 80,000 tons—about the same displacement as that of the *Queen Mary*!

During the all too brief nighttime hours on the surface the submarine's radio had picked up news of Montgomery's landings on the very toe of Italy. After several weeks of heavy bombardment, on September 3 the Eighth

Army launched two divisions across the Strait of Messina and onto the beaches near Reggio. It was over three hundred miles to Salerno. Code-named Operation Baytown, the prelanding bombardment had involved the heavy guns from four British battleships and whole regiments of artillery lined wheel to wheel along the northern shore of Sicily. There were no casualties, apart from a few luckless civilians, and a shell-shocked cheetah that had escaped from Reggio Zoo. The demented animal was shot when it took a shine to an outraged British brigadier. The enemy had long since departed, blocking the narrow mountain roads and so neatly shutting the door behind them.

At Salerno the prime task of the 36th Infantry Division was to secure its beachhead, a defense perimeter of some 25 miles. Like all American divisions at this time, the 36th was a "triangular" division. It comprised three regiments of infantry—in this case the 141st, 142nd, and 143rd—each of three battalions. The regiments were roughly equivalent to the brigades in a British division. For combat purposes each regiment had artillery, armor, and supporting arms attached, which made it into a self-contained or all-arms force called a regimental combat team.*

Walker planned to land two regimental combat teams abreast in the assault. He had to take the high ground, and this meant deploying as quickly as possible onto the mountain spine that came down to the sea on his right flank and occupying the hilltop towns such as Altavilla and Albanella. These towns looked out over the wide expanse of Salerno Bay and the coastal plain; without them, the Americans believed, their forces would be unable to move. Walker had also to advance as far as the bridge called Ponte Sele; this is where, at the end of the first day, his Texans were to link up with the British divisions on their left. General Walker decided to keep the 143rd, his third regimental combat team, in reserve. They were to come ashore behind the assault waves with sufficient momentum and impetus to carry his troops through to their objectives.

For the breakout the American corps commander, General Ernest J. Dawley, had two regimental combat teams (the 179th and 157th) of the 45th Infantry Division on landing craft offshore. They were also available as an "afloat reserve" should things go wrong in the early part of the landings. The 45th Infantry had fought for the first time in Sicily, and its commanding general, Troy Middleton, was pleased with their performance. Like the Texans, the division was a National Guard formation, with its infantry regiments centered originally in Oklahoma, Colorado, and Arizona. It was called the Thunderbirds after the Indian insignia it wore as a shoulder patch.

Once the Americans had broken out of the beachhead, the aim was to throw a line across Italy. This would help them to watch the back of the British corps as it drove hard to reach Naples by the fifth day of the battle and at the same time trap the enemy forces to the south; for they would be

---

*There is a more detailed explanation of the organization and structure of all the divisions that fought at Salerno in the Appendices.

squeezed tight by the advance of the Eighth Army up from the toe of Italy. Later it was envisaged that the Americans and the British would advance in parallel up the Italian peninsula to Rome. At least that was the plan.

On Wednesday, September 8, there was some excitement for the *Shakespeare,* her passengers, and crew. In the early afternoon the officer of the watch observed through the periscope as a convoy of American landing ships nosed quietly into Salerno Bay. A big cruiser appeared over the horizon, and after a furious exchange of signals with the local escorts, the landing ships headed out to sea. By Lieutenant Commander Ainslie's calculations they were some eighteen hours early!

Now at last the great day had come. It was Thursday, September 9. Peter Matterson was looking for the U.S.S. *Joseph T. Dickman,* a 21,000-ton attack transport that in more peaceful days had been the American Lines' *President Roosevelt.* He was to meet—how, nobody had explained—with a scout boat (LCS) supplied by the transport and mark the beach for her troops. Scout boats were fast launches with some armored protection and well-muffled gasoline engines. The operation was straightforward enough. The pilot was to navigate the LCS to within a couple of hundred yards of the shore, take a precise fix, and anchor in the exact center of the designated beach. The craft would then flash a light to seaward of the appropriate beach color code. In Stanbury's case this was red, the northern or left-hand beach for the American landings, immediately to the south of the estuary of the Sele. This river was to provide the corps boundary between the British and American forces.

Much would depend for success—in this instance, accuracy—on the navigational aids that were available in the scout boats. This was something that the British officers had still to discover. The trouble was that the coastline of Salerno Bay, which extends in a gentle arc for some 30 miles, is quite featureless south of the Sele Estuary. Inland the American sector is dominated by a mountain ridge with the highest points being Monte Soprano (3,556 feet) and to its right the perfect cone-shaped 2,000-foot Monte Sottane. From the beach there is a long glacis of wheatfields and vineyards that leads gently into the low foothills and then 7 miles inland ends abruptly in the cliff base of Soprano. This was too far inland to provide an accurate reference point for shoreline navigation unless the equipment was very sophisticated.

A small U.S. Coast Guard cutter left the maneuvering columns of ships and headed for H.M.S. *Shakespeare.* When close to, she lowered a small boat, and a lone sailor pulled toward the submarine. The four pilots collected their gear and said their farewells. H.M.S. *Shakespeare's* role in the Salerno operation was over, and she could now escape to sea to hunt the enemy.

Matterson, as befitting a British officer about to join the navy of a foreign, albeit friendly, power, was impeccably dressed. Tall and slim, he sported a monocle, and his battle dress was beautifully pressed. In a large knapsack he carried his best uniform, boots, and Sam Browne belt, the latter polished and burnished to perfection. Matterson's only gesture to the submarine service was a neatly clipped beard. This, of course, would mark him as unique in any company of brother officers in the engineers.

It was while the four pilots were crammed into the little dinghy that they learned that the Italians had surrendered. They were dumbfounded. Had all the risks they had taken in the past weeks been for nothing? Was Operation Avalanche now going to be no more than an exercise to occupy Italy?

Chapter II

The Gathering of the Divisions

The problem was the Italians. The Italian high command had ousted Il Duce, Mussolini, in a coup on July 25, and they then wanted to surrender, change sides, and become a cobelligerent with the Allies. In the secret negotiations, which began with emissaries sent to neutral Lisbon and then later to conquered Sicily, the Italians believed they had proved their worth simply by ditching Mussolini. But neither the Allied armies nor their countries could have stomached an immediate welcome for their onetime adversary. The issues involved were even more complicated and unreal. Marshal Badoglio, along with other members of his military junta, needed to be convinced that the Allies could protect them from German retribution. Their one desire above all else was to avoid turning their beloved soil into a battleground. To make the Italians feel secure the Allies would have had to reveal the true nature of their plans and the full details of their forces, and there was no guarantee that the plans would not find their way into German hands. The Allies also feared that their own weakness, in the sense of the few divisions they had available, would frighten off the Italians and send them scuttling back to Berlin.

The affair of the Italian surrender must go down as one of the most bizarre, inept, and mismanaged episodes in the history of modern war. Today, with all allowance for time and hindsight, it is hard to understand how Eisenhower and his commanders could imagine it would ease their breach into Fortress Europe. Nevertheless, this sad affair was to have dire consequences for the forthcoming landings at Salerno.

After protracted negotiations the Italians were at last induced, mostly by a series of stratagems that bordered on camp comedy, to surrender. At 6:30 P.M. on the evening of Wednesday, September 8, the announcement of the Italian armistice was broadcast by Eisenhower on Radio Algiers, and at 7:20 P.M. it was repeated by the BBC News Service. The broadcast was designed and timed to secure the greatest possible advantage for the Allies and aimed to delay for as long as possible the wrath of the Germans on the Italians. The surrender had to be announced before the landings, presumably to avoid shedding "innocent" Italian blood, and September 9 had been chosen as D-Day because of the phase of the moon. The army wished to make the most of darkness and to land onshore while it was still night so as to improve their prospects of achieving surprise. From the naval point of view, to make a final or close-in approach and initial assault at night was by no means ideal. There was the risk of collisions from so many ships maneuvering in the darkness or injuries caused by troops missing their footing as they clambered down the scrambling nets. Even more pertinent, to reach their point for disembarkation, the assault ships would have to approach the bay in daylight. This would give the foe ample warning of the armada's intentions.

The Italian high command, paralyzed by the enormity of their treachery, broadcast a confirmation of sorts. The Germans, who had been expecting the Italians to do something like this, swung into action. Their contingency plan, code-named Operation Axis, operated with ease and Teutonic precision. Badoglio and the cabinet made a run for the coast and a fast gunboat to flee into exile.

The Italian armed forces surrendered twice. The first in theory was to the Allies, the second was for real and to the Germans. In the North the intolerant Rommel, who was then in command, disarmed and then herded his Italians toward the Alps and forced labor in Germany. Many escaped to swell the growing ranks of partisans.

Germans in the southern parts of Italy were under the command of Kesselring. He allowed his Italians to go home. Though there was some resistance, the gratitude of the majority knew no bounds as officers and men cooperated to the full with the Germans. In Salerno Bay the 16th Panzers quietly took over the positions previously occupied by the 222nd Italian Coastal Defense Division. This force was in any case on full alert. On September 8 the chief of staff of the Italian XIX Corps informed headquarters, Port Defense Salerno, as follows:

> From 2330 hrs 7th Sept this zone is declared to be in "coastal alarm" following the departure of enemy convoy from Sicily heading for Salerno.

In all the buildup and training for Salerno the assumption by the Allies had been that the enemy would be Italians, though there might be some Germans in attendance. No one seems to have thought through the tactical consequences of the Italian capitulation.

When the Italian surrender was announced, the van of the Allied fleet was in sight of Capri. Lt. Richard Leeke, a platoon commander in 1st Company,

6th Battalion Grenadier Guards, first spotted the island in late afternoon. He pointed it out to the LST's first lieutenant, who in turn brought out a chart and took a bearing. He confirmed it to be Capri, to the north of Salerno Bay, and that the convoy was a bit too far east, that is, near to the mainland. Leeke was appalled by such a casual attitude.

Of course, such considerations were far from the minds of the British and American troops packed into their transports at sea. Almost everybody had heard at least one of the two radio broadcasts. From horizon to horizon assault craft and their escorts echoed to the thunderous cheers of troops delirious with joy. Leeke's Guardsmen sang as if the war were over. At a stroke Eisenhower had blunted the finely honed fighting edge of Mark Clark's troops. Raw young Americans jumped for joy, "*vino* and *signorinas* from the beachhead to Naples."

Other men in the 36th Division thought that the landings would be another "dry run"; yet another exercise after three years of nothing but exercises. The great cry had been they were to be the first American troops to land in Europe in this war; now the fire went out of their bellies.

Many of the British believed it, too—that is, all except the more phlegmatic soldiers, who had learned after four years of war not to believe anything that they couldn't see with their own eyes. In vain officers and "noncoms" in both forces tried to convince the troops that there was still the Germans. Some listened and went about the business of preparing for war. The majority, however, were beyond redemption, lulled into false hopes and expectations.

The atmosphere on some ships became so relaxed that many did not recover. Matterson and the other pilots found such a mood on the Coast Guard cutter as it carried them out to join the fleet. They were taken to meet a jubilant captain, who discussed the Italian surrender at great length. At least the excellent coffee helped wash away some of the staleness of the submarine.

A flotilla of minesweepers fussed by inshore to begin the deadly task of clearing a way through the minefields. Transit boats arrived and took the pilots to their respective attack transports: the U.S.S. *Joseph T. Dickman, Barnett, Carroll,* and *Jefferson.* It was just after two in the morning when Peter Matterson climbed up the companionway and entered the cavernous bowels of the *Joseph T. Dickman.* All around was a hive of activity. Seemingly endless files of troops shuffled past toward the boat stations. The rancid air was heavy with the odors of thousands of men with their sweat, their fears, and their anticipation.

A duty ensign introduced Matterson to the officer in command of the ship's small infantry landing craft, Lieutenant Commander Scanlon of the U.S. Coast Guard.

"Where's my scout boat?" Matterson asked when the pleasantries were over.

"It left ten minutes ago," Scanlon replied. "I'm afraid we got a little ahead of ourselves."

Matterson was mortified. This meant that the pilot boat that would mark Red Beach would be taken in by an ensign who hadn't even the rudimentary understanding of pilotage; but then he wasn't expected to, since he was supposed to have Matterson with him. If he were just half a degree out the troops would land on the wrong beach, which in turn would throw chaos and confusion into the other landings on the right flank. None of the Americans around shared his concern, however. It seemed to Matterson that Avalanche was no longer regarded as a combat operation but rather as a military training exercise in which all the precautions were unnecessary. Everybody had lost interest.

Nevertheless, in the interests of transatlantic relations, Commander Scanlon put himself and his own landing barge at Matterson's disposal. Beyond the stern of the *Joseph T. Dickman*, the early morning air was heavy with exhaust fumes as her landing craft, loaded with the leading wave of the 1st Battalion, 142nd Infantry, circled and awaited instructions. Matterson now planned to lead in the wave himself. If they were to hit the beaches on time they would need to leave immediately.

Scanlon's barge edged away from the *Joseph T. Dickman*. Matterson was half aware of a blur of white faces peering down from above. The last of the regimental combat team waited for their boats. The second wave was already loading. There was very little noise, he remembered afterward.

A yeoman stood on the fantail of the barge and signaled frantically with his hooded flashlights. Scanlon rigged a temporary red light, and the landing craft broke away from the circle and formed in line astern. Matterson thought it one of the sweetest maneuvers he had ever witnessed. As the stern bit into the water and the barge surged forward, Matterson turned to his immediate task.

The coxswain indicated the navigational aids carried on the barge—a single small steering compass, which Matterson thought was probably inaccurate, and in any case only calibrated in 10-degree steps. He was still grappling with the problem as they entered the swept channel through the minefields. They had a 7-mile run into the beach, and Matterson's navigational fix, which he could barely see, was 7 miles inland. An error of 5 degrees would be calamitous.

Pfc. Bill Craig was in the first wave of the landing craft. As he settled down to the run into the beach he checked his equipment and gripped his rifle a little bit tighter. The new wool uniform he had been given in North Africa itched and was already hot and sweaty. Craig was a 24-year-old farmboy from Brownwood. Though a Texan, he had not been a member of the National Guard. Craig was drafted into Company K in 1941, and he had been with them ever since.

So far everything seemed to be going very much according to the plans that his squad leader had explained the previous day. The worst moments had been scrambling down the swaying cargo nets from the high decks into the landing craft below. A fall from that height, weighed down with weapons and equipment, would be fatal. But the squads, aware of the dangers, watched what they were doing, and there were no incidents.

Company K was one of the first away from the *Joseph T. Dickman*. It had taken more than two hours for the barges to sort themselves out into the formation that Matterson had admired so much. By then many of the troops were seasick. Though the sea was mirror calm, the long wait, gasoline fumes, and anticipation were enough to turn the strongest stomachs.

Their seasickness would soon turn to a darker fear.

The landing craft packed with crouching infantry moved inshore. To their front everything was quiet. No shells burst ahead on the beaches, for the high command had decided there should be no preliminary bombardment. This was the biggest blunder of all. There was no provision even for close-in fire support. The navy had offered warships, and Vice Admiral Hewitt, the naval task force commander, had argued vehemently against what he regarded as a foolhardy decision. But Gen. Mark Clark and his staff had studied all the same manuals when students at the War College, and they were equally determined to achieve total surprise. A bombardment from the sea would in their view simply signal intentions to the enemy. The staff and their general had fallen into the classic trap of relating theory to practice. They were shortly to learn that what looks good in the plans can be awful in reality.

The Fifth Army was an Allied army, and the British divisions were under Clark's command, at least in theory. However, their commanders had insisted on a preliminary bombardment of their beaches. They had a monitor, a shallow-draught warship that was nothing more than a platform for its two enormous 15-inch guns, cruisers, destroyers, gunboats, and last but not least rocket-firing landing craft. The latter had been used for the first time in the Sicily landings, where they had proved devastatingly effective.

General Walker had been an instructor at the War College when Mark Clark as a young, aspiring lieutenant colonel had been his student. He supported the view that surprise could be achieved. His Texans had practiced this very maneuver of the silent landing during their final dress rehearsal in North Africa. They had gotten it about right in the end, but some of the first attempts at amphibious operations had proved a disaster.

America's recently created special elite force, the rangers, with all their skills, had their fair share of fiascos too. When Capt. Douglas Scott, R.E., second in command of the 272nd Field Company Royal Engineers (of the British 46th Division), was acting as a company commander in a combined operations school just along the coast from Algiers; General Patton had arrived with his staff to watch the rangers undertake a nighttime landing exercise. Once it was dark, the assembled officers could hear the landing craft at sea. Scott checked his watch; the Americans, thank God, were on time. Patton's profanity was legendary.

The thumping of the diesel engines as they came along the coast got

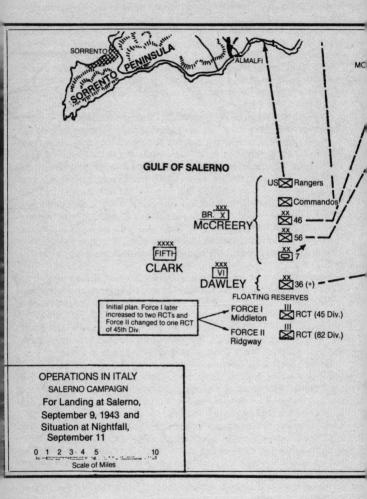

SORRENTO

SORRENTO PENINSULA

ALMALFI

MC

GULF OF SALERNO

US ☒ Rangers

☒ Commandos

BR. XXX
X
McCREERY

XX
☒ 46

XX
☒ 56

XX
☒ 7

XXXX
FIFTH
CLARK

XXX
VI
DAWLEY {

XX
☒ 36 (+)

FLOATING RESERVES

Initial plan. Force I later
increased to two RCTs and
Force II changed to one RCT
of 45th Div.

FORCE I
Middleton

III
☒ RCT (45 Div.)

FORCE II
Ridgway

III
☒ RCT (82 Div.)

OPERATIONS IN ITALY

SALERNO CAMPAIGN

For Landing at Salerno,
September 9, 1943 and
Situation at Nightfall,
September 11

0 1 2 3 4 5   10

Scale of Miles

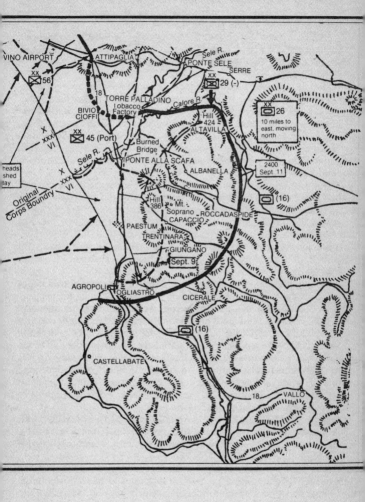

louder and louder. "Blood and Guts" Patton became even more excited, waiting for them to turn into the coast and attack Scott's men, who were acting as "enemy." But they didn't; the craft sailed by.

As Patton heard those distant diesels dwindling into the lovely night air he made one of the more profane remarks for which he was famous: "Jesus Christ!" he said, "do they expect me to drop my f—— pants and sh—— f—— soldiers?"

Scott and the others laughed it off, but all had been around long enough to know that in landing operations you took no chances. Rather the reverse; you gave the troops everything that was available. Amphibious warfare was a hazardous undertaking in which mistakes were bound to happen, and the only way to compensate for or minimize the risk was to overcompensate. This required an abundance of equipment and every military aid possible to ensure that your forces could achieve a landing with the minimum of casualties.

One such aid that had recently become available was the military amphibian that the troops had by then nicknamed the "Duck." In fact, the correct nomenclature is DUKW, which are the initials of the code of description: D (1942) U (amphibian) K (all-wheel-drive) W (dual rear axles). They had arrived in the theater in time for the Sicily landings. The DUKW was built on the conventional 6-by-6 chassis and weighed 7 tons. Its capacity was 5,000 pounds of freight or up to fifty troops. At sea it was capable of 5 knots; on land, 50 miles an hour.

General Walker was anxious also to have some insurance should things fail to go according to plan. While they were still in Oran he sent for Maj. Oran Stovall, who was then the second in command of the divisional engineers. The general asked him to modify some of the DUKWs to carry 104mm howitzers. This required considerable structural alterations to the loading bay of the vehicle to accommodate the wheels and the trail of the gun. There was also the problem of finding a means of lifting the gun out of the DUKW and onto the ground. It taxed their ingenuity, but engineers the military world over are the most resourceful of troops. Stovall designed a collapsible A-frame carried on a separate vehicle, which was capable of picking up the gun and setting it down.

Forty-eight DUKWs equipped to carry 105mm, and a further sixteen with A frames, were loaded onto the LSTs for Salerno. It was a remarkable achievement, made even more so when we bear in mind that Stovall and his team had never seen a DUKW before.

The DUKWs were a godsend at Salerno, but even so, the absence of a naval bombardment was to prove a near-disastrous mistake. At Salerno, the Germans were not only able to calculate where the Allies would land but also when. Ashore Germans from the 16th Panzer Division had only that very afternoon taken over the defenses.

The *old* 16th Panzer Division was destroyed in January 1943. It was part of the ill-fated Sixth Army under General Paulus that was trapped and then annihilated at Stalingrad. The *new* 16th Panzers was reformed in France in

March 1943 around those men who, for various reasons (on leave or wounded, etc.), escaped the fate of their comrades at Stalingrad. The division therefore consisted of some 30 percent battle-tried officers and men; the remainder were recruits and reinforcements.

In May 1943 the division moved to Italy, first to Florence and then to Apulia. Here it completed its training, which by the very nature of an armored formation was in the attack role. At the same time it was brought up to strength, except for its battalion of heavy tanks. The crews were in Germany learning how to handle and fight their new Tigers. They were to be badly missed during the battles for Salerno.

In late August the division moved into its new positions in the Gulf of Salerno as part of the Tenth Army. The last units arrived in the area on August 30th, just nine days before the landings.

The units of the division were fully supplied with sufficient ammunition and fuel to last five days, even longer in some cases. Resupply, especially for artillery ammunition and fuel, was a critical problem because of the effects of Allied air bombardment of the industrial and communications centers in northern Italy. The resupply problem was also made more difficult by the poor road communications in the area. The division's battle headquarters was located just four kilometers northeast of Battipaglia, but it was as much as eighty kilometers to some of the unit headquarters using the local roads.

Maj. Gen. Rudolph Sieckenius, the divisional commander, divided his force into four battle groups to cover the front of the Gulf of Salerno. Each battle group was named after its commander. The chart in Appendix A shows their deployments and composition.

When the commander of the local Italian formations, the lukewarm 222nd Coastal Division, had tried to stand on his honor, he was quietly taken to one side and shot. His men were only too relieved to hand over their weapons to the Germans, vacate their trenches and gun emplacements, and scuttle off to their homes and civilian life.

So the panzer defenses that awaited the Americans in their sector were about as solid as they could be. Along the shoreline, strongpoints, each garrisoned by a platoon of troops, bristled with light and heavy machine guns. These were interspersed with a number of quadruple 20mm antiaircraft guns, their barrels depressed in readiness for their infantry role. The concentrated firepower of high-explosive bullets would be devastating against thin-skinned landing craft and unprotected troops. In the sand dunes 75mm and the dreaded 88mm antitank guns were dug into emplacements. Farther inland, platoons of tanks and panzer grenadiers, in armored half-tracks, were poised for local counterattacks. In the foothills, batteries of mobile and self-propelled artillery looked down on the beaches.

The ground was not completely to the favor of the defenders. Though a map does show it to be an overlooked area with heights for observation and a plain for tank movement, the reality was somewhat different. The high ground lies too far inland to enable the coast to be defended from there, and the plain is rendered unsuitable for the sort of tank warfare the panzers prefer. There are too many ditches and canals, while the high vegetation, in places two or three meters, does not make for "good" tank country.

The price the Americans paid in search of the elusive military goal of surprise was that the German defenses would be virtually undisturbed until the very moment of landing. Indeed, the Germans were almost as well prepared to contest these landings as the Japanese would be at Tarawa two months later. It was a terrible blunder.

Northward beyond the Sele Estuary to the town of Salerno the narrow coastal plain is bisected by a number of river estuaries. To the tidy military mind these acted as boundaries for the two territorial Army divisions that together comprised the British X Corps.

The 56th City of London Division was known as the "Black Cats," after its Dick Whittington shoulder patch. The division was to land two brigades in the assault; each brigade would use two of its three battalions in the first wave. The 167th Infantry Brigade* was to land on the American left between the Sele and the Tusciano rivers. This was called Roger Sector, and the battalion beaches were Amber and Green. Once ashore the spearhead, the 8th and 9th battalions, Royal Fusiliers, would move hard for their main objective. This was the important road and rail junction at Battipaglia, a vital communications center on the route from Naples southward. The brigade's 3rd Battalion, 7th Ox and Bucks, would land in reserve and move to support the attack inland as necessary. From Battipaglia the plan called for the brigade to take the high ground beyond the town and then swing right to link up with the Americans at Ponte Sele, some 7 miles inland.

The 169th Infantry Brigade's landing area was code-named Sugar. This lay between the Tusciano and Asa rivers, and the battalions' beaches were Amber and Green. The brigade had three battalions of the Queens Regiment. The 2/7th Queens and 2/5th Queens were to lead the attack, with the 2/6th in support.

The brigade's objective was Montecorvino airfield. Until this could be secured and made operational, the Allies at sea and on shore would be hard pressed for air cover. All that was available were the meager resources of Fleet Air Arm Seafires from the escort carriers, together with R.A.F. Spitfires and U.S.A.F. twin-boom Lightnings, both operating at the limits of their endurance from airfields in Sicily.

The units that comprised the other division originally came from the northwestern Midlands and the West Riding of Yorkshire. This was the 46th Infantry Division, and its shoulder patch was the oak tree of Sherwood Forest. The first task of the division was to capture Salerno, a dirty, rundown harbor tucked in the armpit of the bay, squeezed between the hills and the seashore. Though it boasted only two small jetties, and both of these had seen better days, they were vital to the success of Mark Clark's plans. He

*The British regimental system is explained in Appendix D.

needed the use of a port with all its facilities intact as quickly as possible. The divisions could not be resupplied over open beaches indefinitely.

The 46th Infantry Division battle plan was complicated. For the operation to succeed it required split-second timing, accurate navigation to the properly designated landing beaches, and above all a strict adherence to the timetable by the succeeding waves of troops. It was vital for the battalions that landed behind the initial assault waves to move inland and secure their objectives as quickly as possible. This in particular meant that the narrow exits out of the Salerno plain had to be in British hands before the end of the first day (or D-Day).

The plan was as follows:

The 128th Infantry Brigade would land first in Uncle Sector, which lay between the Asa and Picentino rivers. The 2nd Battalion Hampshire Regiment would land on the right, Green Beach, and the 1/4th Hampshires on the left, or Red Beach. The 2nd Hampshires as reserve would come ashore on the left. Shortly after first light the three battalions of the 138th Brigade, 6th Lincolns, 2/4th King's Own Yorkshire Light Infantry (KOYLIs), and the 6th York and Lancasters would pass through the Hampshire beachhead and take Salerno. A couple of miles northwest of the port lay the village of Cava and the all-important defile called La Molina, which carried the main road snaking through the hills toward Naples. This low pass was the brigade's final objective for D-Day. That night the division's 3rd Brigade, 139th Infantry were due to land. Its battalions, 2/5th Royal Leicesters, 5th Sherwood Foresters, and the 16th Durham Light Infantry, together with the armor of the 40th Royal Tank Regiment, would lead the march on Naples.

Unlike the Texans, both British divisions had been in action before. Neither could be said to have had a happy war. The Americans, new to war, were eager to be in the fighting. The British divisions for their own different reasons were anxious to put the experiences of North Africa behind them. They had both learned in the process that the Germans were formidable foes. After four years of combat the Wehrmacht meted out harsh treatment to units that were new to battle, especially those rash enough to take chances and their enemy for granted. In fighting the Germans, Montgomery had learned that the key to success lay in the form of overwhelming firepower.

In 1942 the Londoners had first sailed to India. From Bombay they were hurriedly moved into the Persian Gulf and thence Kirkuk and the mountain borders between Turkey, Iraq, and Iran. The division masquerading as the Ninth Army was there as a deterrent should the panzers break through at Stalingrad and swing south toward the rich oil fields of the Middle East.

But it was the Soviets who held firm, and the Germans' own Ninth Army that suffered the defeat. So with the danger passed, room had to be found for the division in the real war. The men traveled by road from Baghdad through Palestine and the Holy Land, the Nile Delta and Egypt, to become part of General Montgomery's veteran Eighth Army. It was the longest approach march to a battle in history. Four thousand miles later the battalions stepped down in time to take part in the last of the messy and ill-conceived fighting that had been the Tunisian campaign. At Enfidaville the division was blooded and mauled when it advanced in a frontal assault uphill against prepared German positions.

After the campaign in North Africa was over, the 201st Guards Brigade, which included the superb battalions of Grenadiers, Coldstreams, and Scots Guards, joined the 56th Division. The Guardsmen had fought the desert war as trucked infantry where there was a need for greater mobility. By this time they were among the first to retrain for the more traditional infantry role, fighting on foot, in readiness for Europe. The guardsmen replaced the 168th Brigade in the division.

The Royal Scots Greys also joined the division. Its Sherman tanks had fought the desert war from El Alamein. This most famous of cavalry regiments, which charged the French at Waterloo, was the last to be mechanized. In 1941 it formed part of the garrison in Palestine, trying to keep the peace between the Arabs and Jews there. It was there that the troopers gave up their gray mounts and turned to tanks.

Of the Allied formations that landed at Salerno on that first morning, the 46th Infantry Division had had the longest war. It had been in France in 1940 and was in the first campaign of all. In May of that year the division was in Brittany on lines of communications duty when the German blitzkrieg changed the map of Europe. The brigades moved north to defend Rouen and were swept up in the rout. Two brigades came out through Dunkirk and the third some weeks later from Cherbourg, St. Malo, and St. Nazaire.

In January 1943 the division landed with the first reinforcements for the British First Army and had fought the terrible winter of the North African campaign. When Rommel broke out of his mountain redoubt and humiliated the Americans at Kasserine Pass, this luckless infantry division suffered too. Some units in the front line stumbled, and much hard-fought-for ground was lost. What added to their ordeal was that the division spent the campaign split into battalion-sized groups and had no chance to build an *esprit de corps.*

In April 1943 the surviving German and Italian troops in North Africa surrendered at Cape Bon. The 46th Infantry Division was reunited, its battalions bruised, battered, and depleted in numbers.

Bad luck hit the division again just before they left for Salerno. While the troops were in Bizerte, they were in a sealed camp, which meant that they were not allowed for security reasons to come into contact with other troops. Though they could write home, the men were told that no mail would be sent to England until their division had embarked upon its operation. In those days enlisted men had their mail censored by their officers. Officers censored their own letters. Also, it was the custom at times like these for security services to make additional spot checks of the mail.

The division was led by Major General Freeman-Attwood, who at the time was one of the youngest divisional commanders in the British Army. He wrote home to his wife saying that he hoped shortly to be in those parts where they had spent their honeymoon, which was innocence itself compared to some of the things other officers were writing. But security pounced on the general's letter, and within a matter of hours Freeman-Attwood lost his command and his career.

With Salerno only days away, the general's dismissal had a serious effect on the division as a fighting force. This was not so much for the ordinary soldier, most of whom regarded generals as objects in the distance to be avoided at all costs. The impact was more immediately felt among the senior fighting commanders and the divisional staff, for together they made a team dependent upon mutual confidence and trust. The teamwork necessary to make a division operate as an effective force on the battlefield cannot be created overnight.

The new divisional commander, Major General Hawkesworth, was proven in battle. He had commanded the splendid 4th Indian Division in the desert campaign. However, he knew little of the overall battle plan, the role that was expected of his division, or indeed the strengths and weaknesses of his own officers and their commands before they embarked for Salerno.

Freeman-Attwood was not the only officer the division lost. While the troops watched from their landing craft, the senior medical officer was called back to the dockside at Bizerte. He was charged with sending home a German microscope. The doctor, a well-loved and popular figure in the division, was escorted from the ship by two burly military policemen. Many who watched could not help but notice that one of the MPs sported a German Luger in his holster.

The division had lost two good officers. Behind both dismissals there was an element of the bitter jealousy and the endless skirmishing for promotion that war brings to a peak. War is, after all, the great opportunity for officers to get above the rank of major, which is as high as most regulars, of whatever nationality, can go in peacetime armies.

There were other problems, too, and these concerned the attitudes of the Americans and the British toward each other. By this stage in the war some of these attitudes had hardened into prejudices, whereby they saw one another as stereotypes.

For the British, the "Yanks" were the soldiers they thought of as crowding into England and their own homes, so the cry of "overfed, overpaid, oversexed—and *over there*" had more than a hint of animosity. The Yanks were souvenir-mad and naïve as well. More than one trooper in the Royal Scots Greys had filled sandbags full of grit from the roadside and sold it to an unsuspecting Yank as the genuine article, "the blood-stained sand of El Alamein"! The British soldier thought the Yank slovenly and ill-kept, extravagant with his supplies and ammunition. He envied him his K rations, comfortable helmet, and warm clothes. Familiarity between the American soldiers and officers was something quite beyond his understanding, as was the American attitude toward race.

The British and American soldiers would join forces to combat their common enemy, the military police, of whatever nationality. Otherwise there was little of what Churchill was later to call the "special relationship" in 1943 in the Mediterranean.

The Americans saw the "Limeys" as a class-conscious army that always stopped the war every afternoon for tea. He could not understand the need for drill, or spit and polish, while he found their customs and traditions old-fashioned as revealed in their regimental dress. The Americans could not fathom why in a so-called democracy a British soldier would be so formal as to say, "Permission to speak, sir?" when addressing an officer. They failed to understand why officers should have their own servant or batman.

It was more often the case that the noncommissioned men of the two nations got along better together than did their respective officers. The Americans respected the fighting skills and experience of the British, did not understand but envied their regimental customs and traditions, and secretly wished that their officers cared as much for their welfare as did the British officers for their men.

Mark Clark was supposed to weld these national diversities and antipathies into a coherent fighting force. The baptism of fire that they shared at Salerno did little to forge such a consensus.

Chapter III

The Special Forces

The British experienced their first taste of what was to come while they were still in their ports in North Africa. In one of the heaviest raids, the Germans bombed the shipping as it massed in the outer harbor at Bizerte the night before the first convoys were due to put to sea.

In an earlier raid, just a few days before, the British corps commander had been seriously wounded. Lt. Gen. Sir Brian Horrocks was an enthusiastic, experienced, and forceful commander. Since August 1942 he had commanded the XIII Corps as part of the Eighth Army. General Montgomery had thought highly of Horrocks, and so he was an obvious choice to lead the X Corps upon its formation at the end of the North African campaign.

That particular evening General Horrocks was dining with the senior officers and staff of the 46th Division when the raid began. The party had hardly stepped outside to watch "the fireworks" when the general was struck down by a piece of shrapnel from an AA shell.

Just a very short distance away, the officers of the 272nd Field Company, Royal Engineers, were enjoying a nice carboy of Tunisian wine with their bully beef. The unit's doctor, Capt. Moran Denis Bergen, an Irishman who spoke with the broadest lilt of his people, was summoned to administer to the general.

The doctor returned some hours later, ashen white and sober as a judge.

"What's the matter, Doc?" Douglas Scott asked.

"Oh, my God," Moran replied, "you should have seen it. It was just like the deat' of Nelson."

"What do you mean by that?"

"Well," said Moran, "when I got there General Hawkesworth was down on one knee; and across his knee like Nelson in that painting was General Horrocks—laid out, blood-stained and all."

Moran went on to explain that some shrapnel had gone through Horrocks' chest and into his back.

"Is he going to be out of action?" Scott asked.

"Oh, yes, he's going home. He's a pretty sick man," Moran replied.

Even in that moment of great pain and physical discomfort Horrocks still managed to retrieve something from the situation. He suddenly opened his eyes and looked up at the group of his senior officers who clustered around Moran and the other doctors.

"Gentlemen," he said, "I don't like the looks on your faces. I can assure you I'm not going to die."

Nevertheless, the British contingent in the Fifth Army had lost its commander and Gen. Mark Clark a trusted and experienced subordinate. A replacement had to be found quickly.

Gen. Sir Richard McCreery, an acknowledged tank expert, and chief of staff to General Alexander in 1942 when he was commander-in-chief in the Middle East, was an obvious choice. Indeed, Alexander, now a full general and commander-in-chief of the Fifteenth Army Group, which comprised the Eighth and Fifth armies, was instrumental in securing his appointment. McCreery, who had returned to England to work on the Normandy landings, was flown back to North Africa without delay.

The Luftwaffe and the Italian Regia Aeronautica constantly shadowed the ships as they sailed north across the Mediterranean. More attacks occurred as the convoys gathered off the northern coast of Sicily. Junker 88 dive bombers and Focke-Wulf 190s swooped on the huge armada. The Luftwaffe, however, failed to penetrate the allied defenses effectively.

Besides the land-based Allied fighter support from the North West African Air Force, there was also the Fleet Air Arm. Admiral Vian commanded the Royal Navy escort carriers of Force V—*Unicorn, Attacker, Battler, Hunter,* and *Stalker.* Their task was solely to defend the invasion forces.

Protecting the escort carriers and providing distant cover for the invasion convoys was Force H, the battle squadron of the British Mediterranean Fleet. Vice Admiral Willis flew his flag in H.M.S. *Nelson.* He had three other battleships—sister ship *Rodney,* together with *Warspite* and *Valiant.* There were the Royal Navy fleet carriers *Illustrious* and *Formidable* and three flotillas, twenty modern destroyers as escort. They had sailed from Malta on the afternoon of September 7.

Adm. H. Kent Hewitt, U.S.N., who was in overall command of the naval side of the landings, with the Western Naval Task Force, flew his flag in the headquarters ship U.S.S. *Ancon.* Also embarked with him was an efficient fighter direction team under the able command of Brig. Gen. Edward House, U.S. Army.

Watching the East Coast and the Adriatic was a second task force. The modern British battleships *Howe* and *King George V*, with an escort of six destroyers, sailed from Algiers for Augusta in Sicily.

Force H did its job. On the night of the September 8–9 it absorbed an attack by 30 torpedo bombers. The fleet inflicted heavy damage on the Luftwaffe and took attacks intended for the invasion forces.

Once the landing craft stood close inshore, however, the Luftwaffe found them easier prey. The LSTs were known as Large Stationary Targets by soldiers and sailors alike. The smaller LCTs came in for their share of the punishment, too. Some landing craft were damaged, and *LCT 624* was sunk with heavy loss of life, just 15 miles off Capri. It was part of a convoy that had already turned toward Salerno.

When darkness fell, the Luftwaffe dropped flares off the convoys and attacked with bombs and torpedoes; but they were able to inflict no more real damage. Indeed, the challenge from the Luftwaffe, which until very recently had controlled the skies over the Mediterranean, was not as heavy or as effective as the Allied commanders had anticipated. The route taken by the invasion force dissected the heart of "Stuka alley." Only a year earlier, Allied convoys suffered crippling losses off Sicily as they tried to fight their way through to beleaguered Malta. But the Luftwaffe had had to divert its increasingly meager resources to meet the air threat from Britain, support the campaign on the Eastern Front, and defend southern Europe.

Anticipated Luftwaffe vigilance alone had been enough to convince the British generals that any hope for a surprise landing in the Gulf of Salerno was an impossible dream.

However, it was not until the van of the invasion armada made its turn toward the coast off the Bay of Salerno that the Germans felt confident they had assessed Allied intentions correctly, since there were a number of bays that had suitable beaches for a large-scale landing.

Montgomery's landings in the South had convinced the Germans that there had to be a second and bigger operation farther up the coast, and Kesselring and his staff were aware that the overly cautious Allies would never venture beyond the cover extended by their own air umbrella. Air power was, after all, their trump card.

The Germans also appreciated that wherever the Allies landed, they would need a port; a large modern and mechanized army could not be supplied indefinitely over open beaches. They knew the combat range of the Spitfire and the location of the airfields in Sicily. A simple arc, the diameter of which represented the Spitfire's range, showed that the Allies had three options in southern Italy. The main port had to be Naples, and to its north was the Gulf of Gaeta. It had good beaches and excellent exits into the flat hinterland, but it was at the extreme range of the Spitfire. Pilots would have perhaps ten minutes over the beachhead if they were to make it home to Sicily with safety. For the Allies it would be the Battle of Britain in reverse. Kesselring had commanded an air fleet at the time. He had understood the frustration of the ME-109 pilots having to break off contact in the skies above Kent to make a run for the airfields across the Channel with fuel gauges reading their life away.

For most of the time the Germans had largely discounted Salerno. The poor exits off the beaches and the towering hills behind would, they believed, be more than enough to deter the Allies. Kesselring favored the Bay of Naples. While he ordered both Gaeta and Salerno to be ready to repel an invasion, he believed that only Naples allowed the Allies to achieve their objective of successfully bypassing the defenses in the South.

While the Allies recognized Naples as their port, they rejected the bay as the site for their landing. Dieppe had shown them the folly of landing in a harbor; it is simply too well defended.

The Germans had anticipated a major landing between September 6 and 9 because the moon would have just entered its second quarter. The announcement of the Italian surrender really gave the game away for both time and place. Eisenhower's broadcast pinpointed the timing of the landing as a matter of hours. It had to be Salerno.

Operation Husky and the Allied landings in Sicily had been preceded by one of the most elaborate and successful deception plans ever. Sicily was an obvious target after North Africa, yet the Allies were able to deceive the Germans into believing that the objective was the Balkans.

Deception at Salerno amounted to little more than a diversionary force, TG 80.4, led by Capt. C. L. Andrews, U.S.N., in the destroyer *Knight*, accompanied by an elderly Royal Dutch gunboat, H.M.N.S. *Flores*, and some coastal craft. Captain Andrews' force left Palermo to demonstrate off the islands of Ventotene, some twenty miles west of Ischia and off Gaeta in the hope the enemy would be convinced they were the advance guard of an invasion force. A second detachment of motor torpedo and gunboats did likewise off the mouth of the Volturno River. There is no evidence that the Germans were at all deceived by the actions of these forces.

Lieutenant Rocholl!* commanded a unit of three armored cars in the reconnaissance regiment of the 16th Panzers. Ever since they had moved into southern Italy the unit had been pestered by the frequent alarms warning of the likelihood of an Allied landing. At 1400 hours on September 8 headquarters had broadcast *Attention Operation Feuerbrunst*. This was the first call to expect an Allied landing; the troops continued with their afternoon rest. Suddenly at about 1630 hours the regiment came on the air again with *Attention Operation Orkan*. This was the code to signal that the invasion convoy was actually in sight. All preparations were made to move immediately.

Rocholl and his team were to cover Salerno; other reconnaissance patrols prepared to watch Castellamare and Vietri. The armored cars were all loaded

---

*Lieutenant Rocholl's diary was first published in 1945 by Alan Moorehead in his book *Eclipse*. I am most grateful to his publisher, Hamish Hamilton, for allowing me to use this material.

and ready to go. Rocholl went across to the company headquarters for his battle instructions and the radio ciphers and learned of the Italian surrender. At first the news came as a shock to him, but afterward he realized that he had foreseen all this and had expected it to happen.

Rocholl was ready to leave. He shook hands with his company commander and other patrol officers and went down, his map case under his arm, to the three armored cars, which were stationed in front of the church. He called his crews and explained briefly the military and political situation, their assignments, and the radio cipher. The crews clambered into the vehicles at his command.

Rocholl fixed the map case into place on the thin armored mantel in front of him and loosened his revolver in its holster; no one could tell how the Italians were likely to behave.

Rocholl glanced around to see that all was ready, then signaled to the other vehicle commanders to start up. The three Daimler-Benz engines roared into life. He led his column at high speed down the main road from Battipaglia to Salerno. Everywhere Italians were standing in groups deep in excited discussions; they had obviously heard of the capitulation.

Rocholl had chosen an observation post on top of the mountain ridge near the sea and to the southeast of Salerno. From this commanding position he had a clear view northwest toward Salerno and Vietri and south-southeast along the entire coast as far as the Plain of Faiano. A section of troops from his own 3rd Company with a heavy machine gun had already dug in nearby. An Italian position that comprised some machine guns and a separate coastal artillery emplacement was below them. The Italians were talking loudly; their voices carried in the evening air, and their unmilitarylike behavior offended the Germans.

With the last of the daylight Rocholl pondered his own deployments. His problem concerned the positioning of the armored cars. He could not leave them on the road because it ran along the forward slope of the hill, and the cars would be too open to fire. Neither could their armament of light machine guns contribute much to the defense line. On the other hand, he did not want them too far away. In the end he placed his radio car facing back along the road and just around the corner from the main observation post; the other two pulled into a culvert.

Darkness descended, and, apart from the still-noisy Italian post, nothing was to be seen or heard. Rocholl ordered a few potatoes to be fried on the Esbit cooker, the Wehrmacht's equivalent of a small field stove. Scarcely had his men started to peel the potatoes when the sergeant from the heavy machine-gun section came running up in great excitement.

"Sir, a dispatch rider has just arrived from headquarters. I have been ordered to take over the Italian position. Would you as an officer undertake this mission?"

Rocholl agreed immediately and set about making his plans. He ordered half of his men to provide cover and to open fire if he signaled, while the remainder accompanied him down to the Italians. He went first to the machine-gun nest. Rocholl told them that their country had capitulated and after being disarmed they could make their way home. It happened just as he had expected. They threw away their weapons and showed their joy that the war was now over for them.

The negotiations with the artillery emplacement proved more difficult. Rocholl spoke first with a second lieutenant, who showed great fear. Rocholl didn't think he deserved to be an officer. When he requested his revolver he handed it over without question.

Rocholl then approached the battery commander, who behaved quite differently. His bearing was that of an officer and a gentleman, and the young German was more favorably impressed. Rocholl explained the situation to him, of which he knew nothing, and demanded the unconditional surrender of the artillery position in the name of the Third Reich.

The Italian captain asked permission to contact his superior officer. Rocholl refused, and the Italian did not seem at all prepared to surrender. The German gave him an ultimatum: Hand over the guns or he would order his own men to open fire.

The Italian quickly came to a decision and handed over his battery. Rocholl's soldiers brought out all the Italian troops, lined them up, disarmed them, and allowed them to leave.

Rocholl returned the captain's pistol, without the ammunition, however. The whole affair had taken less than an hour, and the soldiers returned to the observation post and their meal of fried potatoes. Though they had been ready some while, the potatoes still tasted wonderful.

They were just on the point of clearing up after the meal when they were startled by a terrific explosion. Frying pans and eating irons were hurled aside as the soldiers rushed to man their positions. Rocholl ran to the edge of the hill to witness a terrifying yet beautiful spectacle. The mole in the harbor at Salerno had been blown up by their engineers. Explosion followed explosion, and soon warehouses and numerous small schooners in the harbor were on fire. The warehouses appeared to Rocholl to be empty, for they burned to the ground in no time. On the other hand, a large boat burned the whole night through.

The time passed slowly for the Germans. Though Rocholl ordered his men to rest in relays, they were all too keyed up to sleep at first. Gradually they did settle down and catnapped.

Toward midnight they were disturbed by the sound of aircraft overhead. The soldiers shrugged their shoulders deeper into the foxholes, but Rocholl realized that they were German planes and not the British night bombers that had plagued their lives ever since they had come to Italy. The irregular beats of the unsynchronized engines faded as the planes headed out to sea. The moon shone as a weak crescent very low on the horizon. Rocholl had his excellent night-vision binoculars to his eyes, but he could see nothing. Suddenly on the horizon a formidable anti-aircraft barrage tore skyward. The broad curtain of gunfire showed up clearly the full length of a convoy. Rocholl could recognize especially the anti-aircraft cruisers, for the sound of the multibarreled pom-poms (the British called them Chicago pianos) was quite distinctive.

An hour later a second wave of bombers flew over their position to the sea. By this time Rocholl could clearly see that the entire convoy had advanced far into the Bay of Salerno.

As the landing craft moved toward the minefields the accompanying warships opened fire. The Hunt class destroyers H.M.S. *Mendip* and H.M.S. *Brecon* were probably the first to do so. At 0200 hours they had broken clear of the minefield, and now within a mile of the shore they engaged German batteries.

The British infantry were by this time utterly weary of the sea. Unlike the Americans, who were making a "ship to shore" landing, in which they transferred to assault craft off the beachhead, most of the assault infantry in British divisions were "shore to shore." They had boarded the craft that were to beach at Salerno in North Africa.

There was a timeless bond of sympathy between the crews of landing ships and the men who had been in the North African campaign, who came from the desert; many still had desert sores that refused to heal. The landing craft had made them all violently seasick at first. Nevertheless, regular meals and gallons of hot tea laid on by the Navy had all but reduced some of them to tears.

Many had been cooped up on board ship for at least a week, the last three days of which had been at sea and under attack. The majority of the soldiers traveled in the large LCIs. Landing Craft Infantry displaced 500 tons and had blunt but rounded bows, on either side of which steel ramps or gangways could be lowered to the beach. The forward deck had screens of armor plating to protect the troops as they waited to disembark. Amidships were the navigational and crew quarters, wheelhouse, and the bridge. Belowdecks the men camped out in huge troop spaces, which were equipped with wooden benches like garden seats, or tiers of canvas bunks. Though poorly lit and poorly ventilated, they could accommodate 250 troops each.

Despite their misery and discomfort, the men were not downhearted. Morale was high. The Allies by this stage in the war were used to winning, albeit if there were occasional setbacks and local counterattacks to withstand. The men were for the most part young and fit, their bodies well able to absorb the physical discomforts of shipborne life, especially now that the landings were only hours away. The troops had been briefed by their officers during the voyage, and this gave them further cause for optimism.

Optimism comes from the top, and Mark Clark, the Army commander, exuded confidence, although Salerno was to be the biggest test he had ever faced. Clark had last held command in war when in 1918 he led a company on the Western Front before being wounded.

As we have seen, Clark, who was 46 years old, was convinced that this was a "young man's war." He was part of that new generation of senior officers whom some referred to disparagingly as the "kid generals." Major General Dawley, the VI Corps commander, was nine years his senior at West Point.

Mark Clark had been reluctant to accept Dawley from the first as a corps commander. Clark had discussed the problem with Eisenhower in July while they were planning the landings in Fifth Army headquarters at Mostaganem in North Africa. "Well, Wayne," Eisenhower said, "it's entirely up to you. Tell them you would prefer someone else. This is your baby."*

Clark didn't have the heart to take what he knew even then to have been the correct course of action. He knew that General McNair, his mentor, guide, and patron, had chosen Dawley. They were both artillerymen, and Clark was aware that Dawley was McNair's dearest friend. Clark thought so much of McNair that he told Eisenhower he would sleep on the question. The next morning he told Eisenhower of his decision not to turn Dawley down.

It was a mistake.

Notwithstanding any doubts he had over his corps commander, it was going to be a short campaign. General Clark planned to have his Fifth Army in Naples on September 12, just four days after the first of them were to step ashore at Salerno. He believed in giving his command the complete picture, and so the briefings had been detailed and thorough. How many at the platoon and squad level listened to anything that did not concern them is open to question, however. Had the troops paid attention, they would have appreciated that the key to his battle plan lay with what the general regarded as his trump card, the special forces.

An amphibious landing on a hostile shore is a complex and extremely hazardous undertaking. Success often depends on the attacker securing an objective in advance of the main force. This can mean the capture of a vital piece of ground or the destruction of an obstacle, such as a coastal battery or an airfield. The execution of such missions involves a sense of timing, skills, and training that are often beyond the competence of the normal fighting formation, the infantry of the line. It is at this point that the army commander looks to the special forces that are at his disposal: the paratroopers, commandos, and rangers who have these special skills. At Salerno Mark Clark was interested in the capture of vital ground rather than the elimination of an obstacle.

Clark's original plan for going into Naples was to drop Maj. Gen. Matthew B. Ridgway's 82nd Airborne Division north of Naples along the Volturno and to seize the bridges at Capua. The objective was to keep the German reinforcements, especially the divisions south of Rome, from joining the battle. Clark knew that the crucial phase would occur after the beachhead had been taken. This would be a race. The Fifth Army had to bring in their own reinforcements before the enemy could move troops to defend the lines. The Allies had farther to come and by sea; so the advantage lay with the enemy. The 82nd Airborne had to hold the Volturno until relieved; this was the key to the success of Clark's battle plan.

*Though known popularly as Mark, General Clark's close friends always used his family Christian name, Wayne.

It was fortunate that Clark and Ridgway were good friends. Contemporaries at West Point, they had since attended all the command and staff courses together as students. Ridgway was at first strongly opposed to the operation. Clark sympathized, for he knew that the 82nd would be alone and isolated, but his reasoning clinched the argument. "All right, Matt," he said to Ridgway at the end of one heated discussion, "I know I'm asking a dangerous thing from your precious division, but it is something that will help me to take Naples quickly. At the same time, it is a reasonable objective and assignment for your division."

On September 3 Clark was due to board the command ship U.S.S. *Ancon*; instead he received an urgent summons to join Eisenhower at Fifteenth Army Group headquarters in Sicily.

When Clark arrived at General Alexander's headquarters, Eisenhower, Robert Murphy, the American chief civil administrator in North Africa, and Harold Macmillan, his British opposite number, were already waiting. Clark felt the air of barely suppressed excitement among the group.

Eisenhower took Clark to an empty tent close by and quickly brought him up to date on the latest developments. He told him of the Italian capitulation.

"When you hit the beach the Italians drop out of the war," Eisenhower said.

It was the first that Clark had heard of the affair.

"We've got to drop an airborne division in the vicinity of Rome," Eisenhower said.

"Whose silly idea is that, Ike?" Clark asked.

"Both the British and American governments, the joint chiefs of staff, and the Italians. It's the price to pay," Eisenhower said.

"Well, it won't do any good dropping it in the midst of six or seven German divisions," Clark countered.

Eisenhower explained that the Italians were greatly concerned over what the Germans would do to Rome when they learned of the armistice. An airborne division would put heart into the Italian garrison. Together they would hold the Eternal City until the Allies arrived.*

"Where are you going to get your airborne division?" Clark asked.

"The 82nd, of course," Eisenhower said.

"You can't have that. That's mine!" Clark thundered. "My whole plan is based on that division!"

Eisenhower went into the details of the operation. Brig. Gen. Maxwell Taylor, who was the assistant divisional commander to Ridgway and already identified as one of the rising stars in the U.S. Army, was in the Italian capital at that very moment conferring with the leaders of the conspiracy.

"Wayne, this has been decided by the government," Eisenhower said. "Besides, I know it will please you to know that when it drops, the 82nd will pass to your command."

"Thanks, Ike," Clark said. "That's like having a half share in a wife."

---

*Rome eventually fell on June 4, 1944.

Clark took his leave and hurried back to his own headquarters. He knew that the success of his battle plan depended more than ever upon the speed and skills of the special forces left to him.

On the left flank of the British divisions, units of American rangers and British commandos were to storm ashore at two points on the Sorrento Peninsula. The rangers were recruited from the first American troops to arrive in Britain, and the first complements were selected from the garrisons in Northern Ireland. From a single battalion trained alongside the British commandos and serving with distinction in their role as raiders in North Africa and Sicily, they had expanded to three battalions. They took their name, not from Texas, but from Rogers' Rangers, a crack force of Indian fighters that dated back to the days of the New England Colonies. The battalions were commanded by Col. Bill Darby, who had already covered himself with glory when he led his men in the North African campaign. The colonel and all the men from the original 1st Battalion still wore the coveted green beret presented to those who had "survived" the commando course in the wilds of Scotland.

The rangers had been given a crucial mission. They were to land at the fishing village of Maiori. Then, while one battalion was to secure the beachhead and the open flank, the remainder were to advance quickly into the high mountains, a distance of some 6 miles inland. Their objective was to seize and hold the Nocera defile. This was a pass guarding the entrance to the Plain of Naples. It was a natural chokepoint through which the enemy would have to move the reinforcements it deployed from the North against the beachhead. These would include the Luftwaffe Panzer Division Hermann Göring in Naples and the 15th Panzer Grenadiers in Gaeta. Together with the 16th Panzers at Salerno, they numbered 45,000 troops. In the Rome area and directly under the 11th Flieger Corps headquarters were the 3rd Panzer Grenadiers and the 2nd Parachute Division, another 43,000 troops. Now that there were no airborne units to blow the bridges across the Volturno, the only place where these troops could be prevented from taking the most direct route to the beachhead was the Nocera defile, through which passed the road to Nocera and Naples. It was one of the only two routes through the mountains that embraced Salerno.

There were other German divisions in the area. South of Salerno and blocking Montgomery's advance in Calabria were the 30,000 men of the 26th Panzers and 29th Panzer Grenadiers. Across the mountains near Foggia a further 17,000 men of the 1st Parachute Division watched the Adriatic coast.

Bill Darby told his rangers they would be relieved by the advancing elements of the British 46th Division after some 48 hours. He had even gone to the lengths of obtaining photographs of the strange high-sided Humber armored cars used by their cavalry so that there would be no case of mistaken identity in the heat of battle.

Colonel Darby gave the 4th Ranger Battalion, commanded by Maj. Roy Murray, the task of securing the beachhead and the flanks. This battalion had only been formed in April. It was recruited from GIs stationed in North

Africa. As with all ranger units, the men were handpicked and volunteers. Roy Murray was a 34-year-old Reserve officer who had until then been a company commander with the 1st Battalion.

Darby intended to lead the 1st and 3rd battalions inland to the main objective himself.

The British commandos were ready to land at the marina at Vietri, some 7 miles east of Maiori. Vietri is a little fishing village tucked between the hills and the sea, a couple of miles north of Salerno. Immediately above Vietri was the little village of Cava and the La Molina defile.

Two complete commando units* were to come ashore. Their principal objective was to secure the defile. To accomplish this, the commandos had to be able to do two things. First they had to take and hold the high ground on both sides of the valley; with their training and expertise in mountain warfare they were ideally suited for such a role. Second, they had to prevent the enemy from carrying out demolitions and thus blocking the pass, or indeed from retaking the pass. This was where the weakness of the commandos lay. The main task was to defend the road bridge that spanned a gorge on the edge of Cava. If the enemy destroyed the bridge or held the defile they could pop the cork in the bottle, seal the Allies into their beachhead, isolate the rangers at Nocera, and mop up at their leisure. The commandos did not possess the heavy weapons or supplies of ammunition to withstand a sustained attack, especially if it was spearheaded by armor. It was vital for the infantry division with their tanks and artillery to take Salerno and break through to Vietri and Cava as soon as possible.

This was just one of the many weak links in Mark Clark's battle plan.

No. 2 Army Commando was led by the eccentric but legendary "Mad Jack" Churchill. He was a graduate of the Royal Military Academy at Sandhurst and had served for five years as an officer in the Kings Manchester Regiment. However, Churchill did not find peacetime soldiering to his taste and left the Army. In those last years before the outbreak of war Churchill tried his hands at many things and in his own words "bummed" around Europe. He was a film extra for a while and a financial adviser to a Siamese prince in Paris. At one time Churchill played the bagpipes in Italian restaurants in return for lodging and food. A crack marksman, Churchill also took part in the World Archery Championships before the war.

Churchill was recalled to his regiment and served with them in France in 1939 and the disasters of the following year. He was among the first to volunteer for the special forces that were then being established to raid the enemy coast. Churchill gained the epithet "Mad Jack" for his part in the Vaagsö raid in December 1941. This raid on a fortified harbor in German-occupied Norway was a classical encounter in the history of raiding. Churchill, then a major, was second-in-command of No. 3 Commando. He stood in the leading landing craft playing "The March of the Cameron Men" on his bagpipes as the leading wave drove hard for the beach.

The unit had been rebuilt under Churchill's inspired leadership since the

*See Appendix E for details on rangers and commandos.

St. Nazaire Raid when in March 1942 it had sailed as part of the force that destroyed the *Normandie* dry dock and thereby denied the German battleship *Tirpitz* a haven on the western coast of France. Lieutenant Colonel Churchill had taken his commandos to the Mediterranean in the summer of 1943. They had done a period of guard duty at Gibraltar, in case the Germans chose to respond to the Allies' North African strategy by driving through Fascist Spain, seizing the Rock, and closing the Mediterranean. That danger passed, the commandos landed in Sicily in August in time to march into Messina behind the retreating Germans and Italians.

Alongside them were the Royal Marines of No. 41 Commando, led until wounded early in the action at Vietri by Lt. Col. Bertie Lumsden. This commando unit had been formed the previous year and had landed in Sicily with the initial assault.

The commandos also had to link up with the Americans on their left. This, too, was no easy task, since the terrain was rugged and mountainous. There was always the fear that a determined enemy could infiltrate fighting patrols and thus perhaps create havoc in the rear areas. There was also the narrow, tortuous coastal track to defend. This was the only real link between the two beachheads.

Together the two British commando units formed a sort of brigade and were commanded by Brigadier Bob Laycock; it was known as Layforce.* The relationship between the commandos and the rangers was obscure. Laycock outranked Bill Darby, but their relationship was never defined. Some American books even state that Colonel Darby commanded all five "battalions," though the rangers are shown in administrative instructions as forming part of the X British Corps.†

The aspect of command control between units of different nationalities was another area of weakness in the Allied Fifth Army. The result was that the rangers and the commandos fought separate battles at Salerno, but then so did the British and the American corps.

The two defiles at Nocera and La Molina were the keys to the success at Salerno. There was a further "corridor" through the mountains behind Salerno. It led out along the road to Sanseverino. The British did not consider it of much importance, though the Germans were to prove very sensitive to probes by first the reconnaissance regiment and later the Yorks and Lancasters of the British 46th Division.

The plan required the British to break out of the beachhead and advance through the encircling hills by way of these passes while they were still in friendly hands. From there it was good tank country and a clear road to Naples.

The men who landed on the beaches at Salerno on Thursday, September 9, were destined instead to take three weeks to reach Naples; and 12,000 of their number wouldn't make it.

*Not to be confused with the original Layforce of Commandos, which first operated in the Mediterranean theater before 1942.

†46th Division Signals Operation Order No. 1, dated August 28, 1943.

PART TWO

The Landings

Chapter IV

The Special Forces

The Rangers at Maiori

Of all the troops in the first waves, it was the U.S. rangers who had the easiest time that day. The operation in the hours before dawn proved to be an anticlimax, for there was no enemy to oppose them. The local Italian garrison had resigned from the war, and the Germans had neither the time nor the manpower to guard every beach and cove along the peninsula to Sorrento.

Maj. Roy Murray and his 4th Battalion couldn't believe their luck. Their escort, the British Hunt class destroyer H.M.S. *Ledbury,* had released the landing craft at 0300 hours, and the rangers headed in to a shore that was silent and peaceful. The details on land stood out quite clearly in the bright moonlight. They were the first ashore because it was their mission to seize and then secure the beachhead. Murray and some of his veterans had been with the British and Canadians in the bloodbath that was the Dieppe raid in August 1942. Sicily hadn't been the most tranquil of operations, either. So at 0310 hours, when the first assault boat crunched onto the beach and the troops stormed ashore, it was a pleasant surprise to find the only sound was that of their own making. Not a shot was fired.

Marcel Swank had been on the Dieppe raid. The United States had sent fifty rangers to Dieppe for "on-the-job training." Seven men had died and another 11 were wounded; this was about par for the course in relation to casualties suffered by other units that day. Unlike Murray, who had not even made it ashore, Swank had landed with the Canadian Scottish, fought with them, been wounded, and still thanked the Lord every day for his safe delivery. Swank was a staff sergeant and had just celebrated his twentieth birthday. He had enlisted in the 135th U.S. Infantry under age and joined the rangers when they were first organized in Northern Ireland.

Maiori was both a working fishing village and a seaside resort full of its own importance, though it had no claim to fame other than the fact that now it was the first community to be liberated by U.S. forces in continental Europe. It was one of the few places along that rocky, hostile coast where the mountains did not come down to the sea. It had a narrow beach, less than 800 yards long with a road behind a low wall that clung to the seashore. Maiori comprised a couple of dozen fishermen's cottages and some more substantial dwellings clustered before the hills. The better houses were from the heady prewar days of Mussolini and belonged to the local Fascist Party dignitaries from Naples, who used Maiori as their weekend playground. Some shops, a church, a couple of small hotels, and a jetty with a tiny marina for yachts completed the picture. Its importance had been enhanced by the arrival just a few months before of a detachment of *carabinieri* who had taken over one of the hotels on the seafront as their barracks. There were no *carabinieri* in evidence that morning.

Swank covered the beach in a few bounds, then was over the wall and across the road and into a small olive grove. His section flopped down beside him and took up their fire positions. Swank looked up and counted heads. They were all there, and he was relieved to see the Mexican-American boy doing his job. The kid was brand new to the squad and earlier that evening had a bad attack of nerves. Swank had found him on the *Princess Emma* standing underneath an assault boat davit. The ammunition had just been issued to the platoons. A chaplain had said Mass, and they were all ready to go. The boy was shaking so much that he couldn't load the clip into his Thompson. Swank had gently taken hold of the submachine gun, loaded the weapon, and applied the safety catch before handing it back. They had talked quietly until the time came to board the landing craft.

Swank had a dry landing, but it wasn't the same for everyone. The battalion adjutant, Captain Larbun, was walking up and down the seawall in his GI underwear, helmet, cane, and pistol belt. Swank tried and failed to hold a serious conversation with him.

While the two other battalions started to come ashore, Murray reported to Colonel Darby and took him to the house he had selected for the ranger headquarters. Murray had secured the beachhead and established roadblocks on the coast road. His combat engineers had rigged up some charges to rock overhangs along the road, and these were ready to blow the moment a panzer appeared.

The first reconnaissance patrols were on their way with the sunrise. It promised to be another beautiful day. Company F moved off along the coast road toward Salerno. Their objective was to check a couple of fortified observation posts that had previously been garrisoned by the Italian coastal defense division.

The point platoon had the great fortune to capture a couple of Germans. They were only a mile or so outside of Maiori when the men heard the sound of an approaching motorcycle. They quickly deployed among the rocks and on one of those right-angled bends for which even today this road is notorious, stretched some radio wire across. The motorcyclist hit the wire and broke his neck; his passenger in the sidecar, an *Unteroffizier* (corporal), though cut and bruised, survived the crash. He was hustled off to Salerno under escort while the rest of the company moved on down the road.

It was "first blood" to the rangers.

The observation post was manned by Italians, who had clearly not received news of their own surrender. They opened a brisk fire on the rangers, who scattered for cover. The instinct of a soldier at the crack of a bullet is to drop prone in his tracks. This, however, was drilled out of the rangers and replaced by the automatic response of shooting, not at anything, but to make the "shooter" duck in response to the same instinct. On this occasion the ranger on point fired several quick bursts in the general direction of the enemy as a reflex action. When the enemy ducked, the ranger had gained an edge for himself and his company instead of giving the enemy a second and easier shot.

The disciplined firepower of the rangers soon inflicted casualties on the Italians. Their fire slackened, and survivors of the garrison (it numbered only 20 men under the command of an elderly and very frightened sergeant) surrendered.

It was a different story a mile or two farther, when they encountered the second post and the company's final objective. This garrison at first put up a spirited resistance, and the rangers suffered their first casualties—three men were injured by a mortar shell. Once the rangers began to put their tactics of fire and movement in effect and closed in on the positions, however, the Italians showed they had no stomach for a real fight. Having made their point, they were happy to surrender. The rangers left a platoon behind as a garrison, and the remainder returned to Maiori. The wounded, American and Italians, were placed on makeshift stretchers, which were carried by the prisoners.

Daylight brought the Italians in the little town out in force. They welcomed their American liberators with wine and cheers. At first that day prices were remarkably low, and a bottle of Chianti was exchanging hands for 10 lira, which was about 10 cents. Later, of course, when the Italians realized the error of their ways, a couple of sinister figures cornered the supply and the market. Prices by evening had risen considerably.

It was just after sunrise when the Luftwaffe arrived on the scene. The *Ledbury* opened fire but found it difficult to take any avoiding action because of all the landing craft crowded into the roadstead. Nevertheless, her main battery of 4-inch guns kept the planes at a distance, though the *Prince Leopold*, an LSI, was severely shaken by a couple of near-misses.

Company C of the 1st Ranger Battalion was designated the supply company for the ranger force. The rangers had expanded so rapidly that there had been no time to organize the logistics and support services. John Hummer landed just after daylight with elements of the 83rd Chemical

Mortar Battalion. This unit provided the rangers with their heavy support weapons. The battalions used the 4.2-inch mortar, which not only packed an almighty punch with its high explosive but also could fire shells of white phosphorus. Phosphorus, of course, produces dense clouds of white smoke, and this was its intended purpose, but it ignites as soon as it is brought into contact with the air and can cause terrible burns. The Germans feared the weapon, and their propaganda machine frequently accused the Americans of contravening the Geneva Convention over the use of chemical weapons.

Ranger John Hummer spent some hours along with the other members of his company unloading the mortar shells and other stores that quickly began to accumulate on the beach. Hummer did not really match the image of the rough and ruthless ranger. Still a teenager, he was slightly built; he weighed only 127 pounds and with his Army issue spectacles looked more like a scholar than a soldier. But John Hummer was the only man in his platoon who was fully trained to handle the infantryman's answer to the panzer, the 2.36-inch rocket launcher. This weapon had been introduced in 1942 in time for the U.S. landings in North Africa. It was called a bazooka because a very popular American comedian of the day named Bob Burns used for a prop in his act a fearful musical wind instrument he called a bazooka. The similarity between this and the 5-foot tube of the rocket launcher must have caused an American soldier somewhere to christen this weapon. Nobody at this stage of the war, however, had developed or designed a field case to carry the shells. So John and his No. 2, Bob Olsen, used the old-fashioned gas mask case. Empty, it could hold four rounds quite nicely.

The rangers had some distinctive forms of dress. They had taken the knee-high World War I leggings and cut them down to 5 inches, which were then worn with the short boot. It was also a ranger custom to wear the Army woolen OD shirt and trousers into battle together with a field or combat jacket. In the rangers, fatigues were worn only when training.

A seasoned soldier prepares himself seriously for war. For some it was almost a ritual. Darby, the supreme individualist, allowed his rangers relative autonomy over the content of their pouches and packs during an operation. Before the men had left the LSIs and boarded the landing craft, they were issued three days' rations and two extra bandoliers of ammunition. This allowed for a day's extra rations in case the British were a little later than planned in reaching the Nocera defile. Most of the troops stripped down the ration packs in three piles. The first contained the staple favorites, such as coffee, sugar, and cans of meat and beans. The second pile had those items for trade within the unit—such as hash and stew, for example. The third pile was junk, for you couldn't even give away the hardtack crackers and oatmeal blocks. The ranger had also acquired an empty gas mask case in which would be stored his cigarettes, both those brands for smoking and those for trading, he hoped, with the "natives."

Personal weapons included the Thompson or rifle, ammunition for the Luger acquired in North Africa or Sicily, entrenching tool, and four grenades.

Rangers carried two fragmentation grenades and a couple of the British "contact" or stun grenades.

Once the rangers' transport had been landed onshore, Darby deployed his forces.

He headed inland with the 1st and 3rd battalions, the bulk of his command. The main force moved straight up the rough track toward Chiunzi Pass, which is at the very top of the mountain spine forming the interior of Sorrento Peninsula. On either flank other companies spread out to sweep the ground. For them progress was more difficult over mountainous country with thick woods and deep ravines. A resolute foe, few in number, could stall an advance for hours in land like that. So it was a cautious advance, and the ground had to be searched carefully to make sure no enemy were left behind to raid communications lines.

It was 6 miles, and all of those uphill to Chiunzi Pass. But the rangers were superbly fit, and the reconnaissance elements were in the pass by just after sunrise. Darby and the main force arrived later and looked down on the sprawling plain of Naples and the Nocera defile in the distance. The rangers dug in, and Darby for the first time since he landed radioed Mark Clark on the command ship *Ancon* and told him of the success of his mission.

Roy Murray moved out along the coast road toward Amalfi. He intended to establish his battalion headquarters inland facing the main line of potential threat, which could come across the spine of Sorrento Peninsula. Company C remained in the beachhead completing its supply detail, and Company F watched the right flank. Later that morning it sent the first patrol beyond the old Italian outpost to establish contact with the British commandos.

John Hummer and Company C continued to move the piles of stores off the beach. Some of the men were told to keep a wary eye on the Italians, who hovered like vultures waiting to pick at the carcass. The beach was littered with the two items that every soldier always dumped on landing, his Mae West and his gas mask.

The Commandos at Vietri

Even in the days of the Roman Empire, Salerno was regarded as militarily significant to the defense of Rome. Its defense was the subject of military discourse in what passed in those days for their "war college."

It is a strange feature of the Allied landings there in 1943 as the prelude to their march on Rome that the battle in the first hours increased in intensity from left to right along the bay until we come to the Americans in the south, who had the hardest time of all.

We have already seen that the rangers had an unopposed landing. For the commandos on their right, marine and army, the landing itself was harder and the subsequent hours decidedly more bloody.

The two commandos were embarked on the LSI *Prince Albert* and three British LCIs. Their commanders had enjoyed the lull before the storm by sharing a bottle of vintage port in the officers' bar on the *Prince Albert*. There was the brigadier, Bob Laycock, and his principal staff officer, Col. Tom Churchill; his brother, Jack; and the Prime Minister's son Randolph, who liked to attach himself to the commandos from time to time. Randolph Churchill also spoke fluent Italian and so was really quite useful though he had no specific task in the unit. The commandos being such a strange breed of special forces were not so stiff or rigid as the conventional units. It was easier for visitors to find a role.

It was almost time to gather at their boat stations when Tom Churchill said, "I'm always interested in the code names they give to operations. I wonder why in the heat of the summer here they have called this operation Avalanche?"

Randolph pondered for a moment and replied, "I expect it's because there is an avalanche of Churchills landing!"

Jack Churchill's orders were to take the beachhead, wipe out the batteries, and hold the flanks. The marines were to land behind and move up to take the Molina defile and occupy the high ground on each side.

The destroyer H.M.S. *Blackmore,* sister ship to *Ledbury,* released her charges at 0317 hours, and the landing craft moved inshore. Lt. Tom Gordon-Hemming led his troops in the leading wave of LCAs. He was slightly older than his contemporaries, and at 26 years they considered him to be the old man of the party. Gordon-Hemming was an experienced soldier. He had served for five years as an officer in a famous British infantry unit called the South Wales Borderers before the war and had been among the first to join the commandos in 1940.

Now on this bright moonlight night, Gordon-Hemming followed his instructions to the letter. He turned right at a marker buoy and headed straight for the beach. As they moved in, the first shells from the *Blackmore* rushed past overhead. There was a coastal artillery battery at Vietri. It had been built into the cliff face above the coast road, to which it was connected by a steep and precipitous path. Star shells burst into brilliant white light over the cliff face, and they turned night in the cove into day. These had been fired by a Landing Craft Gun (LCG), an ordinary tank landing craft that had its main deck specially strengthened to mount a couple of ancient 4.7-inch guns, relics of World War I. With their shallow draught these ungainly craft could move close inshore where the destroyers couldn't go and provide fire support on call.

The enemy battery fired off green, purple, and yellow flares (presumably a code for an alarm) and then engaged the warships. Gordon-Hemming sailed to the shore unmolested, perhaps because the guns above couldn't depress their barrels sufficiently. Although the commandos were tensed and braced in expectation, no machine-gun or rifle fire rushed out to greet them.

Despite all the light from moon and shells, the sea under the shadow of the high cliffs was as black as ebony. The commandos in stocking hats and with blackened faces and hands stormed ashore even before the ramps on their craft were properly lowered. In their training exercises in Scotland the commandos had become thoroughly used to wet landings up to their neck and in the middle of winter. So it was a pleasant surprise to step ashore onto the shingle of the little beach at Vietri without even getting their feet wet.

Gordon-Hemming secured the immediate beach while the rest of the commandos passed through and moved on into the little village and the battery. There were no Germans and precious few Italians around. Most of the Italians chose to stay behind their firmly shuttered doors and windows. Those whom Gordon-Hemming did see were very frightened; the women were petrified. As in Sicily they had been told that the black Protestant English would "burn out the Catholics and kill the children."

The coastal battery surrendered without much of a fight, and the village was quickly secured. The battery commander, a German lieutenant, presented his dagger to Churchill to signify the formal surrender of his command. Churchill was touched by this act of military chivalry, for as an officer he deeply regretted the passing of the day of the sword. In fact, Churchill insisted on wearing a sword as part of his commando weaponry. He sported the bayonet frog with the short claymore of the Highland Regiment. He used the cross hilt (rather than the basket hilt), which lay flat against his webbing and had a purple tassel hanging down. Back in Sicily, when General Alexander had inspected the commandos, he had questioned Churchill's sword.

"Sir, English gentlemen with my family name have been to war for a thousand years with a sword, and I don't want to be the first not to wear one," Churchill said.

Alexander smiled and passed on quickly, for the Mediterranean theater and the Western Desert had spawned more than its fair share of unconventional if not eccentric soldiers.

Churchill put the German's dagger to one side and reached into his haversack for his emergency supply of candles. It was time to study his maps and get the patrols out toward Salerno and to deal with a far more urgent problem.

In the hills above and behind Vietri the Germans had some long-range mortars. These began to bombard the beach and shore, and within a short time the fire had become both intense and accurate. Though the marine commandos came ashore relatively unscathed, the follow-up forces, particularly later waves with trucks and stores, had a grueling time. It took the marines some hours to get up into the hills and force the mortar teams to retreat out of range. By then two landing craft had been sunk and a number of others damaged.

Twenty-year-old 2nd Lt. Alex Horsfall found the opposed landing at Salerno an awful shock. He had a bad feeling about this operation from the very first. There had been nothing like the preparation for Sicily, where the marine commandos had spent weeks training for a particular mission. For Salerno nobody seemed really sure what was required of the marines.

Horsfall suffered his first setback the moment his section stepped onshore. The mortar barrage deprived him of his sergeant, a battle-wise and experienced soldier.

The section moved quickly through Vietri. The little narrow streets with their high, grubby buildings were just beginning to let in the first rays of daylight. Horsfall followed the cobbled streets as each led one into another and so up the hill toward Cava. The point team sought what cover they could as they ran from one doorway to the next, their rope-soled combat boots silent upon the uneven stones, and the mat black Sten guns at the ready. They had done it so many times before. The battle school at West Ham, where whole streets in the heart of London's docklands, south of the Thames River had been blitzed into acres of rubble, had become the Army's street-fighting nursery. The local population had been rehoused, the area fenced in, and a couple of tenement buildings restored to some habitability as barracks. The excellence of such training paid dividends at Salerno.

At one point they burst out into a little square; there was a church on the left and a low balcony to the front that looked out over Salerno Bay itself. Horsfall's mind seemed to register the sights, sounds, and flashes of gunfire as the unit turned into Route 18 and ran hard for the defile.

There were some Germans in Cava, and an occasional burst of fire would send the men ducking for cover. A commando fell, shot through the stomach; he was in great pain. Horsfall stopped to administer a shot of morphine when he got a "boot up his arse" from his troop commander, a recently joined officer named John Parsons. Horsfall barely had time to take the capsule out of the man before he was on the move again. Parsons was right, he knew that. The last thing that the section commander can do is lose the momentum of his own assault.

The marine commandos stormed into Cava and cleared the Germans out by gun, grenade, and bayonet. Horsfall led his section to the left and then up into the hills. They were all fit young men, and the pace had not slackened since they had stepped off the landing craft 2 miles and an hour back down the road. Parsons and the other section leader, Johnny Walker, took the hills on the right of the town.

High up on a wooded slope Horsfall came upon a complex of abandoned slit trenches. They were beautifully dug and almost on the position he had marked on his map for the section to occupy. He sent the PIAT team down the track between the trees to a point where they could cover Route 18 and the road to Nocera and Naples. (PIAT stands for Projector Infantry Anti-Tank, the British equivalent of the bazooka.) The rest of the section occupied the trenches. Perhaps if his section sergeant had still been with him then they would have known better than to occupy enemy positions. The enemy would know the exact location of their own trenches.

Capt. Anthony Wilkinson commanded B Troop. They moved into the hills behind Vietri and on to their objective, a little village called Dragonea. It was a stiff climb up the mountainside, but there was a dry riverbed that the marines scrambled up. Dragonea was a tiny hill village with two streets and a few hovels that passed for homes sprawled on the mountainside. Wilkinson led his troops through the village and turned to the right beyond the little square. About a quarter mile farther, the high ground fell away sharply. He deployed his sections into a depth defense. He could see below him the main square of Cava and Route 18 winding between the hills. Wilkinson moved onto the reverse slope of the hill, toward Dragonea; where his troop sergeant major had already established their headquarters. The half dozen men of the headquarters group were hard at it, slit trenches were being dug, the communications were open to headquarters in Vietri, and most important of all—there was a brew of tea ready.

Captain Wilkinson gratefully sipped from a mess cup full of hot, sweet tea and made the report to his colonel. Then he contacted Q Troop, who were on his left and digging in around Dragonea. They were commanded by his very good friend Martin Stott.

They had at the most 12 hours to wait before that defile below them would fill to the sound of the tanks and guns of the 46th Division on its way to Naples.

Chapter V

Uncle Sector: The Landings
of the 46th Division

Brian Coombe was in the first wave of troops to land in Uncle Sector. The 22-year-old lieutenant had intended to become a regular officer in the Royal Engineers, but his intake into the Royal Military Academy at Woolwich was canceled when, in the same month, Germany invaded Poland. He now commanded No. 2 Section of the 272nd Field Company Royal Engineers. His 65 men and eight vehicles would come ashore in 13 different landing craft. Coombe would land in the lead boat and thus be among the very first in the division to touch the ground of the European mainland. His orders were to open up the beach. This meant that his men had to sweep and mark safe lanes through any minefield.

These lanes were not intended for the assault companies. They would have to take their chances as they charged across the beach and into the sand dunes beyond. It was their job to push back the enemy defenders and secure the beachhead. It was Coombe's job to open up the routes for the subsequent waves of infantry, together with the vehicles and the support weapons.

Coombe had traveled to Salerno in an American LST though not all its load of troops were intended for the first wave. Their turn to land would come later in the day. Shipboard conditions were crowded and uncomfortable. LSTs were really designed to transport armor for short distances and so had little by way of space or amenities for troops belowdecks. The heat in the holds where the vehicles were stowed and the men were supposed to sleep was unbearable. The food was normally C rations, for the ship's galleys could not supply so many people.

The U.S. crew had been very anxious to do all they could for the soldiers, especially, it seemed, to compensate for it being with no liquor on board. On D-Day the Americans gave all the men in the first wave hot coffee and doughnuts. The doughnuts were lovely and hot, the most delicious that Brian Coombe had ever tasted.

Just after midnight Coombe and his team shook hands all around. The farewells were very dramatic. As they were the first troops away, the men stepped straight into the LCAs, and then the little assault craft were lowered down into the sea.

Every one of the LCAs got away safely except the craft in which Brian Coombe, who was supposed to be leading the other craft into the beach, traveled. It was stuck between the deck and the sea, where it stayed for a little while—though it seemed like hours to a fuming Coombe—before the swaying craft was lashed to the ship's side. The troops reached out and clambered up the scrambling nets and back onto the deck. They were so loaded down with all sorts of equipment that this proved quite tricky. On the deck they learned that somehow a cable had snagged the propeller of the LCA and it was now hopelessly entangled.

The other LCAs had disappeared into the night.

There was nothing for Coombe to do but return to the wardroom he had left so dramatically just a short while before and seek consolation in the excellent coffee and doughnuts.

Coombe knew what to expect, but it was still embarrassing to be greeted with cries of, "God, you've turned up again! It's a short war!"

And what was even worse, those who weren't part of the first wave had finished the coffee and doughnuts.

The propeller was soon freed, and Coombe and his men clambered down the net, easier than going up, and into the landing craft. Once clear, the coxswain steered a course to the stern of the mother ship, where all the other LCAs were still forming into their circle.

A flotilla of minesweepers led the way into the beach. They had their sweeps out to port and moved in line abreast. Close to the beach each craft turned and reversed course. Seven ships in the flotilla would sweep a channel approximately half a mile wide on each course. By the time they returned to the starting point, theoretically a channel a mile wide had been swept through the minefield.

The German defenses were now thoroughly alerted. Batteries of 88mm guns opened fire on the LSTs. The first salvoes scored a direct hit on *LST 357*; a number of the crew and 25 soldiers were injured.

Admiral Connolly, U.S.N., was the senior naval officer in Uncle sector, in the command ship U.S.S. *Biscayne*. The latter, a converted seaplane tender, moved forward and laid a smoke screen between the LSTs and the shore to cover the backup waves while they were still embarking their troops. Three Hunt class destroyers steamed to within a mile of the shore and bombarded the enemy positions. Landing craft support ships then escorted the assault craft all the way into the beach. The LCGs took a fearful pounding as they engaged the Germans at small-arms range, but between them the destroyers and gunboats caused the enemy bombardment to slacken considerably.

Just before the first wave hit the beaches, the rocket ships sent their salvoes. These were ordinary tank landing craft with superimposed decks on which were stacked rows of rockets. Each craft carried about 1,000 5-inch rockets. These were electronically fired in salvoes by the commanding officer, who sheltered in a little steel cupola above the wheelhouse. Every other crew member sheltered below decks to avoid the sheet of flame that the rockets threw out.

The contribution of the landing craft rockets (LCRs) to the Battle of Salerno lasted less than 5 minutes, but it was devastating. The effect of the fire of a thousand rockets in a small area is roughly the equivalent to the fire of 30 regiments of artillery or 30 cruisers each with a broadside of 12 6-inch guns.

The sight of these monsters in action defies description. There are the whistling roar and trails of arching fire as numerous salvoes hurtle shoreward. The deafening thunder of hundreds of simultaneous explosions as the projectiles detonate the minefields and obliterate the defenses blocks out all other sounds. Now, the ground struck by the salvoes burst into gouts of orange flame, which lit up the predawn sky. The few Germans who survived the bombardment were seen dazedly coming out of their holes.

Subsequent salvoes hit farther inshore as the ship moved forward at about 3 knots until its pods were empty. The tricky moments came later for the crews as their craft reversed course slowly away, alone, unarmed, and suddenly terribly vulnerable. The sailors tried to ignore the threat of enemy retaliation as they gingerly moved around the still smoking rocket pods checking for misfires.

The Americans had no faith in this absurdly ingenious device and refused to use them. There were sufficient rocket craft to fire the way onto each British beach.

The leading waves were under orders to land on those beaches that had been attacked by the rocket ships. On the left-hand beach (Uncle Red), the 1/4th Hampshires took casualties on the final run to the shore. The German batteries were out of range of the rocket fire and in their turn fired deadly accurate air bursts just over the open landing craft.

The crowded infantry squatted in the darkness, surrounded by their thoughts, fears, and one another. At this moment of trial they sought protection and comfort from the nearness of a comrade and the plywood side of the landing craft. For the first time, perhaps, they were made starkly aware of the relentless compulsion of the military machine, which had collected, trained, and then molded them into an efficient killing unit and at the appointed hour set them down on the beaches of mainland Europe. Once the leading companies of the battalion reached the shore, like a well-oiled machine they stormed across the beach toward their initial objectives.

Trouble began with a tiny navigational error. The rocket craft that was to blast the way ashore for the 2nd Hampshires fired its salvoes on the wrong beach, and the rockets intended for Uncle Green fell on Sugar Amber. The leading wave of the 2nd Hampshires followed orders and the rockets. They landed south of the Asa River and onto the beach used by the Queens Brigade of the 56th Division. The repercussions unraveled like pulled wool from a sweater, and the results were nearly calamitious. Sugar Amber became hopelessly overcrowded, and the leading elements of the 5th Hampshires followed their 2nd Battalion onto the wrong beach. However, the heavy weapons and vehicles of both battalions, which came ashore in later waves, attempted to land on the correct beach. Thus the rifle companies were separated from their own desperately needed support of mortars, antitank guns, and heavy machine guns. The latter couldn't in any case land properly because the German defenses on Uncle Green were still intact, and the rifle companies were needed to pry the defenders out of their positions.

The main target that the offending rocket craft had failed to destroy was an enemy strongpoint that the Italians had called the Magazzino and the panzers Lilienthal. The Germans had taken it over the previous afternoon and in the short time available to them had improved its defenses. It fairly bristled with machine guns, mortars, and the older coastal defense pieces left by the Italians.

Sugar Amber became even more congested as with clockwork regularity the succeeding waves of landing craft arrived off the beach. Some of the boats, unwilling to mill around and wait their turn under fire, came northward past the Asa River. The result was that the Hampshires had companies on both sides of the river, and the Lilienthal blasted away at every new target that came within its range and arc of fire. Some of the Hampshire companies became horribly confused, and casualties began to mount.

Brian Coombe had come ashore as planned with the 1/4th Hampshires on Uncle Red Beach. He had been very conscious of the fact that he would be among the first to land and was determined to do it properly. But his actual arrival on the mainland of Europe was the reverse and quite undignified. He slipped on the wet and greasy ramp and fell head over heels onto the beach.

The sappers started to clear lanes across the beach. A standard lane according to engineers is about 8 yards wide. Coombe worked alongside his troops. Tall and slight, he never wore a helmet (they gave him the most blinding headaches), but instead wore his service cap. The most useful thing he carried was the long bayonet, the sort used in World War I. He found this, with its 3-foot blade, the best way of prodding for mines.

Three men with mine detectors moved slowly up the beach, and with them came another three men prodding the ground with their bayonets, searching for wooden mines or booby traps. Coombe was not too worried about the latter, since the Germans hadn't had enough time to do anything elaborate. The mine detectors were fairly primitive. They would pick up a fair lump of metal, but the Germans also had wooden mines where the only metal was probably the firing pin. In addition, if the mine was at any depth, the detector wouldn't pick it up.

It was the *Schützenmine* that the men really feared. This was an antipersonnel mine that when tripped forced a canister containing shrapnellike steel balls about three feet into the air. When the canister exploded it had a lethal range of about two hundred yards. The British and Americans called it the "S" mine; the fighting troops called it the "debollicker."

The men working on the outside of the lane had little reels of tape on their backs. As they moved forward the tapes unrolled, and another sapper would peg the tape down with colored markers.

It was a slow and ponderous business for the sappers to clear a lane across a beach, and not the least of their worries was the enemy shellfire, which caused a steady trickle of casualties. As Coombe had suspected, the Germans had sown most of their mines among the dunes and the exits of the beach.

The point platoons of the Hampshires had already worked their way along the tracks that led to the main Salerno road. German S mines and artillery had taken their toll, but the resistance was not nearly as severe as that experienced on their right flank.

Whether on land or at sea, it was, of course, impossible to account for every mine. LCT 570 was moving under orders to the beach. She carried six priests of the Royal Artillery. These were 25-pounder field guns mounted on a tank chassis. They got their name because of the high cupola, which the gun commander occupied, shaped something like a pulpit.

Leading Seaman Turner, the coxswain, was down in the little wheelhouse below the bridge; it was a tiny enclosed affair with a solitary porthole in the front. It gave the coxswain a rather obscured view out over the ramp and bows of his craft. Turner, a 21-year-old farmboy from Lincolnshire in England, was on his second operation; for he had arrived in the Mediterranean in time for Sicily.

LCT 570 emerged from the smoke screen into the curtain of 88mm fire and steered for the shore. Turner could see very little and was relying on course instructions from his skipper in the open bridge above him. Suddenly there was a big dull boom, and Turner was thrown against the ship's wheel. The landing craft stopped dead.

"We hit a mine, Coxswain!" the skipper shouted down through the voice pipe.

"What are you going to do?" Turner asked.

They were about the same age, and Turner didn't consider this a time to stand on formalities. The skipper came down from the bridge and discussed the situation with Turner, who was his leading hand. The mine had blown off the bows of the landing craft and in the process had inflicted heavy casualties among the soldiers, though none of the landing craft's crew had been hurt. Seven of the gunners were killed, and another 20 were wounded. Three of their guns were badly damaged, and one had disappeared entirely. The double bottom of the landing craft had stopped it from sinking like a stone.

An attendant motor gunboat came alongside and transferred the dead and wounded. The skipper ordered the surviving soldiers to join the gunboat. By this time it was daylight and Turner could see quite a number of mines bobbing in the water around them. They were perhaps a mile and a half from the shore. While the first lieutenant and the spare sailors fired at the mines with rifles that had been discarded by the soldiers, Turner and the skipper discussed their predicament. Both aware of a previous incident when a sister boat had broken in two and her skipper in the stern section had towed his own bows into port, they decided to try to beach the boat stern first; the engines were undamaged, so they had all the power they needed. Turner brought *LCT 570* around and pointed the stern at the beach.

LCT 570 moved slowly, very slowly toward the shore. They had gone about half a mile when suddenly the craft gave a great shudder and they heard the sound of collapsing metal.

The engine room crew were already on their way up to the deck when the skipper gave the order, "Stand by to abandon ship!"

A gunboat came alongside, and the crew stepped across. They watched as *LCT 570* slowly turned over and settled by the shattered bows. The remaining guns fell into the sea, and the stern rose momentarily into the air before *LCT 570* disappeared.

Chapter VI

The 56th Division

Sugar Sector and the Queen's Brigade

By 0255 hours the minesweepers of the 12th Minesweeping Flotilla had swept a channel through which the leading Hunt class destroyers and LCGs moved in to soften up the defenses.

Capt. N. V. Dickinson, R.N., was the senior naval officer for these beaches; and his command ship was the *Royal Ulsterman*, an LSI. Dickinson dispatched the first wave of the Queen's Brigade toward the shore, and they landed about 10 minutes late, at 0340 hours.

The "Black Cats" stank of coffee. These men, who had all been in the Middle East for some while, wore khaki drill (KD), a lighter-weight tropical uniform, which had been bleached almost white by the relentless desert sunlight. The final collapse of the Axis in North Africa had yielded a vast amount of war booty, which included tons of poor-quality Italian coffee. The staff, fearing that the soldiers would stand out against the green European terrain had all their KDs stained brown. Great cauldrons of boiling coffee were prepared, some in North Africa and others on the ships en route to Salerno, and their KDs "dunked" in the evil brew. The result was an unevenly brown-stained uniform smelling of coffee.

Even this smell was overpowered by another. As they approached the shore the soldiers from North Africa could smell Europe. For so long they had lived with the perfumeless scrub of the desert that the scent of the greenery ashore was overpowering.

The main difficulty in Sugar Sector was overcrowding and congestion as men and machines spilled in from Uncle. Nevertheless, the Queen's were able to push inshore against light but stubborn resistance. These beaches remained the quietest in the whole of Salerno Bay. By 0630 hours the first of the big LSTs were coming right to the shore and unloading straight onto the beach. This is called "dry ramping."

The real problems came with the two beaches Amber and Green in Roger Sector.

Maj. G. F. H. Archer commanded the headquarters company and was the unit landing officer with the 8th Battalion of the Royal Fusiliers. A 26-year-old Regular Army officer, Archer had been commissioned into the Royal Fusiliers in 1936 upon graduation from Sandhurst. He went to France in 1940 with the 2nd Battalion but was transferred home just before the German blitzkrieg to take command of a company in the 8th, which was a territorial battalion. He had been with them ever since.

They had sailed to Salerno in the relative comfort of the *Glengyle*, an LSI (*L*), Landing Ship Infantry (Large). *Glengyle*, 10,000 tons of assault ship bristling with landing craft and guns, was a Royal Navy ship that could lift a full battalion into battle. Her gravity davits held three LCAs apiece, whereas the gravity davits found in most other ships carried only one.

Archer left the *Glengyle* at midnight with the first wave of LCAs. He and his party of eight regimental policemen were to organize the fusiliers onshore and direct them by company inland to their respective forming-up positions. The policemen carried empty jerry cans in which they had cut holes to represent the companies—one hole for A Company, two for B, and so on. The idea was to light these and so signal the companies onto the correct part of the beach.

It had been a considerable relief to Archer to discover that the beaches in his sector were not mined. Some marvelous air photographs taken just 24 hours before had been dropped to the ships. The photographs showed a German soldier and his girlfriend walking arm-in-arm along the seashore.

The first wave into Roger Sector had a quiet passage all the way to the beach. Archer and his team leaped out of the craft and ran straight across the sand to the shelter of the dunes. There was some spasmodic fire, but the forward companies were scuttling past on their way to the battalion's initial objective, the coast road. Archer stood up and looked around to get his bearings. He couldn't recognize any of the landmarks, though he had spent hours on the *Glengyle* studying the air photographs.

Archer knew they had to be on the wrong beach as there wasn't anything that looked even remotely like the landmarks. Unbeknownst to him, the beachmaster had decided to bring the fusiliers ashore 1,500 yards south of their intended beach.

In the meantime, Archer, still confused, told his group to stay put while he ran inland after the first wave until he could get his bearings. He took his unfortunate batman with him as escort. A batman was an officer's servant. In times of peace or when the regiment was out of the line the batman looked after his officer, cleaned his quarters and kit. In battle the batman acted as the officer's runner, prepared his meals, and dug his slit trench. This allowed the officer to concentrate on the more important tasks of leading his men without having to worry over his personal administration. As a system it has worked extraordinarily well. In Archer's case he had a batman who was older than the others, a perfect "gentleman's gentleman" in camp but a little slow in war.

It was harvest time and in the air photographs Archer had noticed a field of hay stacked around poles, rather like Indian wigwams. He walked onto the field and in the bright moonlight recognized the shapes of the hay stacks. Archer turned to his batman. "My God, I know we're not where we are meant to be!" Archer said as they hurried back to the beach.

It was too late. The policemen were already laying out the tapes and lighting the little containers of gasoline in the bottom of the jerry cans. There was nothing that Archer could do about it, because the ramps of the landing craft bringing the second wave were already grounding on the beach.

At this precise moment a German battery with 88mm mortars and heavy machine guns, which had survived the initial barrage by remaining quiet, suddenly roared into action. While the machine guns and mortars hammered at the fusiliers, the larger guns took on the landing craft that were still some way out to sea.

The target of the German guns were three LCTs loaded to the limit with the Sherman tanks of A Squadron, Royal Scots Greys. The tanks under the command of Major Stewart were the armored support for the fusiliers.

Leading was *LCT 397,* commanded by Sub-Lt. Lew Hemming. He had started the journey from Bizerte as "tail-end Charlie" because he was the junior of the three commanding officers. But earlier that night the Greys had decided that the craft were loaded in the wrong sequence. Their squadron commander wanted the tanks on Hemming's craft ashore first. They couldn't switch the tanks around, so they had to change the order of the ships. Hemming, who until this time had been taking life easy at the end of the line, suddenly found that as lead ship he now had all the responsibility for navigation. Hemming thanked the good Lord that he had John Simon as his first lieutenant. Simon was a mathematician whose navigation was perfect.

LCT 397 carried a load of five Sherman tanks and a "D8" bulldozer in front. Each Sherman had a 3-ton Bedford army truck to pull ashore, and there were a couple of jeeps and some additional 3-tonners at the rear of the vehicle deck.

An LCT was 200 feet long and fully loaded weighed over 800 tons. In this condition it had all the sea-keeping qualities of a floating piano.

Their orders were to land the tanks at H + 20;* so Hemming had begun the 12-mile run into the shore shortly after midnight. Just ahead of them Hemming watched another LCT that was of particular interest. It carried the regimental guides and was scheduled to beach 10 minutes ahead of the Sabre squadrons of Sherman tanks. The guides were traveling in an LCT Mark IV. This was a more recent boat than Hemming's Mark III, longer, bigger, and

---

*H hour indicates the precise hour of the attack or the start of the operation. So H + 20 means 20 minutes after the operation has begun.

broader in the beam. However, since it had the same power plant, the Mark IV was a knot or two slower. Hemming began to overhaul his bigger brother and so drew the Greys' attention to this dilemma.

"Do you want to land in sequence or land on time?" he asked. It was the sort of problem that the planners should have spotted, but then everything was done in such a rush at Salerno. There had been neither the time nor the opportunity to take account of contingency plans to cover a breakdown in the master plan. At this level the operation was planned from start to finish in three weeks. The Allies had three years to get ready for Normandy and still mistakes were made there.

The Grey pondered a moment. There was no way he could ask the advice of his squadron commander in LCT 391 astern. It had to be his decision.

"Well, Lew, it's better for us to land in sequence," he replied.

Hemming ordered his helmsman to alter course and reduce speed. The signaler flashed the message to the LCTs who were following in line astern. Hardly had this been accomplished when there was a tremendous explosion and a pall of black, oily smoke hid the spot where the LCT Mark IV had been. Lew Hemming couldn't tell whether it had sunk or not, but he guessed she had probably hit a mine.

He turned to the soldier standing alongside on the crowded bridge. "Well, I'm sorry, old son. You're on your own because I don't think your guides are going to be there," he said.

Both agreed that the LCTs might just as well be on time now.

Hemming brought his LCT back onto the original course, and the speed picked up again to their best, a respectable 8 knots. A German air raid started. The night sky filled with flares, and occasionally a bomb dropped around them. The greatest threat seemed to come from the falling shrapnel of exploding AA shells.

An assault craft loomed up out of the darkness and kept station abeam of Hemming's boat. It contained the beachmaster.

"Is this 397?" an anonymous voice sounded through the darkness and a megaphone.

"Yes," Hemming replied.

"You're not to beach as originally intended," the voice ordered and then added by way of explanation, "There are some German guns waiting for you."

"Aye, aye," Hemming replied. "Where shall we go?"

"Move to the north," the beachmaster ordered, "and land there if you can. There is an assault boat burning on the water. You should be all right if you come in on the other side of it."

Lew Hemming gave the order to turn to port, and the LCT turned 45 degrees until they were beam onto the beach. He was followed by the other two craft, moving in sequence, first 391 and then 346.

It was at this point that the Germans let rip with everything they had. Either their battery commander had realized the LCTs were going to move away and out of his arc of fire, or he just couldn't resist the fat, juicy targets of three LCTs broadside and less than half a mile out to sea. The 88mm high-velocity shells rushed by. Hemming had been at sea long enough to know that he couldn't stay beam onto the beach. He had to present the smallest target to that battery, fast; either he showed his bows or his stern to the Germans. He had to reach the beach, so the decision had to be hard-to-starboard and back on course.

He called down the voice pipe, "Get back on the original course, cox'n. Stay on that course whatever happens."

John Simon, the first lieutenant, left the bridge and ran along the catwalk above the vehicle decks to the bows. It was his duty to lower the ramps and direct the tanks and trucks out of the ship and away to the beach. As Simon ran along the catwalk he frantically waved his right arm clockwise above his head. The tanks below were waiting for that signal. As one the engines roared into life. The Wright-Cyclones of the Shermans were not renowned for their silence, and the well deck echoed to their roar.

Sailors passed between the vehicles knocking out the shackles that anchored the tanks and trucks to the big eye bolts in the deck.

The starboard pom-pom, a 20mm Oerlikon with a flat trajectory of 1,000 yards, took on the Germans. Hemming didn't have enough crew to fire both of his cannons. The one mounted in the port wing of the bridge remained silent.

Hemming called down for full emergency speed, and he kept calling until the LCT shuddered from stem to stern and sparks were pouring out of the exhaust funnel behind him.

He was absolutely certain that the LCT would be hit. Exposed as he was on the bridge, which boasted nothing more than some thin plate and splinter matting as protection, he didn't have much hope for his own survival. It seemed like forever, but it was perhaps only a couple of minutes later that he realized why the Germans were not hitting his LCT. They couldn't depress their guns low enough, and instead the shells were ripping through the rigging literally within feet of his head.

The Germans missed Hemming but hit 391. She got caught on the turn and while still beam on to the beach. The landing craft was hit five times in rapid succession. One shell struck the turret of the tank on which Major Stewart was sitting, though miraculously he survived.

LCT 391 caught fire immediately and within a very few moments had rolled over and sunk. Most of the soldiers who took to the water swam for the shore; some were picked up by a couple of motor launches. Three soldiers were killed; two were troopers, and the third, a young lieutenant named Hutcheson, had joined the regiment just a few days before they left North Africa.

The third landing craft, *346*, managed to avoid trouble by turning a complete circle. She had started to make her original turn to port as the first shells plowed into her consort. Her quick-thinking skipper decided to complete the circle and come in again rather than swing to starboard. When the LCTs were full loaded they were slow and ponderous craft, which answered the helm in their own good time.

Meanwhile, Hemming drove hard and straight for the beach, but they were no longer alone. A British destroyer had spotted their plight and steamed alongside. This was H.M.S. *Laforey*, a destroyer leader armed with six 4.7-inch guns. She engaged the battery in a most spectacular fashion. An ammunition dump onshore blew up with a shattering explosion. The whole area became shrouded in smoke and dust. At a range of 800 yards, battery and destroyer exchanged shot for shot before the German guns fell silent. The *Laforey* then limped away to lick her wounds. She had taken five hits. A shell had burst in the boiler room. There was a 3-foot hole at the waterline. One stoker was killed and some other men badly wounded. The *Laforey*'s commander, Captain Hutton, signaled his consort, H.M.S. *Lookout*, to take his place.

In the meantime, *LCT 397* had hit the beach, and John Simon had sent the ramp crashing down. It seemed to Hemming to be taking a long time, and nothing was happening. He was waiting for the armor to start rolling so he could move his craft farther up the beach as the load lightened. By now a host of small-arms and mortar fire was sweeping the area. From his vantage point on the exposed bridge Hemming watched as other landing craft were hit and men ran up the beach, many falling.

Unable to contain his patience any longer, Hemming left the bridge and ran along the catwalk to the bows to see what was causing the delay. The bulldozer hadn't come off yet, and Hemming's unreasonable fear was that unless it got off soon, nothing would get off. They could not have this charmed existence much longer.

By the time he reached the bows, training, experience, and above all, discipline had reasserted themselves over fear. He gazed down on what was obviously the problem. The blades of the bulldozer were only inches shorter than the width of the exit from the landing craft. She had to be teased gently free of the boat, and John Simon had everything under control. Hemming walked carefully back to his bridge and paused en route to exchange farewells with the Greys' troop leader in the first Sherman. He spent the next fifteen minutes totally absorbed in the intricate task of inching forward in response to the tanks and trucks leaving the craft. When Simon signaled that the last vehicle was away, Hemming rang down for full speed astern. Ramp down, for that could be winched back at their leisure, *LCT 397* wriggled free of the grasping sand and swung out to sea.

LCT 397 made its way back through the crowded anchorage as dawn revealed the squalor of the debris of war floating around. Pieces of ships and equipment and pieces of men, too, danced in unison a macabre ballet in time to the wash of the passing ships.

Hemming could not help but think that although both soldiers and sailors had shared those moments of absolute fear and terror under fire, for the Navy their job, at least for the present, was over. For the Army it had only just begun.

Chapter VII

The 36th Division

The 16th Panzer Division had two reinforced companies covering the four beaches in the U.S. sector. Most of these troops were at strongpoints constructed close to the shoreline. They were originally intended to bolster the local Italian defenses, but now that they no longer existed, the Germans were at a disadvantage, for their infantry (in this instance panzer grenadiers trained to operate alongside tanks) was now in static defense points. There was not sufficient infantry remaining to operate with the tanks in a local counterattack role. The panzers had sited some additional machine guns and mortars to cover the likely exits from the beaches and had put down single concertina barbed wire.

Field artillery was dug in around the foothills below Mount Soprano. From these positions they had a commanding view of the shoreline and beaches. Panzer engineers had cut down a grove of pine trees near the medieval watchtower at Paestum. This improved the arc of fire for the field guns inland, to the railway and Route 18. As a parting gesture, the fallen trees were booby-trapped.

The Americans were about to pay the price for allowing the enemy the luxury of leaving his shore defenses virtually undisturbed until the moment of landing. Rumors persist to this day that as the first elements approached the shore a loudspeaker from the sand dunes roared out in English, "Come on in and give up. You're covered." This did perhaps occur but in a quite different context, as we will see later.

Peter Matterson and Lieutenant Commander Scanlon led the first wave in toward Red Beach. They passed the gunline provided by the 5-inch batteries

on the U.S. Navy destroyers *Bristol, Ludlow,* and *Edison.* From that point on
the landing craft were on their own. To the left the bay had come alive with
the sound and fury of battle as broadsides from the naval support ships in the
British sector thundered away and German batteries fired in defiance. To the
American front the beaches were quiet; there was neither sound nor
movement.

Matterson's navigation had been near-perfect. Despite the most primitive
of instruments he was just 50 feet in error as the first wave approached the
beach. The pilot craft were less than a mile offshore, and their job was done.
Scanlon's boat slackened speed, and the leading wave of the 142nd Infantry
swept past. In the bright moonlight the troops looked remarkably casual and
relaxed. It was just before 0330 hours, and the landings were on time.

The first boats "bottomed" together, and their ramps ground into the
gentle surf. German guns opened fire as one. Flares shot into the sky and
turned night into day; machine-gun and mortar fire raked the landing craft
and the surf. Matterson stood and watched, aghast with horror. Never had he
seen anything like it. Landing craft simply disintegrated, their wooden
frames overwhelmed by a hailstorm of fire at the front and on the flanks.
Other boats, caught a little way out, drifted helplessly, sailors and infantry
obliterated by air bursts.

The tragedy of the act numbed their senses, and it was a moment or two
before Matterson could grab the handset of the boat's radio to summon up
fire support for the second wave.

Pfc. Bill Craig and other men from Company K didn't even get their feet
wet. Their coxswain had kept the throttle wide open and rammed the boat
hard onto the sand. As the men ran up the beach they suddenly realized they
had landed right in front of a pillbox. Any minute now, thought Craig as he
joined a group that scattered to the right and hopefully out of the arc of fire.
Nothing happened; perhaps there weren't enough personnel of the 16th
Panzers to be at every defense post. However, the next one along was
manned, and Craig for the first time in his life heard the unique sound made
by bullets directed toward him. It was and remains an unnerving sound,
though we of today's generation know of the phenomenon of the sound
barrier. On first hearing it, a novice like Craig *knows* it is a lethal sound,
knows that it was much closer to his head than it actually was. Even to the
trained ear of the veteran the sound masks the muzzle report and confuses
the ear over direction. The sound that Craig heard in those dark, early hours
on a beach in Europe has never been copied in a movie theater, and probably
never can. But Craig will tell you, for that morning on the beaches below
Paestum, he became a veteran; the sound that resembles it most is the
cracking of a bullwhip in the hand of an expert.

A salvo of mortar shells burst close by and stitched a line across the sand.
Craig tried to hold onto his reason and remember all that the instructors had
told him of battle—lie still, place your hands over your helmet, and breathe
easily. The air around filled to the tortured whine of shrapnel, and the
platoon suffered its first casualties just a hundred yards into mainland

Europe. The German panzer grenadiers who manned the mortars knew their weapons and the terrain. Systematically they plastered the beach from shore to dune, and the Texans started to pay the bloody butcher's bill for Salerno.

In the face of such intense fire the assault companies were decimated. Nevertheless, they gradually worked their way up the beach and on into the blessed sanctuary and refuge of sand dunes. All they had against the mortar pits and machine-gun nests were hand grenades. The volume of fire pinned them to the dunes.

A hundred yards offshore a landing craft that had been converted into a close support role opened fire. Their original orders were to hold fire until daylight, unless fired on first. There were four such craft, one for each beach. These were small boats carried on the davits of the attack transports. They were lightly armed, with two rocket launchers apiece and smoke pots. The first was to silence the machine-gun fire on the beach and the second to provide cover. Designated LCS (S), Landing Craft Support (Small), they were handy craft but didn't pack a big enough punch. Even so, the boat off Red Beach, under the command of a young ensign, valiantly entered the fray. He discharged his rockets at the enemy beyond the dunes while his .50-calibers engaged the enemy strongpoints.

The nearest American destroyer was the U.S.S. *Ludlow*. Known as "Lucky Lud" in the fleet, she had negotiated the minefield and was steaming just 1,500 yards offshore. Her gunners were remarkably quick, and within minutes shells from her main battery of 5-inch guns were winging their way shoreward. Even so, the amount of help she could give to the already sorely pressed troops on land was limited. The German batteries were using semiflashless ammunition, so they were almost impossible to pinpoint while the *Ludlow*'s gunnery control had no idea how far the U.S. infantry had advanced.

What added to the misery of the men onshore was that there was no sign of the second waves. These should have long since passed Scanlon's boat, but all Matterson had found was an ensign in the scout boat gamely showing a red light some 200 yards off-station. Matterson corrected the direction and then went off in search of the missing second wave.

They reached the minefield and still there was no sign of the landing craft. These boats should have landed 7 minutes behind the first wave.

Scanlon was convinced they had missed them; there was no reason for them to be this far back from the shore. Peter Matterson was equally adamant. "Not with my eyes and my night glasses," he snapped. "They're not here."

Eventually they found them. The landing craft were milling around on the seaward side of the minefield. Apparently a couple of LCAs had struck mines on their way through what was supposed to have been a swept channel. The patrol boats that marked the entrance to the channel had taken it upon themselves to stop any more boats from moving inshore until after daylight, which was still an hour away.

Some of the LCAs were Royal Navy boats. Their coxswains were not at all happy about taking an order they knew had to be wrong. The fact that it came from the U.S. Navy didn't help matters, either. Some of these craft had already set off with their troops for the shore by sailing *over* the minefield and trusting to Providence that their shallow draught would be protection enough.*

Matterson persuaded Scanlon to do the same with the American LCAs. They herded a group together and headed inshore, with the U.S. Navy's threats of dire consequences against Scanlon and the U.S. Coast Guard ringing in their ears; for the patrol boats remained adamant in their refusal to allow the landing craft to proceed inshore.

The little force successfully negotiated the minefield, but by then the night sky was beginning to lighten and Scanlon was anxious to give his brood all the help he could as they approached the shore.

"It's getting light, Pete," he said. "Let's make it dark again." The LCA carried some smoke pots on the stern, and Scanlon set these off. It was a good idea in itself, but the trouble was that every landing craft commander in the area who had smoke canisters did the same.

It was about the most dangerous thing they could have done, for by this time the Navy had relented, and the third wave was approaching the shore. As they entered the rolling bank of thick, choking smoke, the marker boats disappeared from view and confusion reigned. There were numerous collisions, and those that came out of the smoke were totally disoriented.

Scanlon came across a number of these landing craft, full of infantry, milling around leaderless, frightened, and confused. They all seemed hesitant to run the last gauntlet—the zone of fire into the beach itself. He took the scout boat to within hailing distance of one LCA.

"Coxswain, take that lot in!" ordered Matterson.

"I don't think they're ready for us," replied the sailor.

Matterson must have looked an awesome sight dressed in battledress, brilliant white Wellington boots, steel helmet, monocled, and bearded. "Get in!" he ordered.

American infantry cheered, and the coxswain started toward shore. The other craft followed.

On some beaches, the fire was so heavy that the landing craft turned back out to sea. Control craft and others manned by resolute men like Scanlon and Matterson promptly turned them around and sent them inshore. Others simply dumped their human cargoes in deeper water and left them to wade ashore. This meant that radios were swamped and useless. Communications between shore and ship did not function, and the confusion intensified.

Onshore the Germans were putting to good use the town defenses of Paestum. The Doric columns of the ancient Greek temple were fire-resistant, while the blunt ramparts of the old city provided excellent cover.

---

*Lieutenant Stanbury also found elements of waves two to seven at about 0545, waiting some three miles offshore. These he mustered and led onto the beach.

Constructed of Etruscan blocks, the wall extended for some 5,000 yards and in places was 50 feet high.

Near to the beach was a 50-foot medieval stone watchtower. It was too close to the shore to be engaged by naval gunfire. From this vantage point panzer grenadiers had mounted machine guns that swept the beaches. Observers in the tower were in radio touch with the batteries inland. They brought down a rain of lethal mortar and artillery fire.

From the beaches the Americans ran for cover in the scrub and the irrigation ditches beyond the duneline. Infantry moved forward in small groups toward the railway, which was about one and a half miles inland.

Herman Newman was a captain in the 1st Battalion of the 141st Infantry. As operations officer, he was responsible for loading the landing craft. It was his task to fit weapons and ammunition, food, water, and people onto a limited number of landing boats. Above all, he had to ensure that the battalion landing team would be able to fight as it landed. Newman assumed the worst in all his planning. He believed nobody and worked on the assumption that the beach would be lined with "Krauts."

It was just as well that he did. The day had started badly for the 141st, and it didn't really get any better. One platoon of infantry was dropped into the sea when wires snapped and its LCA tipped in the davits. A soldier carried between 75 and 80 pounds of weapons, ammunition, and equipment. Very few survived.

The password on the American beaches was "Hearts of Oak." This was chosen in the belief that the Germans would find it a difficult phrase to repeat. But as Herman found later in the day, the Germans could say it as well as the Americans.

The landing craft approached Blue Beach, and Herman watched as a pair of multiple 20mm cannons in the duneline swept across the water like a fan. Just before the shells reached his boat the guns traversed back the other way, and the boat sailed down the alley between the fire to the beach.

It was still dark as he stepped onshore, though the beach was constantly lit up by flares and exploding shells. All the training in the world couldn't prepare these troops for such a baptism of fire. Their craft had carried the headquarters detail with the battalion CO and the radio operators. Some of the enlisted men were hit as they ran up the beach while machine gun and mortar fire dispersed the remainder of the party. Some men hugged the sand dunes for cover while Newman led a small group through the coarse scrub down an embankment and into a foul-smelling irrigation ditch. Just a short distance to their front were two German positions, both very active. One had a machine gun, and the other was a mortar team.

Newman was armed with a .45 automatic pistol, which was next to useless in this situation. He grabbed a rifle off one of the signalers and told his own orderly to cover his back while he crawled up onto the embankment and tried to pick off the machine-gun crew.

Newman eased up the bank through the reeds until he could see the machine gun to his left. He settled himself and was just about to squeeze the

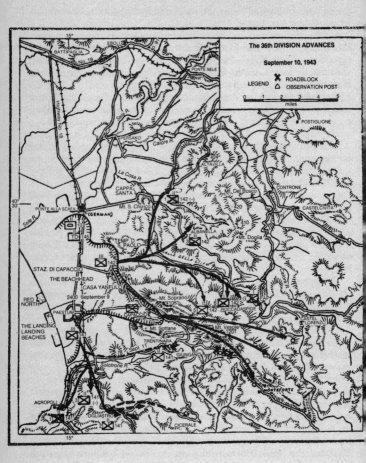

trigger when he suddenly felt straw being piled on his back. He looked up to see his orderly kneeling above him, in full view of the Germans, with a bundle of straw and reeds in his arms! Herman swung the rifle and knocked his orderly into the ditch and then slithered down beside him while he explained the facts of life—in this case, fire and movement—to the soldier.

At that moment a couple of men with a rifle grenade joined them in the ditch. Newman decided to try again. He ordered the new men to engage the mortar while he tackled the machine gunners. With a last withering look at his orderly, Newman moved carefully onto the embankment and opened up on the machine-gun team. The fire from an unexpected quarter seemed to unnerve them, for they scuttled back toward the railway. The rifle grenade, intended for use against tanks, was pretty ineffective in that role, but against an open mortar pit it could be lethal. The second shot fell into the pit, and the mortar ceased firing.

Newman ran up over the embankment and across the swampy ground to the mortar pit, the grenade team right behind him. They found two soldiers standing beside a damaged mortar. One of them was bleeding profusely from wounds in his arms and legs; the other, who supported him, was unarmed. Newman, who spoke a little German, found that the two soldiers were Austrians from Linz. They belonged to the Pioneer Company and had been sent to occupy the position just an hour before the first assault wave hit the beach.

He packed them off to the rear under escort and collected his team together. By this time the Germans had pulled back, and the first waves of the battalion were able to move down onto their initial objective outside Agripoli.

They were the lucky ones. The other waves of the 141st were pinned down for much of the daylight hours by heavy and persistently accurate German fire, which later closed the beaches in that sector. Newman moved behind the leading company. There was little resistance except for an occasional round of sniper fire and more numerous shells and mortars.

Newman sited the battalion command post on the slopes below Agropoli, and the commanding officer together with his headquarters team comprising the Operations, Intelligence, and Communications personnel settled down to the business of war. The problem was that the subsequent waves of the combat team were caught some 400 yards inland. Enemy fire pinned the Americans down, and the companies lost their cohesion as men hurried to find what cover they could. The Texans could advance only in twos or threes. Intense mortar and machine-gun fire made it impossible for larger groups to form and operate.

In the meantime, on the beach, men from the 11th Engineer Combat Battalion were completing their first task of the day, which was to clear the minefields. Dee Winn, a 24-year-old corporal, had been with the unit since its National Guard days; he landed with the third wave of the 141st Infantry. He came in on an LCM, a small landing craft that could carry a light tank or a couple of jeeps.

A tremendous amount of shellfire was hitting the water all around. Winn comforted himself with the thought that if a shell landed near him, he would know very little about it. He had 5 pounds of explosives strapped to his back.

Their wave sailed into the curtain of enemy fire, and there was carnage. On all sides there was a wall of flame. Great gouts of water doused some, but these were quickly overwhelmed by successive salvoes. The noise of the barrage was unbelievable; it assaulted the ears and drove breath from the body. Four LCAs were knocked out; two simply blew up. Bloody fragments of men and material splattered Dee Winn's boat and unnerved the coxswain. "They're going to get us if we keep going!" he yelled.

Staff Sgt. Lee Lester was the ranking man on board. He reached out and steadied the tiller bar on course. "Well, they'll get us for sure if we go back," he said, "so let's go on in."

The boat grounded about 100 yards out, and the men quickly splashed ashore through the knee-deep shallows. The beach was still being swept by a fair volume of small-arms fire, but Winn's squad took no casualties in its mad dash across the sand to the haven of the dunes.

Winn set the squad to work sweeping the exits of the beaches with their mine detectors. As with the British, it was a slow and carefully coordinated effort between "prodder" and "sweeper." The work required that the men expose themselves, and the squad began to suffer casualties.

All the while waves of landing craft touched down, and fresh groups of troops, together with the first vehicles, began to move up the beach and head inland. By sunrise the Americans were just ashore. With the first streaks of daylight the Germans launched their local counterattacks spearheaded by tanks.

Bill Craig and the survivors of Company K had made some 500 yards inland before they were pinned down. A couple of tanks appeared from around the corner of a house and started to fire on the beach. The infantry had nothing to fire back with and so could do little more than get down behind a rock fence and wait for their own artillery to make it ashore.

Their experience is typical of what happened on the American beaches in the hours before dawn. The "T" Patchers were hit by a resistance that not only far exceeded their expectations but also was much tougher than that experienced by the American divisions that landed in North Africa and Sicily. Enemy fire had so disrupted the initial assault waves that the subsequent advance inland bore little resemblance to that laid down by the planners.

PART THREE

The Beachhead

D-Day: Thursday, September 9

Chapter VIII

The Special Forces

Ranger Force

The Americans of the 1st and 3rd battalions of rangers spent most of the day digging their slit trenches along the ridgeline and high ground to either side of Chiunzi Pass. Volcanic ash, in places to a depth of 4 or 5 feet, provided the topsoil and the problems for the rangers. On the one hand it was extremely easy to dig, but its fine, sandlike composition, almost like a black powder, caused frequent cave-ins. The men's experience told them that a near-miss from an enemy shell or mortar could bury a soldier in such a trench. So they dug shallow trenches and then gathered the limestone rocks to build ramparts or parapets to the trenches. These were equally dangerous in their way, for a bullet will ricochet off a stone parapet but simply bury itself in one made of earth.

As the men dug and constructed their foxholes throughout that long, hot day, they stopped occasionally to take in the breathtaking view. Behind them was Salerno Bay, now a scene of frantic activity, but the ships and the landing craft looked like toys in a children's paddling pool. To their front was the magnificent panorama of the Plain of Naples. On the left skyline, the city glistened in sunlight reflected off the shimmering water of the Bay of Naples behind. The rangers had excellent observation of the vital Highway 18 as it wound its way out from the city and passed through the Nocera defile, where they should have been. The defile lay about 3 miles away to their right front. Why Colonel Darby did not go all the way to this natural chokepoint and his military objective remains a mystery. Darby certainly was a law unto himself and did not see fit in any signals to explain why he had stopped at the Chiunzi. Neither did Fifth Army headquarters on the command ship *Ancon* query or challenge his deployment. It certainly wasn't enemy opposition, because the two battalions had not seen a German that morning. However, had Darby moved his battalions onto the defile the Germans could easily have cut off his line of communications and retreat to the sea. There were not enough rangers to hold both Chiunzi and the Nocera defile, and the former was the high ground.

Later that afternoon a patrol of three German armored cars probed toward the pass. The high whine of their gears as their engines labored up the mountain track from the plain betrayed their presence and gave ample warning to the rangers.

A bazooka team moved toward beyond the outpost line and fired in ambush. Two of the armored cars were destroyed and their crews captured; the third reversed furiously down the hill and out of range. The crew members who had survived the ambush were captured and interrogated by the rangers. They belonged to the Reconnaissance Battalion of the Luftwaffe Panzer Division Hermann Göring. The division was based in Naples and in the process of reforming after the mauling it had received during the campaign in Sicily.

Commando Brigade

The commandos were having a sticky time in Vietri. Germans in the hills between Vietri and Salerno had the village under observation and brought down harassing fire with monotonous regularity. Commando casualties began to mount. Small patrols of panzer grenadiers infiltrated back into the narrow streets on hit-and-run raids. Not all of these were successful by any means, and a number of men were wounded and captured. One, a young lieutenant with a nasty leg wound, spoke quite good English. Tom Gordon-Hemming chatted while they waited for a landing craft to take the German to one of the hospital ships in the bay.

"The Italians surrendering! Well, you are the lucky ones!" the young officer said in a bitter and sarcastic manner. "Now, we, the Wehrmacht, are the lucky ones. We no longer say for you the war is over, but for you the war is Italians. You have the Italians on your side," he concluded, "Lucky fellows!" Gordon-Hemming was left in no doubt about the German's contempt for his one-time Axis partner.

Colonel Churchill had ordered No. 2 and No. 5 Troops from his commando to guard the right flank, and they were deployed on the outskirts of the village. They looked over Route 18 as it climbed out of Salerno. There wasn't much space between mountain and sea, though the cliff face was less severe at this point. Houses clustered along the road, and narrow, pebbled streets with impossible gradients led down to the shore.

Lt. Joe Nicholl was a history undergraduate at Cambridge at the outbreak of war. Now he commanded a section in No. 2 Troop, and they were ordered to cover the two 6-pounder antitank guns that had taken up positions in the little tree-lined square, which in better days had been the social center of Vietri. From there they could command the road into Salerno.

And there were problems from that quarter for the commandos, for it wasn't the tanks and armored cars of the 46th Division that drove out of Salerno to greet them, but two Panzers. By this stage in the war every Allied soldier who came into contact with a German tank automatically described it as the one most feared of all, the monster Panzer Mark V, the Tiger. In fact, there were no Tigers with the 16th Panzers at Salerno, or indeed with any of the other formations that later appeared on the scene.

The tanks that came against the commandos on the first day were Panzer Mark IV Specials. With their long-barreled 75mm gun and additional armor they were more than enough to handle.

No. 2 Troop's antitank guns opened fire at 900 yards. The range was too great, and though the shells scored hits, they bounced off the tank's face-hardened armor plating. The second tank, which was following behind, swung off the road and plowed into a cottage. The building collapsed around it, and from its hull-down position the tank opened fire in support of its leader. High-explosive shells slammed into the trees and burst with devastating effect. The little square filled to the scream of shrapnel, and a number of men were killed or wounded. Peter Lea, the unit's Intelligence officer who was standing at the rear of the square, died instantly. He had rushed out of his operation's room when the warning of the tanks had been received and apparently had forgotten to take his steel helmet. Tragically, he was hit in the head. A gifted and popular young officer, he had already been decorated for gallantry and would doubtless have had a brilliant career if Fate had given him the chance.

While Joe Nicholl saw to the wounded, the troop's other section commander, Lt. Pat Henderson, with some of his men in doubtful but faithful attendance, set out to take on the panzers. Henderson had gotten his hands on a PIAT. As mentioned earlier, Projector Infantry Anti-Tank was the British equivalent of the bazooka, and in the right hands a PIAT was a startlingly effective weapon. The trigger released an enormous spring, which crashed into the base or tail of a missile, exploded a propellant charge, and sent it hurtling off toward its target. The PIAT needed brute strength to cock; it weighed 30 pounds and had a kick like a Missouri mule. It would penetrate the armored skin of any tank, provided the range was less than 100 yards. The first batch had reached the commandos just before they left Sicily.

While the section brought down covering fire, Henderson worked his way forward. He got down behind a low wall in front of the house and opened fire. The lead tank had started to move forward when Henderson fired his first round. The shot fell short and bounced on the road in front of the tank. Now thoroughly alarmed and angered by the man's impudence, the tank crew turned their full wrath on Henderson. They couldn't depress the barrel low enough, so they opened fire on the house in the hope that it would fall around him. At the same time, Henderson had to stand up so he could reload the PIAT. The spring could be compressed only by unlatching the shoulder pad, standing on it, and levering the barrel until the spring had withdrawn into the body to the point where it is held in check by a simple catch mechanism. Replace the shoulder pad and the weapon is ready to fire. Henderson fired again and then a third time. Though he hit the tank, the shot failed to penetrate. Every time he stood up to reload, his devoted section smothered the tank in small-arms fire. This at least stopped the tank commander from using the machine gun mounted externally near his hatch. At the same time, shells screamed into the house, and more and more masonry came tumbling around Henderson. The fourth and last PIAT round penetrated the tank. Now the crew clearly decided that discretion was the better part of valor, and so with thick smoke pouring from a jagged hole in the side, the tank limped slowly back down the hill. The second tank covered the line of retreat and then quickly followed suit. Lieutenant Henderson was awarded the Military Cross for this action.

In Vietri itself as the morning wore on, more of the local population ventured out from behind their closed shutters. British soldiers always have a soft heart whenever they come across children. The youngsters of Vietri ate chocolate, many for the first time in their lives, and the first contact across a cultural divide was made.

Tom Gordon-Hemming had two great interests in life. The first was cricket, and the second was his religion; he was a devout Roman Catholic. He stopped and talked to the parish priest, their common language being Latin. Gordon-Hemming asked the priest to say a Mass at which he could serve at the altar. The priest was only too happy to agree, and that afternoon the church was filled to capacity. The word had quickly spread, and the people had flocked to a service held against a backdrop of gunfire as the battle for Salerno increased in intensity.

A number of the commandos who could be released attended. Private Davidson was Gordon-Hemming's batman. Davidson stood close by with his Sten gun cradled in his arms. He couldn't let his officer out of his sight, not even to serve Mass.

When the service was over, the priest turned and addressed the congregation. He spoke with great passion, and much of it was way over Gordon-Hemming's head, though clearly it was good, for the people smiled every time the priest said, "*Grazie*, Capitano."

Thereafter the Italians were remarkably friendly and hospitable toward the commandos. Some of the Italian men offered to help by acting as porters, and others revealed where some German weapons were hidden.

The marine commandos in the hills passed a largely quiet day. They improved their trenches, cleaned themselves and their weapons, and caught up with sleep. Toward the end of the afternoon a couple of reconnaissance vehicles from the 46th British Infantry Division moved out of Salerno. Marines from a dozen vantage points looked down as the armored scout cars felt their way gingerly through the defile, around a hairpin bend, and out of sight. Alex Horsfall breathed a great sigh of relief once the cars had passed by his position. "We're not in the front line anymore, someone else is in front," he thought.

A short while later a ranger patrol came over the hill and down among the trees to his position. Horsfall chatted easily with their officer while the men had a break and cautiously sipped the steaming mess cups of tea that appeared as if by magic. It was good not to be alone, to know that other friendly forces were not too far away. The rangers left to return to their own unit, and, as if on cue, the reconnaissance cars returned through the defile, moving quickly and with evident purpose. A sense of unease permeated the marines. Men quietly climbed back into the foxholes and checked their weapons. Spare ammunition was laid within easy reach, and Horsfall walked quickly around the trenches. The air was heavy with anticipation. All the while the valley reverberated to the sounds of the big guns at Salerno.

Chapter IX

The 46th Infantry Division
and the Battle for Salerno

Since the first landing there had been no letup in the tempo of operations on the beaches below Salerno. With the daylight, more and more troops came ashore, and the beaches were increasingly busy. One man who was ashore with the first waves was Eric Way, a Congregationalist Army chaplain. As soon as he stepped on land the Reverend Way set up an altar right on the beach. This remarkable young man had a tremendous influence over the troops as they passed by on their way inland and to battle.

Capt. Douglas Scott, R.E., was concerned. He had heard nothing from his two junior officers since they had landed. Brian Coombe had by this time moved farther inland. Hugh Lock, the other junior officer, landed under fire with B Company, 1/4th Hampshires. Their LCI was an American craft, and the skipper, seemingly anxious to be free of his passengers and danger, had ditched them some distance from the shore. The radio had been swamped, and communications were impossible.

Once ashore, Lock had moved inland quickly. It was his task to reach Route 18 and make sure as the troops moved up that the bridges were safe and not about to be blown up by a retreating enemy.

Douglas Scott had also sailed in an American craft. *LCT 142* was commanded by Lt. (J.G.) George Laythrop, who until the war had never sailed a boat in his life. The United States Navy took him to the Pacific Coast and trained him on *LCT 142*. Laythrop then took the craft through the Panama Canal, across the Atlantic, and into the Mediterranean, no mean feat for even a seasoned sailor.

George Laythrop had arranged for a breakfast of eggs and bacon on the bridge, a farewell feast. As a special treat he dumped a good dollop of jam right on top of the egg. Scott never quite forgave him for that!

Scott was ready for war. Like most British officers about to be confronted by the possibility of a dunking, he had put the "French letters" to a use never envisaged by the London Rubber Company. All his maps, codes, secret and semisecret stuff, together with his compass, anything that was going into the water was tied into a "soldier's friend" and the end firmly knotted.

Then Scott strapped the low, oblique air photograph of his landing beach, which some intrepid pilot had taken a day or two before, to his forearm and rolled up the sleeve of his khaki drill jacket. He went up to the bridge to say goodbye to George Laythrop. The two had become firm friends during the five days they had spent at sea.

The LSTs were magnificent as they unloaded the early waves of troops into the LCAs. The ships remained motionless so that the heavily laden men had a safe passage down the scrambling nets. Sapper Smith certainly appreciated the gesture. He was a big man—6 feet, 5 inches and with the weight to match—and he needed all his strength that day. Smith clambered down the side with a "Yukon pack" on his back. This was an H-shaped frame made from 2 by 1 timber with canvas slats. Strapped into the middle was a mighty case of atamol explosives. The whole lot weighed about 150 pounds, and although another man carried the detonators, the other members of the team gave Smith a wide berth.

LCT 142 passed through the line of motionless LSTs and into the German barrage. The 88mm and coastal artillery were firing air bursts over the LSTs, Scott thought, to knock the troops off the nets. By the time their craft had reached the shore the volume of fire had increased; it was murderous.

At about this time Admiral Connolly took the U.S.S. *Biscayne* close to the shore and bombarded a German battery that was shooting up his landing craft. Broadsides from *Biscayne*'s 5-inch guns soon silenced the Germans, and she returned to her proper station. Thereafter the admiral was known as "Close-in Connolly."

Laythrop rammed the LCT onto the beach as hard as he could. In those precious few moments before the rattle of chains heralded the lowering of the ramp, Scott tried to collect his thoughts and to drink in all the fantastic sights and sounds that assailed him on all sides. Try as he might, he could not rid his mind of a certain element of unreality. "Am I really here?" he thought. He felt tremendous elation. Despite the violence and the imminence of death, it was also thrilling.

With his Thompson at the ready, Scott led the charge out along the ramp and into the sea. A momentary fear about depth, for Scott was a little on the short side, and then the cold shock of water up to his armpits. Soaked through, he waded to the shore, the attachments of "French letters" floating in front like so many sausages.

Scott included in his group the company's splendid sergeant major, Charlie Dean, and Scott's faithful batman, Bert Muncy. They were about midway up the beach when the volume of fire forced them to the ground.

Shellfire and mortars had cratered the beach into a lunar landscape, and the taped lanes through the minefields had been obliterated. There was no sign of Brian Coombe.

The group inched forward on all fours trying to keep below the bursts of small-arms fire that slashed the air above them. Suddenly Scott felt something pulling at the hairs on his left forearm. With a chilling realization he knew it had to be a trip wire. There was a "plop" in the air above, loud and distinct above the gunfire. Scott's mind had just registered the thought that it was a dreaded German "S" mine.

There was a blurred sight of something in the air and then a blinding flash and shrapnel whined into the sand. Scott was the only one in the group to be hit. Shrapnel peppered his back and shoulder, and a slightly larger piece went through the left cheek of his bottom and came out again. The sharp pain caused him to leap to his feet. The others followed suit, so Scott, laughing aside his wounds, ran hard for the dunes.

While the group caught its breath, Scott looked around. Casualties were mounting. One of the unit's trucks, a 3-ton Bedford loaded to the axles with explosives, had just come off an LCT. Scott watched fascinated as the vehicle roared across the beach. A sergeant he knew well was leaning high out of the hatch in the cab looking for a route around the craters, the driver seeking a purchase in the sand without spinning the wheels but desperate to make even the slight cover offered by the dunes. Other men contributed their weight and their shoulders to the sides, trying to keep the truck moving. But an engine strained by too many punishing miles, too much war, and no four-wheel drive lacked the power for the job. A salvo of shells straddled the truck, and it went up in flames with a resounding roar. The sergeant, driver, and the sappers around were killed instantly.

By now German tanks were appearing, and as the sun climbed higher, so the enemy fire increased. With the improving light, more of the beach unfolded to the observers in the hills.

Scott and his command team moved out behind the Hampshires. They passed through the olive groves and into the tomato plantations. The Italian farmers had just taken in the tomato crop, and the fruit was everywhere, piled into great shocks and covered with straw. Some of the tomatoes must have been there for a time, because they were beginning to rot.

Soldiers ran from one stack to the next, seeking whatever cover they could as they crossed the open fields. Shot and shell crashed into the tomatoes, and it wasn't long before most of them were splattered over the field and the soldiers. The stained coffee brown KD uniforms, which had run in the seawater, now took on a ghoulish appearance. Everyone looked like a casualty.

At about this time the 5th Hampshires, the brigade's reserve battalion, was trying to cross the Asa River and move on to their designated assembly point inland. They hoped their vehicles, heavy weapons, and first-line ammunition would meet up with them. Like most units that morning, their radios had failed after immersion in the sea. The battalion moved in separate groups. Two of the companies were well to the front and out of contact with battalion headquarters, which together with C and Support companies had crossed the Asa and were now moving to the rendezvous. The men tramped down a lane later known as Hampshire Lane, a narrow track with high stone walls on both sides. The order of march was Charlie Company in the lead, Headquarters Company and Support Company in the rear.

They had gone about 600 yards inland and were still in the lane when suddenly they were hit head-on by a German counterattack. Three assault guns with panzer grenadiers in half-tracks tore into Charlie Company. The noise of the battle and especially the tremendous roar of the barrage had masked the sound of the enemy's approach. Though surprise, was mutual since neither knew of the existence of the other, it was carnage. The guns crushed through the columns, then ground men beneath their half-tracks. Soldiers tried desperately to climb the walls to escape the slaughter in the lane, but they were caught in the hail of fire from the half-tracks, only to fall back wounded and dying beneath the very tracks they sought to escape.

Support Company established a defense line and deployed out of the death-trap lane by the time the panzers had plowed through to the battalion headquarters. There the surviving Hampshires held out until the panzers were dispersed by naval and artillery fire.

Late that evening D Company found its way back into the now sadly depleted battalion fold. It had spent the better part of the day east of the Asa River, and though cut off from the rest of the battalion it was unmolested by the enemy. The first day at Salerno had cost the 5th Hampshires 40 killed and more than 300 wounded or captured.

In Uncle Sector the first of the big LSTs were beaching when the front line was barely 200 yards inland from the beach. Some ships were hit repeatedly as they moved inshore. LST 385 took five hits from German 88mm and still managed to discharge her cargo. Once beached it would take an hour and a half to two hours to unload these ships; they sat there like stranded whales, and many were hit repeatedly.

The tale of LST 375 was typical. The ship was hit twice on the way in, and this started gasoline fires. Once onshore the tank deck had just been emptied when she took another shell right through her open bows; the shell burst against the elevator. The skipper took LST 375 out into the roadstead for repairs rather than take up valuable beach space. The crew rigged the elevator and had just about gotten the last of the trucks from the top deck onto the tank or main deck when it collapsed under the weight of a heavy truck. It took most of the day to clear up the wreckage, and then LST 375 moved inshore a second time. That evening the Luftwaffe bombed the beach and hit LST 375. Nevertheless, the next morning she unloaded the last of her cargo, her wounded, and her dead before limping back to North Africa.

The fighting elements of the 6th Lincolns had crossed the Mediterranean split up in nine different ships to minimize casualties. Charlie and Dog companies sailed in LCIs and landed just after dawn. The other companies and battalion headquarters traveled in the more comfortable LSTs and did not come ashore until later in the morning.

The Lincolns were a dyed-in-the-wool territorial Army battalion, men who had volunteered for part-time soldiering in the days of peace; and at this time in the war they were far from happy. The North African campaign had proved an ordeal, and in the last days they lost their beloved commanding officer, Lieutenant Colonel Myrtle, who was killed in action. He was succeeded by the second-in-command, Major Barrel, who saw them safely through to the end of the campaign. In the way of the territorial Army many hoped that Major Barrel's appointment would be confirmed and the command kept in the family. However, since the high command believed that many of these territorial Army units needed the benefit of a regular officer's experience, Lt. Col. David Peel-Yates was sent to take command. He was a regular officer in the South Wales Borderers and had previously been on the staff of First Army headquarters.

Peel-Yates was 6 feet, 4 inches of efficient fighting machine. He was a dedicated and totally professional soldier. But it did take the commanding officer and the battalion a little while to come to terms with one another.

Nobody was more aware of the early frictions than Oliver Hardy, the battalion Intelligence sergeant. He worked very closely with the CO as a key member of the battalion's tactical command team. Hardy had grown immune to the jokes made about his name, especially as he was small and slightly built, the very opposite to his film star namesake. Hardy had been with the battalion since its territorial Army days in Grantham. A neat, precise man, he had been brought up a pacifist, like so many of his generation. Hardy was 23 years of age and married. The first war casualty he had seen was his wife's father, killed when the Luftwaffe combed the ordnance works in Grantham.

The Luftwaffe were active over the beachhead as the battalion headquarters LST moved inshore, and orders were passed for all troops to get belowdecks. Hardy led his squad of six men down from the open and exposed main deck. They were caught in a companionway between two watertight doors that were locked tight when the alarm bells sounded. Confined in the steel coffin, the men could hear the melee as the close-range guns on the deck above hammered away. The hull bulged and buffeted to the concussion of near-misses from bombs and shells. Hardy was petrified; they were trapped, battened in, and nobody knew they were there. The steel walls seemed to close in as if to entomb them. He remembered it later as the worst and most terrifying moment of the war.

When the raid had passed, the doors were opened. Hardy felt they had been there for an hour, but when he checked his watch it was no more than 10 minutes. Even so, it was with a sense of tremendous relief that he made his way down to the vehicle deck and his 5-cwt office truck.

The LST made two attempts to come ashore at Green Beach, but the German guns that still controlled the exits were too much for such a lumbering target. Eventually the ship came in on Red Beach. It was 1330 hours, and they were about 4 hours late in landing.

As Hardy took his utility truck ashore, a song from his school days came to mind, "When It's Nighttime in Italy." He hadn't thought of that song for years, and it wasn't one he particularly enjoyed. But as he drove down the ramp and dry-shod onto the sand, it wouldn't go away.

Later in the afternoon on that first day, the vehicles and trucks of the leading battalions came ashore. Pvt. Doug Parker drove the pioneer truck that belonged to the 6th Lincolns. The rifle companies had come ashore during the morning, and he was anxious to link up with his mates. Parker was a builder from Skegness in Lincolnshire, England, and though a skilled craftsman, he had stayed with the pioneers of his own local territorial Army battalion rather than transfer into the sappers.

The pioneer truck was loaded with explosives, mines, demolition fuses, and heavy tools. It was the first vehicle onto the LST and therefore the last off. Parker had spent the whole voyage on the top deck of the LST rather than with the other drivers deep in the bowels of the ship. It was only with the greatest reluctance that he had moved down to the vehicle deck. In one sense he was sorry to leave the American LST. The crew had looked after them as well as they could, and their generosity had been overwhelming. He hadn't seen so much sugar since the war began, and the food was good and plentiful.

The old Bedford was "clapped out." The windshield had been removed in North Africa because it would reflect in the moonlight and so give their position away. Parker couldn't remember the last time the engine had fired on all four cylinders.

The Bedford was parked at the far end of the landing ship at the bottom on the lower deck; so when the other vehicles started up, he collected all the fumes. The ship shuddered frequently as shrapnel peppered the decks and hull from near-misses. Parker could hear his own batteries of 40mm high up on the bows blasting away at an unseen enemy.

The battle on the beaches was remote to the men who waited to leave the ship. In the hangar decks the vehicles had a ghostly aura, their shapes and forms outlined in the dim blue filtered lights set into the deckheads. Parker gently pressed the accelerator and tried to identify the origin of a knocking he hadn't heard before. He couldn't and so dismissed it as of no great consequence. Instead he checked his Thompson, clipped a magazine into place, and stuck his helmet under his seat, where it would be of more use protecting his vital parts. Like most British soldiers, he hated the helmet. He had no faith in its "protective qualities," and at the same time it gave him the most fearful headaches. It never seemed to fit properly but always bounced around and got in the way.

He pulled his brown floppy beret down over his right eye. The distinctive Lincoln regimental badge, "The Sphinx of Egypt" stood out clearly. The regiment was known as the "Yellow Bellies." Like so many pieces of military folklore, the origins are obscure. It certainly wasn't for any past misdemeanor on the field of battle. The tunic of the officers' mess dress had a yellow facing representing the sands of Egypt, and this is one reason given for the name. Another explanation is the Lincolnshire is renowned for its potatoes and thus the soldiers ate vast amounts of the vegetable, which often has a yellow hue.*

The vehicles were now inching their way slowly forward, springs and axles creaking as they rode over the eyebolts and shackles that lay discarded on the decks. The columns moved in response to sets of red, green, and yellow traffic lights. These were operated from a control room which, rather like a producer's booth in a broadcasting studio, gazed into one of the huge holds through thick glass windows.

Parker bumped and jostled his way out of the dim hold and into the bright, hot day of battle. Shells were still tearing into the beach, and the air was heavy with the acrid smell of smoke. The LST alongside had been badly hit and was on fire. No vehicles were leaving her holds.

He gunned the motor across the sand and followed the battalion signal truck in front. They moved into the dunes, came to a stop, and waited. Parker was afraid to turn off the engine or leave the cab in case the faltering engine stalled. Eventually other vehicles in their convoy arrived, and they moved out to join the battalion.

Even this was easier said than done, for though the beaches were still under shellfire, the roads inland were clogged with traffic. Parker inched his vehicle forward. The roads were narrow and unmetalled, with deep ditches on both sides. To men used to the wide open spaces of the North African campaign, this was a new experience. Trucks, some as the result of poor driving, soon seemed to ditch themselves, effectively blocking exits from the beach. Traffic control either by local units or the MPs was almost totally lacking for much of the day.

Immediately on landing, the Lincolns, together with the 2/4th Kings Own Yorkshire Light Infantry, joined with the remnants of the Hampshires and came under command of the latter's brigade. The first need was to clear out the Germans who still controlled the exits from Green Beach, even at the expense of the advance into Salerno itself. This required the battalions to hook right southward and take the Germans in the flank and rear. It took the Lincolns the rest of the daylight hours to complete their part in the operation.

The countryside near the beach was flat and densely covered with vineyards, orchards, and groves of citrus. Observation was possible only from the roofs of farm buildings, and there weren't too many of these around. It was difficult to arrange close fire support from the artillery except on targets that had been identified by the leading infantry. This was risky, because the ground was so cluttered and confusing that the infantrymen were not always

*See Appendix D for a more detailed account of regimental folklore.

sure where they were in relationship to the map. More than one artillery stonk landed on friendly forces before the battle for the Salerno beachhead was over.

In such close country the actions of the Lincolns that afternoon resembled a game of hide-and-seek. No one had any idea where the Germans were, and they, if the truth be known, were equally confused about the Lincolns. Oliver Hardy did his best to keep the situation map up to date, but it was a pretty hopeless job. It was a long, hot, frustrating afternoon composed of a mosaic of vicious little fire fights, often involving no more than a section of troops who could invariably hear more than they could see. By the time they had reached the general area behind Green Beach the Germans had in any event quietly slipped away.

In the late evening battalion headquarters moved to Odelle Monache Farm, a strongpoint the enemy had only recently evacuated. Sergeant Hardy followed the line of jeeps into the courtyard and had just stepped out when a Thompson burst cut the air above his head. Men scattered, and Hardy ran toward the man who had fired. He was the driver for the battalion's second-in-command and had taken up a position in the doorway to the main house.

"What's the problem?" asked Hardy.

"There's a German down there," replied the man, pointing his Thompson in the direction of an olive grove that abutted the farmyard.

"How many?"

"I saw only the one."

"Right," said Hardy, "keep his head down until I can get around on the other side."

Hardy moved around behind the trees and came up quietly behind a figure he could just make out in the evening light, crouched behind a pile of stones.

Hardy got right behind him. The man stood up slowly, and when he heard the Thompson cocked he raised his arms in the air.

"Who are you?" demanded Hardy.

The man claimed to be an American war correspondent. He wore an American helmet, but the rest of his outfit was a discolored blue denim suit. To Hardy it was not unlike the uniform worn by the Hermann Göring Division.

The man handed across his press credentials and explained that he had come across from the American sector but had lost his bearings. He was looking for the British Corps headquarters.

The correspondent was very shaken. He had spent most of the afternoon hiding out from the Germans, and the nearest he had come to being killed was at the hands of the British.

Sergeant Hardy took the American into the farmhouse and to his commanding officer, Lieutenant Colonel Peel-Yates. Between them they questioned the correspondent closely on what he had seen that day and then fed him before an escort conducted him to divisional headquarters.

Chapter X

The 56th Infantry Division:
The Black Cats Ashore

Salerno was the first landing in World War II that the British had made against German resistance, and the difference was immediately apparent. In North Africa and in Sicily the assault waves had by midmorning moved well inland and taken the battle out of range of the shore. In Salerno at this time the front line was only a few hundred yards inshore. Naval support ships were firing on "targets of opportunity"; there were plenty of those.

One such ship was *LCG 8,* commanded by Lt. John Pitt, R.N.V.R. (Royal Navy Volunteer Reserves), who before the war had worked in the National Provincial Bank in the main square in Bournemouth, England. The LCG (Landing Craft Gun) had a complement of two officers and 10 enlisted men, with one officer and 22 men of the Royal Marines to man the guns. Reggie Lane was the marine officer. He and Pitt were old friends, for in one of those strange quirks of fate that war so frequently produces, they had both worked for the same bank and branch. Pitt had traced the history of his two ancient 4.7-inch guns through their serial numbers. They had come off what in those days was called a torpedo boat destroyer and had last been fired in action in a night engagement in the English Channel. That was in the summer of 1918, just a couple of months before the end of World War I. Pitt and *LCG 8* had been at Sicily, but they had nothing like the targets that the beaches at Salerno presented.

At their top speed of seven knots they bore in for the shore to attack a German battery that was causing problems at the beaches above the Sele Estuary. The day was already hot and very sunny, but visibility was obscured by a sea mist mixed with the smoke that hung like a pall in the heavy, breathless air.

Inshore was the lovely early-morning smell of Europe. It reminded Pitt of marmalade on toast.

Pitt had the help of a bombardment liaison officer (BLO) on board. This officer, a captain in the Royal Artillery, advised the Navy on which targets to attack. In return for his services Pitt was to beach his craft so that the BLO could then go ashore and link up with the forward observation officer. The task of these exceptionally brave men was to liaise between the front line and the artillery support both at sea and onshore as the battle moved farther inland.

LCG 8 had been in action since before daylight in support of the Division's beaches. She had already destroyed one German battery, and there were a few holes in her upper works to show for her troubles. Pitt intended to land his BLO immediately after he had completed the destruction of a second battery. In order to bring both his guns into action (they were mounted one behind the other and not superimposed), he had to turn beam onto the shore.

The shell struck low and at the rear of the small open bridge. Every member of the bridge party was a victim of the shrapnel that scythed its way through men, the screen, and out into the sea beyond. Pitt was standing at the front of the bridge and was shielded by the BLO, who was caught climbing the bridge ladder, having picked up his kit from the little cabin below. He took the full force of the impact and died instantly. A young seaman also died, and another, Pitt's signaler, had his leg blown off. The first lieutenant was down, too. Pitt staggered to his feet; a fragment had sliced through his knee.

Some sailors helped to clear away the dead. Luckily there was no fire. A marine who had some training in first aid came up on the bridge and did what he could. He bandaged Pitt's knee and applied a tourniquet to stem the bleeding. The leg was by now quite numb, so Pitt leaned against the bridge screen and continued to command his ship. Reggie Lane joined him on the bridge, and the gunfire control on the main deck was left in the very capable hands of the marine sergeant major. Only when the battery had been silenced did Pitt take *LCG 8* out of the action.

The Algerine class minesweeper H.M.S. *Cadmus* came alongside. She was acting as an escort at the time and had a doctor on board. Pitt, his first lieutenant, and the other wounded were taken off and transferred to the hospital ship *St. Davids* and later to a hospital in North Africa. Reggie Lane, like most Royal Marine officers, had a watchkeeping certificate, which meant that he was professionally competent in navigation and seamanship, and so he commanded *LCG 8* until a relief officer joined later in the day. For keeping his ship in action though badly wounded, Lieutenant Pitt was awarded the Distinguished Service Cross.

In the meantime, on the Black Cats' beaches, Eighth Battalion Royal Fusiliers had destroyed the German strongpoint that had proved so trouble-some in their sector. Their commanding officer had dispatched Z Company to carry out the task. This had all come as a surprise to Corporal Fox and others in the company, for as the battalion reserve they hadn't expected to be in action so soon.

Cpl. Alfred (Ginger) Fox was 5 feet, 4½ inches tall, came from Oldham in Lancashire, and had bright red hair. Since the outbreak of the war had found him as a waiter in Bournemouth, he had served in the 11th Battalion of the Hampshire Regiment Royal Jerseys and the Seaforth Highlanders before joining the Royal Fusiliers.

With his height Fox had found amphibious warfare training sheer hell. It was even worse for his close buddy, Corporal Newman, who was half an inch shorter. On exercises in North Africa, nine times out of ten their landing craft would hit a false bottom formed by a sandbank, and the two corporals would step off the ramp and go under. Corporal Newman was convinced the Navy did this deliberately. When this happened the others had great difficulty dissuading the little man from wading back out to the boat. It had become a battalion joke, as these little things so often do in wartime.

As their landing craft had approached the beach at Salerno, Fox sensed the anxiety in the crowded boat. He turned to his friend and said loudly, "Corporal Newman, for goodness sake, when you get off this thing hit something firm because we ain't going to have time to argue!"

The men were still laughing as the ramp went down. The two corporals jumped together and promptly disappeared beneath the surface.

Corporal Fox was deadly with the Bren light machine gun. He and his number two on the gun, Pvt. Harold Fish, a coal miner from Yorkshire, moved out on the flank with the other Bren teams to provide covering fire. They were a good pair and had been together since they were drafted in Bournemouth.

The company had taken the German strongpoint with bayonets. The Bren teams had kept the Germans' heads down all the way in to the first position. The company commander, Capt. Henry Filler, was killed leading the charge. A sergeant and a number of privates had died too in that frantic run across the sand.

Fox had lost one of his best pals in the attack. Pvt. Freddy Eddington had joined the Army on the same day, they had been together ever since, and he had lasted for perhaps ten minutes in the war.

Fox, locked into his own private grief, looked around the German positions. They were awful sights, for some of the enemy had been caught by the naval bombardment, and they were a sickening mess. One young German officer was a bloody pulp from the waist down. He spoke some English, but all he could say through clenched teeth was, "Kill me. For God's sake, kill me."

Major Archer, as beachmaster for his battalion, continued to direct the troops and vehicles onto the beach, and supplies began to pile up. Everything was coming more quickly than he expected, and there didn't seem to be enough people around to keep it all moving.

It also was Archer's task to change the order or the sequence in which men and materiel came ashore, depending on the priority and needs of the battle inland. Word had come back that the battalion's right-hand company had met tank opposition. Support Company had four of the new 6-pounder antitank guns. Each was mounted on a high-sided Bedford truck called a portee. Archer dispatched the guns and then moved across to the gun emplacement to send Z Company to link up with the rest of the battalion.

While he was with the company another messenger arrived from the adjutant. The commanding officer had been wounded. Since the second-in-command, who was with the vehicles of B Echelon, had yet to arrivê onshore, Archer as the third most senior officer followed his guide inland to assume temporary command of the battalion. He left word with his regimental police sergeant to brief the second-in-command as soon as he landed.

In company with his batman (who in battle served as escort and runner), he walked off the beach and along to the lateral road about half a mile inland. On the way he passed two troops of Greys, all eight Shermans bogged down up to their driving wheels in a muddy field. There was one unit that had yet to make the transition from North Africa to Europe in mind as well as in body.

Farther on and across a field, near a little hamlet called Ponte di Ferro, Archer saw his antitank guns. He counted four. They were all there, burning. Two of the guns had been knocked off their portees, ammunition exploded, and all around he could see the still forms of the dead.

The sound of battle grew louder, and Archer, his batman, and the guide started jogging. They came across the CO of the 7th Battalion Oxfordshire and Buckinghamshire Light Infantry, the 167th Brigade's reserve battalion. He was sitting in a ditch on the side of the road with his tactical headquarters, a small group who were the forward headquarters with the commanding officer. They were drinking tea. Archer asked him if he knew what the latest situation was, but he hadn't the foggiest idea. His forecast of events, however, was gloomy, and he confirmed Archer's growing fears that the battle plan was beginning to come apart at the seams. The chances of the brigade reaching their D-Day objectives and linking up with the Americans on their right across the Sele River were becoming more remote by the hour.

A few hundred yards down the track, Major Archer at last came upon his own tactical headquarters. The adjutant was relieved to see him and quickly explained the battalion's position. Their advance was stalled by the German tanks. The Greys had failed to get into the act since they had tried to deploy off the road and had bogged down. The battalion's own antitank guns had rushed forward, too far forward, and had been ambushed by the German armor.

It is the dream of every young regular officer to lead his battalion. Major Archer was no exception, but this was hardly the best moment to assume command. He thought for a moment and was about to issue orders when the second-in-command jumped down into the ditch.

The new officer took over the battalion, and Archer stayed to listen to the orders so that he would have a clear picture of the battalion's objectives.

Then he returned to the beach, now the new second-in-command, to organize the B echelon—the supply and administrative base.

Z Company had in the meantime moved forward and, at Ponte di Ferro, changed places with B Company, which was on the battalion's right flank. Ginger Fox and the rest of the 16th Platoon were out on the point. They passed the still-smoldering remains of the ambushed antitank guns. Their lieutenant ordered Fox's section to scout forward while the rest of the platoon moved into a field to provide cover.

Fox took his section in the ditch and off they went. Besides Harold Fish he had three riflemen and a lance (acting) corporal with a PIAT. The latter was of Italian parentage and was afraid the enemy would treat him as a traitor. "If I get captured, the bastards'll kill me," he said, moaning.

The little group had not gone very many yards when they heard the sound of German tanks moving up the road. They crouched low into the ditch. A tank opened fire on the men in the field where some of the soldiers had taken cover behind haystacks. There were a lot of casualties.

One of the riflemen in the ditch incautiously raised his head and was spotted. The three tanks in front of them opened fire, and shrapnel plowed into the bank at the back of the ditch.

Alfred Fox felt a searing pain in his back. He turned to Harold and asked, "Are you all right?"

"No, I got hit in the shoulder," Fish said.

Fox looked around. The rest of the section were dead. Nearest to him lay the Italian lance corporal. Fox reached out and grabbed the PIAT, together with a bag of rounds.

"Now we're in a mess, aren't we?" Harold asked.

"Aye."

"What are you goin' to do?"

Fox could hear the tanks, which had started to creep forward. Everything was quiet in the field where the rest of the platoon had deployed.

"They're moving," Harold said.

Fox looked for his Bren gun. The color drained from his face as he realized with horror that he had left it on top of the ditch. He could see it pointing defiantly at the German tanks. His eyes even registered the fact that the safety catch was off and it was set on automatic.

What happened next was a nightmare. There was no explosion at all. To Fox it sounded like an almighty vomit and a black mass of oil had rolled over the edge of the road, and as it rolled, it was fired. A wall of flame seared across the ditch and burned the grass on the other side. The flaming oil burned the shirts and the skin off their backs. It devoured the oxygen and left them gasping for air and gulping fumes into their lungs.

The Bren gun suddenly started to fire. The flames had reached the butt, and the heat had done the rest. It startled the tank, because the flamethrower momentarily ceased.

As if in a dream, Fox grabbed the PIAT, which was already cocked and loaded. He had fired a PIAT once, on a range in North Africa. Since he was a little man, the recoil had nearly broken his shoulder. Now he didn't even have a shirt to cushion the impact.

Corporal Fox fired just one shot, and he hit the German tank on the ring at the base of the turret. It was a Panzer Mark III converted to carry a flamethrower. Fox's round must have penetrated and caused damage. The tank driver let in the clutch and reversed at speed, straight into the tank behind. Unnerved by the experience, all three tank drivers withdrew their vehicles down the road. An angry tank commander in one used his machine gun to spray the still-burning ditch where Fox and Harold Fish were creeping away on all fours. A couple of rounds gouged chunks out of Fox's buttocks.

The two decided to separate and so divide the German fire when it came time to get out of the ditch and make a run for cover. Alfred Fox was by now in considerable pain and shock. He ran back down the road and past the mess of the ambushed antitank guns. A little farther on a voice said, "Hello! What are you doing here?"

Alfred looked up and saw a machine gunner from the Cheshires. There was a whole platoon of them dug into a field, the heavy water-cooled Vickers machine guns ready mounted on their tripods and dug into shallow pits.

"Do you want some fruit and cream?" the machine gunner asked.

"Fruit and cream?" Alfred asked incredulously. "Yes, please."

The Cheshire pulled a large can toward him and deftly slit the lid with his jackknife. Then he reached inside his weapon pit and poured in some canned milk before handing it to Fox. Everyone on the gunline seemed to be eating, Alfred noticed.

"Where did you get this lot from?" he asked.

The Cheshire pointed to the burned-out wreckage of the antitank guns. The contents from one of the portees had spilled out into the field, and there were cans and NAAFI rations everywhere.

Corporal Fox made his way down to the beach and an aid station. The first person he met as he stood in line with the other walking wounded was Harold Fish.

Badly burned on the elbows and back, with flesh wounds in his back and buttock, Corporal Fox was evacuated onto a hospital ship and out of the war for six weeks. During that time he was not aware of the significance of his actions: He had blunted a German tank attack and had turned the enemy back when they were only a short distance from the sea.

In November Cpl. Alfred Fox was awarded the DCM for his actions at Salerno. It was the biggest surprise of his life, and it wasn't until he read the citation that he even remembered the incident.

It had taken two hours to dig the eight Shermans of A Squadron of the Scots Greys out of the field. Bulldozers had been brought in from the beach, and everybody lent a shoulder, from the brigadier downward.

Once free, the tanks moved in support of the 8th Battalion Royal Fusiliers. The tanks that Corporal Fox had so bravely engaged were reported to be on the move again and advancing down the road. To avoid a head-on clash, Captain Williams, the acting squadron commander, took his tanks inland to hit the Germans with a left hook. He moved carefully and sought only the firmest ground on which to advance, and the maneuver worked splendidly. The lead tanks came across the Germans, stationary and broadside on at a range of 500 yards. The surprise was complete. The crew of one Panzer Mark IV was actually standing on their tank and looking to their front.

Sergeant McMeekin commanded the leading Sherman, and his gunnery was excellent. Within minutes he had destroyed the Mark IV and a still-smoking Mark III armed with a flame thrower. Lieutenant Compton, the troop leader, came in support, and between them they destroyed a third flamethrower and exchanged shots with the last of the Mark IVs, which was by this time in full retreat.

Sergeant McMeekin was awarded the Military Medal for this brilliant action.

German resistance along the beaches that day was patchy. With only one division to watch a front of more than 30 miles, it could hardly have been otherwise. So while the 8th Fusiliers had a grueling day, their sister 9th Battalion had a clear run all the way into Battipaglia.

There had been some initial resistance when the battalion hit the beaches, but this had soon been overcome. There was no sign of the battalion vehicles coming ashore from the landing craft, which now lined the water's edge; so the men commandeered and "liberated" what was immediately at hand. On tractors and trailers, horses and carts, wheelbarrows and bicycles, the battalion pressed hard inland. Spirits were high, and the fields of tomatoes allowed them to give full rein to their London humor. "Get yer luvly tomatoes!" and similar cries were bandied back and forth along the lines.

The only armor ashore that was available to protect them were the Bren gun carriers of their own carrier platoon. Fusilier Harris drove the platoon commander. The worst moment of the day had been when they hit the beach. Though the sappers had marked out lanes across the beach to the dune with white tape to indicate the areas that had been swept clear of mines, the LCT on which they came ashore was nowhere near such a lane. Harris at the wheel of the first vehicle to leave the ship hesitated until his platoon commander thumped him on the shoulder.

"Go on! You got to bash on!" he yelled.

So Harris let out the clutch, and the little carrier lunged forward and careened across the uncharted sand. Harris sat there frozen with fear waiting for the mines, but the vehicle chose its own crazy course; and with the platoon commander laughing hysterically all the way, they reached the safety of the duneline.

The carrier platoon moved ahead of the battalion and screened their advance along the road into Battipaglia; the town was occupied by nightfall.

On both sides of the 9th Battalion, other units had failed to take their objectives. The 8th Battalion reached Santa Lucia, and the Ox and Bucks passed through their positions to maintain the momentum of the advance. In the fading light of the day German resistance had stiffened, and the advance had stalled.

On the left of the now very exposed 9th Battalion, Royal Fusiliers in Battipaglia was another yawning gap caused by the failure of the 169th Queen's Brigade to secure the airfield at Montecorvino and the higher ground beyond.

The first part of the day had gone well enough. The 2/6th Queens, who had been given the airfield as their objective, had landed smoothly on beaches to the left of the fusiliers and soon were marching inland. In support were two Shermans belonging to C Squadron of The Greys and the 25-pounder guns of the Royal Devon Yeomanry.

The tanks were the first onto the airfield with the infantry of the leading companies. At first it all went their way. The Germans were clearly caught unawares and suffered as a consequence. While the infantry scuttled in and out of the hangars, the tanks shot up the aircraft parked around the field.

Part of the perimeter of the airfield was formed by Route 18 on the northern edge and a small road that led off down the west side to the main entrance. Route 18 passed the airfield by way of an embankment. This gave the Germans a commanding view of the ground, and it allowed them to recover their composure. From these positions they were able to pour a withering fire on the advancing infantry. In front of the embankment the field had been harvested, and some Germans dug in there to hold a forward defense line.

Eric Fulbrook was a corporal with C Company of the 2/6th Battalion of the Queen's Regiment. He soon found himself in the thick of the action. He had waded ashore that morning loaded down like a packhorse. Besides his own personal equipment of entrenching shovel, Thompson, spare magazines, and grenades, he carried an additional small pouch of Bren gun magazines loaded with tracer, a form of incendiary bullet whose trajectory is made visible by a luminous glow. These help a machine gunner to adjust his aim. Every man stepped ashore with two large packs. One contained his personal kit; the second had 2-inch mortar bombs. Both packs were dumped on the beach. These would be collected by the supply elements in the battalion. The personal packs would be stored until the rifle companies came out of the line. The pack and mortar shells provided an immediate supply of ammunition.

Fulbrook was worried about his own personal pack because it contained his hair-cutting instruments. He was the company barber and had cut everyone's hair on the day before they landed. It helped take the men's mind off the fact that their landing craft spent that day in company with others steaming back and forth in sight of Capri.

C Company started the action in reserve and waited on the edge of the airfield before being called into action. A German attack pushed the leading platoons back, and C Company moved forward to retake the lost ground.

The impetus of their charge took the Queen's back into the hangars and huts on the southern side of the field. Fulbrook fought alongside another corporal named Belsey. Everyone knew Belsey to be the unluckiest man in the battalion. In North Africa he had been a company quartermaster sergeant, and on the verge of promotion to sergeant major he was caught selling blankets to Arabs. Belsey was busted to corporal. This was but the most recent disaster to befall him in a military career dogged by ill luck. A phlegmatic man, no matter what happened to him his response was, "Just my luck," a catchphrase known throughout the battalion.

The platoon moved out from the forward edge of the last hut and were met by a hail of fire. A machine-gun burst caught Belsey flush in the head. He was just a yard or so in front of Fulbrook. As the impact of the shots spun him around, Fulbrook heard the words, "Just my luck" as Belsey hit the ground.

The survivors raced for the cover of a drainage ditch and cowered in its bottom while the Germans kept up the fire. There was no way forward or back. The platoon commander, Lt. Charles Alverson, crawled forward and ordered Fulbrook to get his section out along the ditch and try to outflank the enemy.

The section scrambled along the bottom of the ditch until it ran out in the middle of the field. A little way to their front were some large "wigwams" of sticks on which the hay had been hung to dry. Among these were a couple of persistent snipers and a machine-gun nest. Fulbrook ordered the section to give him supporting fire while he ran forward to the cover of the first wigwam. From there he reckoned he could lob a grenade into the enemy gun position. At his word the section lifted their weapons over the edge of the ditch and opened fire. Fulbrook was on his feet in an instant and ran across the dry, stubbled field. He zig zagged, as laid down in the infantry manual on field tactics, to confuse the enemy's fire.

A sniper caught him. Fulbrook thought he had been hit by a mortar bomb or something similar. He seemed to float high in the air and then, like in a slow-motion movie, float to the ground. The bullet from the sniper had in fact hit his back pouch in which he carried a grenade. That had exploded and the blast tore all his kit and clothes from his body. What saved him was his shovel, which took the full force of the blast.

Even so, Corporal Fulbrook was grievously-wounded. He carried a spare clip of tracers in his pocket. They had gone off and torn a hole in his thigh, which opened to the bone, and there was a gaping hole in his chest.

While he lay there bleeding, naked, and helpless, the sniper put another round into him for good measure; it scorched through his stomach wall. Fullbrook lay there for the rest of the day, the Germans daring anybody to respond to his cries and attempt a rescue.

Only by evening was the battalion able to stabilize its position and push the Germans back to the northeastern corner of the field. The troop of Greys from C Squadron had fought hard throughout the day and had taken on German armor whenever it appeared. There were too few Allied tanks available, however, to influence the scale of battle decisively in favor of the Queen's. The Greys for their part lost four tanks simply blunting the German attacks.

D Company of the 2/6th Battalion had spent a thoroughly miserable day. While the battle had raged back and forth on the far side of the field, the Germans had kept them pinned down in the hedgerows. A continuous bombardment of shells and mortars had frustrated the company every time it tried to move into the battle. Casualties began to mount.

Toward late afternoon the battalion CO Lieutenant Colonel Keighley, wisely withdrew D Company, for they were suffering needlessly. The men pulled back across the road and into a vineyard, where they attempted to dig in. Cpl. Frank Peart found, along with everybody else, that this was well nigh impossible because the ground was rock hard. So they dug some shallow shell scrapes and pulled the vines down over themselves as camouflage. They lay there and ate the grapes.

The action at Montecorvino airfield seemed to vindicate the Greys and their criticism of the use made of them by the 56th Division. The commanding officer of the Greys had begged the respective brigadiers to keep his squadron intact so that their numbers could influence an engagement. Tanks were more effective if they were used in mass. This was especially the case with the Sherman, which was outgunned by the German tanks. But the three saber or fighting squadrons had been given one each to the three infantry brigades in the division.

The divisional commander had also allowed his brigadiers to use the tanks at their own discretion. After all, the advice of a cavalry colonel could be considered biased, since no commanding officer likes to see his beloved regiment broken into bits and distributed at the whim of the infantry. This was yet another round in the battle over tactics, which the British Army's infantry and cavalry fought bitterly throughout the whole war.

The 167th Infantry Brigade had listened and followed the advice of the cavalry. As we have seen, even though A Squadron was down to eight tanks, their intervention at Ponte di Ferro was extremely successful. The Guards Brigade had yet to land, but they intended to use B Squadron in a similar manner and keep their tanks together.

But Brigadier Lyne, who commanded the Queen's insisted on parceling C Squadron by troops to his battalions in the field. At Montecorvino he was wrong, for the tanks thus dispersed were too few in number to swing the action in favor of the infantry.

Such a deployment had another weakness. A troop has three tanks and is commanded by a lieutenant, often young and inexperienced. With the Queen's this young officer had to advise a lieutenant colonel commanding a battalion on how best to use his tanks, in itself a recipe for disaster.

Some hours later a stretcher party came upon Eric Fulbrook. He was still alive. Private Egleton, a medical orderly, lived near him in Reading; he slapped shell dressings on his gaping wounds and pulled him back into the ditch for shelter. Every movement was agony for Fulbrook, though the men were as gentle as they could be. They gave Fulbrook a "Victory V" cigarette, but his pain was so bad that he drew back so hard on the cigarette that it burned through to his fingers.

The stretcher bearers took him to the edge of the airfield where there were some hovels with chickens pecking in the dust, where the wounded lay patiently waiting their turns for attention. The chickens were bomb-happy. Every time a shell burst and the ground rocked from the concussion, they would leap into the air with fright. This provided the men with some lighter moments in the midst of their suffering. Some Italian peasant women were assisting, and a couple of Italian soldiers helped carry the stretchers into a hovel that served as an operating room.

Corporal Fulbrook had lain out in the open field for the best part of the hot summer's afternoon. The sun had baked his open wounds and burned his face, and he was desperately thirsty. He begged the Italians to give him just a sip of water to moisten his parched lips, but wiser counsel prevailed. The battalion medical officer cleaned him up as best he could and drugged him against the pain.

After dark a couple of Bren gun carriers, specially adapted to carry stretchers, clattered over the cobbles and into the farmyard. Eric Fulbrook was strapped onto one of these; the pain had eased as he floated on a cushion of morphine during the short drive to the beach. There he joined the rows of wounded waiting their turn outside the divisional casualty clearing station.

Corporal Fulbrook remained in the hospital on the beach for three days of operations and blood transfusions. On the third night he was carried out to a landing craft, which took him to a hospital ship in the bay. After many months of hospitalization in North Africa he was sent back home to England. His active part in the war was over.

While men fought and died to secure the beachhead, others poured ashore throughout the day. The additional infantry, such as the 201st Guards Brigade, were intended as reserves of the last resort, but it was hoped they could be held in readiness to lead the breakout the next day.

The men of the 6th Battalion, the Grenadier Guards, were dressed in long KD trousers and angola (a corruption of angora wool) shirts, helmets, small packs, and webbing equipment. They carried 48 hours' worth of rations (bully beef, cheese, chocolate, hard candy, biscuits and tea) and mosquito nets. Lieutenant Leeke was dressed exactly the same as his men except that he carried a Luger, dagger, map case, and field glasses and wore the new black beret that the officers had just been issued. He carried his helmet; as with all officers in the brigade he had the liner inside made to measure by his hatter in London.

The orders were to proceed to the concentration area, which was a couple of meadows just a little way inland behind the sand dunes. Apparently the whole brigade had heard the same, for the men of all three battalions walked up the path between two damp ditches filled with rushes. There was no method to it; the battalions were all mixed up with one another. Scots,

Grenadiers, and Coldstreamers jostled each other in a long, winding herd of humanity, carrying bicycles, Bren guns, and mortars. It was like leaving a football field with the crowd after a big game.

Eventually they came upon a group of deserted farm buildings where people stood directing the traffic. Suddenly Leeke found himself almost alone, with the crowd down to just a trickle as the grenadiers moved on to their concentration area. Everyone was cool and efficient as the battalion rapidly dispersed first into company and finally platoon groups. Leeke led his platoon into an area by a small road where the men were hidden by towering tobacco plants. In front of them was a large orchard with the most delicious apples; he allowed one man from each section to pick the fruit.

It was still very noisy. The Germans shelled the beach while the naval guns and a battery of self-propelled 25-pounders nearby were shooting inland just over their heads.

Leeke got bored and so strolled a little way down the lane and discovered the headquarters of the 169th Infantry Brigade. It consisted of the brigadier, his signalers, the Intelligence officer, and a truck. Leeke went up, leaned over the tailgate, and tried to glean some information, but apparently that was the one thing they lacked.

Shortly he saw for himself evidence of the battle then being waged for control of the airfield. A German truck passed by, driven by an English corporal, and Leeke counted some unhappy prisoners sitting in the back. Then a carrier came swaying down the road, the tracks clattering over the uneven surface. It carried wounded on stretchers, both German and English, and pulled into an aid station opposite the orchard. A captain in the Queen's was lifted out, and Leeke caught a glimpse of a pale, twisted face, a left leg hanging awkwardly. The officer's trousers were torn and soaked in blood, and a field dressing had slipped from his groin.

Leeke returned rather thoughtfully to his platoon.

Orders came down from brigade. The battalion was to march as quickly as possible in the direction of Battipaglia, which was on the other flank, and to support the fusiliers in their attempt to push farther inland. Leeke was lucky to have the leading platoon, for though he had to concentrate on directions at least he didn't have to eat another man's dust.

The Guardsmen marched in single file along a road running parallel to the sea. It was crowded with carriers, Sherman tanks, jeeps, and signalers. They passed their own battalion headquarters digging into a ditch and just a little farther up the road a factory with a solitary but very tall tower. Leeke thought the latter was an excellent but rather obvious place for an observation post.

The platoon reached its allotted position, which was to guard a ford over the Tusciano River, and the men started to dig their slit trenches.

The platoon commanded by Lt. Freddie Fraser passed by; they were all very gloomy. A shell had struck a carrier, killing and wounding four men, including Lance Sergeant Emery, a popular section commander.

There was a farm close by, and Leeke strolled over to search the buildings, but they were empty and derelict. Coming out of the farm he saw the factory tower receive two direct hits. Leeke learned later that Lt. Michael Ridpath, the mortor platoon officer, had been seen by a German Mark IV climbing the tower. He was killed and a second officer, Capt. Edmund Vaughan, wounded in the chest and blinded by shock.

The platoon sat down to a meal of fried bully beef and freshly picked tomatoes. Leeke then sent the men in batches to bathe, wash, and shave in the Tusciano. Despite the sound of the guns it was a peaceful scene.

Toward late evening Leeke enjoyed a final cup of tea and a pipe, chatting with Sergeant Thomas, his platoon sergeant. They had done the rounds, posted the sentries, and quiet had fallen on the platoon area. Leeke was looking forward to a good night in a dry ditch when they got new orders to move farther ahead and up the river immediately.

How typical of war. The men wearily gathered themselves and their possessions. The first platoon set out with the darkness.

By the end of the first day the British X Corps were ashore with 23,000 troops, 80 tanks, 325 guns, and more than 2,000 vehicles of all shapes and sizes. The corps, landing on a 7-mile section of the beach, had been given the objective of securing a beachhead that embraced the town of Salerno, the airfield at Montecorvino, the passes out of the plain, Battipaglia, and Eboli. The corps had failed to meet almost all of these objectives, and the Germans were still in possession of some vital pieces of ground.

It had been a day of confusing actions, with most of the battles at battalion level or below. For the higher commands at brigade and division, both ashore and afloat, it was a day of rising tensions made more acute by want of accurate information. For the highest commands at corps and army afloat, it was a day of nagging doubts and uncertainty.

General McCreery had sent the divisional tactical headquarters ashore during D-Day. However, X Corps tactical headquarters remained in the command ship H.M.S. *Hilary* until September 12. McCreery was convinced she was the best focus for land, sea, and air communications.

In spite of the ferocious fighting—much of it, as we have seen, at very close quarters—casualties on the British side were remarkably light. The 56th Infantry Division had losses of 195 men, and the 46th had 350 casualties, the majority coming from the Hampshires.

Worst of all, perhaps, no firm contact had been made with the Americans across the Sele River. The mere existence of the Sele River underlines the fact that from dawn on the first day the Allies fought two quite separate battles at Salerno.

Chapter XI

The "T" Patchers'
Battle for Paestum

Daylight had revealed that the British X Corps had a sharp fight on their hands. However, the first hours of that fateful morning were to prove even more of an ordeal for the Texans in the U.S. VI Corps. At first they were in a desperate plight. Of their four beaches, only Red Beach was safe from enemy small-arms and close-range fire. Even then, the bigger batteries inland were still zeroed in on the beach, and salvoes slammed into the sand with frightening and depressing regularity. The watchtower at Paestum was making life extremely difficult for those troops trying to come ashore on Green Beach. The Germans were finally ousted when elements from the beach unloading parties, drawn from the 531st Shore Engineers Battalion, downed tools, picked up their rifles, and drove them out at bayonetpoint.

Yellow and Blue beaches were to remain veritable death traps for some hours to come, swept as both were by enemy small-arms and artillery fire. The 141st Regimental Combat Team was still in a difficult situation. The 1st Battalion remained split, with the bulk of the rifle companies pinned down and isolated on the right. The 2nd and 3rd battalions had been able to move off the beach but could make little progress against the superior firepower of the Germans. Neither could the GIs contact the warships for fire support, though the radio operators tried for some time.

Heavier artillery was also causing mayhem in the sea lanes and the shore approaches. Landing craft and DUKWs, afraid to run the gauntlet of fire, milled around without purpose or direction, so that timetables and unloading sequences became hopelessly confused.

Daylight also allowed the Germans to throw their tanks and self-propelled guns into the attack. At first they fought in small groups or even individually but were inadequately supported by the Infantry; however, there were no American tanks yet ashore to oppose the panzers.

The original plan had called for Shermans to be unloaded at 0630 hours on Blue Beach. As the LSTs approached the shore their neat formation was devastated by enemy artillery fire. Ships were damaged, and there were a number of casualties. The ships withdrew and were not able to land their tanks until 1330 hours, when they came in on Red Beach. Even then they had to be escorted in by a couple of destroyers, which engaged the enemy batteries and in the process offered themselves as targets.

Allied firepower, in the form of naval and some air support, became increasingly effective. At 0825 the British monitor H.M.S. *Abercrombie* opened fire in support of the Texans with her 15-inch guns at a range of 2,500 yards. Her guns were directed by a naval spotter aircraft.

The cruiser U.S.S. *Savannah* made contact with her fire-control party ashore at 0914. She brought her main 6-inch batteries into action at a range of 17,450 yards and drove off a tank attack against the 141st above Yellow Beach.

Initially, however, the absence of tanks or artillery ashore meant that German armor had to be fought by the infantry, so there can be little doubt that if the Germans had launched more substantial and better-coordinated armored counterattacks the American beachhead would have been in desperate straits.

The reserve battalions of the assaulting infantry regiments together with the 143rd RCT and the supporting arms that landed that day still had to fight their way ashore against an enemy still entrenched in their defense positions. This was something they had not expected to do, since it was the task of the first wave to clear and secure the beaches. If they thought about it at all, the GIs thought in terms of landing first and then later perhaps a battle. They were not mentally attuned to the immediate assault role. So they took casualties and arrived late and invariably in the wrong place, which added to their confusion.

In all their training and preparation for Salerno very few soldiers really took the thought of combat seriously. Until they have experienced combat, it is not their nature to do otherwise. While their officers planned on the assumption that the enemy on the beaches would be Italians rather than Germans, the ordinary soldier felt it to be another training exercise.

The Italian capitulation had added to the air of unreality by causing confusion and misplaced optimism. The men *talked* about invasion and combat, but to a marked degree they were victims of their own propaganda. The soldiers were so indoctrinated that they really never doubted that the firepower of the Navy's big guns and the bombs of their invincible Air Force would "blow the hell out of the beaches" should the enemy attempt to stop them.

When the assault craft carrying Company K of the 143rd RCT approached the beaches, the trouble was that the firepower came from the land. Their landing craft milled around for some hours, and when eventually they headed inshore it was to land on Red Beach rather than the intended Blue Beach. By this time as they drifted in and out of the smoke screen amid the ghastly flotsam of war, the sense of adventure had faded and the grim physical realities of combat had taken its place.

All this was especially true for the younger soldiers. Pfc. George Bailey had just turned eighteen and had started off his military career in the National Guard as a bugler. He was now a radio operator, alone and frightened, as cocooned in their own fear, they moved through the enemy barrage and the landing boat grounded on the gravel. His eyes saw but his mind refused to register as the boat alongside took a direct hit and fell apart, spilling men and equipment into a frothing red surf.

They needed no urging to leave the landing craft; neither did the crew. The coxswain and his bowmen came with them. There was no way they were going to take their boat back out through that terrible slaughter.

There were people all over the beach; everywhere he looked George Bailey saw confusion and pain. Another salvo of mortars stitched their way across the sand, and the men threw themselves down and buried their heads in their hands. The company first sergeant started to raise hell. "Get off this beach!" he yelled over and over again.

Discipline reasserted its control, and Company K rose from the sand and ran inshore. With the others, George Bailey ran across the beach and away from that nightmare.

Ike Franklin landed with elements of the 3rd Battalion's Headquarters Company. Since the war began, he had gone up the ranks to sergeant and back down again, twice. He was now a medic, and it was his job to make sure that the radio link between the rifle companies and the battalion aid station worked. He came ashore at Red Beach equipped with his walkie-talkie radio, a medical aid bag, and pouches, in which he carried his rations, a change of socks, and some extra bandages. There was a large red cross prominently marked on his helmet and his right arm.

Franklin owes his life to a German machine gunner. The landing craft grounded on the beach, and Franklin was the first to step off. He looked up, and there, just a hundred yards away in the sand dunes, was a German machine gunner. Before Franklin could react, the German pointed to his own helmet and arm and signaled him to hit the beach.

As if in a dream, Franklin hit the sand at the water's edge, and the machine-gun bullets ripped into the crowded landing craft. Eight men died in as many seconds before a chance shell took out the German. It was probably a German shell falling short that killed the gunner who had saved the life of an American medic. Franklin saw it all and, like so many who experienced traumatic events, couldn't register the violence of the action.

Franklin picked himself up and made his way across the dunes, through a field of tomatoes, and down into an irrigation ditch. He was thirsty, and so he took his canteen cup and filled it with the water from the ditch. Reaching for his pack, he took out a sulphur tablet, dropped it into the water, and gulped it down. There were some other soldiers in the ditch.

"Aren't you supposed to wait for that to work?" one asked.

"I may not be alive to have it then, but I'm thirsty now," Franklin said.

"I hadn't thought of that," the soldier said. He reached down and did the same.

Franklin moved across another field and then spotted a soldier he recognized as being with the signals outfit attached to the battalion's headquarters. The man told Franklin that he had seen the aid station in an olive grove less than a couple of hundred yards away. By the time Franklin had found the unit, the first wounded were already being brought in from the battle as it progressed farther inland.

Pfc. Arnold Murdoch was in Company K and came ashore on Red Beach a little later. At 28 years of age, this factory laborer from Corsicana, Texas, was older than most men in his squad. Arnold was a kind and gentle man who was totally and utterly bewildered by anything military, and a man already hit by tragedy, for his young wife had died before the division had come overseas. Though Arnold Murdoch even saluted corporals, because he didn't know any better, he had one saving grace: he was the sweetest shot in the company. They had given him the Browning automatic rifle (BAR) because he was a natural shot and had an affinity for this particular weapon.

The Browning automatic rifle, which had been used in World War I, was the U.S. Army's answer to the British Bren gun and the most excellent German MG34, and not a very good answer at that. Because an American infantry section was routinely equipped with rapid-firing automatic rifles, the War Department didn't see the need for the additional firepower of a light machine gun. The result was that the U.S. Army never had a decent light support weapon for use at squad level throughout the war.

It was Arnold's own fault that he was in the landing craft that particular morning. He had hurt his ankle in the final warm-up exercise in North Africa, when he had fallen down a hill. He had been offered the opportunity to come in with the transport later in the day. But Arnold believed it was his duty to stick with the squad, even though there wasn't going to be any fighting. After all, the platoon commander had explained everything in his briefing on the ship. They would land on Blue Beach, march a short distance inland, and take up their positions on a mountain called Soprano. They would be there perhaps for a couple of days, and then they could expect the Germans to counterattack. Arnold couldn't remember what was supposed to happen next, but he reckoned that his ankle would be fine by then; so he elected to go in with his squad.

On the run into the beach Arnold and his assistant BAR gunner, Jack Partley, were constantly told to sit down, but neither could contain their enthusiasm or curiosity for what was happening all around. "Murdoch," Jack yelled, "them damned shells are landing out there! Stand up and look!"

Arnold ignored the stares of those around and stood up and looked out. He saw a shell burst in the water just a short distance away. The water went straight up in the air. For all the world it reminded him of the spray from an uncapped fire hydrant.

Ahead of their boat was a minesweeper, which they gradually overtook. Somebody on her bridge had a bullhorn and talked to the landing craft as they passed.

"The beaches are dead ahead!" the metallic voice boomed out. "Good luck!"

Arnold wondered why he should wish them luck. Did the minesweeper know something he didn't?

By this time Red Beach was becoming so congested that the landing craft were having to wait in line and to jostle for a place to set down their ramps. Some started to unload a little way out from the beach.

Arnold Murdoch stepped gingerly off the ramp and splashed ashore. It wasn't too bad; the water came just up to his knees.

Shells were landing thick and fast on the beach. Murdoch's section looked for cover and huddled behind an armored bulldozer until the driver leaned out of his cab and yelled above the noise of the engine, "Don't hang around me, fellas! I draw flies!"

The squad moved across the beach and played it by the book. They ran a few steps, hit the ground, got up, ran a dozen more, and hit the ground again. But Arnold couldn't run properly, and by this time he was in considerable pain from his ankle. Neither could he wait on the beach for a truck or jeep to give him a lift; the gunfire was too heavy, and his section needed him. So he stumbled and fell, stumbled and fell, all the way up the beach through the sand dunes and into the damp, marshy ground beyond. All the while salvo after salvo crashed into the ground.

War is a time-compressing experience, and men move from baptism to a veteran condition in a remarkably short period of time. One of the things that they learn very quickly is to identify the salvo directed at them in particular. Arnold was well into the marshy area, a little behind the rest with the exception of Jack Partley, when Arnold's instinct told him that the next salvo was more personal. He had been taught always to fall with his hand on his rifle. But on this occasion as he threw himself forward his injured ankle caught in some tufts of weed, his leg twisted under him, and down he went with the BAR falling from his grip. Arnold covered his head with his hand and tried to squirm his way into the soft protection of the marsh, but he knew he was going to get hit—he just knew it.

A shell burst in the air, and shrapnel slammed into the ground around him. One chunk almost tore his left leg off. Smaller fragments of shrapnel punctured his back and his arms.

At first Arnold felt nothing. He took a moment to gather his senses and clear his head after the numbing detonation of the shell. It was when he tried to scramble to his feet that it hurt. A wave of pain pressed him back into the earth, and he screamed out in agony.

Arnold lay there and hollered for help. Four times he called for a medic until he couldn't yell anymore because it hurt him so. When he yelled it put pressure on the injured nerves, and waves of pain coursed through him.

A medic (the Texans call them "pill-rollers") finally came up to him. "I heard you the first time," he chided.

The medic turned him over gently and examined the shattered leg. He quickly applied a tourniquet to the fleshy part of the thigh and rushed off to find help.

Arnold lay there for a couple of moments and then looked up to see Jack Partley bending over him. The same shell had sent fragments into his arm, and he too was in considerable pain.

"Do you want me to take the gun, Arnold?" he asked.

"Yeah, go ahead," Arnold said.

Partley bent down to pick up the BAR, and Arnold watched as his face froze. It was a lump of twisted metal and splintered wood, so misshapen neither could tell one end from the other.

"Forget it, Jack," Arnold said. "Get yourself off the beach."

Partley was clearly reluctant to leave his buddy, though his own wounds had him hopping from one foot to the other.

"Jack," Arnold said, "you can go back and find that pill-roller and send him back here."

"I can do that," Jack said.

He ran back in the direction of the beach, still clutching his injured arm. Arnold noticed that Partley had left his rifle behind, but he didn't have the strength to call after him.

With his good arm Arnold tried to reach across the front of his combat shirt for some cigarettes, but his hand came back a sticky red mess. Instead he reached into the other pocket and pulled out his New Testament. He opened the flyleaf and read what his wife had written shortly before she died: "I love you. I'll meet you in heaven."

Arnold started to pray—it wasn't something he did very often. He tried to remember how the Catholics made the sign of the cross, did something similar, and prayed out loud. "Well, listen, God, if you'll help me to get back and out of this, I'll try to be a better man, in Jesus' name. Amen."

He had heard the Catholics use the last phrase, and it did seem appropriate. Arnold kept repeating this simple prayer, over and over. In its own way, it did bring some ease to his pain.

How long he had lain there, Arnold couldn't tell; he seemed to lose all count of time. He did what the medic had told him to do and every so often eased the pressure of his tourniquet.

The shells seemed to be falling with less frequency, and lines of troops picked their way inland. Some of the curious looked and stared; the others, the frightened, averted their eyes as they moved past the prostrate forms that littered the ground.

An officer (Arnold thought he was a colonel, but he wasn't sure) stopped and leaned over him. "Son," he said, "I wish I could help you."

"Sir," Arnold said, "I don't think you can."

At that moment the medic reappeared, accompanied by another one who carried a folded stretcher.

"Do what you can for the soldier," the officer ordered.

The medics gently cut away the leg and the sleeves from his uniform and eased him out of his clothes. Arnold braced himself and looked down at his leg.

Just below the knee it was hanging by a few threads of sinew and bone. It was almost literally torn off. "Well, that's that," Arnold thought and tried to imagine life on one leg. The medics poured sulpha powder on his wounds, placed a shell dressing on his leg, and bound up his arm and back. They took the rifle discarded by Partley, broke it down into two pieces, and used them to fashion a splint for the leg. They gently lifted him onto the stretcher and then set out for the beach and straight onto a landing craft. There were other wounded, and gradually the deck began to fill up. Nearby was a German who lay white and still on a stretcher, a couple of shell-shock cases slouched nearby, oblivious on the deck.

Perhaps Arnold dozed, but it didn't seem very long before, with much bumping and scraping, the landing craft announced its return to a mother ship. Lines were attached, and the little boat was winched up its davits to the level of the main deck above. A couple of white-coated doctors scrambled into the boat. One turned to examine Arnold; he was then joined by an older man.

"Sir," Arnold said, "if you can save my leg, I sure would appreciate it."

"I wouldn't even think about losing your leg," the surgeon replied. Thus encouraged, Arnold relaxed. He felt the prick of the needle into his skin and nothing more.

While Arnold Murdoch was being prepared for surgery, the LSTs of Convoy FSS2, which had come in from Bizerte, approached the beaches. They gathered speed for their final run-in. Above their low bows the great doors were already partly open and the ramps down, for most of these craft had earlier released their cargo of DUKWs ("Ducks") for the shore. The vehicles are aptly named. There is almost a farmyard scene as they swim from the warm protection of the bow doors, their legs tucked beneath them.

Onshore the Germans, few in number, began to pull back toward the lower slopes of the hills inland. The GIs, seeking to maintain their pressure, thrust forward in a series of separate and uncoordinated small-unit actions. While the Germans tried to regroup their main forces, lighter screening troops turned at bay snarled into the counterattack, probing for the weak spots and trying to knock the Americans off their stride.

All the while the forward fighting formations of the Texans increased in strength, as troops singly, by pairs, or in small groups worked their way forward toward the railway line. This was the main point of reference, and from that they found their way to the battalion's forming-up area farther inland.

The battalion aid station was on one side of an olive grove, and the companies were deployed around the far side and beyond. After linking up with the battalion, Company K dug its foxholes at the forward edge of the olive grove and close to a dry stone wall. The ground was hard, and in the hot sunlight it was backbreaking work. Pfc. George Bailey and the others in his squad worked bare-chested. The men didn't make much progress because many regarded it as an unnecessary chore; after all, they were bound to move forward before too long, and all that effort would be wasted.

At the first sound of the tank tracks, there was a concerted rush for the half-completed foxholes; men grabbed shirts, helmets, and weapons and dived for cover. Bailey looked down into his foxhole and saw the battalion commander there. This wasn't the time or the place for military protocol. "You're in my damn foxhole . . . sir!" Bailey screamed.

The colonel got out and went in search of his own.

As the noise of the tanks increased, word came along the line, started no one knows where. From hole to hole the whisper was, "There are six Tigers heading this way. They have just cut the 142nd to hell."

A bazooka team of two men moved out and took up a position behind a stunted, gnarled olive tree on the edge of the open field. Back in his foxhole, Bailey gripped his rifle a little tighter and wished, like so many others, that he had dug a little deeper.

Two tanks moved across the open field and began to drop shells into the olive grove. The first volleys whistled around the ears of the men working in the aid station. The medics had not even considered the need to dig foxholes.

Ike Franklin sheltered behind an olive tree with a couple of other men. He tried to raise some artillery on his walkie-talkie, but it was useless. The radio waves were full of crackling static, which, when it cleared, rebounded to the crowded calls of half a dozen stations, all fighting to be heard.

A second and third volley of shots burst over the aid station. One shell was directly above the tree under which Franklin crouched. The tree was split asunder by the blast, and the two men with him were mutilated, one decapitated. Franklin staggered away in blind horror and disbelief. There wasn't a scratch on him. "Dear Lord," he thought, "that is twice in as many hours."

By this time one of the tanks had strayed a little too close to the bazooka team, whose presence was still concealed from the panzers. The tanks had now spotted the main infantry positions and were about to open fire when the bazooka crew fired first.

The projectile hit the tank right on the bow machine gunner's position. Though it didn't penetrate, the shot did some damage. The tank reversed from the field, its retreat guarded by its still healthy but cautious brother.

After the excitement was over, the company moved to its allotted position, which was to act as the reserve force for the regimental combat team. The men dug in about 400 yards southeast of Casa Vannulo, where General Walker had already established his command post.

General Walker had stepped ashore on Red Beach with his command team a little after 0800 hours that morning. It had taken their landing boat more than 5 hours to make the 12 miles from ship to shore. Delays, uncertainties, and congestion in the sea lanes had all helped to prolong what should have been a short sea journey.

Maj. Armin F. Puck was with the general. Puck, known throughout the division as "the sheriff," was the provost marshal. Though only 29 years of age, he had crowded into his life a degree from the University of Texas and a couple of seasons as a Triple-A minor-league baseball player with the Kansas City Blues. War service had included escort duties for Gen. George Marshall and British F.M. Sir John Dill at Fort Blanding. This was not his first visit to North Africa and the Mediterranean. He had traveled as part of the escort for Sen. Henry Cabot Lodge when he visited North Africa and General Montgomery before Alamein.

Now as they moved in toward the shore, Puck could tell that all was not going according to plan. The enemy artillery was too heavy, and the volume of machine-gun fire indicated that the assault battalions ashore were still having difficulties.

The landing craft passed through the curtain of fire unscathed, though the young coxswain, like so many that day unnerved by the experience, had needed the steadying hand of the commanding general himself on the tiller over the last few hundred yards.

The coxswain wanted to come ashore with them. He had no desire to take his boat back through that hail of fire and said so in blunt terms.

General Walker was equally blunt. "No," he said, "I think you had better turn that boat around and go back to your ship."

"I don't know where it is," the coxswain replied.

"You'll find it, son," Walker said.

The coxswain dropped the ramp, then unloaded his party into water that was waist deep. They had about 75 yards to wade to the shore. Clearly he had decided to run the gauntlet back out to sea while his nerves held, for by the time the command party had stepped onto dry land, the boat had gone.

Puck had waded ashore ahead of the main group. He was anxious to see how his military policemen were standing up to their baptism of fire on the beaches. Puck had first recruited and then trained the division's policemen. It was their task to keep the men and the vehicles flowing. Like the beach work parties, they had no opportunity to take cover from the bombardment.

Sergeant Wallis, one of Puck's top squad leaders, was at the water's edge to meet the command party. Puck checked with him to be sure he knew exactly what was expected of the military police detachments. Their orders were to clear the beach of all traffic and troops. Then they were to move to the forward companies to provide traffic control as necessary and establish prisoner-of-war collection points.

Wallis pointed out the direction of the railway station at Paestum. "Sir, you're supposed to go that way," he said.

Puck moved briskly ahead of the main group. The beach was still under occasional artillery fire. He had just about reached the duneline when Puck saw a German Luger in front of him. It lay in the sand, right in his path.

"Don't touch it!" somebody yelled. "It's booby-trapped!"

Puck reached into his shirt and pulled out a K ration. He stood back a few yards and hurled it at the Luger. The ration hit the pistol squarely on the handle, and though it leaped into the air, nothing else happened. Puck reached forward and picked it up. He hadn't been in Italy five minutes and already had acquired a Luger.

It was about a mile and a half to the area that had been designated for the divisional command post. The path took them along the north side of the ruins of the ancient Greek settlement of Paestum, which now showed the scars of this, its most recent military encounter.

General Walker set a quick pace and marched tight-lipped. He hadn't liked what he had seen so far and was anxious to reach the command post so he could exert some control on the battle. There had been too many landing craft milling around out to sea. The beaches were too quiet and devoid of the right sort of activity. He had expected to see the engineers laying the wire mesh trackways and clearing all the beach obstacles, but none of this had been undertaken on Red Beach. Most disconcerting of all, as they moved inland the battle was waging fiercely all around them. He had hoped that by this time the Germans would have been pushed back, well past the railroad.

As they came to the railroad station the party came under mortar and machine-gun fire. Charlie Walker, the general's son who was acting as his aide, stumbled over his own feet and fell. Puck and Carl Phinney (the supply officer) reached out, got him by his arms, and dragged him for about 15 yards before dumping him down out of harm's way. Like all the officers in Walker's command, Puck would follow Walker into the very jaws of hell, but he wasn't about to have "his butt shot off wet-nursing his baby boy." Another shell burst in the exact same spot where the son had stumbled.

The German barrage increased in intensity and volume. The command party crouched down behind a low stone wall as the mortar shells plowed into the ground around them. There was a tree growing out of the wall on their side, and Puck was holding onto it for dear life. The tree seemed to offer something solid—life and hope, perhaps—in a world of turmoil.

General Walker was also trying to grab hold of the tree, but Puck's vicelike grip would give him no room. Finally and totally exasperated, Walker said, "Puck, quit fucking around. Turn that tree loose and let me get a hold of it!"

Despite the intensity of the bombardment, Puck knew that if the Old Man said "fucking," that was serious!

After a while, the German bombardment eased. The command party ran the last hundred yards to the railroad station and regrouped. Walker climbed up the station stairs and viewed what he could of the battlefield. It is terrible for a general to be in the middle of his battle without any means to influence the events around him.

The railway line was completely devoid of Americans for as far as he could see, which was perhaps a quarter mile or less, for the morning haze still hung heavy in the air. Walker had heard over the radio, however, that battalions of both the 142nd and 143rd RCTs were inland and to the northwest beyond the highway and the railway. He could also hear and see something of the battle that was still being waged for the exits off Blue and Yellow beaches.

German tanks were making another drive for the beaches. Though his three battalions were ashore, Col. Richard J. Werner found that without heavy fire support there was little the 141st RCT could do. Even while his naval gun observer on the beach was still trying to call in naval support, five tanks managed to break through. The tanks overran an isolated company of the 1st Battalion. Those men who stayed in their foxholes or got down in the irrigation ditches were unharmed, even though the tanks rolled over them. However, many tried to run for it and were either run down or shot.

The timely arrival of field artillery and the first naval shells finally helped disperse the German tanks. The GIs had been fortunate, for if the Germans had been able to mass their armor it would have been a different story.

General Walker and his divisional command group, which at this stage could offer to the battle no more than a combat patrol comprising a number of rather elderly and unfit officers, moved north along the railway line toward Casa Vannulo, a farm across Highway 18, which was immediately inland from the railway. Between the two was a low embankment and a ditch.

As Walker and his team approached the farm, the owner, Signor C. Vannulo and his family, all dressed in their best Sunday clothes, came out to meet him. Walker established his command post among the substantial farm buildings, one of which was an especially large tobacco warehouse. There among the racks of drying tobacco General Walker prepared to exert his measure of control over the battle. Regimental liaison officers got to work immediately, and within a short while his unit commanders began reporting to him in person. Other staff officers concentrated on the situations map, which soon took shape.

However, before General Walker could get down to his job, he had a further ordeal to face. The Germans launched another tank attack. At about 1145 hours 13 Panzers—Mark IIIs and Mark IVs—came down Highway 18 from the north and moved against Casa Vannulo and the divisional command post itself.

Walker sent one of his officers back to the beach with instructions to bring up artillery posthaste; then he led his team across the road and into the ditch beside the railway. From there they watched the German armor come within range. Bazooka teams from the 142nd and 143rd RCTs kept the tanks at bay. Already the message seemed to have spread, and the panzers were showing a healthy respect for these new weapons. In the meantime, help of a more substantial nature entered the fray.

It came in the form of the Cannon Company of the 143rd Infantry, or rather in one of its guns. The Cannon Company was equipped at this stage of the war with the old French 75mm of 1914 vintage, mounted on a White half-track. Their role was to give close artillery support to the infantry; they were not intended for the antitank role.

John Whittaker, a first lieutenant, commanded a platoon of three such vehicles, but there was only one immediately available for action on the beach when word reached him of the tank threat at Casa Vannulo. One half-track had yet to come ashore, and the third sat forlorn and immobile with a vapor lock. In any case, even if its cursing sergeant could have coaxed some life into the stubborn motor, it still had to be dewaterproofed. This was a time-consuming but absolutely essential job before any of the ordinary vehicles (DUKWs, of course, were immune) could proceed into battle. Trucks and armored fighting vehicles had verticle exhaust attachments that allowed them to "wade" ashore under their own power. In order to protect the more exposed parts of the engine and other vital parts, a rubberized solution was used to seal the vehicle and make it watertight. After the vehicle had landed, this solution had to be stripped away; otherwise the engine would soon overheat.

Whittaker, a 23-year-old onetime semipro baseball player and law student, hopped aboard the only serviceable vehicle and rode it into battle. Once through Paestum, Route 18, tree-lined and straight as an arrow, stretched before him, but visibility was obscured by the heat haze and smoke that hung in the windless air. He moved through columns of infantry plodding down the highway and within a short distance came to a stop. Whittaker could just about make out the shape of a tank to his front. He jumped down and moved to the side of the road, where he could see some officers in the ditch.

A shell whistled between his head and the vehicle before plowing into the head of the column of infantry some 200 yards behind. Those who survived the appalling mess moved quickly off the road. The left-hand column jumped into the ditches between the road and the railway while the right-hand column, unscathed, deployed in an extended line beyond the road.

Whittaker stood where he was in the highway and directed the fire of his gun. The French 75mm might be old, but it still could crack out a rapid rate of fire, three rounds a minute. They destroyed the lead tank, and this forced those behind to deploy into the field on Whittaker's right; as they did so, the panzers had to expose their vulnerable sides to Whittaker's fire.

Fresh support arrived in the form of a 105mm howitzer belonging to the 151st Field Artillery. This gun was towed into action by a DUKW, and it deployed on the track that led from the highway to Casa Vannulo. The combined fire of the howitzer and Whittaker's 75mm broke up the panzer assault; five tanks were destroyed, and the remainder beat a hasty retreat.

In the midst of the action Walker was amazed to see a DUKW come from behind the German tanks and bounce across the field and back onto the road, where it roared at full speed into the safety of the American lines. It was carrying the radio set for use in communicating with Army headquarters aboard the *Ancon* in the harbor. Walker had sent Carl Phinney to the beaches to find it and rush it through to the command post. Phinney and the driver had lost their way and come in from the wrong direction; but fortune favors the brave, and they had driven into and out of the field of fire without a scratch.

By about this time the development of the division's beachhead was at last beginning to progress. This was despite the fact that only two (Red and Green) of the four beaches were open and able to receive landing craft, and artillery fire still was landing on all four. Men and materiel were coming ashore in substantial quantities, while inland, control and discipline were bringing order to the earlier confusion.

Beachmasters used loudspeakers to encourage the landing craft milling at sea to bring their cargoes of men and materiel ashore. They probably shouted phrases such as, "Come on in, we've got you covered!" This is a rational and reasonable explanation of the earlier myth of the Germans "greeting" the first Americans ashore.

The only unit still in deep trouble was the 1st Battalion of the 141st RCT, which was isolated on the right. The other battalions had at last started to move inland, backed by heavy artillery support. However, the 1st Battalion, its headquarters, and its scattered companies were destined to remain pinned down for the rest of the day, some still to the seaward side of the railway tracks.

In the early afternoon German tanks came swinging in from the south in one last attempt to reach the sea, only to be turned back by a desperate defense. Even then, some of the forward positions were badly mauled and troops isolated. A couple of squads' worth of men from Company B took cover in a drainage ditch only to find that when the enemy tanks fell back they halted about 50 yards away. This effectively isolated the small group from the remainder of the company. The heaviest weapon among them was a BAR, so Lieutenant Hill, the platoon commander, ordered them to hold their fire and not reveal their presence; their survival depended on it. One of the men, Pvt. Truman A. Rice, was seriously wounded, his legs and thighs rent by shrapnel. There were no medics with the group, and though in the most intense pain, Truman remained still and quiet. The slightest sound would have alerted the Germans to their presence. He died shortly after 1400 hours in great pain but without having uttered a sound.

German positions on Mount Sottane above the beleaguered troops made any movement impossible. Naval gunfire was able to help ease their predicament a little by screening some of the German batteries and preventing the enemy from launching further attacks. Until dusk, however, it was a stalemate for the 141st RCT.

Elsewhere, naval gunfire was beginning to make a bigger contribution to the land battle. As in the British sector, destroyers steamed close to the beach, providing direct fire support. Naval parties ashore and spotter planes helped direct the guns of the cruisers farther out at sea. Much of the artillery that had managed to come ashore in the late morning was now joining the battle in support of the hard-pressed infantry.

The 105mm howitzer of Battery C, 132nd Field Artillery, was lowered from the assault ship into an LCM, and the six-by-six truck that was used to pull the gun came down after. The two were then connected up on the LCM. This was a complicated and delicate task, not made easier by the fact that it had to be done while it was still dark. It was well into the morning by the time the LCM came ashore on Red Beach. An LST was burning furiously on the beach alongside, so the men lost little time unloading from their LCM and driving inland. Military policemen directed them into an apple orchard just above the ruins at Paestum.

One of the great qualities of American soldiers is their ingenuity. They can throw away the rule book and function by sense or feel, or "by the seat of their pants." It is no simple affair to bring a battery of artillery (which consisted of four field guns or howitzers) into action, and there are set rules and procedures to be followed. However, all of these take time, and that was in short supply on the American beachhead that day. The gun was in action before the trails had been adjusted or a pit dug. Forward observation officers had come ashore with the first waves of the 142nd Infantry. Those still alive were already calling down fire missions.

The rule book went out the window in another sense too that morning. The LCMs bringing the guns and trucks ashore had the capacity to carry only one unit each. Though the craft left their mother ships in groups comprising a complete battery of guns, they soon became separated in the chaos and confusion of the shipping lanes and the mayhem at the seashore. So the guns arrived at the position individually and just extended the firing line. The first mission was fired in early afternoon, when there were nine howitzers in the battery.

Their target was a group of tanks, which they attacked at a range of 3 miles. Stripped to the waist in the hot afternoon sunlight, the six-man crews serviced their guns and smothered the enemy tanks in fire. The shells, each weighing 40 pounds, were rammed into the breech. Firing at a rapid rate, the gun captains ignored using the plunger between rounds and instead employed the shortcuts that their training had taught them. Of course, no howitzer is designed to fire in an antitank role. Neither, however, can panzers take the volume of artillery that such a battery can deliver. The Germans were forced to pull back, cursing their own impotence to counter such overwhelming firepower. Without the Luftwaffe to control the skies and the Stukas to dive-bomb such batteries, they had no answer to American artillery. Later the howitzers were switched to a counterbattery role as the forward observation officers tried desperately to pinpoint a German mobile 88 battery that was still this late in the day firing on Red Beach.

All the while the missing guns, crews, and the service and supply detachments arrived at the orchard. The supply detachments went into action without delay, replenishing the shells on the gunline. Nine further separate missions were fired in support of the infantry that day.

Later in the afternoon the first of the heaviest guns, the 155mm howitzers of the 155th Field Artillery Battalion, came ashore on Green Beach and moved to a position just a mile north of Paestum. Sergeant Ward Gable commanded one of these guns. He was just 20 years old and came from Forth Worth, Texas.

The guns did not fire that afternoon, but at one stage there was fear that some German tanks pressing the 142nd Infantry were on the point of breaking through. The order came down to swing the guns out onto a left traverse and to lower the barrels for a point-blank shot. Gable listened over the headset as the battery commander issued his final instruction: "You'll see some tanks come over that hill, and they ain't going to be ours."

Gable thought it would at least be a novel experience to fire these monster pieces over open sights. Normally they can throw a 95-pound shell over 25,000 yards.

The master sergeant passed down the gun line and handed each captain a thermalite grenade as a precaution. This was a grenade about the size of a beer can with a pull pin at the top. It was an incendiary device that, when lowered down the barrel to the bottom, would dissolve the block and breech. It was the easiest and at the same time the most effective way of immobilizing the gun.

Fortunately, the German threat did not materialize.

Chapter XII

The Texans Consolidate
Their Beachhead

Despite occasional alarms, the Americans were now firmly ashore. They had blunted the heaviest of the German counterattacks and were making progress inland. However, their superiors on the command ships at sea had little idea of the true state of affairs in the land battle. Communications between shore and ship were practically nonexistent, and very few details reached Mark Clark and Dawley. Only fragments of reports came their way, confused words taken down from wounded officers and men evacuated from the beaches. Since these men were in pain and often in shock, such reports were disjointed and frequently incoherent. Boat crews from the first waves came back with wild stories of mass slaughter and disaster.

Maj. Oran Stovall saw what effect wild stories could have on the morale and spirit of the soldiers. He was the troop commander on the *Marnix*. When the first of their landing craft returned, many were in a battered condition with dead, wounded, and dying among their troops and crew. They took off the casualties, patched up the boats, and replaced the crews where necessary before sending them inshore with the follow-up waves. But even such prompt and firm action could not prevent the rumors of the dire deeds onshore from spreading and causing consternation among those who waited their turn to land.

It was hardly surprising that both Dawley and Mark Clark came to believe that the situation ashore was much worse than it actually was. What added to their frustration was that technically the forces were still the responsibility of the Navy, and Admiral Hewitt had yet formally to hand over command of the land forces. It was established procedure in landing operations of this nature that the troops be firmly ashore and the forward edge of the battle inland and beyond the direct support of naval gunfire before the *admiral* would ask the *general* to assume responsibility for the command of his own forces. Until such time Dawley took his instructions from Admiral Hewitt rather than General Clark.

Unable to restrain his impatience, General Dawley left his ship at 1300 hours to make a personal inspection of the beach. He took with him just one other officer as escort. Not only was this act strictly against the "protocol" of command, but Admiral Hewitt wasn't even informed that the corps commander had gone ashore.

Hewitt did, in fact, send two messages to General Dawley that morning. The first, sent at 1000 hours, ordered him to assume command of the troops ashore, not because the Navy felt they had discharged their duty, but because communications from the 36th Division to the ships at sea was nonexistent.

A second message (both were sent by patrol boat for fear that the Germans might decipher the codes) contradicted the first. At 1200 hours Hewitt ordered Dawley to remain on his ship to confer with General Middleton about an early commitment of his 179th RCT into the land battle.

The second message reached Dawley's LST at 1500 hours and before the first, which thoroughly confused the corps staff. In any event, at that time Dawley was ashore and in Walker's divisional command post seeing things for himself.

This didn't exactly help matters because, until Dawley was to assume formal command, General Walker was responsible to Admiral Hewitt for the tactical operations on the beachhead. It was just as well that none of the American senior officers took any of this formality too seriously. In the German Army, however, and as we shall see later, a similar administrative confusion was to cause mayhem in the relationship between Tenth Army and OBSUED, Kesselring's headquarters near Rome.

Hewitt's first message finally reached Dawley's ship at 1520 hours, and a staff officer rushed inshore to find the general.

Dawley was given the message at Walker's command post. He decided to undertake a thorough investigation of all the front-line deployments, friendly as well as enemy forces, before assuming command. The only problem was that he had just two staff officers ashore, and Walker had none to spare. This meant that Dawley was forced to operate from the beginning on a shoestring, acting as his own Intelligence and operations staff officer. Dawley embarked on a punishing personal routine, which was not only a silly decision on his part but also one that was to cost him dearly later.

Military action is unpredictable, for what looks good in the plans can appear awful in reality. Dawley had not anticipated assuming effective command at this point in the battle, but clearly it was in need of direction from on high. This could not come from the headquarters ship, U.S.S. *Ancon*, because of the breakdown in communications. This for Dawley was the decisive moment of command; he should have seized command with both hands and asserted his authority over the battle. Instead he delayed the moment of command and so revealed those elements of indecision and uncertainty that no commander can have and survive. In subsequent days Dawley's punishing routine and Spartan headquarters were to undermine his ability to think on his feet and to issue clear and decisive orders. He sowed the seeds of his own downfall.

The reason there was so much confusion and chaos with radio communications was that the signals unit had failed to arrive at the divisional command post with all the equipment in working order.

It is the task of a unit called the message center to land first and establish and maintain communications until the divisional signals net can be established. The first message center team, three privates with a corporal in command, left the *Marnix* at 0100 hours. A DUKW was lifted over the side, and the team made their way ashore immediately behind the initial assault waves. The DUKW carried a new RC299 radio, developed by a factory in Detroit. The radio measured 5 feet by 5 feet; it sat big and fat in the back of the vehicle and made the DUKW an even bigger target. The team was intended to land on Blue Beach, but it was closed; eventually two hours later they came ashore on Red Beach in the midst of a particularly nasty mortar barrage. The corporal stopped the DUKW behind the dunes to get his bearings for the station at Paestum. One of the men checked the equipment and found it shot through by shrapnel.

This was the unit that Col. Carl Phinney had found and rushed through to the divisional command post. Though he knew its condition, he hoped that something could be salvaged, but they had risked their lives for nothing. The set was wrecked.

A second message center team left the *Marnix* at about 1000 hours. Virgil White, a 23-year-old technical sergeant, was on board the DUKW. It took them 2 hours to reach the beach. White found traveling in a DUKW to be like sitting in a wash tub on a lake; they bounced around a lot. They tried to come ashore on Green Beach, but like most others were diverted to Red, where they had to wait in line before the DUKW could come ashore.

The beach was under fire, and White watched as a salvo of mortars came across the sand and into the path of a couple of 2½-ton trucks that had just come out of an LCT alongside. The trucks blew up in a solid sheet of flame. Virgil White realized the DUKW was three times their size!

Eventually they were able to move forward, and the first person they met was an Italian peasant, who accosted them and offered a drink from his bottle of wine. He claimed to be from Chicago!

White pulled the DUKW into the yard at Casa Vannulo and parked against the tobacco barn. It took the men a short while before they finally had communications with the command nets out to sea.

Divisional headquarters was by this time a hive of activity. Bert Carlton was a first lieutenant in the 143rd Infantry Regiment. His job was to act as liaison officer between his regiment and divisional headquarters. He was there that afternoon when the Luftwaffe began to concentrate in earnest upon the American sector. Focke-Wulf 190s, equipped with underwing bomb racks, came in low and fast over the crowded anchorage and the beaches to drop their bombs inland before zooming up and away over Mount Soprano. By the time the aircraft had dropped their bombs, the anti-aircraft fire from the fleet had tracked them inland. The shells invariably punched empty air, and it was the troops on the ground who suffered. They caught a double dose: German bombs and American shrapnel.

There was an unofficial rush to mount machine guns on jeeps and trucks to provide additional anti-aircraft fire. Carlton had picked up a German Spandau MG42 and a couple of belts of ammunition off the beach. Capt. Harry Stokes, who commanded the antitank company, didn't have a machine gun for his jeep; so between them the two officers fashioned a mount and eagerly awaited the next German air raid. The jeep was parked a little way out in the field of tomatoes behind the barn.

They didn't have long to wait before an FW-190 came screaming in low for the hills; a couple of black things dropped away, and the bombs burst across the highway. Little bright sparks flashed along the wingtips and splats of dust spurted up from the ground. Stokes swung the gun and let rip with a long burst. The distinctive sound of the Spandau's high rate of fire rose above the noise of other weapons, against all of which the enemy plane seemed impervious as it climbed unscathed toward the heavens.

Stokes' jeep drew every piece of small-arms fire around, and the two officers flung themselves to the ground.

When it was over, Bert Carlton looked up and caught Harry Stokes' eye. They nodded, scrambled to their feet, and made their way back to the now bullet-ridden and very sad-looking jeep. Between them they took the gun and the ammunition and dumped all of it in the nearest irrigation ditch.

The general came out of the tobacco barn, looked at them, and laughingly said, "I thought you boys knew better."

No detailed report is necessarily correct. It is just the first report that contains hard information—that is, goes into detail; whether that detail is correct or accurate is another matter.

The first detailed report reached Mark Clark on board the *Ancon* a little after 1700 hours. The news was nowhere near as bad as he had feared. For the first time since H Hour that morning he could afford to relax just a little and to discuss the operations that were necessary to expand the beachhead.

Toward the end of the day German resistance declined remarkably, and the Americans were able to push forward to secure some important objectives. The 601st Tank Battalion and the 645th Tank Destroyer Battalion arrived. Both were from the 45th Division, and their presence made an immediate difference. The 3rd Battalion's 143rd Infantry pushed forward and secured the village of Capaccio just southeast of Mount Soprano. John Whittaker's half-tracks formed a roadblock at the far side of the town.

This in effect represented the center of the American line, with the 143rd RCT astride Monte Soprano and part of Monte Sottane. To their right the 141st RCT was able eventually to move out with the darkness from the positions where they had spent the daylight pinned down. As they moved forward to lock into the right flank, they came upon gruesome evidence, in the form of burned and wrecked enemy vehicles, of the effect of naval bombardment.

The weakness lay on the left flank. Though the 142nd RCT was firmly entrenched in the foothills below Albanella, this was a long way from where their left-hand battalion was meant to be deployed. These were the nearest American troops to the British, and they were still 7 miles from the Sele River. The right-hand battalion of the British corps, the fusiliers, were a further 3 miles beyond the far bank.

As the effects and sounds of battle died down with the sunset, the Germans broke off contact. They left the Texans holding a beachhead that had a perimeter of some 12 miles and a depth of 4 miles at its deepest.

As a parting gesture, the German pioneers (or engineers) blew the bridge on Highway 18 over the Sele River. The two corps of Mark Clark's Fifth Army were now separated.

In the gathering darkness, staff officers and soldiers worked through the night. The big tents were up, lamps glowed inside, and their harsh glare fought against the blackout. Behind the tobacco barn, generators mumbled, and the high-pitched hum of a dozen radios showed the divisional signal's team keeping a night watch. The main command post was heavy with the rich aroma of Havana tobacco. The Texans liked their cigars, none more than Walker as he talked over the day's events with his senior advisers.

In another corner of the big tent a young officer worked away oblivious to all that was going on around him. Capt. Vince Lockhart was the assistant personnel officer at the divisional headquarters. This 28-year-old National Guard officer was a journalist by profession, and in part he was chosen for his present assignment because of his gift for words. Vince was required to write up the division's recommendations for awards and decorations. However, it was another aspect of his work that kept him at the keys of his typewriter that evening. He also had to compile the battle casualty reports. The list made for depressing reading, especially as there were so many names he recognized from his days in the Texas National Guard. The division had suffered some 500 casualties, of which about 100 men were killed. To a more dispassionate eye such casualty figures, though higher than those of either of the British divisions, were still relatively low, especially for an operation as fraught with peril as an opposed amphibious assault. The belief that the first day at Salerno was bloody has developed largely because the higher commands cocooned on board ship and starved of news from the front, painted a picture of an inordinately difficult day out of ignorance.

There was much that had to be done before the position could really be made secure. One was to clear the chaos from the beaches. On Red Beach in particular, there was a veritable mountain of boxed ammunition and supplies of all shapes and sizes. These lined the seashore and in many places were stacked in untidy piles several feet deep into the sea. There was no room for landing craft to let down their ramps.

In part these problems were undoubtedly caused by the fact that the beaches had been under shellfire throughout the day. However, men who had been detailed to unload the ships had in many cases drifted away inland either in search of shelter or battle, and this left the boat crews to become their own stevedores. On some of the bigger LSTs the stores had been loaded in the wrong order in Oran or Bizerte, and this caused further delay.

The LSTs of convoy FSS2 should by now have been on their way back for a follow-up load. Instead they littered the shore waiting to be unloaded. It was to be midnight on September 12 before the last of these had cleared the beachhead.

In the succeeding days, the landing craft were to exert a critical influence on the land battle. Though the first convoys did sail on schedule to pick up the reinforcements planned, there were far fewer ships than had been expected. They left an anchorage at Salerno that was already experiencing its first air raid of the night.

Admiral Hewitt was concerned that the enemy had the *Ancon* pinpointed. In daylight like a queen bee in the hive, she was the center of activity, and if that weren't enough, her bulk and the forest of aerials that festooned her superstructure were even more of a giveaway. After dark Hewitt ordered *Ancon* to change her station and then moved some destroyers and a cruiser close by as additional anti-aircraft protection. The *Ancon* was not an easy ship to protect in such a crowded anchorage.

Lt. Peter Matterson of the Royal Engineers was safely ensconced on the U.S.S. *Joseph T. Dickman,* where he had already become something of a personality. He had been prepared to compromise over dinner and eat with the American officers at what he regarded as the totally unreasonable hour of 1730 hours. But he was mortified by the absence of afternoon tea in the wardroom; this he regarded as uncivilized. Matterson went to the bridge to register his complaint in person to the captain.

Though the *Joseph T. Dickman* carried many thousands of tons of war freight, tea—neither Indian nor Chinese—wasn't included in her manifest. The problem was solved, however, when they signaled a passing British destroyer. A small boat was lowered and a 10-pound box of the best Chinese tea was exchanged for a couple of canned hams from the *Dickman*'s wardroom.

Salerno was to witness the best and the worst characteristics of the Anglo-American relationship at work before it was over. This, however, must rank as one of the strangest.

The part played by the two navies in support of all the operations during D-Day was important. This was especially the case in the American sector, and it was acknowledged as such by a senior Army officer onshore. Brig. John

W. Lange, who commanded the 36th Division's artillery, sent the following message:

> Thank God for the fire of the blue-belly navy ships. Probably could not have struck out on Blue and Yellow Beaches. Brave fellows these, tell them so.*

Salerno marked a departure in the annals of World War II in Europe. For the first time the British and Americans came across German troops who defended their positions with a desperate yet thoroughly professional ferocity. Later such resistance and military competence came to be considered normal, both in Italy and in northwestern Europe. But it was encountered for the first time in September 1943 at Salerno. The fact that such a "discovery" was made by Allied troops who were going into battle for the first time made it even more of a traumatic experience.

---

*Samuel Eliot Morison, "Ludlow Action Report," *U.S. Naval Operations in World War Two*, Vol. IX, pp. 270.

PART FOUR

The Pause

Chapter XIII

The Germans

Lieutenant Rocholl's patrol watched the British landing from the high ground above Faiano. Even at some distance and in the dark it was not difficult to pick out the various stages of the battle.

There was no mistaking the British rocket craft. The ground around the Germans shook and reverberated to their terrifying explosions. Rocholl couldn't see the leading waves of the landing craft, but he knew they had to be close to the shore when the machine guns along the dunelines opened fire.

Rocholl wrote out his reports and faithfully recorded the events that his radio operator transmitted to divisional headquarters.

With the dawn Rocholl took his team and moved into the abandoned Italian battery position. As the sun rose, early-morning mist rolled back to reveal the panorama of Salerno Bay packed full of Allied shipping. To the young Germans who rejoiced at such a target there was also a darker fear, for they could not but tremble at the magnificent spectacle of such enemy power concentrated in one place. Gradually this incredible scene slipped from view as British destroyers hurried to lay the smoke that would screen their movements from the eyes of Rocholl and others in the hills above.

Just after 1000 hours, Rocholl witnessed a strange event. A little convoy emerged from behind the smoke and headed toward the small harbor at Salerno. The convoy stopped a few miles from the shore, and a single small landing craft—Rocholl focused his binoculars and counted some dozen men on board—moved toward the destroyed mole. The landing craft came to within yards of the mole unmolested; then an 88mm gun battery located in the slopes behind him opened fire. Shells fell all around the little boat, but it seemed to bear a charmed life. Rocholl watched as the stern bit deep into the water, the bows came around, and the landing craft scuttled back to the company of its brethren.

Not long after, the first British shots began to fall around Rocholl. At first he feared that his observation post had been discovered, but then he realized that the enemy must have been observing the harbor incident. Somebody on ship or shore had an idea where the 88mm battery was located and was determined to give the area a good pasting.

In the late afternoon, a British reconnaissance patrol caught Rocholl and his party unawares and at a tactical disadvantage. The enemy, wearing rubber-soled shoes, had infiltrated into a position that overlooked the gun pit; though they were few in number, the vicious rat-a-tat-tat of their Bren gun displayed both their determination and intentions. There was nothing more he could do. The observation post's position was compromised, and the best thing now was to join up with the armored cars, which they were able to do.

Rocholl led his armored cars through the now destroyed and deserted city of Salerno. Headquarters had ordered him to take up a position at the sanatorium. The tires of their eight wheels sang across the cobbles, squealing their protest as the cars swerved to avoid the craters and debris that pockmarked the street. The lieutenant cocked the Spandau 42 on its mounting beside him and urged his driver on faster.

It was like a ghost town. Skeletal buildings stood out stark and ominous in the light of the setting sun, casting bizarre shadows across the main street. The British artillery bombardment from the guns on ship and on shore had reduced much of the old town to rubble. The streets close to the harbor had come in for special attention; there seemed to be very few houses that had survived the holocaust of shot and shell.

Rocholl noticed the shops, their windows smashed and their contents strewn on the pavement along the looters' paths. There were, however, other matters of more immediate concern to him, for he had no idea how far the British had advanced. It was a ghastly feeling to drive through the empty streets waiting for the first belch of flame and the screaming shot that would be an antitank gun in ambush. The muzzles of his guns swung through their arcs, seeking the enemy in doorways and windows, but nothing impeded their progress.

Rocholl was amazed and very puzzled. He could not understand why the *Tommis* were not in Salerno. As a reconnaissance officer he knew his division's deployments, and there wasn't that much to impede the British. The German troops on the beaches and forward of the highway were there to buy time, nothing more.

Rocholl knew a couple of officers in his regiment, older and more battle-wise than he, who had fought the British in the desert. They had spoken frequently and very disparagingly of their caution and reluctance to take chances. Perhaps it was true? A surge of hope and optimism flooded his thoughts. They could be defeated and sent reeling back into the sea.

The three armored cars drove the length of the city and then swung right and up the steep hill that led to the sanatorium. There Rocholl intended to establish his new observation post. The hospital looked out over the bay, and its unsurpassed views would expose every movement in the plain below. A lot of men in the course of the next few days were to die for possession of this vital ground.

Rocholl swung past the little gatehouse over the bridge and into the gardens of the sanatorium. The road, still climbing, curved in a broad, right-handed sweep to the main buildings at the top of the hill. The cars came to a stop, and Rocholl briefed the crews. Drivers topped up the fuel tanks with the last of the gasoline from the jerry cans stowed in the racks. Radio operators netted in the radios to headquarters and reported their location. A silence descended upon the scene, punctuated by the hum of the radios and the ticking of contracting metal. Rocholl was on the point of sending a couple of men to check the heavily shuttered building when a door creaked open and out walked a figure in black. It was the local priest. Father Caruccio beseeched the young officer to leave the hospital and to give thought to the sick and not to make this place a battleground.

"What a strange conception of war these Italians have," Rocholl thought. Still, the obvious sincerity of the priest was not lost on the young officer. Rocholl ordered his sergeant to have a quick look inside the building and report as quickly as possible.

Within a few minutes the sergeant reappeared and reported that the hospital was full of people, and not just the sick. "Half of Salerno must be crammed into those corridors, Herr Leutnant," he reported. Like most Germans, he had scant respect for Italian resolve and believed that they had only themselves to blame for their country becoming a battlefield.

Rocholl had not the slightest intention of acceding to the priest's request, though he admired his courage for speaking out—that took some guts. Red Cross flag and Geneva Convention or not, "hospital hill" was just too important to be discarded. He was on the point of launching into a discourse on the fortunes of war when the matter was taken out of his hands. A message came through ordering Rocholl to take his detachment to reinforce the roadblock on the outskirts of Battipaglia. The cars moved once again and retraced their route through the town and out into the countryside. It was already quite dark as they sped through the little villages that dotted the lower slopes of the hills. They were some distance from the battle zone, and there were more people on the streets, gathered in little groups outside cafes. Some waved to Rocholl and threw flowers onto the armored cars shouting, "*Viva* Inglese!" The Germans did not disillusion those who had once been their allies and who now presumed the British were already on the march to liberate Italy.

The patrol pulled in behind the roadblock. Rocholl climbed down from his turret and talked to the antitank-gun commander, who was standing beside his weapon. The armored cars deployed off the road and dispersed, ready to lend the weight of their firepower should the enemy appear. Rocholl mounted a motorcycle and rode off toward Eboli and regimental battle headquarters to make his report in person, but he was unable to find it because it had been moved in the meantime.

"So much for military efficiency," he thought as he quartered the country-side looking for some sign of the regiment. Angry and frustrated, he abandoned his search and returned to the roadblock. The quartermaster was waiting for him; he had brought them rations, mail, orders, and the new location of headquarters.

The patrol was to return to regimental battle headquarters once they had eaten. Rocholl went with the quartermaster, leaving his sergeant to bring the vehicles later. By the time Rocholl had reported, it was 2300 hours. He came out of the farm building that served as headquarters to find his three cars neatly parked and festooned in their camouflage nets. Rocholl had a quick bite to eat and then climbed into his bedroll, which had been laid out beside his armored car. They all slept like the dead.

Even while these men slept, Wehrmacht and Luftwaffe divisions were on the move. Kesselring's first reaction to the landings at Salerno had been to order General der Panzertruppen Heinrich von Vietinghoff, who commanded the Tenth Army, to retreat northward toward Rome. Now even at the end of the first day, the idea was beginning to crystallize that the Allies had presented him with the opportunity of doing the reverse. Though it would take more than 24 hours for all the necessary authorities to approve, Kesselring intended to launch a massive counterattack to throw the Allies back into the sea. Like most of his contemporaries in the German high command, Kesselring was terrified by the maritime strategy of the Allies and their ability to spring surprise from the sea. In the case of the Italian peninsula, with its long and vulnerable coastline, he feared the *amphibious hooks* that land large numbers of Allied forces onshore, would outflank his defenses, and trap his divisions.

For the first couple of days, the news from the Salerno beachhead could not have been more favorable. Kesselring was an optimist (he was affection-ately known as "Smiling Albert"), but on this occasion he could hardly believe his good fortune. The *Tommis* and the *Amis* had come ashore where he had more or less expected. The divisions that had been identified were not the veterans of the Eighth Army that had earned the respect of the Wehr-macht. Instead, the Allies had sent in a green American unit and two British divisions that the Germans held in low esteem. On top of this, they were led by a general who was experiencing his first taste of command in the field. From the German viewpoint, the situation at Salerno could hardly have been more favorable.

Over the succeeding days the German plans began to take shape. From the Tenth Army down through the panzer corps headquarters to the divisions in the beachhead, these plans were increasingly influenced by the mistakes they noted the Allies had made.

The Allies had failed to land with sufficient forces to give them the necessary impetus to take the high ground. Even worse was that the beach-head was flawed. There was a significant gap between the corps, and confusion between the British divisions. These vulnerable points were begging to be exploited. The beachhead lacked depth, too, so that even if the Allies did have more troops waiting to land from the ships in the bay, there was no room for them to deploy into such a shallow area.

At the end of the first day a depleted 16th Panzers had the British and Americans pinned to the floor of the ampitheater formed by the mountains that encircled Salerno Bay. In anticipation, Kesselring ordered Von Vietinghoff to gather his forces for the kill.

There were two factors in the Germans favor. First, Montgomery's troops were advancing so slowly from the south. For a week the British 5th Infantry Division had sweated its way along the torrid western coastal highway. There had been little to oppose them, for the German high command had already decided that Calabria was expendable strategically and tactically. The main problem was demolitions and roadblocks of every sort, sown with mines. It would be unfair to make light of the enormous problems that confronted the troops. The nature of the countryside made it impossible to bypass obstacles, and so the speed of the advance northward was dictated by the sappers, whose task it was to repair the roads destroyed by the enemy. Awkward bridging equipment had to be moved forward over narrow and congested roads.

In desperation they tried an interception from the sea when a reinforced brigade landed at Pizzo and attempted to cut off the battle group of the 29th Panzer Grenadiers, which was the rear guard. It was the misfortune of the landing forces to hit the beach at the precise time that the panzer grenadiers were retreating through the town. Surprise was lost, and the Allied force found itself fighting for its existence. Had the landings been a day earlier, they might have achieved something, but it was a messy affair and the casualties were heavy.

By the time the Allies were fighting for the beaches at Salerno, Montgomery's infantry were closing on Nicastro. They had advanced 100 miles since landing at Reggio and were 200 miles from the American right flank, the 1st Battalion 141st RCT, at Agripoli.

Kesselring, convinced that Montgomery would not try any startling new moves, ordered Von Vietinghoff to leave the minimum forces necessary to make life difficult for any advance in Calabria and concentrate on Salerno. He intended to destroy the beachhead at Salerno before Montgomery's Eighth Army could threaten the German flank.

The Germans gauged Montgomery's mood precisely, for on the evening of September 9 he sent a message to Alexander that began:

> My divisions are now strung out and the infantry . . . must be rested. Am halting main bodies of divisions on the line Catanzaro to Nicastro. . . . Divisions will then wind up their tails and have two days' rest. . . .

General Alexander replied in no uncertain terms on September 10:

> It is of the utmost importance that you maintain pressure upon the Germans so that they cannot remove forces from your front and concentrate against Avalanche. . . .*

The second factor the Germans had in their favor was that many of the troops they had available were those the Allies had allowed to retreat safely out of Sicily. In so many ways the great tragedy of the Italian campaign was Sicily. It was the first invasion and the big mistake. When the Allies launched Operation Husky and landed along the southeastern coast of Sicily, the Germans had taken the enormous gamble of moving troops by way of the Straits of Messina onto the island and into a probable death trap. The high command accepted the probability that very few of these troops would leave Sicily. Yet, as it happened, 40,000 Germans, 62,000 Italians, 97 guns, 48 panzers, and 17,000 tons of ammunition and supplies crossed the Strait of Messina northward under the noses of Allied air and naval forces.

At the time neither Eisenhower, nor his subordinate Alexander, nor his prima donna army commanders Patton and Montgomery appreciated the true significance of Sicily. If only an operation similar to that at Pizzo had been launched in mid-July rather than early September, the Germans could have been sealed into southern Calabria and Sicily.

Such a military reverse could in turn have exerted a significant influence on the German high command, for in the Wolfsschanze or "Wolf's Lair," Adolf Hitler's command bunker deep in the forest heartland of East Prussia, another battle was being fought. There were those, led by Rommel, still the folk hero of the Wehrmacht (and the new commander-in-chief of all German forces in northern Italy), who believed that the Italian peninsula could not be defended. He was convinced that the Allies, with their overwhelming firepower, command of the seas and the skies, and seemingly unlimited resources, could land anywhere on the Italian peninsula and so turn the flank of the strongest defense. Rommel's contempt for the Italians knew no limits. He proposed to the Führer that the German armies fight a series of delaying actions all the way back to the North, where the mountains were their most formidable. He was quite prepared to write off Rome, the Pope, and the Vatican in the process.

Kesselring was opposed to such a strategy and favored holding Italy as far south as practicable. Air-minded, he saw possession of the complex of airfields around Foggia, which lay directly across the Apennines from Salerno, to be an important asset. From bases such as these, armadas of the Allied heavy bombers would be able to open a new front in the air war against Germany, for they could strike at the targets in the South. These were resources and capital assets, factories and the like, that had been moved into

*C. J. C. Molony, *History of the Second World War*, Vol. V, *The Mediterranean and the Middle East* (London: H.M. Stationery Office, 1973).

the southern part of the Reich out of the path of the bombers based in England. To defend the new targets would in turn force the Luftwaffe to divert precious fighters away from the Ruhr, Berlin, and the industrial North, where they were already locked into a titanic struggle with the Flying Fortresses of the U.S. Eighth Air Force and the Lancasters of the RAF Bomber Command. The Luftwaffe, Kesselring knew, lacked skilled pilots in sufficient quantity to fight the air war on two fronts.

There were other considerations to be taken into account. Kesselring as a theater commander was beginning to experience the problems that resistance movements can cause to an army of occupation. If the Germans abandoned southern Italy to the Allies, this would allow them to use the ports along the Adriatic coast to support Tito and his partisans in Yugoslavia, give aid to the Greeks, and set the Balkans on fire. The Yugoslavs had already proven to be the biggest beneficiaries of the Italian capitulation. They had acquired enough arms from those occupation divisions to make the transition from a guerrilla force to a regular army. As the pace of the Soviet offensive in the East gathered momentum while the Anglo-Americans prepared to strike from England in the West, the Germans could ill afford to police an increasingly turbulent southern flank.

Of course, Hitler, who by temperament hated to give up any territory, was already persuaded in part by Kesselring's arguments. The feeble Allied strategy in the Sicilian campaign had given further weight to Kesselring's position.

Salerno was now to become the opportunity for the Wehrmacht to destroy the Allies and their resolve to invade Europe. The British and American troops pinned down in the foxholes and trenches in their narrow and congested beachhead were the ones to reap the bitter harvest of their commander's flawed strategies in Sicily and the German desire to inflict a crushing blow against their amphibious landings.

Chapter XIV

The Expanding Beachhead

From the moment the first troops stepped ashore at Salerno, it became a race between the two armies, Allied and German. The need for the Fifth Army was to rush reinforcements and to build up their firepower so they could break out of the vicelike grip of the enemy in those encircling hills. The critical factors were the landing craft—their sea time; the time to unload; and above all, their capacity. The latter was a matter of numbers of LSTs to carry the men and the supplies from the ports of North Africa and Sicily to the beachhead and the numbers of LCTs to ferry the goods from the attack transports in the bay to the troops on the shore.

Mark Clark had gone into the battle knowing that there were not enough landing craft to furnish his needs at Salerno. Battle damage, Montgomery's needs, and the requirements of other theaters had denuded the total available. Clark had wanted to land with two divisions in the U.S. VI Corps; he had enough craft for one and a third divisions. The absence of port facilities aggravated the problem, for, as we shall see, everything the Allies needed had to be manhandled ashore over open beaches. All Mark Clark could so was pray for fine weather. Even the slightest change for the worse would whip up the waves and create a swell. In such conditions cargoes could not easily be transferred from freighter to landing craft, and no skipper likes to beach his LCT through a surf.

The Germans had to move their forces by land and over somewhat shorter distances, so this gave them an immediate advantage. To reinforce the hard-pressed 16th Panzers, Von Vietinghoff had elements of four divisions, all of which were within striking distance of the beachhead. This was known to the Allies, for Ultra* had told Clark to anticipate 39,000 German troops in the area, including an armored division on D-Day and 100,000 three days later.

Unlike in Sicily, Von Vietinghoff decided not to contest the beaches but to build up his forces and then, from the advantage of the high ground, attack the Allies downhill, which would give the Germans the impetus to set the Allies running.

The battle was to be in the hands of two panzer corps headquarters, both of which were drafted into the area for the purpose. The XIV Panzer Corps would look after the northern battle involving the Special Forces and the British divisions of the X Corps. The LXXVI Panzer Corps were to handle the operations against the Americans south of the beachhead.

The Germans, however, had their own problems. The first and most pressing lay with the condition and quality of their own divisions. Experienced and veteran they may have been, but some were in disarray.

The XIV Panzer Corps had Luftwaffe Panzer Division Hermann Göring in Naples. It had been badly knocked around in Sicily and North Africa. The division had an effective strength of under 15,000 men. It had just 30 tanks and 21 assault guns that were operational, but it was well blessed with ample field artillery. Its panzer grenadier regiment was not even in existence, so the division was weak in infantry. As compensation Von Vietinghoff attached two battalions of infantry from the 1st Parachute Division, then stationed in Apulia.

The 15th Panzer Grenadier Division was deployed in the Gulf of Gaeta to the north of Naples and was in an even worse plight. It had an effective combat strength of about 12,000 men, but there were just seven tanks and 18 assault guns to support them.

Though both divisions set out on the evening of September 9 for Salerno, their advance to battle was fraught with difficulties and delays. The German military presence in Italy had never been popular there. In the halcyon times of Axis victory it was harsh, overbearing, and suspicious, while in the later days of adversity and setbacks the Germans had acquired the reputation of abandoning Italian troops on the Eastern Front and in North Africa.

Now the long columns of German trucks and armored vehicles encountered hostile Italians. Bitter crowds in the teeming streets of Naples slowed the pace to a crawl, and there were many angry scenes. The 15th Panzer Grenadiers had a similar experience in Baronissa, where the units became isolated and separated. In both cases, the division's arrival at the beachhead was spread over a period of two days, which meant in turn that they were committed to the battle piecemeal.

The divisions coming in from the south not only had farther to travel and

---

*The German coding machine that had come into British hands even before the outbreak of war. Brilliant work by the deciphering experts allowed the enemy order of battle to be forecast with great accuracy.

over more hazardous terrain, but were also victims of German bureaucratic blunders.

Though ordered to move, the 29th Panzer Grenadiers remained immobilized near the Gulf of Policastro in Calabria throughout the period of September 9 and 10. The division had no gasoline. The Tenth Army had been in existence for only a short while and had yet to acquire a quartermaster organization. All logistics were still in the hands of Kesselring's headquarters at OBSUED, and they had neglected to inform the Tenth Army where the fuel dumps were located.

The divisional commander, Gen. Maj. Walter Fries, had tried to contact the Tenth Army's headquarters, but because the latter was such a new formation it had still to receive the full complement of signals troops in the signals regiment. Those who had arrived were poorly trained and had little or no experience.

When the Tenth Army was first created in Italy, the needs of a signals regiment were not regarded among the highest priorities. After all, Italy was an ally, and the local civilian telephone exchange was considered adequate for a while, at least. The loss of such facilities was but one of the many prices the Germans had to pay when their forces became an army of occupation in Italy.

Neither could the divisional commander requisition local stocks. Italian gasoline was of very poor quality and quite unsuitable for almost every type of transport used by the Wehrmacht.

To make matters worse, some 240 cbm's of gasoline had been sunk in the port of Sapri on September 8 when a German naval officer, convinced the Allies were about to land in overwhelming strength, panicked and scuttled the tanker *Taute*. This had encouraged an equally ardent Wehrmacht officer onshore to put the local fuel dump to the torch.

Von Vietinghoff remained in blissful ignorance of the plight of the 29th Panzer Grenadiers until the general major turned up in person at army headquarters hot, flustered, and very angry.

Fuel was then sent south by every available means. The 16th Panzers had to provide it from their own reserves, which reduced their effectiveness in battle. Some was even moved by air to Sala Constina.

The 26th Panzers, though not so badly afflicted, had precious little fuel to spare, and they had the farthest to come, since some of their units had been fighting the Canadians on the eastern or Adriatic coast. It was also a panzer division in name only, for the operation in Calabria had not been considered suitable for tanks. So of its two tank battalions, one was back in Germany reequipping with the new Mark VI Panzers or Panthers, and the second was attached to the 3rd Panzer Grenadiers in the flat country south of Rome. The division had in their place the 1st and 4th Battalions of the parachute regiment. Its tank battalion left Rome for the beachhead but would not arrive in the area until September 16.

The units had other problems to contend with in their forced march across the Apennines to Salerno. In the more remote mountain passes, convoys were ambushed or roads blocked. Before the capitulation, the Italians had two million men under arms in Italy alone. Many of these had moved into the hills to swell the ranks of the partisans. With their weapons and knowledge, they were a welcome addition. Thus emboldened, the partisans became increasingly active behind the German front line. Convoys had to be escorted and important installations from supply dumps to bridges guarded, and this took troops away from battle.

Even so, the major problems the Germans encountered in moving their forces to the battle area were caused by the unwelcome attentions of the Allied air forces.

Road and rail communications into the Salerno area were hammered by medium bombers. At the same time, the Mitchells and Flying Fortresses of the Strategic Air Force bombed the two main crossings over the Volturno River at Cancello and Capua, and American Liberators of the Middle East Air Command pounded the airfields at Foggia.

Despite the fact that the Luftwaffe operated from air bases so much nearer the beachhead, they were unable to intervene in any successful fashion in the land battle. They were critically short of aviation fuel, which rationed the time their planes could stay airborne; in net terms this alone canceled out their supposed advantage of time and distance.

Allied air cover proved to be most effective. Clear weather at high altitudes permitted incoming German aircraft to be spotted, and the Lightnings and Spitfires fought the air interception battles and kept the Germans at bay. Throughout much of the time, however, there was a haze at low altitudes and over the sea and beaches. This enabled Focke-Wulf-190s equipped with bomb racks to launch hit-and-run attacks on these targets.

The Royal Air Force contributed two wings, each of five squadrons of Spitfires, to the air battle at Salerno. The fighters operated from adjoining landing strips bulldozed out of the vineyards near Falcone in Sicily. From there the beachhead at Salerno was at maximum operating range. The planes were equipped with 90-gallon overload or drop tanks, which actually doubled the amount of fuel carried internally.

Wing 324 consisted of mixed squadrons of Spitfire Mark 5's and Mark 9's. Only the latter were fast enough, once they had jettisoned their drop tanks, to catch a Focke-Wulf-190, provided the pilot had the advantage of height or the FW-190 had bomb racks which, even empty, increased his air resistance.

The Mark 5 Spitfires were much slower than the Mark 9s but still had a considerable deterrent value, as the Germans couldn't really tell the planes apart.

The wing had come in with the North African landings in November 1942 and so by this time ought to have been a seasoned and veteran force. However, many of the senior pilots had exceeded their operational tours and were assigned to nonoperational jobs for a rest. Many of the best pilots had been killed ground strafing in Sicily.

The perilous game of strafing saw the loss of more aces in both the British and American air forces than any other form of flying. Low-level onslaughts were often against obsolete aircraft or occasional road convoys and were never worth the loss of a skilled pilot. The pilots themselves dreaded such missions where, instead of pitting their skills against another in the sky, they were offering themselves as targets to every ground gunner within range.

Air cover at first and last light over the beachhead was provided by the carrier-based Seafires. These were the vital times that the RAF wings could not cover due to night landing and takeoff difficulties at their strips in Sicily. The drop tanks added a ton to the weight of the Spitfires, placed enormous strain on their frail undercarriages, and caused aerodynamic complications with the trim and flying attitude. Clearly Spitfires thus equipped caused enough problems in daylight.

The Seafires (naval versions of the Spitfires) operated off the escort or Woolworth carriers of Admiral Vian's task force. The carriers, obtained for the most part on Lend Lease from the United States, were converted from mercantile hulls in various stages of construction or from completed ships in the earlier versions. They were high and unwieldy vessels and soon revealed the most appalling seakeeping qualities. Some of the early types carried great amounts of ballast; this initially was made up of 1,800 tons of concrete and 1,000 tons of seawater. The carriers displaced 15,000 tons and carried between 18 and 24 aircraft and more than 50,000 gallons of aviation fuel.

The ships were capable of 20 knots, and the Seafires needed a 30-knot start to get off them; the extra 10 knots was counted on to be supplied by a head wind. Off Salerno most days there was hardly any wind, and deck landing accidents played havoc with men and machines. It was hardly surprising that the sortie rate dropped from 265 missions on D-Day to 56 sorties by the fourth day of the battle.

The Strategic Air Force supplied nine squadrons of Lightnings. These were American twin-fuselage long-range fighters; they provided the combat air cover from 10,000 to 14,000 feet. The Seafires patrolled at 12,000 to 16,000 feet on the north flank, while the two RAF wings flying 20- to 30-minute missions over the beaches between Salerno and Agropoli flew at a height of 16,000 to 20,000 feet.

The task of providing general air cover was complicated by two further factors. The first was the considerable haze over the battlefield. In part this was caused by the weather conditions, but also the movements of the battle, vehicles and dust, guns, shells, and smoke contributed to the pilots' problems in identifying their targets.

The beachhead had no radar, and therefore there was no advance warning of enemy air attacks. Contact with enemy aircraft was by visual means only. Allied pilots found Luftwaffe fighters difficult to spot if underneath because of their very effective camouflage, while those above were to be avoided since they had the advantage of altitude and thus speed.

The warships were also having a strenuous time. The cruisers and destroyers were close inshore during the day performing their many bombardment duties while at night the gun crews had to be alert for air raids. The methodical Germans had already established a pattern of launching their heaviest raids just before dawn and again just after dusk, when the skies were clear of marauding Allied fighters.

The ships had to adapt their routine quickly to the 24-hour battle. The anti-aircraft cruiser H.M.S. *Delhi* was an elderly lady of 1918 vintage that had been converted to her present role in 1941 by a New York shipyard. The accuracy of her shooting soon became legendary. The cruiser averaged two enemy planes a day, and this measure of success resulted in a highly competitive spirit among all her gun crews. The ship's company asked their skipper, Captain Peachy, to be allowed to remain continuously at action stations. The ship's routine was altered accordingly.

Bombarding most of the day and at action stations throughout the night caused other problems, too. Destroyers such as H.M.S. *Brecon* could not use their galleys, as the diesel oil tank for cooking had to be drained to avoid the risk of fire. The sailors went the first couple of days without hot food and their beloved tea until someone hit on the idea of using a steam poker. This was a perforated copper tube at the end of a steam-filled copper hose, a makeshift affair normally used for heating the water in the wardroom bath. The sailors found they could make soup and cocoa, and boil water for tea; it was even possible to make porridge after a fashion. While *Brecon* remained at Salerno, the officers' bathroom became the galley.

The mighty ships of Force H, Britain's Mediterranean battle squadron, left the beachhead at the end of the first day and moved out to intercept the Italian battle squadron. At 0300 hours three new battleships, *Italia, Roma,* and *Vittorio Veneto,* with six cruisers and eight destroyers under Admiral Bergamini, left Spezia and steamed south to surrender.

The Germans were not about to let such a rich prize escape unpunished. They lured the fleet westward and off its course by false signals and thereby kept it in range long enough for the Luftwaffe squadrons based in the South of France to set out to bomb it. A new squadron had recently arrived in Marseilles. The planes were armed with a new kind of controlled bomb. This forerunner of the cruise missile was to wreak havoc in the Mediterranean. Their first major victim was the admiral's flagship, *Roma.* The Italians lured by false hope believed the planes were Allied; they neither opened fire nor took evasive action.

A bomb struck *Roma* with such force that it penetrated to her forward fuel storage before detonating. Fires swept uncontrolled through her forwards and below her bridge, wiping out the main turrets before it reached the magazines. *Roma* blew up and sank with the loss of 1,500 men, including her admiral.

Later on September 10, the rest of the Italian squadron rendezvoused with the British fleet, which escorted them to Malta. It was ironic that the battleships *Warspite* and *Valiant* should be with Force H; a quarter century earlier they had escorted the surrendering battleships of the Kaiser's navy into Scapa Flow.

The next day, September 11, Admiral Cunningham was able to send one of those famous naval signals that punctuate so much of British history:

> Be pleased to inform Their Lordships that the Italian battle fleet now lies at anchor under the guns of the fortress at Malta.

Elsewhere the Allies were demonstrating maritime supremacy and in their own way helping to make the beachhead at Salerno secure. An idea came from the Italians toward the end of the long discussions concerning their capitulation. There were very few German troops garrisoned at Taranto; the Italians suggested that the Allies seize the port and use its magnificent naval base for their own needs.

Eisenhower, Alexander, and Cunningham planned to carry elements of the British 1st Airborne Division from Bizerte to Taranto. It was to be called operation Slapstick. Initially it was hoped the landings would promote confusion and uncertainty and help things at Salerno. Later it was intended to feed into the port two of Montgomery's divisions and the headquarters of V Corps to exploit an advance inland to take the airfields at Foggia, 80 miles away over the mountains.

Very much an afterthought, it lived up to its code name. Like so much of the Italian campaign, the idea was sound; but it lost its edge in practice. The four cruisers of the 12th Cruiser Squadron together with the fast minelayer H.M.S. *Abdiel* and the U.S. Cruiser *Boise* carried the airborne troops. If loading a landing craft was difficult, the cruisers presented almost insurmountable problems to the harassed staff officers, who had little idea of the amount of space available or the clearance between decks to store equipment. The code name Bedlam would have been more appropriate.

The force landed at Taranto unopposed. The only casualties came from the tragic loss of *Abdiel*, which hit a mine while swinging at anchor and sank with heavy loss of life.

Once ashore the "red berets" lost no time moving quickly inland. The paratroopers had not been able to bring their first-line transportation with them; so they were largely immobile. Lacking heavy weapons, they could do little but probe forward gently. At first the enemy was nowhere to be seen, and by September 11 the paratroopers had secured two other valuable ports on the Adriatic coast, Bari and Brindisi. A couple of LCTs with a squadron of the Greys embarked would have made all the difference, for it was good, open country and the enemy had very few tanks in the area. The tanks with paratroopers on their backs could have brushed opposition aside. Instead the Germans, in the form of their own parachute division, resisted any further advance.

Operation Slapstick made little or no impact on Salerno, where Mark Clark was already seeing his plan to be in Naples on the fifth day as hopelessly optimistic. After spending more than 24 hours offshore, the last of the corps reserve was disembarking not to break out but to plug the holes and gaps in a still dangerously thin and shallow beachhead.

The first elements of the 45th Division had reached the main anchorage at 0150 hours on September 10, exactly two months after it had invaded Sicily. Mark Clark's instruction was for the division to provide the floating reserve for the Fifth Army, and therefore the exact time and place of its deployment was indefinite. Because of the shortage of landing craft only a portion of the division, comprising the 179th RCT, two battalions of the 157th Infantry, and some additional artillery, were able to move on the first departure.

The problems involved in getting the division to Salerno had been considerable. In the Sicilian campaign the Thunderbirds had been part of the U.S. Seventh Army, and switching armies can be an administrative nightmare. Patton's Seventh Army was required to equip the 45th Infantry with sufficient war supplies to last 24 days. The only problem was that nobody in Army Group headquarters had seen fit to warn the Seventh Army; so the "indent" from the Thunderbirds came as a surprise since the Seventh Army had "heard on the grapevine" that the need would be for one week of supplies only.

The division was in bivouac at Trabia, and the staff planned to load the troops at Termini Immerse. The landing craft—British LSTs and American LCIs—were those available from Montgomery's operation, and he was loath to release them until his troops were well established ashore; this was as much a consideration of time and stockpiles as it was the depth of the advance. Consequently, the first group, 16 LSTs and LCIs, did not arrive unti' September 7. It was only by working around the clock—to load 10 LSTs simultaneously requires 250 trucks alone—that the first convoy sailed on time.

The Fifth Army told the division to expect a second group, 32 LSTs. This was clearly far more than they had anticipated, and it meant that more of the division could be embarked than had previously been thought. While extra troops were organized at Trabia, the division also arranged loading facilities at Palermo. This required switching truck routes and supplies, special trains and troop convoys, and a new traffic-flow system for Palermo. Only seven LSTs sailed into Palermo, and one arrived at Termini.

The after-action report of the division states that through the entire loading, both at Palermo and Termini, the staff had constant problems with each British captain of each British LST.

The report complains that the ships arrived with some 50 to 75 tons of cargo still on board. This consisted of British ammunition, sacked coal, and various types of "impedimenta" that had not been removed during Montgomery's landing. All these had to be cleared from the ships before the loading could begin.

At first the British captains flatly refused to accept any American bulk cargo. This completely upset U.S. plans, for the Americans intended to take sufficient supplies to sustain each shipment for seven days after its arrival in Italy, in addition to a gradual buildup of supplies for the required 24 days.

The division G4, the chief supply officer, in his report said bluntly that each British captain took delight in raising any technicalities that might delay the loading or harass the technical quartermasters in the loading process.

Despite these and many other problems, the division loaded its combat teams. The regiments were once again stripped for action. The service companies, barracks bags, administrative equipment, and many vehicles were left behind. The man, the pack on his back, ammunition to shoot, and rations to eat were all that went.

The division arrived off Salerno in time to experience one of the many nightly air raids. Though the troops might not have envied those fighting onshore, they learned that they could not dig a foxhole in a steel deck.

The divisional commander, General Middleton, who had his command post on *LST 404*, was ordered to bring the 179th RCT ashore. Originally this was planned for 0300 hours, but the mist was so thick and the anchorage so crowded with ships riding almost shoulder to shoulder that it was postponed until 1140 hours.

By the next morning the mist had cleared; so the LSTs and LCIs inched their way through the anchorage and pulled right up on the beach, or alongside the pontoon bridges, which the engineers had constructed some 50 yards into the water.

The situation in the beachhead had improved considerably insofar as the threat of German artillery was concerned. However, all the beaches were still badly congested by the inability or failure of the Army to provide sufficient troops to clear them of stores and unload waiting landing craft. One beachmaster went so far as to refuse to accept any landing craft that were not accompanied by work parties.

The Thunderbirds came in on what once had been Blue Beach, 3 miles south of Paestum. Though they had been through all this before in Sicily, the men were jittery, chain smoking as they watched the silent landscape or sat entombed in the bowels of their LST.

At exactly 1140 hours, landing platforms bit into sand and shingle, and the great steel doors swung wide. Sunlight streamed in as drivers inched their vehicles forward in low gear to the ramps. On the LCIs, infantry slung their equipment over backs and onto shoulders and crowded around the hatchways. Many an anxious eye was cast shoreward as they gazed out over the beach. The mountains seemed to start within yards of the sea and reach right into the cloudless sky.

There was no enemy activity; it was quiet, perhaps too quiet. "It's a cinch," said a sergeant from the 179th. "There ain't no Krauts at all."

He was right. Ahead of them the 36th Division had spent a long and frightening night full of anticipation of what the morning might bring. The Texans had expected more determined resistance, climaxed by a panzer counterattack. Instead the Germans had broken off contact and seemingly melted away. It all came as a very welcome surprise.

So even while the Thunderbirds tramped inland and into war, the Texans expanded the beachhead. On the right flank the 2nd and 3rd battalions of the 141st moved farther into the hills above Ogliastro and took up positions to command Highway 18 as it entered the plain from the south. The 1st Battalion had needed the time to reorganize after its experiences on D-Day, but it now moved inland, climbing up the steep slopes and rock-strewn paths into the hills behind Trentinara to block the road through to the plain.

While the 143rd RCT remained in reserve near Capaccio and confined its activities to patrolling the upper Calore River, the 142nd RCT moved forward to attack Hill 424, Altavilla, and Albanella.

All these operations were completed with deceptive ease.

The 2nd Battalion advanced on Roccadaspide to protect the right flank of the regiment and crossed the rugged slopes of Mount Soprano. The 3rd Battalion took the center line and had Albanella as its objective. The battalion struck out from Tempone di San Paolo and moved over open country, across the Lusa River and up the slopes to the Albanella road. There was some desultory machine-gun fire but nothing really to impede its advance. The battalion occupied the town by 2000 hours and established its outpost line of defenses.

The left flank of the regiment was protected by the 1st Battalion, which moved northeast toward the Altavilla hill mass. In the critical days of the Salerno battle, the conflict was to sweep back and forth over the Altavilla hills. The hills comprised two peaks, Hills 425 and 315, which were joined by a saddle. From Hill 424 a third, unnumbered hill comes into view, jutting up on the eastern side of the saddle a half mile to the south. Behind this hill and 424 runs a rough ravine. The town of Altavilla sprawls on the southwestern slope of Hill 424 and in itself is unimportant because the high slopes of the hill command the little town.

It was a long, hard march for the battalion. The Americans didn't make life any easier for themselves by taking a long time to sort things out and get moving. General Walker was already noting with growing concern that the time between orders being issued and their being carried out was too long. He knew the Germans would not continue to allow them that luxury indefinitely.

The result was that the 1st Battalion had reached only the edge of the slope some two and a half miles southwest of Hill 424 by the time night fell. The men bedded down where they could and prepared to continue the advance at daylight. They lacked a sense of urgency, and perhaps their own regimental command did not appreciate that Hill 424 was such a vital key. From different points on the hill it is possible to see the entire Salerno plain, eastward into the upper valley of the Calore, north into the corridor between the Sele and the Calore, and west into the valley between Altavilla and the La Cosa hills.

The next morning the battalion completed its deployment and moved into Altavilla itself. The only approach to the summit of Hill 424 is by a steep, stony path about 9 feet wide sunk between near-perpendicular rock and earth walls up to 6 feet high. Terraced fields and olive groves shield the path from view. Company A set out along the path, reached the summit of 424, and dug their foxholes. Company B occupied the hill ground above the road, while Company C dug in along the southern slopes. Battalion head-quarters and Company D remained in the town. Except for occasional shells there was little German activity. Patrols ranged as far as the Calore River, but they saw no evidence of the enemy.

The RCT now held a line some 8 miles inland, and its commander was well pleased with the performance of his troops. At the end of D + 1—Friday, September 10—the regimental commander, Col. John D. Forsythe issued the following message to his men:

> We have landed successfully against heavy odds. We have lost several good, brave men but your conduct has been marvelous. Your initiative and ingenuity in a difficult situation has only increased my faith in you.
>
> Remember your communications and your security.
>
> Remember your concealment.
>
> The worst is over. Collect your company or battalion, your platoons and squads, and we are more than a match for all that can meet us.

Chapter XV

Quiet Warnings

Across the Sele River on the British corps front, the reserves who had landed after the main assault on D-Day spent their second day in mainland Europe attempting to capture those initial objectives still held by the enemy.

In the center the Scots Guards moved up and prepared to attack a large tobacco factory. The attack was ordered for later in the evening. The 3rd Battalion, Coldstream Guards, moved up on the left flank and prepared to aid the 2/5th Queen's onto the Montecorvino airfield. Once again the gallant Queen's were involved in a furious fire fight for the airfield. Within the first 24 hours of their war here, the Queen's had lost five company commanders and 170 men, almost all in the fighting for Montecorvino.

When the Coldstreams arrived at Montecorvino in the afternoon, the Germans had gone. However, the airfield, which had cost so much to take, still was unusuable, for it was completely dominated by German artillery in the hills 3 miles to the north.

The 6th Battalion, Grenadier Guards, were under orders to make for Battipaglia in support of the fusiliers. Their approach march had begun the night before, and it had been a most uncomfortable affair. The guards, in common with all the Allied soldiers who were still on the low ground, had a new experience that night. No account of the fighting in those early days of the campaign would be complete without mention of the mosquitoes. These were no ordinary mosquitoes that the troops met at Salerno. In clouds of thousands, they were active not only by night but in broad sunlight, too. And they bit through every form of protective clothing that anyone could devise.

Lieutenant Leeke and his platoon followed the twisting river in the moonlight. On their left was the sound of heavy firing, and Leeke realized that No. 3 Company was meeting opposition. Their only means of keeping direction was the stream, which also was the happy hunting ground of the mosquitoes, attacks from whom the Guardsmen endured in stoic silence. They also had to keep crossing the stream, the Tusciano, which was no more than an open sewer, so everyone became very wet and smelly, but it was the only way to ensure that they moved forward rather than sideways. At one point, during a short break, Leeke and another officer stopped in a thicket and by hooded flashlight compared notes and maps. They cautiously smoked a cigarette in cupped hands before rejoining their platoons. Another junior officer, Lt. Freddie Fraser, the Master of Saltown, who commanded a platoon in the company, was sent forward on a reconnaissance patrol, but he found nothing and returned.

By this time the men were very tired. The night before had been sleepless for them, cramped on the landing ships, and now tempers were becoming short. The company plodded through the night in weary silence, each man lost in his own thoughts. Suddenly they stopped; a group of officers ahead of them were talking. Leeke stumbled forward to the sound of the voices to find that they had at last reached their destination.

The moon had set and so in complete darkness the platoons began to dig their slit trenches for a defensive position. Dawn found them still digging, and for the first time they could see the surrounding country. Lieutenant Leeke sketched their position; he later drew it into his journal, and it is reproduced below.

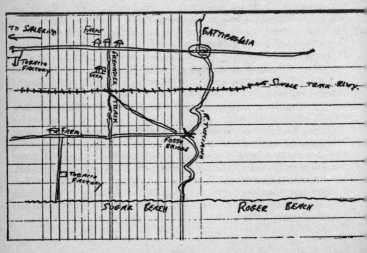

They were guarding a dirt road leading to the Fasso bridge. Most of Leeke's platoon were dug into an area of thick bamboo, which grew along the riverbank. The company manned their weapons and were on alert for half an hour and then retired behind the bamboos, below the level of the bank. Leeke left six men in the forward trenches on guard behind the Bren light machine guns.

The Germans peppered the area with shellfire, and one shell fell on company headquarters. It wounded the company runner, a pleasant, fair-haired young Guardsman named Harris. Leeke ran over to see if he could help. Harris had a stomach wound and looked awful. Guardsman Barnham, Leeke's servant, bound up the wounds with a shell dressing.

Leeke returned to the platoon and sat on the edge of a trench with Sergeant Thomas. They discussed events and shared a can of hard candy. The young officer felt reasonably confident that they were in the right position; a night march to a new location across difficult and unfamiliar ground is every young officer's nightmare.

It must have been about midmorning when they heard the sound of tracks coming down the road from the direction of Battipaglia. Leeke peered out from behind the bamboo expecting to see the battalion's carriers. Instead there were three German half-tracks, not 50 yards away; he counted the soldiers who were peering out of them.

Someone opened fire with a Bren gun, and Leeke dropped down into his trench as the whole platoon at the position came to life. Above the racket he could hear a voice, almost on top of him, bellowing orders in German. Three German heavy machine guns began to scythe through the bamboo, first at random and then, in response to further gutteral words of command, systematically up and down. Leeke crouched low in the slit trench, knees drawn up under his chin, looking grimly at Sergeant Thomas. Heavy slugs slashed the bamboo above his head, and he wished that something could be done; the Brens had long since ceased their chatter. Unfortunately they didn't have the PIATs with them, and even if they had the PIATs would have been of little use against a moving armored half-track.

Suddenly, and for no apparent reason, the Germans broke off contact and retreated back down the road. This was to become part of the pattern of events at Salerno.

The Guardsmen, thankful for small mercies, crawled out of their trenches, and Leeke counted the damage. It was a miracle, but not a single man in his platoon had been hit, though others had suffered casualties. Leeke resited some of the trenches while Barnham went off to forage for breakfast. He returned with a couple of eggs and a cold chicken from somewhere, Leeke knew when not to ask too many questions, and they sat down to breakfast.

The carriers arrived to take the wounded to the aid station. Information came about casualties to date. Leeke listened to the names of the officers killed and wounded; all were his friends. It seemed they were losing the best officers fast.

The order came to move, of course just when the tea was nearly ready. The men marched off moodily, munching biscuits and trying to stop the mosquitoes from diving into their tea. The word was passed down the line that reinforcements were ashore and the tanks were advancing. The column moved up a trail (it reminded Leeke of a charming country lane) later to be known as Grenadier track.

The traffic was considerable. Captain Pat Britten, who commanded Support Company, drove through in his jeep, leading the 6-pounders, and Guardsmen scrambled along the banks to avoid the portees and the jolting guns. They stopped at frequent intervals and ate the apples, apricots, and figs that grew all around. Leeke made use of one halt to disappear into a tobacco field with a spade, for the first time since the boat and in mainland Europe, which seemed like ages ago but was only 26 hours.

The companies crossed the railway and came up to the first major obstacle—the main road. Just before the junction the track passed some cottages, and the men deployed quickly into the fields. Leeke and another officer were to cross the road with their platoons; the third was to remain there as reserve with company headquarters. As the officers discussed the details a house nearby was hit by three shells. Leeke thought that crossing the road, straight and broad, would be no picnic.

Leeke lined up his platoon as if for a race and led the first section across at double time. More shells were landing all around, but the men paid no heed to them. They came upon a gate with a padlock. Lance Sergeant Storey blew off the lock with his rifle, and within a second or so the squad was in the comfortable cover of a thick orchard, with tobacco growing around the edge. The rest of the platoon arrived, and Leeke ordered them to dig their slit trenches in a wide semicircle with the road as the diameter while he went off to talk to the other platoon commander, Lt. Freddie Fraser, who was very worried; he had lost some men crossing the road nearer the buildings. There were some other houses nearby, and they both felt they ought to search them, but the shelling made this too dangerous. Leeke rejoined his platoon.

The shelling died down, and Leeke began to feel unpleasantly isolated. The troops dug shallow slit trenches, or shell scrapes, and ate the apples growing all around. German artillery was firing on targets behind them, some shells landing on the beach or the railroad, while others hit much nearer, on the road.

On the front of the 46th Division, the panzers were already resisting fiercely. The reconnaissance regiment sent the armored cars from B Squadron out once more to the Cava defile. They ran into German mortar and artillery fire at the Cava bridge and made an orderly withdrawal on the commandos at Vietri, who were thus given some warning of the forthcoming attack.

The 6th Battalion, the York and Lancaster Regiment, had deployed beyond Salerno and had been on the road to Sanseverino the previous evening when it ran into a solid wall of German resistance. The beaches were still in considerable confusion, and though most of the town was in British hands, the port of Salerno was under almost constant shellfire.

Nevertheless, unloading continued. One LCT returned on the Friday after effecting temporary repairs to her loading cables, which had been damaged the day before. The unloading started again, but with the first heavy truck, the cables snapped completely. As a last resort another LCT came alongside in the bay, and the now urgently required ammunition trucks were driven across steel hatchway covers from one ship to the other, each driver seizing the moment when the two ships leveled in the swell.

Mark Clark came ashore on that first morning and toured the beachhead. He was most anxious to establish his own Army headquarters on land as soon as possible, but he had to curb his impatience. The first priority had been to have Dawley and his corps headquarters fully ashore and operational, and this still was not functioning properly. Even so, Clark brought his signals staff with him that morning to look for a suitable location for the Fifth Army command post. They decided on a house called Baronissi villa. It was large, imposing, and still relatively intact after the battle had passed by. The villa was located close to the estuary of the Sele River and on the seaward side of the railway and main highway. It was convenient enough for him to reach the British corps headquarters but more importantly was in the American sector and close to Dawley. Mark Clark had strong reservations about Dawley and believed he would need support if all did not go according to plan.

General Clark was also anxious to select a spot to bring the 157th RCT ashore. These two battalions with their supporting artillery were all that was left of the floating reserve. He spent some time discussing this and other matters with his two American divisional commanders, Walker of the 36th Infantry Division and Middleton of the 45th Infantry Division, and was tremendously enthused by the apparent lack of enemy activity. Indeed, the situation looked so good that he sent a message to General Alexander saying he would soon be ready to break out and advance on Naples.

Later that morning, Mark Clark climbed into his jeep and set out for the British corps headquarters. "Sheriff" Puck provided an escort, and two military police sergeants, one British and the other American, traveled with the general. It was too dangerous to use the highway, and in any case the bridge over the Sele was still being repaired. Instead, the small convoy wound its way along one of the numerous jeep tracks that had by now appeared. Their route took them along the shoreline and its immediate hinterland, which had by this time been transformed by the paraphernalia of war. There were mountainous dumps of gasoline, food, and ammunition, among which tractors and trucks toiled away, seemingly moving material from one dump to another.

There were other evidences of war, too. The debris of the previous day's struggle littered the landscape. Abandoned equipment was everywhere: German antitank guns, which attracted the idle and curious; a multiple AA machine gun, its mount twisted and blackened barrels distorted to the sky; a pack discarded by some young soldier, probably hot and frightened, still waited the return of its owner. Little mounds of spent cartridges, evidence of some action by a squad or group, were crunched into the shingle by the passing jeeps.

Later they were to become firm friends, but on this first morning in mainland Europe Clark was not particularly looking forward to his meeting with Gen. McCreery. Part of the problem was that he didn't really know anything about the British troops under his command. (Within twelve months Mark Clark had had sixteen nationalities in the Fifth Army.) The Fifth Army had begun life under his command as a training organization principally for American divisions coming into the North African theater. Clark had pressed Eisenhower for it to have a combat role and with this had also come its internationalization. On more than one occasion since it began to prepare for war, he had wished that it was all American or all British troops going into Salerno. The complication of commands was incredible, and the logistics problems ate deep into the flexibility of his forces.

The British had different food, the American ammunition wasn't any good to the British because it was of a different caliber, and both armies had their own trucks. Though Clark never expressed his misgivings to Eisenhower, it was his personal view that Salerno had been made a mixed command because if these, the first landings on mainland Europe had failed, then both countries would have shared the blame.

Moreover, Clark did not find Dick McCreery an easy fellow to get along with. He had all the reserve and mannerisms of a typical British cavalry officer. However, Clark knew his war record. McCreery was a good and tough soldier who had already displayed great qualities of leadership in battle and was a brilliant staff officer. In the coming days and indeed throughout their time together in the Italian campaign, Clark found it a great source of pleasure and security to have such an experienced subordinate commander.

McCreery always told Clark exactly what he thought, and that morning he explained in no uncertain terms the strength of the German resistance that the men on his front were encountering. Unlike the Americans, the troops of the X Corps, from the special forces on the left through to the fusiliers on the right flank, were in contact with the enemy. McCreery was convinced that the battle for the beachhead was about to begin. He doubted the ability of his hard-pressed troops to break out and link up with the Americans at Ponte Sele, let alone reach Naples in four days.

The British corps commander was also concerned about the rangers. He knew that deployed on the Chiunzi Pass they were in the wrong position, and it was probably just as well because there was little prospect of the armored cars from the reconnaissance regiment of the 46th Division reaching Nocera, which had been their original objective. They would have been isolated and presumably destroyed. Even on the Chiunzi he believed they

The Port of Salerno as seen in prewar days, from Vietri.

A British Beach on D Day. A 40mm light anti-aircraft detachment stands by to repe[l] Luftwaffe attacks. In the background a Dukw has just disembarked from a U.S. Nav[y] LST.

A Landing Ship Tank (LST) of the U.S. Navy unloads its infantry from the 36th Division into a Higgins Boat for the run to the beach.

U.S. Army six-by-sixes are loaded from a transport into an LCT for the run to the beach.

British Infantry land from a U.S. Navy LST on D Day. The beach is shrouded by the smoke screen that caused the Allies more problems than it did the enemy.

A Sherman of the Scots Greys together with British infantry from the Royal Fusiliers on the road to Battipaglia. The smoke in the background is from an ammunition ship bombed by the Luftwaffe.

Youthful members of the Panzer Division Hermann Goering who surrendered to British Commandos in Vietri during the first hours of the battle on D Day. These men almost certainly were recruited into the division from the Hitler Youth.

A couple of German tanks from the 16th Panzers that had been destroyed by the 6 pounder anti-tank guns of the 8th Battalion Royal Fusiliers. The tank in the foreground is a Mark III Special equipped with a flamethrower.

German prisoners from the Panzer Division Hermann Goering being escorted to the POW cage. The enemy appear defiant, disciplined, and not at all downhearted.

Men of the 1/5th Queens Regiment on patrol in the vineyards close to Montecorvino. The photograph is probably a reconstruction.

Breakout! U.S. infantry from the 3rd United States Infantry Division move along Route 18 in pursuit of the retreating Germans.

A 155mm howitzer of the American army in action in the bridgehead.

General Alexander, Commander of the Fifteenth Army Group, picnics on the beach during his visit to the Tenth British Corps on September 15.

Lt. Gen. Mark Clark, Commanding General of the Fifth Army, with Air Marshal Coningham, RAF, who commanded the Allied air forces in Italy, walking along a prefabricated beach road in the American sector.

General Mark Clark greets General Montgomery of the Eighth Army on the latter's arrival at the Salerno beachhead.

Lt. Col. "Mad Jack" Churchill, Commanding, No. 2 Army Commando, being briefed by the corps commander General McCreery for the attach on Pigoletti. Churchill is wearing his famous claymore short sword.

Men of the 6th Battalion Royal Leicesters from the 46th Infantry Division marching through Salerno toward Vietri, to relieve the Commandos in the Cava Defile.

The viaduct at Vietri, which was under enemy shellfire throughout the nine days of Salerno and is showing the scars of that bombardment. An anti-tank gun and a truck from the 46th Infantry Division can be seen on the bridge.

A mortar platoon from the 46th Infantry Division is seen in action in the town of Salerno.

were terribly vulnerable and in need of reinforcements and heavy-weapons support.

McCreery also shared Mark Clark's concern over the gap on the right flank and the low, flat country between Battipaglia and the Sele River. The two generals discussed the problems in considerable detail before Clark returned to the American sector. He had determined to reorganize and redeploy the VI Corps as quickly as possible across the river and also onto the high ground.

General Dawley protested most strongly when Clark outlined his orders, and well he might, for he ended up with a longer front to defend with less troops at his command.

Mark Clark ordered a battalion task group to move to Maiori by sea as soon as possible to support the rangers and thus come under the command of the British corps. The 1st Battalion of the 143rd Infantry was at that time the division's reserve infantry and bivouacked at Vannulo. The battalion, commanded by Lt. Col. Walker, son of the commanding general, prepared to move. The remainder of the task force consisted of a company each of medium tanks, tank destroyers, and shore and combat engineers, together with a battery of field artillery. The task force was placed under the command of Brigadier General Wilbur.

It took a while to organize the troops, their equipment, and the LCTs and LCIs to transport them from Red Beach to Maiori. The advance guard arrived shortly after dawn on Monday, September 13.

Clark had also decided to shift the VI Corps boundary across the Sele River to link up with the British and to use the 157th RCT to plug the gap. Clark hurried back to the *Ancon* to make the necessary arrangements to bring the 157th RCT of the 45th Infantry Division, the Thunderbirds, ashore on the beaches north of the Sele River. When he issued the instructions, the general was informed that the Thunderbirds were already ashore and on the southern side of the river. Clark was astounded and furious that this had happened.

Admiral Hewitt explained the circumstances. He had been under orders from naval headquarters to return the landing ships immediately and all he could do in the absence of Clark was to dump the troops and their stores on the nearest convenient beach.

The 36th Divisional Combat Engineers had been working around the clock to replace the bridge across the Sele, but it was not until September 11 that the 157th RCT were able to cross over and into what had once been the British corps front.

At 2210 hours on Friday, September 10, the big attack transports, having completed the unloading of troops and supplies for the Southern Attack Force, departed for North Africa. Peter Matterson sailed with them; his part in the battle for Salerno was over. The convoys were ordered to proceed to Algiers and there await further instructions, for there was a possibility that they might be required to bring in reinforcements.

At about this time the 179th RCT set out on its long approach march to battle. Earlier that afternoon General Dawley had ordered General Middleton to send that combat team to block any German threats from the direction of Eboli.

Colonel Hutchins, who commanded the 179th RCT, waited for darkness to cover his move and then ordered the columns to advance. At 1930 hours the first troops stepped out along Route 18. They marched northeast as far as a road junction just south of Ponte Alla Scafa, where the columns turned and headed northward toward the crossing over the Calore River. A mile farther, the advancing troops split. A southern column led by the 2nd Battalion continued north-northeast across the low hills on the west bank of the Cosa River before turning northeast over the rolling ground below Altavilla and Hill 424. The main column, led by the 3rd and 1st battalions; Battery B, 160th Field Artillery tanks; and tank destroyers turned off north to the Calore River just above its junction with the Sele. Their orders were to move up the Sele–Calore corridor toward Highway 19 and the high ground at Serre, having swept the terrain for signs of the enemy. At Serre they would rendezvous with the southern column, and the yawning gap in the middle of the Fifth Army would, it was hoped, be filled before the Germans could capitalize on the Allied mistakes.

While the southern column branched quietly away into the night, the northern column soon hit trouble. Ahead of them flames lit the darkness as the Germans blew up the pile and plank bridge across the Calore in the faces of the advance guard. Colonel Hutchins quickly deployed his forces. The infantry scattered into the tobacco fields on either side of the track while the tanks and tank destroyers moved into position to cover the crossing. Combat engineers rushed forward and began feverishly first to reconnoiter for and then to build a new crossing point over the river.

It took the engineers a couple of hours, but in that time they had done a magnificent job. About a half mile downstream they had thrown a pontoon bridge across half the river. It spanned the deep water on the southern side, then disappeared in the shallows near the opposite bank. Others worked to complete a bypass of the broken bridge.

Colonel Hutchins wasted no time but set out across the river with his infantry, light vehicles, and guns. He ordered the armor to join him as soon as the bypass had been completed; but they never crossed the Calore.

Once on the other bank the RCT was in unknown and hostile territory. Men waded knee deep across the river and then back onto the road. The point teams and scouts fanned out ahead, for there had been no prior reconnaissance of this ground.

The column marched silently on through the night. They passed Persano, the walled villa and stables, once the royal hunting lodge of the Neapolitan kings. It stands on a knoll and has a commanding view of the ground to the Calore crossing.

Hutchins quickened the pace. Already the first streaks of dawn were lighting the night sky, and he was anxious to reach the objective before daylight. The column turned northeast and marched into the gently rising ground of the "upper corridor," with its large fields lined with tall trees. By now the column had moved some 10 miles into "no-man's-land," an outrageous defiance of the enemy.

Throughout the length and breadth of the great ampitheater-like plain of the Sele, long columns of troops tramped into the front line. What had begun, however, as the march to a breakout had now become a desperate race to seize the best ground and shut the door tight in the face of the panzers that were poised to swoop down from the hills.

PART FIVE

Days of Crisis:

The German Counterattack

Chapter XVI

Chiunzi and the Sorrento Line

War is not a smooth succession of dates and places interspersed with actions tied up neatly like so many parcels. War is confused, hard to understand, and for the commanders in the field, fearfully difficult if not impossible to control.

This was Salerno in those hectic, crowded days in September 1943.

For those of us who were not there, it is hard to get under the skin of the fighting soldier; to understand how it was going for those men whose individual courage, endurance, and sacrifice were given day after day without tangible hope of it ever ending; for this was the reality behind the shifting lines and arrows on the newspaper maps at home.

There is not the space to place the full record before you and to describe all the deeds, even of those who have already been introduced in this book. Instead, in the following chapters I have selected just a few episodes that reflect the nature of the fighting. They help tell the tale of Salerno.

During the next phase of the battle for Salerno, when the Germans counterattacked the beachhead, both sides suffered from major disadvantages, though in the end those of the enemy were to prove more enduring. The Germans were unable to concentrate their divisions in sufficient force to drive against the beachhead and smash the defenses through a coordinated offensive. Instead, we have seen that for a variety of reasons, some of their own making, such as the lack of signals and communications troops in Army headquarters and the failure to ensure an adequate fuel supply, the Tenth

The German Defense of the Salerno Beachhead*

Parent Formation	Battle Group Commander, Main Units (Initial)	Sector	First Arrival/ Approx. Completion	Facing Allied Formations
Hermann Göring Panzer Division	*Haas* (Col. Haas, 1st Pz. Gren. Regt. H.G.)	Roads, Chiunzi–Maiori; Nocera–Vietri; S. Severino–Baronissi–Salerno	Sept. 10–13	46th Div., Commando Bde, Ranger Force
	2/1st Pz. Gren. Regt. H.G.			
	2/115th Pz. Gren. Regt.			
	3/115th Pz. Gren. Regt.			
	H.G. Reconnaissance Bn.			
	Composite (tank) Bn. H.G.			
	Panzer Regt.			
	3 Bn. (assault guns) H.G.			
	Panzer Regt.			
	Artillery, Engineers			
	Becker (Major Becker, 1st Parachute Regt.)	Road Chiunzi–Maiori	Sept. 12	Ranger Force
	3/1st Parachute Regt.			
15th Panzer Grenadier Division	*Stroh* (Col. Stroh, 71st Werfer Regt.)	Road, S. Severino–Baronissi–Salerno	Sept. 10–12	46th Div.
	129th Pz. Gren. Regt.			
	215th Pz. Abteilung			
	71st Werfer Regt.	Area S. Mango		
	Artillery, Engineers			
	This group passed under comd. of H.G. Pz. Division			

Division	Units	Area	Date	Opposing Division
3rd Panzer Grenadier Division	*Moldenhauer* (Major Moldenhauer, 29th Pz. Gren. Regt.) 1/29th Pz. Gren. Regt. 2/67th Pz. Gren. Regt. detached from 26th Pz. Div. 103 Reconnaissance Bn. 103 Pz. Abteilung (assault guns)	Area Salerno	Sept. 13	46th Div.
29th Panzer Grenadier Division	*Ulich* (Col. Ulich, 15th Pz. Gren. Regt.) 1 and 3/15th Pz. Gren. Regt. 26th Reconnaissance Bn, Artillery; Engineers	Altavilla–Albanella–Controne	Sept. 10-11	36th U.S. Div.
	Krüger (Lieut.-Col. Krüger, 71st Pz. Gren. Regt.) 71st Pz. Gren. Regt.	Area Eboli	Sept. 11	45th U.S. Div.
				56th Div.
26th Panzer Division	2/9th Pz. Gren. Regt. 1 and 3/4th Parachute Regt. 129th Reconnaissance Bn. Artillery; Engineers	Polla–Sala Consilina	Sept. 12	VI U.S. Corps front

*C. J. C. Molony, *History of the Second World War*, Vol. V, *The Mediterranean and Middle East* (London: H. M. Stationery Office, 1973).

Army was able only to send troops piecemeal into the fray as they arrived at the front.

Even so, by the end of the third day the panzer divisions had a wedge driven deep between the American and British positions on the beaches and were launching repeated attacks.

The Allies should by that time have been firmly established onshore and well able to absorb whatever the enemy was able to hurl at them. From the very first the landings should have been no more than a calculated risk for the Fifth Army.

Since just before the outbreak of World War II, Britain had been in possession of the means to break the code of the standard German radio enciphering machine called Enigma. This intelligence system was called Ultra, and it was without doubt the most extraordinary intelligence coup of the war. Ultra had provided the Royal Air Force with priceless data on Luftwaffe deployments during the Battle of Britain and had made a major contribution to winning the U-boat war in the Atlantic.

The intelligence provided by the Ultra system told Mark Clark where the German divisions in Italy were deployed. He knew that the 16th Panzers were the only forces in the area other than some very second-rate Italian coastal defense formations. German reinforcements could come only from forces such as the Panzer Grenadiers near Gaeta, the Luftwaffe Panzer Division Hermann Göring in Naples, and the Rome "garrison." Ultra even told Clark about the general condition of these divisions and that most were short of their panzer battalions.

So what had gone wrong for the Allies? The original assault, which had been intended to achieve such bold things, had instead turned into a nightmare. It had changed to the defense of a long, thin strip of sweltering, mosquito-infested coastal plain.

The Italian surrender had been a muddled affair that at the end of the day worked more in favor of the Germans.* Its announcement by Eisenhower, as we have seen, simply gave the German high command warning of an imminent invasion, while at the same time Mark Clark was deprived of the 82nd Airborne Division for the landings.

The Fifth Army failed to land sufficient forces with the right impetus of armor and gunpower to take the initial advance straight onto the high ground. Additional problems were caused by the use of too many troops who were not adequately trained in amphibious operations.

Finally, the 16th Panzers, though dispersed over a wide front in ad hoc battle groups, were still able to thwart Allied intentions. Their counterattacks took the steam out of the Allied advance and destroyed the Allies' momentum and in some cases their confidence. The result was that from the

---

*A further tragedy concerned the thousands of Allied troops who were prisoners of war in Italy. They were ordered by the Allied high command to stay put in their prison camps and wait for the Allies to reach them. Instead, the Germans rounded them up and took them to Germany. A potential and very valuable source of trained manpower was lost.

advantages of the high ground, Von Vietinghoff's Tenth Army divisions had no trouble attacking a beachhead that was too shallow and too thinly garrisoned. Over the period of eight days from Saturday, September 11 until September 18, when Kesselring called a halt, the Germans hammered away at the defenses. There were times when the issue seemed in doubt as the line buckled and the Allies fought with their back to the sea.

The Overseas Service of the BBC was about all the men in the line could pick up on their radios. Naturally, the news was strongly slanted in favor of the British, and this irritated the American troops considerably, especially when they heard broadcasts that Montgomery's Eighth Army was dashing up the "boot" of Italy to their rescue. Nothing could have been farther from the truth. Montgomery's advance through the mountains of Calabria was hopelessly bogged down by his dependence on the roads. Despite Alexander's almost daily efforts to prod the Eighth Army into some speed, the Germans' rear guard had the British and Canadians nicely bottled up as long as their general was unwilling to take the risk of striking out and away from the major routes to bring some force to bear on the battle for Salerno.

In the meantime, the men at Salerno knew there were problems, but the true nature of their predicament became apparent only when they listened to the BBC news broadcasts. The daily bulletins described a desperate battle for the beachhead with the Germans trying to drive the Allies back into the sea. The ordinary soldiers, whether they were in the line, a gun pit, or servicing the needs of the fighting, were not aware of such high drama. For them Salerno became a series of fights as the Germans struck first at one point and then another along the line. Everywhere was in range of the Germans' guns, so there were no rear areas relatively safe from the battle.

The ground dictated the fighting and so, for both sides, it was a battle of infantry; neither could find enough to fill their needs. On the Allied side engineers and truck drivers, company clerks and even bandsmen shouldered rifles and moved into the front line.

Salerno was hot and dusty, and by the fourth or fifth day, since the troops had had no proper sleep, it became intensely wearying, and mistakes were made. Perhaps the biggest strain, as in all closely fought, intensive battles, was the noise. The continuous, stupefying noise of battle induces fear, and being frightened for a prolonged period is very draining. It is an experience for which men can never be trained or prepared. All that commanders can do in such circumstances is hope that discipline will prevail and that perhaps being afraid of being frightened, and showing the fear, will be the biggest fear of all.

Considerations such as these, of course, became even more critical when such a large part of the army in the field was composed not of seasoned troops but of British and Americans who were relatively new to war.

Once the counterattacks had started, Ultra could not offer any real assistance to Mark Clark and his commanders in the field. Instead it served to keep Churchill and the high command informed as the battle ebbed and flowed. They were able to follow everything through the daily briefings that came from the home of Ultra at Bletchley Park in Oxfordshire. Churchill agonized during those days and at times feared another Gallipoli, the operation that had ruined his political career in World War I. His was the greater relief when he knew before Alexander and Mark Clark that Kesselring had ordered the Tenth Army to break off contact and retreat to the winter line north of Naples.

Colonel Haas commanded the 1st Panzer Grenadier Regiment of the Luftwaffe Panzer Division Hermann Göring. Haas created a number of battle groups, each built around a battalion of panzer grenadiers but also including supporting arms, and sent them into battle. They hit the commandos and the rangers first.

For the rangers, of course, the German attacks were as much a daily reality as for the main body of the Army in the plains and hill flanks at Salerno. However, the pattern of their war was small engagements at close range with little thought for the niceties of combat. A constant backdrop was the artillery bombardment as the Germans sought to keep the rangers' heads down and away from the defile of Nocera. Behind their barrage the Germans poured men and materiel through the bottleneck to the main battle at Salerno.

It seemed that the Germans, judging by the ferocity of their attacks, were very much aware that they could not ignore the rangers. So long as they held Chiunzi Pass, their presence posed a threat. One of the prime specialist tasks of the rangers was to act as a raiding force. They could have caused mayhem in the rear areas and along the enemy's main line of communications, so it can be argued that the rangers by absorbing such attacks diverted German forces from other and perhaps more critical areas of the battle. By the same token, however, the rangers had to be reinforced, and the loss of a complete battalion battle group* with all its supporting arms from the operations south of the Sele was serious.

Once the Fifth Army had failed to break out and link up with the rangers at Nocera as planned, the role of the special forces changed completely. Now they were required to guard the left flank and the back door into the X Corps and keep the Germans from infiltrating across Sorrento Peninsula.

Initially the rangers defended a ridge of mountains around a small valley that opened into the bay at Maiori. However, Roy Murray and the men of his 4th Battalion gradually expanded the base of the beachhead farther westward into Sorrento, and by September 12 his forward companies were looking down from the high ground above Castellammare.

A squad of men from the reconnaissance patrol got bored one morning as they looked over the shimmering sea and golden sands beneath them, so they decided to have a look at Castellammare. They walked into town and boarded a streetcar, which took them into the central square. Nobody seemed to

---

*Lieutenant Colonel Walker's 1st Battalion, 143rd Infantry, together with its tanks, artillery, and supporting arms.

notice them; for the resigned, docile Italian civilians, a uniform was a uniform by this stage in the war; especially since all his hopes for an end to the fighting had been dashed in the aftermath of the capitulation. The squad had bought some ice cream cones and wandered out of the square when they were suddenly spotted by a couple of "headhunters," German military police in a patrol car. With a screech of tires and pursued by a hail of fire from half a dozen Thompsons, the latter accelerated away to summon assistance. At this point the rangers decided discretion was the better part of valor and beat a hasty retreat to the hills.

When he heard of the incident, Murray applauded the initiative but then pointed out that as a reconnaissance, all they had learned was that there were probably more Germans than Americans in Castellammare!

Such initiative, if not unconventional behavior, was typical of the rangers and especially of Murray's 4th Battalion. They liked to be different, and so *all* the men in the 4th grew moustaches just to promote a little *esprit de corps*. Darby objected strongly, but Murray was equally determined to have his way, even if it did mean disagreeing with the man he admired most of all. There were a couple of men who didn't want to grow them, but if Darby had found one without a moustache he would have ordered everyone to follow suit, so the whole battalion had moustaches.

For the most part the companies were either split into small groups guarding roadblocks covering every conceivable approach across the peninsula, or battle patrols that went out looking for trouble. More often than not, their opponents were men from the German 3rd Battalion, 1st Parachute Regiment. It was indeed a clash between elites as battle patrols fought it out to the bitter end, for neither side was inclined to surrender. This suited the rangers, for if headquarters didn't want prisoners, then they didn't take prisoners.

This wasn't the glamorous part of the front, and Murray didn't have any newspapermen around telling him how to fight the war; so they fought the war the special forces way. Circumstances were often such that it was too difficult to take prisoners. The rangers were thin on the ground, and men could not be spared for escort.

Manning the roadblocks was a miserable and frequently dangerous chore that fell to the lot of everyone in the battalion at one time or another in the campaign. One night Sgt. Marcel Swank was in charge of a roadblock. He had a motley bunch of people from the headquarters company with him—truck drivers and the like. The night was as black as hell; he could hear a jeep climbing up the pass in low gear—the sound was unmistakable. Slowly but surely the little cats' eyes, which were the pinpoint convoy lights, came into view, and a voice from deep inside the dark and the canopy said, "Is that you, Sergeant Swank?"

"Yes, sir!" Swank said, recognizing the voice of Colonel Darby.

"How's it all going?", the colonel asked.

"Just fine, sir," Swank said. "Everything is just fine!"

Swank was proud that the colonel knew his name. Darby was a remote figure who distanced himself from both officers and men. Marcel Swank remembers Darby* as a man of few words, yet the men worshipped their commander. The rangers had absolute faith in him. He was referred to as "El Darbo" (never, of course, to his face).

What made Darby's style of leadership so strange is that in special forces the reverse is usually the case. In small, closely knit, elite units who embark on hazardous enterprises, the barriers between officers and enlisted men are invariably reduced. This is in part to do with the personalities of the men who are attracted to such enterprises and because the casualty rate tended to be very high.

In all his time in the rangers, Swank could remember only one occasion when Darby showed any familiarity. A group of them had gathered one evening in Amalfi outside the house that Roy Murray used as the battalion headquarters. There was a young ranger, Cpl. Johnny Wezkinsky, who was a classical guitarist. Though this music was a departure from the usual country and western, the men would gather around to listen to Johnny's music.

Colonel Darby walked down the street and came out of the darkness into the circle of light, listened for a moment, and said, "Corporal, can you play 'Dark Eyes'?"

Johnny played "Dark Eyes," and the colonel stood there, stone still, until he had finished.

"Thank you, Corporal," Darby said, and he disappeared again into the night.

Swank had to make frequent journeys into the hills to the left of Chiunzi Pass to haul ammunition from the beach at Maiori to the companies from the 4th Battalion that held that part of the line. This morning he made the run in his jeep and trailer with a 1-ton carrier for company. As they drove out of Maiori and up the steep track behind the town, a group of children playing at the roadside broke off their game to run alongside the vehicles and beg for cigarettes and candy. Swank indulgently threw out some goodies and ordered his driver to press on. They left the children behind scrambling in the dust and the dirt when the air filled with the very distinctive sound of incoming artillery. On the right-hand side of the road there were some rock overhangs inside of which were natural caves; the Americans abandoned their vehicles and took cover.

The salvo burst with a frightful crash on the road, perhaps 400 yards behind the vehicles. When the dust and the noise had settled, Marcel Swank looked back to see the children sprawled in the road, and looking like discarded rag dolls.

The men turned the vehicles around—no mean feat on this narrow track—and raced back to help. No one appeared from the town, for by this time death and war were commonplace in Maiori. One child, a little girl, was badly hurt in the arm; another, a boy, sat there with his legs a bloody mess. A

---

*Col. William Darby was killed in action in Italy shortly before the end of the war while leading a combat team of the 10th Mountain Division, U.S. Army.

slightly older boy was yelling at the top of his voice. Swank ignored him, for nobody who bellowed that loud, he thought, could be badly hurt. Instead Swank turned his attention to another little boy, who lay there dazed with shock; where his eye had been there was now a red-black hole. Swank picked him up and drove to the aid station; the other vehicle brought in the remaining casualties.

The aid station was inside a little white stone church that nestled close to the hillside. Next door was a pleasant little pasture. Swank ran into the church, but the child died in his arms even as he reached a doctor. "Take him out back, Sergeant," the doctor said wearily to a shocked Swank.

In the little pasture behind the church a row of dead GIs were laid out waiting for burial. Swank gently put the child alongside the American soldiers and returned to the war.

Chiunzi Pass was by this time known as the "88 Pass" or "Hellfire Pass" because of German 88mm artillery fire. It certainly must rate as one of the hottest and most deadly spots on the Salerno front. The rangers had a couple of 75mm guns on half-tracks that belonged to their cannon company. For 18 endless days, the daylight hours became one long duel between the cannon company and the German 88s in the valley below. A half-track would run up to the top of the pass, fire a round or two, and reverse like fury before the German shells crashed into the road.

By their third day in Europe, John Hummer and his company had made the long, hard climb into the pass. They had been relieved of their supply duties in Maiori once the support elements had arrived and the Italians found there was money to be made by laboring for the Americans.

Hummer occupied a slit trench just to the right of the pass and down a little way on the reverse slope. Above him and below the crest was a naval observation team from the Royal Navy. They directed the gunfire from the supporting warships, especially the monitor H.M.S. *Roberts*. Armed with two 15-inch guns, she could lob a shell of enormous weight and with unerring accuracy into Nocera. The gun captain in the main turret of *Roberts* had been a boy seaman in 1916 at the Battle of Jutland.

Hummer was perfectly safe there except for the off-chance of a direct hit from the plunging fire of German mortars. He had exchanged his bazooka for an M1 carbine and had dug his slit trench in some poor Italian's vegetable plot, so he was never short of herbs, onions, or tomatoes to help season his stews.

The rangers found the 4.2-inch mortars of the 83rd Chemical Mortar Battalion splendid weapons. Everywhere the rangers went, the mortars were able to accompany them in full support. Roy Murray was convinced this mortar was the best artillery around, for it could fire different kinds of ammunition, had the range of the 105mm howitzer, and could go places the howitzer couldn't.

September 13 was to be the crisis day in the beachhead. It was known as Black Monday to all who were there. On that day the rangers received the promised reinforcements of the 1st Battalion, 143rd Infantry. The advance party from Company A met the rest of the battalion on the beach at dawn and took them to an assembly area in the town. In the meantime, Colonels Walker and Darby set out with a small command party to look at the ground. Just after 0830 hours the Texans started the long 6-mile trek up to the pass. Most of them still felt distinctly groggy after an uncomfortable night in a tossing landing craft—generally Texans don't like the sea. Nevertheless, morale was restored to a degree by great steaming mugs of the force's elixir for all ailments, Army coffee.

The battalion came under fire even while it was still behind the front lines. By way of a special welcome to the front, German mortars stitched a pattern along the road and through their ranks, and then the forward company was ambushed by a German patrol that had infiltrated from the north. Any doubts that Colonel Walker or his men had about their need to be in Sorrento Peninsula were quickly dispelled. It took a two-company assault to force out the enemy, and this caused even more casualties, in addition to those suffered earlier.

The battalion reformed, and, while the first trickle of wounded moved back down the mountain, the rifle companies deployed off the track about 1,000 yards short of the summit. There they moved up to the ridgeline in the center, a saddle-shaped feature with high hills on both sides. The rangers held the mountain wedges and the Texans the ridges. Beneath and behind them, the artillery and support companies deployed into their own fire positions.

Such is the fog of war that while the 143rd Infantry was moving in to support the rangers, Roy Murray was desperately trying to get his battalion together from their scattered outposts, for that morning Darby had received an SOS from General McCreery. It came in the form of a polite and hopeful request for a battalion to help the hard-pressed commandos at Vietri, where it seemed the Germans were on the point of breaking through and rupturing the defenses.

Murray got together men and trucks at Amalfi and that afternoon set off to "rescue" the commandos at Vietri. The convoys stopped on the outskirts of the town as the vehicles negotiated the Vietri bridge, which was held firmly in the sights of German mortars. Swank had been to Vietri on a number of occasions and knew this obstacle intimately. He called it the "How's-about-it-now bridge" because of the question asked by the phlegmatic British military police who controlled the traffic and in between mortar bursts would ask of the drivers, "How's about trying it now?"

By the time the rangers had pulled their big 6-by-6's into the town and reported to the brigade headquarters, the emergency was over. Murray and his men stayed the night and enjoyed a liquid evening with the commandos before returning whence they came. The battalion moved into the line above and to the left of Chiunzi Pass and spent the next 12 days in continuous contact with patrols of German paratroopers.

Chapter XVII

The Commandos

The commando brigade had technically come under the command of the 46th Infantry Division on D-Day and looked forward to being relieved by the infantry. The commandos had achieved their objectives in seizing Vietri and the high ground to the Cava defile, but they had neither the manpower nor the fire support to withstand a concerted enemy onslaught. In addition, the commandos carried all their food and immediate requirements for the battle on their back, and three days was about their limit without resupply.

However, on Friday, September 10, their headquarters was informed that there could be no such relief. The North Midland Infantry division was heavily involved in securing its beachhead and in pushing the Germans back in the hills behind Salerno.

So the commandos prepared to meet the enemy as best they could. The commandos' positions were strong, for they held the high ground and were in touch by patrol with the rangers on the left flank. Churchill's Army commandos had secured Vietri and linked up with the Lincolns of the 46th Infantry in the Cava defile.

On the second day, a number of the enemy were observed approaching Vietri from the north. The Germans opened fire with Spandaus on troops moving in the streets while others set up a heavy machine gun. Churchill clambered up onto the roof of the brigade headquarters and directed the fire of the Bren guns and mortars onto the enemy. He was in his element, and within a short time a direct hit was scored. The colonel watched as several Germans were seen to hurtle through the air in a burst of high explosive.

For Anthony Wilkinson and his troop of Royal Marines high on the hill above Dragonea, the first German probe came about midday and was easily contained. Then the German mortar barrage began, slowly at first, but it built into a towering roar of flame and noise as they saturated the hilltops and the terraces below. The slit trenches that Alex Horsfall and his section had occupied were smothered in mortar fire, and he was among the first casualties. Shells bracketed Horsfall's trench, and the young officer was "blown up"; to this day he remembers nothing about the incident. The first thing that Horsfall remembers thereafter was when he regained consciousness in an Army commando dugout in Vietri, some hours later.

The Duke of Wellington had been sent by Churchill with his troop to support the marines in the defile. He had gone forward on reconnaissance after the mortar barrage and brought out the survivors of Horsfall's section together with the wounded, who had been carried on makeshift stretchers. Although there was not a mark on his body, Horsfall was bleeding from the ears, and the medical officer diagnosed a fractured skull—not that Horsfall could understand much because he was by this time totally deaf.*

Meanwhile, the Germans launched attack after attack against the commandos. Wilkinson and his men watched the Germans assemble in the main square in Cava, move out, and climb the terraces. He brought down naval and artillery fire, but they kept coming. The ground simply swallowed up the defenders; every hilltop needed a picquet or small detachment to deny it to the enemy, and there were not enough troops to cover the thickly wooded valley floor and the terraced slopes.

The grenadiers of the Luftwaffe Panzer Division Hermann Göring came forward blindly. Mostly young men, they had green-painted faces and hands and wore yellow and green camouflage smocks, which made them extremely difficult to see. They advanced yelling their division's battle cry, *"Hoch! Hoch!"* The commandos, completely unmoved by such theatricals, steadily picked them off once they had come within range.

For a while it was slaughter, but then part of the section that occupied the terraces below was hit by a furious mortar barrage, and some of the commandos fell back in confusion. The Germans poured through the gap, broke into the village of Dragonea, and A Troop was surrounded.

The reserve troop (Q Troop), which was positioned ready to launch its own counterattack, stormed down the hill and into the village. Martin Stott was killed at the head of his men, and Wilkinson saw a section leader lieutenant hurl a grenade at a group of advancing Germans. One of the latter fired his machine pistol and cut down the young officer even as he and the others were killed by the grenade.

---

*That night Horsfall was lashed in a stretcher to a truck and driven to the main casualty station in Salerno before being evacuated on a hospital ship to North Africa. Fortunately he did not have a fractured skull, but his eardrums had been blown in by the explosion, and blood was oozing out. Once the tissues had healed his hearing returned, and some weeks later he hitched a lift back to the commandos.

Wilkinson had only quick flashes and glimpses as the action ebbed and flowed around his position. In the right hands, the British Army's entrenching shovel is an ideal weapon for close-quarter fighting, and the commandos excelled in its use. Another commando bayoneted a German in classic textbook style.

In many senses this first major encounter between the German division and the commandos was a clash of opposites. The commandos were professionally ferocious troops who were above all trained to kill, especially in close combat. The young panzer grenadiers belonged to a division with a fancy name and were fiercely patriotic National Socialists. The Germans had little training or experience in warfare of this sort, for most of them were flak gunners who had been drafted into the field division, or men trained to guard airfields.

The battle ended when a German shouted an order from the terrace below, and the grenadiers fell back behind a curtain of mortar shells. Though Wilkinson was left in possession of the field, all he had to hold the position were the remnants of two troops of commandos. Six officers and 120 commandos had occupied the hill, and now there were only 50 commandos, a troop sergeant, and one other officer besides himself.

Captain Wilkinson had lost his two section subalterns. Hawkward had been killed, and Stewart was wounded and awaiting evacuation. The only other officer was Peter Haydon, who had just turned 19 years of age and six months before still had been in school. Haydon had been badly wounded early in the engagement and been brought into Wilkinson's headquarters but had refused to be evacuated. Though he had half his buttocks shot off and kept fainting from pain and loss of blood, he stayed with the position.

Wilkinson regrouped his forces and moved his own headquarters back about 100 yards because the Germans by then had his position pinpointed. The Germans came again that afternoon, but on this occasion the commandos held them at bay by withering machine-gun and small-arms fire. Peter Haydon shot a number between fainting bouts. He was later awarded the DSO for his action; at nineteen years of age he was the youngest officer ever to receive the award.

Brigadier Laycock decided to reinforce the marine commandos, so Churchill sent Nos. 1 and 3 troops to occupy the heights to the north of Dragonea and thus extend the line. They prepared to move out at dusk. First, however, they had to negotiate the wretched viaduct bridge to the west of Vietri.

Joe Nicholl found that the only way was to load six men at a time onto the carriers and run the gauntlet. The art lay in gauging the distance between the vehicles and in taking the bridge at a speed greater than the Germans could land their mortars. This meant cranking up the carriers and charging the bridge at a run while the men held onto the swaying, bucking machines for dear life. All the carriers made it that evening, though the Germans had tried hard enough to score a hit.

Nicholl and his section climbed into the hills, the terraces lit by bright moonlight. Midway up the hill, they collided with a German fighting patrol. At first there was some confusion because the commandos didn't know whether these were their own marines falling back or Germans who had broken through the front.

Another section commander, Guy Whitfield, challenged a figure in the moonlight; the guttural reply was enough, and at a range of 20 yards he dropped him neatly with a remarkable pistol shot through the head. In the confused, close hand-to-hand fighting that ensued, the commandos were supreme. A number of the enemy were killed; seven wounded were taken, including one officer; and four prisoners were captured by another group at bayonetpoint. Eight automatic weapons of various types were collected, together with many belts of ammunition.

The commandos pressed on, and No. 1 Troop moved onto the western slopes. No. 3 Troop's headquarters occupied a monastery on top of the hill, while the troop's two sections dug in on the northern and eastern slopes.

Joe Nicholl saw his men dig in on the terraced slopes and then set up the rotation for guard duty. He lent his watch (it had been a 21st-birthday present) to his section sergeant, Willis, who was with the machine-gun post on the terrace below. The two had agreed to spell each other, and Willis had the first two hours of guard duty. Nicholl settled down and went to sleep.

Dawn found the commandos with a splendid view of the front. The first thing they spotted was a mixed force of approximately 30 tanks and armored vehicles lining up in Marini, a little village across the other side of the Cava defile. Obviously the enemy was gathering forces for a major counterattack. The gunners were alerted and within minutes the first shells burst with great accuracy on Marini; the surviving armor beat a hasty retreat northwards toward the hill village of Lagnetto.

The enemy retaliated by once again drenching the hillsides with mortar fire. This time they singled out the monastery for special attention, and the masonry came tumbling down as the building shuddered from the shell hits. A number of men were wounded by shell fragments, as were Italian refugees who had sought sanctuary in the monastery.

The Germans infiltrated the defense positions of the commandos throughout the long day. Even though there was a small picquet on each hill top it wasn't enough, for the close country of ravines and wooded slopes restricted observation and fields of fire. The Germans were thus able to send fighting patrols who, having evaded the outposts, would then shoot up the rear areas before escaping. If the commandos could have established strong-points in sight and sound of one another—and in that country one is talking of no more than 100 yards apart—perhaps the Germans could have been stopped. But there were just not that many commandos available in the brigade.

The hill at Dragonea is 1,500 feet high and has precipitous slopes. The problems this created for the evacuation of the wounded and the resupply for the front line were considerable. Though in general the men were reasonably well supplied with ammunition, they soon began to run short of food and water. Wilkinson's main problem was a shortage of water. Toward midday he sent a patrol into the valley to fill the water bottles. Fortunately the Germans did not spot them, and they all returned safely.

In the Cava defile (or "Happy Valley," as the commandos now cynically called it, for it was anything but happy; it was instead a place of terror and death), the Germans tried on a couple of occasions to burst through the defenses with their tanks. The commandos, both marine and army, held on grimly throughout the day. The troops commanded by Lieutenant Parsons of the Royal Marines and Captain the Duke of Wellington were now in the front line as the Germans tried to break through into Salerno.

Vietri came in for continual bombardment throughout Saturday, and there were many casualties. Brian Lees, the Army commandos' medical officer, had established his medical post in one of the few houses in Vietri with a deep cellar. In the middle of the afternoon a couple of commandos came in carrying a pathetic burden, a little girl who had been caught in the chest by a shell fragment. They laid the girl down on the rough table that Lees used for operating, and the doctor cut away the thin, blood-splattered cotton dress. Lees and his team of orderlies tried their best, but the child never rallied and died an hour later.

A direct hit demolished the headquarters bunker of the marines and wounded their commanding officer, Lieutenant Colonel Lumsden, very badly in the thigh. Others were caught, too, when the roof of the bunker collapsed around them, and for a while the marines had no radio communications.

Toward evening the 46th Division sent the first infantry to relieve the commandos. The 6th Lincolns and the King's Own Yorkshire Light Infantry moved into the hills, and the commandos came down into Vietri for a rest. A company of the Lincolns took over from Anthony Wilkinson's unit; they seemed to be double his numbers in strength. The commandos buried their dead and marched into Vietri.

Wilkinson's batman was really a little old for commando service, and before the war he had been a "gentleman's gentleman." But on occasions such as these he was worth his weight in gold. He had arranged a most comfortable bed for his officer, a grand four-poster with a feather mattress. Wilkinson hardly noticed as he tumbled between the sheets, fully clothed, to sleep for the first time undisturbed since Wednesday, four days before.

It wasn't to be a long sleep, for the Germans launched a major attack on the 139th Infantry Brigade front to the northeast of Salerno. Panzers came rumbling down the road from Avellino, and, though the first assault was contained, things looked serious. The Lincolns and the KOYLIs were sent across to reinforce the line, and at 0830 hours on Sunday, September 12, the two commando units moved once more into the hills above Vietri. The only reinforcements they received were a section of two Vickers heavy machine guns manned by the 2nd Battalion, the Royal Northumberland Fusiliers.

They had come up as divisional support troops with the Lincolns and the Light Infantry and had remained at Dragonea. Brian Lees and his medical orderlies had gone with them and set up his aid station in the front line in the village of Dragonea, for there were just not enough men available in the commandos to provide stretcher parties.*

The troops of Royal marines and Army commandos were now mixed with one another. Wilkinson found that on his right flank the line was held by the Duke of Wellington and his troop rather than marine commandos. Joe Nicholl was ordered to take his men back to their old trenches, which they had previously occupied to the left of Dragonea. There were marines on each side of his small force.

The commandos endured a terrifying afternoon of mortaring. Wilkinson was injured by a salvo that burst around his tactical headquarters. The incident left him totally deaf, and he had to rely on his troop sergeant major, Tom Morgan, to tell him what was happening.

The barrage lasted on into the night, and then in the early hours of Monday, September 13, the Germans attacked.

Joe Nicholl awoke as soon as the crack of the mortars ceased. A young commando named Chick Burn shared Nicholl's trench. Silence descended, and the commandos manned their weapons—they needed no prompting from their section sergeants to "watch your front." Suddenly the Germans were into the forward positions. A German appeared, and Nicholl caught a glimpse of a parachute smock as the enemy fired. Burn fell back; the buller had gone through his steel helmet and killed him instantly. Nicholl emptied his Browning automatic at the German, who disappeared behind a rock.

Men in the forward positions fell back, and Gordon-Hemming ordered his troops to reform behind a long, low stone wall on the reverse side slope.

This was a maximum effort by the Germans, and along the line the commandos were forced to give ground and retire from Dragonea. Brian Lees took the wounded into a cellar where they could not be seen and had all-round cover. Some civilians told him what was happening outside, but in any case by the sound and direction of the small-arms fire he realized that the Germans were in the village. He could not leave the wounded, some of whom were seriously hurt, so Lees decided to lie low and await events.

Many of the wounded, however, were still with the forward sections in the line; the fire had been too heavy for them to be evacuated to the aid post in Dragonea. Butch Denby was in Alf Branscombe's section; Denby was a very big man who came from the Midlands in England. He had been badly hurt by shrapnel, which had laid his back bare to the bone. When the order came through to withdraw, Branscombe as his corporal made the big man as comfortable as he could.

*By this stage in the battle No. 2 Army Commando had had one officer and four men killed, and 33 wounded. The marines in No. 41 Commando had had heavier casualties; three dead and five officers wounded, together with 74 men wounded.

"We're going to have to leave you here, Butch," he said. "Everything will be okay. The Germans will treat you all right."

"All right be buggered," Butch said. "If you're going back, I'm going back."

Denby struggled to his feet, picked up his rifle, webbing belts, and pouches and went back with the marines, his back a quivering hunk of glistening, raw meat.

For a while, it was touch and go. Joe Nicholl and his section took shelter behind the stone wall on the reverse slope below Dragonea as the German barrage suddenly increased.

Major Lowrie, the second-in-command, came up to organize the position. German mortar shells crashed into the treeline and sent slivers of wood hurtling through them. One caught Lowrie in the throat. Sergeant Hill screamed out in pain, "I've lost my arm, I've lost my arm!"

Nicholl tried to help Major Lowrie. It was a horrible wound; each pulse-beat splashed out blood, which pumped onto Nicholl as he squeezed the morphine from a tube into a vein. It was too late; Major Lowrie's life blood drained away, and he slumped back and died in Nicholl's arms.

A forward observations officer from the artillery came up and called for defensive fire down on their own positions and men, which was a tactic of last resort. The 71st Field Artillery, which was by this time in support of the commandos, performed magnificently. While the commandos hugged the ground, intense and extremely accurate fire caught the Germans in the open, and they were decimated.

The British bombardment lifted at 1230 hours, and the commandos, led by Major Parsons of the Royal Marines and the Duke of Wellington, stormed forward to counterattack a by now thoroughly demoralized enemy. An hour later the line had been restored, and Brian Lees and his wounded were rescued in Dragonea. The men dug in, and the wounded were evacuated. The night's action had cost No. 2 Commando alone five officers and 21 men killed and 43 men wounded.

The Germans opened up with yet another bombardment. This one lasted a further two hours, but as the shellfire died away there was no new attack; clearly the panzer grenadiers of the Haas battle group had had enough.

At dusk on September 13 the Yorks and Lancasters moved into the hills and relieved the commandos. The weary troops marched back into Vietri and returned to the same houses they had occupied before. The quartermaster provided them all with a change of clothing. It was the first time since the landing on Thursday morning that Anthony Wilkinson had been able to change; his Army issue vest, black with sweat, had disintegrated. Some of his hearing had returned in one ear, but in the other he was still completely deaf.

Brian Lees spent the night shuttling back and forth to Salerno evacuating the wounded into the 46th Division field hospital. By this time the battle was reaching its crescendo along the whole front, and they could spare him only three ambulances.

The following morning the two commando units were moved by truck through Salerno and into an area just below the village of Pigoletti. The men dug slit trenches in an olive grove and slept the day and the constant German bombardment away.

They were joined in the rest area by the survivors of a section from No. 1 Troop. These commandos had occupied the far left flank position above Vietri near the village of Pandonani and when the Germans launched their offensive were completely cut off from the rest of the force.

The section had made its way down to the coast road between Vietri and Maiori in the hope of getting around the flank and rejoining the commandos. In the darkness they were mistaken for Germans and came under heavy mortar fire. So they turned around and headed cross country toward Maiori. They came to the beach at Cetara, where they attracted the attention of an LCI that was moving close inshore. The captain picked the men up and dumped them ashore the next morning on Amber Beach at Salerno, where they found the rest of the commandos.

Chapter XVIII

The Battle for Salerno

"I am not satisfied with the situation at Avalanche. The build-up is slow and they are pinned down to a bridgehead which has not enough depth."* These terse sentences, taken from the message that General Alexander sent on the evening of September 12 to the chief of the Imperial General Staff in London, point accurately to the Allied predicament at Salerno.

The strands of this fluctuating defensive battle, however, are difficult to unravel, though after a week's bitter fighting it was eventually to swing in the Allied favor. Salerno was never the neat battle so loved by those military historians who look for lines and arrows on a map to describe the situation. Salerno was typical of modern conventional war, a messy affair of small-unit engagements spread across an often ill-defined and constantly changing front.

The 46th Infantry Division at times was to hold the narrowest of bridgeheads as its battalions clung grimly to their positions in the difficult wooded hill country behind the town. Units of the 16th Panzers now reinforced by the battle groups from the Hermann Göring Panzer Division continued to probe into the Cava defile, exploring for a weak spot between the Lincolns and the commandos.

On the afternoon of September 11 the Germans launched a major counterattack down the Baronissi road, which was at the center of the British division's positions. The panzers hit the forward companies of the Sherwood

*C. J. C. Molony, *History of the Second World War*, Vol. V, *The Mediterranean and Middle East* (London: H. M. Stationery Office, 1973), p. 299.

Foresters at Ponte Fratte, where audacious infiltrations by the enemy forced the British troops to fall back more than a mile. Two companies from the battalion of Leicesters were ordered forward to assist in the counterattack, and this incident reveals the nature of the fighting in this sector. The Leicesters advanced along the heavily wooded slopes, lost their way, and failed even to make contact with the Sherwood Foresters. Even their own battalion assumed they had been lost to the enemy. Instead the Leicesters, living up to their regiment's reputation of the "fighting tigers," held on to an advanced position deep in enemy country, where for three days they waged a private war against the Germans. At one time they even drew water from the same well as a unit from the panzer's reconnaissance regiment. On the third night, having run out of food and ammunition, they regained the British line, bringing with them 42 of their own wounded and suffering the final indignity of being shelled by British guns. In the meantime, the Durhams were taking up positions on Hospital Hill, on the northern outskirts of Salerno. They stripped the Red Crosses from the sanatorium, removed the patients, and set up their positions. Farther south, the 1/4th Battalion of the Hampshires dug in on the high ground called White Cross Hill, named after the survey mark on the summit.

All of the battalions were in the front line, and they were subjected to a constant barrage of enemy mortar and artillery fire. The British soldiers also had to be on constant guard against the German combat patrols as, heavily camouflaged, they infiltrated down the dry riverbeds and through orchards and woods. One evening a strong enemy unit caught the main force of the Leicesters in the middle of their evening meal. The Leicesters dropped their mess equipment, sprinted for their slit trenches, and opened a brisk fire on the equally surprised Germans, who had no idea the British were in that position. In what became known as the "steak and kidney battle" (presumably that was what the men were having for supper), the Leicesters held their ground, and the Germans retreated from the field.

All these actions were fought against a constant barrage of shellfire, but the British were suited to that aggressive and dogged defense in which they show their best qualities. For the first few days, the 46th Infantry Division endured the enemy onslaught in the stoic manner that so epitomizes the British soldier with his back against the wall.

On September 13 sapper, mortar, and machine-gun companies were used as infantry, for by this time the rifle companies were considerably reduced in strength. In the rear echelons the battalions armed their cooks and clerks, while administrative units dug defensive positions and manned their weapons pits. Some ground was given, and it was a return to the legend of the "thin red line" where the British infantry, the redcoat of history, has prepared to make his stand as the inner perimeter held firm.

In the southern part of the division's front the Hampshires had been bombarded frequently, but the Germans had not yet made major attacks. The Hampshires had carried out aggressive patrolling, but compared to other areas it had been a relatively quiet sector. This was soon to change.

Just about midnight on September 14, when the Hampshires were on the point of relieving their company on the crest, the Germans poured down a terrific mortar barrage, and a battle group from the 15th Panzer Grenadiers swarmed into the attack. The Hampshires, caught in the open and at the worst possible moment, were overrun, and White Cross Hill, which afforded a splendid view of the battlefield, was lost. This invaluable feature now became the scene of some of the most bitter fighting on the beachhead. Successive and increasingly costly attacks were launched by all three battalions of the Hampshires, but to no avail. Though some made it to the crest, none could hold it against the determined counterattacks. In fighting more reminiscent of the trenches of World War I, the Germans clung firmly to their prize. British commanders became obsessed by White Cross Hill. Even when Ultra told them that the Germans were going to break off the battle and retreat behind the winter line (the defensive positions along the Garigliano River, where Kesselring intended to hold the Allied advance for the winter), the depleted commandos were thrown into the fray, but they failed to take White Cross Hill.

This form of defensive fighting was quite different to that which the division's reconnaissance regiment had anticipated and trained for. They should have been in the vanguard of the advance, seeking out the best routes forward and feeling for the weak points in the enemy defenses. On September 10 they attempted just that when a unit from B Squadron, led by Peter Mason, probed its way into the Cava defile while A Squadron advanced as far inland as Materno without encountering the enemy; so they returned to their base at San Mango for the night. When they moved forward the next morning, however, they found the enemy ready for them and lying in ambush at the point that had been the limit of the previous evening's patrols. A Squadron's armored cars returned the fire and knocked out a couple of Spandau machine-gun pits. Their squadron commander was on the point of ordering a full assault when they were ordered to withdraw. The decision had been made to prepare for the defensive operations that by then had been seen as necessary.

During this defensive phase the reconnaissance regiment continued to send out patrols by day as well as listening patrols by night. For the latter, the reconnaissance regiment would send perhaps two or three men on a stakeout in no-man's-land during darkness. They were to provide early warning of an attack or just observe enemy movement; it was nerve-racking. At the beck and call of every infantry battalion in the division, the regiment's troopers crawled out beyond the perimeter and into the unknown to learn the enemy's intentions.

For those men and units who had to move from Salerno into the Cava defile, there was one particular hazard to negotiate. As at Vietri, there was a bridge that led into Cava. It spanned the railway cut and became known by the local garrison as "Gauntlet Bridge." The stone parapet had been battered down, and in places there were gaping holes through which German machine guns fired on fixed lines from across the valley. Vehicles could negotiate the bridge only one at a time because the structure was so unsafe. The trick was to wait for a burst and when it stopped to "go like hell" in the hope that the enemy didn't have another belt of ammunition ready. It was a little like Russian roulette, as some had already found out; an abandoned jeep and an overturned motorcycle were on the bridge, evidence of a bad night. Douglas Scott was there that morning with Ian Keelan, his company commander, trying to inspect the bridge supports. The machine-gun fire was particularly heavy. Suddenly a young officer strode onto the bridge and with complete disregard for the fire climbed into the jeep and drove it away. The route was now clear, but, as if that weren't enough, he returned, picked up and mounted the motorcycle with ease, though it was heavy and awkward to handle. He kick-started the "bike" and rode it off the bridge. Scott watched and wondered where the boundary between bravery and foolhardiness lay.

The Lincolns were in that sector holding the line alongside the commandos. Oliver Hardy was able to organize the battalion's operations room and indicate some semblance of order on the situation map. As a territorial Army soldier he was proud that his unit was fighting alongside the elite commandos. Hardy was a cautious man, never bigger than war, and he went about his work quietly and efficiently.

The Lincolns were conscious the whole while that there was nothing behind them but the sea. The landing craft were always there in the bay. It began to be a joke that they were waiting to take them off only if the Lincolns could reach them. However, any movement in the open drew a barrage of enemy mortar and artillery fire.

The Lincolns' headquarters was established in a large house on the hill above Vietri; it was comfortable enough, but for the forward rifle companies it was a completely different picture. The terrain was terrible, the days hot and dry, and there never seemed to be enough drinking water. The battalion had made a couple of attempts to probe forward, but Baker Company had come sadly unstuck near the village of Alessia, their attack had failed, and they lost some good men. Against the incessant bombardment, there was little the Lincolns could do but hold on, patrol hard to retain the local initiative, and watch for German infiltration.

The Lincolns respected the Germans as soldiers. Opposing formations in the front line often develop something of an affinity, and this is sometimes reinforced by an event or an experience, as it was for the Lincolns. In the North African campaign a patrol had been caught out in the open in no-man's-land and badly mauled by the Germans. One of their wounded was tended by the enemy medics, who placed him on a stretcher and, before they fell back, signaled to the Lincolns to pick up their man.

At Salerno, everywhere was the front line, and for those who had to travel between the rear areas and the rifle companies it was just as uncomfortable in many respects as manning a slit trench. One stretch of Highway 18 just outside Salerno was always under enemy shellfire; it was a nightmare having to negotiate the half-mile section of road. Doug Parker did it a couple of times in a day and never got used to that journey in the old Bedford, which he had named "Betty," after his wife. Each time the military policemen signaled for his turn, he gunned the engine and prayed the whole way that the motor wouldn't let him down. On most occasions he carried ammunition from the beach to the battalion in Vietri, where it would be unloaded and taken on to the rifle companies. For this second part of the journey they would use jeeps, mules, or even, for some of the more isolated platoons, man-pack it into the line. Sometimes just to have a change Parker would stop the truck on the way back into Salerno from Vietri, run across the road, and take a quick dip in the harbor. There was one particular place that was a favorite spot, for the rock overhang shielded the bathers from the landward side, so there was little or no chance of the Germans hitting them with mortar fire. Stripped naked, he would join the other drivers in the sea and for just a little while frolic and horseplay. It was a fool's paradise, for there was no real escape from the constant barrage. Though the shellfire never seemed quite so bad because it was more impersonal than small-arms fire, nevertheless, if someone had said, "I'll guarantee you six months of life, no more," he would have taken them on at that time. Such a guarantee seemed to offer more than the life expectancy at Salerno.

There were rumors, too, the whole while. The most popular was that they couldn't hold the beachhead and that the division was going to withdraw. The plan was that the artillery were to withdraw to the beach first, and then the infantry would withdraw through them. Such stories became common.

The Lincolns had no radio link between battalion and its B Echelon; they had to rely on direct contact. One day Sergeant Hardy had to go to the echelon to pick up some documents. He rode on the back of a motorcycle driven by the orderly-room clerk. They were midway along the notorious section of Highway 18, and the motorcycle was going as fast as it could when German shells laced the road and chased after the frantic pair. A couple of shells fell ahead of them, and they rode the motorcycle straight into a ditch. Shaken, wet, and bruised but profoundly relieved to be alive, Hardy sheltered below the bank and waited for the bombardment to cease. The orderly-room clerk lit two cigarettes and gave him one; it was only afterward that Hardy remembered he didn't smoke.

It was also Hardy's job as Intelligence sergeant to find a safe route from the battalion headquarters through to the coast road that led westward out of Vietri to Maiori. This was to be used by a battalion of rangers due to arrive as reinforcements. It was the middle of the afternoon when Hardy and another soldier set out on their mission; the sun burned through his helmet, and he felt as if his head were encased in an oven. They found a route that would be under cover for most of the time, though there was no way around the bridge. The rangers would have to negotiate the bridge and run the gauntlet of enemy fire before they could get to Vietri.

The route back to battalion took them along the railroad and through a cut. On the side of the track there was a large water tank gushing water. Hardy couldn't resist this chance. "Here, hold my Tommy gun," he said to his companion.

Hardy took off his steel helmet and stood under the water. Seemingly from nowhere a few local people rushed out with a towel and when he had finished helped to dry him down.

The sappers, like the reconnaissance regiment, found themselves initially with little for them to do in line with their principal assignment—in their case, engineering. Brian Coombe and his section helped to improve the communications from the beach to the immediate hinterland and built a few jeep tracks to ease the traffic flow.

Douglas Scott went to find a medical officer to have his own shrapnel wounds treated. He didn't want to bother his own unit's doctor, who was by this time working with the main divisional field hospital. Walking behind the dunes, Scott met a young Royal Army Medical Corps doctor who had his bag with him.

"Look Doc," Scott said, "can you just have a quick look at this, please?"

"What's the matter?" he asked.

"I've got some shrapnel in my shoulder, my back, and my bum," Scott said.

The doctor walked with him to where the engineers had their rear echelon. Scott stripped, and the doctor set to work cleaning out the tiny bits of shrapnel, which by this time had started to fester.

While the doctor worked, the two men talked. Scott found that the doctor had lived near his parents' home in South Wales and had even dated one of his sisters. They had never met for Scott was in the Army at the time.

Then the sappers were called to become infantry. The Sherwood Foresters had been roughly handled by the 3rd Battalion of the 115th Panzer Grenadiers, Hermann Göring Division. The problem was that with every battalion in the line there now were no reserves of infantry. At the time the sappers were available. Their engineering skills would not be used until the breakout was on and the Allies were advancing on Naples.

The sappers moved up to the high ground east of Ponte Fratte. Though trained as infantry after a fashion, they had little practical experience in such work. The men in the company weren't youngsters. The engineers were a territorial Army unit, which many of the men had joined before the outbreak of the war. Many were in their thirties, so Brian Coombe as a junior officer probably was one of the youngest in the unit. Most of the soldiers and nearly all the senior NCOs had been tradesmen or skilled craftsmen before the war. They worked hard building bridges and roads and clearing minefields, and they did it superbly well, but they weren't particularly adept as fighting soldiers.

At last light the vehicles took them to the bottom of the hill they were to occupy. When it was dark the sappers scrambled up the hill and relieved the Sherwood Foresters. The latter had been there for a couple of days and were ready for a rest after being in such a lonely and exposed position. The infantry lost no time leaving the hill, and the sappers settled into their new and accustomed role. The first thing they found was that the slit trenches were only about 3 feet deep, and they went down into solid rock.

It was almost as if the Germans knew there had been a relief and that a fresh and untried unit occupied the line. With the dawn came the mortar barrage. It quickly built up to a terrifying crescendo, and the hilltop was smothered. They began to suffer casualties immediately, and when Coombe organized his stretcher parties they too became casualties. What made it worse was that they had only small arms, rifles, and Bren light machine guns; they had no mortars with which they could hit back. After an hour and a half there were some 40 casualties and no end in sight to the bombardment. No one seemed to be in charge. Everyone, officer and soldier, crouched low in the makeshift trenches. Gradually the sappers moved off the hill and took up fresh positions lower down the reverse slope. The battalion commander of the Sherwood Foresters was absolutely furious that the ground had been lost to the enemy. However, little could be done about it, for the sappers had been ill prepared for such a personal and terrible baptism in front-line battle.

The senior engineer officer with the division wisely sent them back to the beaches, where he found them manual work (building a jeep track) very quickly. This was a necessary tonic to get everybody occupied and back into shape again very quickly.

For those on the beach or farther inland, one feature of the division's battle that remains firmly in their minds was the magnificent fire support provided by the monitor H.M.S. *Roberts*.

This strange but lethal warship was in her element. She was moored so close inshore that Douglas Scott, who saw her almost daily, couldn't understand how she hadn't run aground. To give her main battery even greater elevation the crew had pumped out the starboard ballast tanks, which gave her a decided list. Every time the *Roberts* fired her massive broadside, she rolled and was practically awash. But the old lady was magnificent, and the men ashore were convinced she was worth at least a regiment of field artillery. Watching the red balls of fire that her 15-inch shells traced through the night sky like angry comets was one of the best morale boosters.

Even though there were crises on land, the landing craft continued to bring the precious cargoes ashore from the freighters, which were now moored some 6 miles at sea and beyond the range of German artillery. Lew Hemmings and his crew had been at his work without a single break since the first landing. Indeed, the landing craft worked 24 hours a day. Empty trucks were reversed onto the vehicle decks, and then Hemmings would put to sea armed with a manifest of the supplies needed and which ship was likely to have them. Once alongside, the freighter's crew would drop a cargo by net into the back of the trucks, and Hemmings would return to the shore.

If the beach party was waiting they would drive the trucks ashore; otherwise Hemmings and his crew would do the job. In this fashion the landing craft would make six or eight trips a day, regular as clockwork. Hemmings felt that at times the schedule was like that of a railroad.

There always seemed to be a panic on the beach, and though the days merged into a single sweaty blur of unremitting toil, the Germans never seemed to be very far inland. Every time they beached the landing craft the sounds of battle seemed very near. The troops who toiled on the shore frequently gazed inland, and their apprehension was infectious.

On the fourth day of the battle, there was a desperate need for 25-pounder artillery shells. The beachmaster gave Hemmings the manifest of those ships loaded with ammunition. Despite the urgency of the request, Hemmings could find no artillery shells on the ships that were listed as having them.

When he had been to four freighters and received the same negative answer, he moved alongside the fifth and climbed aboard to speak to the captain.

"No, my ship carries no ammunition," the captain said.

"Well, according to the manifest, you do," Hemmings said.

"That's as may be," the captain replied, "but when we were in port loading, the dockers wouldn't handle the shells because they weren't paid extra money."

Many of the freighters were loaded at ports in England and then sailed in convoy for the Mediterranean and the beachhead at Salerno.

Hemmings went on searching until he found a freighter with the shells. It made his crew very bitter because the men onshore were screaming for ammunition. What were they fighting and dying for if those at home behaved in such a fashion?

Chapter XIX

Battipaglia and the Tobacco Factory

On the 56th Division's front, which stretched from the outskirts of Salerno on the left to the ground between Battipaglia and Eboli on the right, the German counterattacks over the following days probed for the weak spots; there were plenty of these, for there were not enough troops to man the line. They struck hard at the Queen's who were by now dug in on Hill 210 across the railroad and above the airfield at Montecorvino. Between the Queen's and the fusiliers around Battipaglia, the line was thinly held by the three battalions of the 201st Guards Brigade. In the center of their line a vicious battle was to be fought for possession of what became known as the Tobacco Factory, which was a couple of miles west of Battipaglia. This was a tomato processing plant that occupied a slight rise in the ground and thus had a commanding view.

Another popular spot for attacks was along the corps boundary where, to the right of the fusilier brigade's line beyond Battipaglia, the front was held by ad hoc formations from the reconnaissance regiment and engineers pressed into the battle as infantry. However, it was with the guards at the Tobacco Factory and the fusiliers dug in defending the vitally important communications center at Battipaglia that the days of crisis began in this sector.

German pressure against the 9th Battalion, Royal Fusiliers in Battipaglia started at dawn on Friday, September 10. The two rifle companies of fusiliers, which had moved out and deployed along the Castel Lucia heights to the northeast of the town, were forced to retire into Battipaglia. They had been caught in the path of the advance by all three battalions of the 64th

Panzer Grenadiers and their supporting armor. In this initial phase it was almost pure blitzkrieg, with the fusiliers being the *Schwerpunkt* or point at which the main thrust of the attack hits the defenders. They left half their men on the hill dead as the survivors retreated into Battipaglia. The panzer grenadiers then spread around the town and sealed the fusiliers into the trap.

German tanks moved in, and the panzer grenadiers infiltrated through the 6-foot-high tobacco crop that covered the fields nearby. In the hills above, mobile batteries of 88mm artillery began a house-by-house demolition, but as long as the 6-pounder antitank guns survived, the tanks were kept at bay. As many as four different crews manned the guns; each crew was knocked out by shrapnel and machine-gun fire one after the other, only to be replaced with fresh men who knew full well the fate that awaited them.

By the early afternoon the last of the defenders' antitank guns had been knocked out, and at the same time the enemy was reinforced by the first troops to reach the battlefield and the 16th Panzers. The 1st Battalion of the 3rd Parachute Regiment, previously attached to the 29th Panzers in Calabria, moved straight into the fray at Battipaglia.

Fusilier Harris had parked his carrier in a narrow side street, and the crew took cover in a building on the seaward side of a main street that consisted of a row of two-and three-story houses with shops on the ground floor. The house was empty, and there was not much furniture. Though the survivors from forward companies had already retreated into the town, the reconnaissance platoon attached to battalion headquarters had not received any orders other than to get under cover. In circumstances such as these the men brewed the inevitable cup of tea and stoically endured the German bombardment.

With the antitank guns gone, German armor moved right onto the front-line defenses. Fusiliers fought with desperate bravery, firing their Bren guns from the shoulder into the tank slits, but to no avail.

A very popular young officer was reported missing at the bridge into Battipaglia. He had been a film actor who had become quite famous. He starred in public information films, one in particular entitled *Next of Kin,* in which he had played a soldier who had given the game away. In England, this former actor had joined the 9th Battalion, but just before it left for overseas service he was sent to join a staff headquarters in India. There he was thoroughly miserable, and so when the battalion appeared in Bombay en route for the Middle East, he had persuaded the colonel to arrange for his recall. In the middle of the afternoon, he and a platoon held the bridge as the only escape route open for the battalion. German half-tracks and infantry swooped on the position and overwhelmed them. He disappeared and was never heard of again.

Above the cacophony of noise that was the German bombardment of Battipaglia, Fusilier Harris and his driver, Frank Dewar, heard the sound of tank tracks coming down the main street toward the house in which they had found shelter. Dewar had an orange-colored sticky bomb, about the size of a football. It was a sophisticated form of Molotov cocktail. The idea was to drop it into a vehicle, where it would shatter and immediately burst into flame.

Harris crouched under the low stone balcony, and Dewar stood poised to drop the bomb at his signal. The tank came nearer and then stopped right outside the house.

"Now?" whispered Frank.

"No," Harris replied, "wait a moment until the hatch opens."

Harris stole a quick glance, and just at that moment the hatch opened and out popped a British artillery observation officer. The two fusiliers eased back into the room, and the tank—Harris recognized it now as a Stuart light tank—drove on down the street. The gunner officer will never know how lucky he was not to get a Molotov cocktail down his neck.

Shortly afterward Lieutenant Carter, their platoon commander, appeared on the scene. "I think it's time for us to make our departure," he said. "If you make your way down out of the town you should come across the guards. We'll be in touch again."

There wasn't much else to be said. The two men packed up their gear and went out by the back door of the building. They scrambled over a low brick wall and dropped down into the little side street where Harris had parked the carrier. Both men reached into their pouches for a couple of grenades, pulled the pins, and dropped them into the vehicle before running off down the road. A blast of fire and flame followed by the sound of exploding ammunition marked the destruction of the carrier.

They turned into the main street and hugged the doorways, for the area was alive with machine-gun fire. Harris looked back and saw a couple of tanks about 300 yards away blasting the houses at point-blank range with their main armaments while the bow machine gunners hosed the street with fire.

They spotted a couple of men from their platoon caught behind a low wall on the opposite side of the road.

"Come over this side!" Harris yelled. "It's your only chance!"

"No, we can't," Jim Bootley, a particular friend, replied, "we can't make it!"

"The sods are not going to get me as a prisoner," Harris swore.

"Me neither!" Dewar said as he scampered over the rubble and into the next doorway. Harris knew that if they lingered, the Germans would be certain to capture them. Their only hope lay in escape.

They passed a big house on the edge of town that housed the battalion headquarters. There were rows of stretchers outside, for it was doubling as the regimental aid post. The chaplain and the doctor were working among the wounded, oblivious to the battle.*

Harris and Dewar, now joined by two more fusiliers, crossed the railway lines and found their way to the Tusciano River. There seemed to be very few

---

*The chaplain and doctor elected to remain behind with the wounded and were subsequently taken prisoner.

other fusiliers on the same mission. The banks of the river were overgrown with tall reeds and matted vegetation. The little group pressed on as quickly as they could, moving in single file.

They had gone a quarter of a mile, or slightly less, when the reeds at the top of the bank suddenly parted and they were looking down the wicked barrel of a Bren gun.

"Fusiliers?" a voice demanded.

They had reached the outpost line of the guards.

"You'd better come out and meet our RSM," a Guardsman said.

Harris never thought he would have been so relieved to meet "the Brigade" (as the Guards were known by the rest of the Army).

One of the Guardsmen (they were grenadiers) took the four fusiliers down a little track to a farmhouse near a bridge. There they met the imposing figure of the guard's regimental sergeant major.

"Ah, well," he said, "you chaps will be useful. As far as I know we're going to attack later this afternoon, so you had better come with us. Had any food yet?"

"No, sir," Harris said.

They were led away and given a generous helping of compo stew and some steaming mugs of tea.

Later in the afternoon the Guardsmen prepared to attack. They were joined by what seemed to be the best part of a full squadron of Sherman tanks from the Scots Greys. The tanks had had an awful time because all the roads from the beaches inland were extremely narrow so they could advance in single file only and the deep ditches on either side had stopped them deploying off the roads into the fields. They were like whales stranded on a beach.

All the Germans needed was a single well-sited 88mm antitank gun to hold up a whole regiment of armor. The Greys knew the enemy tactic. They would wait until the tanks had advanced a good distance down a road and then "roll up" the lead tank with the first shot. Nevertheless, the Greys persevered, even though they knew that each time the lead tank would be hit.

Hugh Massey, who was second-in-command of B Squadron, the Greys, found the Salerno campaign frustrating and wasteful in armor. The tanks always had to move forward slowly in low gear, so the noise from the engines was terrific, betraying their presence long before they came into sight. And it wasn't easy to spot an 88mm gun because the shell traveled with such velocity that it invariably struck its target before the crew had even seen the flash from its muzzle.

The squadron moved into position and lined a track toward Battipaglia. Massey and the other commanders could see nothing but olive trees in front and so were totally dependent on radio for news of the action. But with headsets clamped over their ears they couldn't assess events by listening to the sounds of battle. The tanks were fighting the action deaf.

No. 2 Company of the grenadiers forced a way close to town, and a reconnaissance group linked up with a few remaining fusiliers, who were in uncertain possession of its southern end. At that particular point the panzer grenadiers moved in from the north, cut the road, and threatened to overwhelm the guardsmen.

Suddenly word came over the air that the Germans had broken through. The tanks trained their 75mm guns roughly in the direction of the bridge over which the Germans would have to advance and loaded with high explosives. When word came to fire, the tanks opened up as one and sent round after round in the direction of the enemy. The massed fire of the Greys stopped the Germans at the bridge, but because of the close nature of the fighting there were casualties among the Guardsmen as well.

Later that evening Harris and the other fusiliers who had moved in with the Guardsmen were ordered to reassemble at the crossroads just outside the village of St. Lucia.

In the fading light of the evening there appeared to be a couple of hundred fusiliers at the crossroads. They were all that remained from the battalion.

"Baldy" Reid, their former platoon sergeant but by then with the battalion's administrative troops in B Echelon, came to where the carrier platoon was standing.

"Is this all there is?" he asked.

There were about a dozen left out of the original 30 men.

"Yes," Harris said, looking around him.

"Where are my boys? Where are my boys?" Reid cried over and over again. When training in England, he used to curse them up hill and down dale. Now he was heartbroken.

R.M.S. Hollis took charge of the men. Patiently but firmly he sorted them out and reorganized the survivors—there were less than half a battalion—into new rifle companies. There were some officers, junior officers, and a company commander or two who together with the senior NCOs were able to provide the nucleus of a fighting force.

The men were fed and then told to dig in around the crossroads at St. Lucia. To their right was a canal.

"Who's beyond the canal?" Harris asked.

"The Americans should be," somebody replied.

"Should be! Fine!" Harris said. "But are they or aren't they?"

Nobody seemed to know.

There were a couple of the big new antitank guns, 17-pounders, about 50 yards behind the fusiliers while the division's support troops, the 2nd Battalion, Cheshire Regiment, moved some of their Vickers heavy machine guns into the outbuildings of the farm.

The headquarters of the 167th Brigade had watched and monitored the tragedy of Battipaglia throughout the day, though they were powerless to intervene.

Earlier that morning John Gerber, one of the battalion's officers, arrived in a jeep at the headquarters to try to get hold of a radio. The brigade signals officer got into the jeep with him to go to see what was wrong with the battalion's radios. They were ambushed on the outskirts of Battipaglia by a trio of German half-tracks and killed.

Among the tightly knit little group of officers that comprised the brigade's fighting headquarters, none had shown more alarm and despair than 23-year-old Captain David Appleby, the Intelligence officer. He had been commissioned into the 9th Battalion at the outbreak of the war and had only recently left them for his tour of duty on the staff.

Appleby went down to St. Lucia, where the survivors from the battalion were gathered, staying for a while and then with the onset of night returning to brigade headquarters. On occasions such as these Appleby rode a motorcycle—and very carefully, indeed. It was bad enough to ride without lights, but one of the major perils of the night came from his own side, who had the habit of placing a line of antipersonnel mines across the road.

Although a lot of good friends from his old battalion had been killed or were missing that day, Appleby concentrated on his job. One of the extraordinary things among the younger officers and men was their acceptance of tragedy. People whom Appleby knew well were dead, but he did not feel the same pangs as he would today. There was an acceptance of these things, not because their experience in war had hardened them, for at that time the fusiliers had not been exposed to it much. It was probably because young people are extraordinarily adaptable; they accept these things in a way that older people never would.

On his way back, Appleby met somebody trotting up the track toward him. The figure had come from the direction of the Sele River, across which the night sky reverberated to the sounds of incessant and heavy gunfire. Appleby stopped the motorcycle and asked the man where he was going. Never pausing for a moment in his stride, the figure responded, "We aint' no infantry, sir," and the American disappeared into the night.

Appleby sat there bemused. He had heard stories about the U.S. Army and its overspecialization, wherein a man would do his job and no more. The young captain shook his head in amazement. In the British Army when it came to a crisis, everyone was infantry.

Major Archer, the headquarters company commander of the 8th Fusiliers, was also abroad that night. Ever since the landing at Salerno had settled down he had commuted from B Echelon to the companies in the front line, which was to the right of Battipaglia. He had heard of the disaster that had struck the 9th Battalion and had stayed in his own battalion headquarters, which was located in a small farmhouse, to see if there would be other developments.

When dusk came, the front seemed to quiet down; so Archer decided to return to B Echelon, which was close to the beach and near brigade headquarters. On the way back he passed a lone Sherman from the Greys. It was parked, black and menacing in the middle of the road, as if in anticipation of a further breakthrough on the front. Archer maneuvered his jeep around the obstacle and paused to exchange a few words with the earphoned head that protruded from the turret. The driver's hatch opened and an anonymous hand held out a steaming mess cup of sticky, sweet tea. The mosquitoes homed in on it like bees around a hive. With practiced ease Archer swept the cup clear of insects and placed the liquid to his lips. It tasted of gasoline and oil fumes and the mixture of smells that come from the belly of a tank, but it was, nonetheless, good and hot.

Archer pressed on to B Echelon, parked his jeep, and strolled in in time for the usual evening meal of compo stew and local vegetables. He had just joined the quartermaster, the regimental sergeant major, and the chaplain with his meal when all hell broke loose. Archer and the others looked up in alarm as a great burst of firing shattered the front, and guns along the line responded. The heaviest firing, artillery and machine guns, he was sure was coming from the 8th Battalion front. The brigade staff captain came running over from headquarters.

"Sir," he said, addressing Archer, "there's a bit of trouble on the 8th Battalion front. The brigadier's not sure what is going on. Would you find out?"

Archer ran for his jeep and drove as fast as he could for the battalion's headquarters.

David Appleby knew exactly what was going on, for in the midst of the heavy firing he met a whole group of men milling down the road. He jumped off his motorcycle and directed them into a field. With the help of some senior NCOs and a couple of junior officers he quickly sorted them out. There were about 50 fusiliers from the 8th Battalion who had fled from the tremendous barrage of fire that had overwhelmed their positions. The men, for the most part somewhat sheepish, wanted to return, but in the moment of blind panic they had discarded their weapons. There was no way that Appleby could lead unarmed men on a dark night into a front line that by then might be occupied by the enemy.

Just a short distance across the field was a battery of 25-pounder field guns. Appleby found their officer and asked him for all his gunners' personal weapons, rifles, and submachine guns. Naturally enough, the gunners were not at all happy about this, and a shouting match began between the two officers until Appleby produced the clinching argument: "Either you give up your rifles and let them take them up to the front," he yelled, "or you can keep your rifles and use them when the Germans come here!"

The gunners handed everything over, and Appleby led the fusiliers back toward the front line. They hadn't gone very far when they came upon a little tent on the side of the road. Inside there was a fusilier, fast asleep. For about half an hour that fusilier had been unknowingly the most advanced part of the British Army. The man snored away, quite ignorant of the part he had played, and Appleby had no intention of disturbing him.

Headquarters of the 167th Brigade had also alerted Lt. Aidan Sprot, the Intelligence officer in the Scots Greys, that the enemy was attacking and making for the beaches. All the saber squadrons, reconnaisance troops, and tanks of regimental headquarters moved out immediately and took up fire position.

There was a steady trickle of infantry coming back down the road, so Tim Readman, a troop commander, stood in the middle of it. When the men asked him the way to the beaches, he replied in his calm, unhurried way, "You're going the wrong way. The beaches are over there," pointing to the front line.

They all turned around innocently and walked back toward the front.

At about this moment Major Archer at last found the battalion headquarters. It had been moved from the farmhouse to a position a few hundred yards nearer to the beach. He learned that the leading company apparently had been hit hard and some of the troops had fallen back, though much of this was rumor because they couldn't raise the company commander on the radio. There were quite a lot of stragglers around, and the commanding officer was convinced the report was accurate. He planned to use the reserve company to move forward and reoccupy the position.

Everybody in the battalion headquarters was desperately tired; even the commanding officer fell asleep in the middle of his own briefing. Archer, who seemed to be the only one who had noticed, prodded him awake.

Archer moved forward with the reserve company and came across the company commander still in his own command post, but now with Appleby. Archer now learned that apparently the front line had suddenly received a tremendous battering from their own 25-pounders. The barrage had unnerved the men, especially since it came from their own guns, and they had abandoned their trenches and gone streaming back toward the beaches.

The Germans had failed to spot the disorder, and so no real harm was done, though there can be nothing so demoralizing and disconcerting for infantry than to be shelled by their own side.

In the early hours the battalion sent out a strong fighting patrol to restore their own superiority over their part of the front line and confidence in themselves.

It was becoming increasingly obvious that mistakes were being made because men were reaching the limits of their endurance. Very few had had sufficient sleep on the voyage from North Africa, and they had now been in the line for three days. For some it had been a week or more since they had enjoyed an unbroken period of sleep.

The fusiliers returned to the position, and the battalion headquarters to the farmhouse. Archer, luckier than most with a relatively secure slit trench in B Echelon and thus the chance for some hours of rest most nights, spent the remainder of the night at the battalion headquarters so the CO could catch up on his sleep.

The next morning they regrouped and later in the day were joined in the headquarters by Brigadier Gascoigne, who commanded the Guardsmen. They all climbed into the farm loft to see the Scots Guards make their second attempt on the Tobacco Factory. The first had ended in failure.

The Tobacco Factory was really the key to the whole position. (As mentioned earlier, this wasn't a tobacco factory at all but a storage depot and a canning plant, mostly used to process tomatoes.) Standing on a slight rise in the ground, this complex of buildings, which also included some old Army barracks, sat astride the main road and railway line. Whoever held the factory controlled the line of communications between Salerno and Battipaglia, together with much of the surrounding countryside. It was absolutely vital to the Germans, for it threatened their only transverse supply route; its loss would require a considerable detour around the hills inland when both time and fuel were at a premium.

The buildings had been surrounded by a spiked iron railing 8 feet high and fortified into mutually supporting strongpoints with interlocking arcs of fire. They covered an area of about 3½ acres and were formidable obstacles.

The Scots Guards had launched their first attack in daylight and without artillery support and had paid the price for their impetuous assault. It was rumored that, deeply mortified by their failure, they apologized to the brigade commander and asked his permission to try again.

Word came from brigade headquarters that the Germans had largely abandoned the factory, so it was decided the Scots Guards should try again the following evening. By this time the 56th Field Regiment, Royal Artillery, had laid down a healthy barrage. The attack was timed to start at nine-thirty on that bright moonlit Saturday night.

Three companies were to mount the attack. G Company was in the center and had as its objective the Tobacco Factory. The right flank company* took the right, with the main Battipaglia–Salerno road as their objective, while F Company, on the left, had as its objective a white farmhouse at the main crossroads to the west of the factory.

Anthony Philipson, who led a platoon in F Company, moved forward at the head of his men as the barrage reached its crescendo. They reached the railroad embankment, where Philipson met another officer, Lt. Ralph Dollard, who had just made a quick reconnaissance. He reported the Germans were present in considerable strength with armored cars and Spandau machine guns. The earlier Intelligence reports appeared to be wrong. They were debating whether to attack, because the men would have to advance across an open field, when the brigadier came running up to them from the fusilier headquarters.

"You've got to attack! You've got to attack!" he ordered. "The people on the left are already moving on the tobacco factory." The order was given, though Philipson was convinced it was a mistake.

The barrage lifted off the target and shifted its fire to the areas immediately behind, while the platoons of F Company moved in an extended line into a field of bamboo. Bayonets were fixed, and the Guards advanced with their rifles at "high port"—it was copybook stuff.

---

*In times past the tallest men in the Guards were placed in the grenadier companies, for they would be able to throw grenades the farthest. These companies always guarded the flanks of the battalion, right and left. The custom has remained to this day to have a right flank company and a left flank company among the rifle companies in the Guards.

As if the bright moonlight wasn't enough to contend with, the Germans had set fire to a huge silo behind the white farm. It turned night into day.

Philipson wanted to put down smoke, but there wasn't time; they had to keep up the momentum of the attack. The Guardsmen came out from the bamboo and started across the last 300 yards of open field that led up to the farm. The Germans had knocked out the bottom stones of the stone cowsheds to provide machine-gun ports. The Spandaus opened up on the advancing Guardsmen; the bullets, coming knee high, bowled them over like tenpins. The company was slaughtered. Philipson looked around and could see only Captain Weston-Smith, the company commander, and a couple of men still on their feet.

They got to within 50 yards of the buildings when the survivors had to hug the ground. Philipson lay there hoping the silo would burn itself out so they could retreat. He was angry and frustrated. They couldn't attack a solid stone wall and machine guns with just infantry.

The sounds of battle died down, and some Germans emerged from the rear of the buildings and started to prod the bodies, which lay scattered like so much chaff across the field. Philipson lay face down and feigned death, but a burly grenadier rolled him over and the game was up; with hands held high above his head he was led off into the German position.

The young officer was taken into a building and put with a number of other prisoners. From out of the darkness across the field there came the unnerving sound of a man crying. The crying went on for some time. The noise almost tore them apart, for they were already in a state of shock, and it sounded like an animal in pain. A panzer lieutenant approached Philipson and spoke in rather strange English:

"One of your wounded is out there. Will you go back with two of my stretcher bearers?"

Philipson was impressed. This was chivalry of the highest order, and he immediately consented and gave his word as an officer not to attempt escape.

The German lieutenant, two stretcher bearers, and Philipson stepped outside, and immediately shots rang out from the survivors of the company who had regrouped at the railroad embankment. "Stop! Don't fire!" Philipson yelled.

The firing stopped, and a couple of unfortunate Guardsmen who had taken cover in the bamboo came out thinking that the farm had been captured, only to find themselves guests of the Wehrmacht.

They picked up the wounded man, who lay about 100 yards from the farm and was very badly hurt. The German took Captain Weston-Smith and Philipson, the two officers they had captured, by motorcycles back to their battalion headquarters. There they joined other officers from the battalion. It had by all accounts been a disastrous night. Nearly the whole right flank company had been overrun by German tanks and captured,* and the Tobacco Factory had been abandoned after a bitter battle.

---

*Only the company commander, one other officer, and 12 Guardsmen escaped capture.

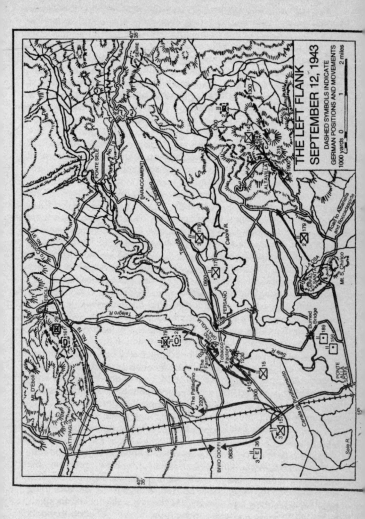

The Guards officers received first-class treatment from these front-line troops. The next morning an officer approached them while they were finishing a breakfast of coffee and black bread.

"Would you like to see where you were?" he asked.

He took the prisoners to an observation post that was just below the crest of the hills and showed them the panorama that was Salerno Bay. Philipson could hardly believe his eyes. There beneath him was the house they had attacked, and farther back behind the railroad embankment he could clearly see his own men—and all of this without the aid of binoculars. No wonder they were receiving such a pasting in the plain below.

Philipson, angry and bitter, was led away to start his two years as a prisoner of war. He felt the attack should never have been carried out without tank support. It was a disastrous mistake to attack across 300 yards of floodlit field without even the means of keeping the enemy's head down with supporting fire. Anthony Philipson also marveled that he had survived that terrible night attack when so many others were killed.

After the failures at Battipaglia and the Tobacco Factory it was decided to withdraw from this salient and so shorten and, it was hoped, strengthen the line. The Guards battalions, in particular, were in a horribly exposed position, for the Germans were pressing them on three sides. The Grenadiers spent the entire following day—Sunday, September 12—under increasing German pressure. The line was very thinly held in places and the country tailor-made for infiltration tactics, at which the panzer grenadiers were in any case so very good. The Germans showed courage and efficiency that gave the Guardsmen gloomy prospects for the following campaign.

Lieutenant Leeke spent a nervous day watching the great stands of tobacco in front of them and waiting for dusk and the chance to withdraw. He took a fighting patrol out at one stage to sweep the tobacco and, it was hoped, put the Germans off their stride. At the end of the sweep Guardsman Banham took a sniper's bullet through the shoulder. The bullet spread out when it hit his equipment, making a hole the size of a silver dollar just below his collarbone. Although they were in full view of the enemy, Leeke dropped his rifle, pulled out his commando knife, and cut away the remnants of Banham's equipment and shirt. He applied a field dressing to the wound and then scurried back while the platoon gave what covering fire it could against the unseen sniper.

Toward evening Leeke heard the sad news that Francis Wigram had been killed by a mortar bomb. The death of friends, Leeke felt, was always the worst part of war. He could stand the shelling, bear the sight of disfigured corpses, and resist fear of the enemy in an attack or on patrol. But something changes when someone very close is killed violently, suddenly, and unexpectedly. Somehow Leeke had never thought that Francis Wigram would be killed.

As soon as it got dark, the retreat began. First the 17-pounders were hooked on to their vehicles and pulled, creaking and jolting, on the rough ground back over the railway. They were followed by the 6-pounders, the company transport, and finally the tanks, a troop from B Squadron, the Greys. Each Sherman rumbled back along Grenadier Track up the bank over the crossing showing black and enormous against the evening sky.

Sitting in their trenches with packs on and clutching their weapons, the grenadiers, serving as rear guard, felt lonely and isolated. The Guardsmen looked toward Leeke, and he looked at his watch. The minutes dragged by, and suddenly the sound of heavy firing came from the right flank. "My God," thought Leeke, "the Germans have seen the tanks withdraw. They know we're retreating. We shall have to do it under fire." But the Brens and the Spandaus quieted down, and at last the time came to move. Leeke and his platoon moved out and then waited just over the level crossing as the counterattack platoon, just in case the Germans followed them. He stood there with the carrier platoon commander, who was covering the withdrawal. Men came trooping back in single file, Grenadiers and Coldstreams of the different battalions mixed together. Just at the top of Grenadier Track was a jeep with the commanding officer sitting motionless on the hood and occasionally looking at his watch. The men walked past him, calling out from time to time what company they belonged to.

At last no more came. Leeke got his platoon together and followed down the Grenadier Track. Midway they passed the Shermans standing silent sentinel and covering them as they moved to the concentration area. Leeke found he was back near the bridge where the half-tracks had shot up his platoon. Was it just 48 hours before?

They marched on a little farther and moved into an arable field, part tobacco and part tomato. The 6th Battalion, Grenadier Guards, was now the corps reserve.

In the words of their brigade commander, "There was very little to be done except to hold on at all costs to what we had got until further troops were landed, or until the presence in the vicinity of the Eighth Army made itself felt."

Chapter XX

Altavilla and the Sele–Calore Corridor

The tactics employed by the enemy during the four days of counterattack (Saturday to Tuesday, September 11–14) made full use of their advantage in position and mobility. Tanks and assault guns, closely supported by infantry in half-tracks, concentrated quickly at exposed parts of the line and made quick stabs. If a particular attack did not offer the opportunity for further exploitation, the enemy withdrew to his original position, re-formed, and moved off to strike in another direction. These were the classic tactics of blitzkrieg in the field, a formula that had worked before for the panzers.

The disaster that hit the American sector on Saturday, September 11, was in part caused by the fact that significant numbers of troops were advancing and therefore not in prepared defensive positions when the Germans struck.

The corps plan Dawley had devised was sound enough. He had three columns on the move. On the far left the 157th RCT had crossed the Sele River into the British sector and was to move inland and attack Eboli, which lay about 8 miles from the Sele. If the Americans could take the town, the German positions in and around Battipaglia might be exposed. Such a threat could be enough to pry the enemy from Battipaglia, and then the British in turn could threaten the German grip on Montecorvino.

On the right flank the Texans had taken Altavilla with deceptive ease and now were poised to swing on to Hill 424 and thus dominate the ground all around.

In the center Colonel Hutchins and the main force of the 179th RCT was to continue its advance up the Sele–Calore corridor to Ponte Sele, where they could cut Route 19 and the main German supply lines.

The vital ground in the American sector was the flood plain between the Sele and the Calore rivers. The plain forms a corridor of low ground starting at Serre, a village 12 miles inland that nestles at the foot of the hills. The corridor descends gently to the junction of the two rivers, just 5 miles from the sea. This was the obvious line of advance for any defender in launching a counterattack against a beachhead, yet its significance did not become apparent until the first troops were on the ground. Mark Clark and his Fifth Army staff had largely ignored the feature and never appreciated the importance of Persano as the key point in any defense against an armored thrust through the corridor. Persano was a hamlet squatting on top of a low hill that had a commanding view of the plain, particularly the crossing point over the Sele River. Instead they had looked beyond to Pointe Sele, the point where the two corps would link to complete the beachhead perimeter, the Americans coming through the high ground to the right from Altavilla, and the British completing the pincer movement by way of Battipaglia and Eboli.

Against such determined thrusts, the Germans were able to deploy only odds and ends of units. They were part of Von Doering's 79th Panzer Grenadier Regiment, together with some companies from the 3rd Parachute Regiment, the 26th Reconnaissance Battalion, and some of Ulich's group from the 29th Panzer Grenadier Division. Later in the day more of that division entered the fray with the arrival of the Krüger Battle Group and the remaining troops from the 79th Panzer Grenadiers.

During the night-long approach march of the 179th RCT on September 11-12 the first contact was established between the Thunderbirds and the 56th British Division.

Capt. Daniel B. Allen was the artillery liaison officer attached to the 2nd Battalion. The scouts of the leading companies had lost direction once they had crossed the Sele River, and the companies wandered around the area. It was a very dark night, and there were very few features that the scouts could use to check their position. In circumstances such as these, it is very easy to become disorientated and lost. It wasn't long before the battalion command group also became lost; it didn't have the faintest idea where it was or where the rifle companies were. A halt was called while the units sorted themselves out, so Captain Allen decided to make his own personal reconnaissance; Staff Sergeant Prickett, the battalion sergeant major, went with him. They set out, marching on a northwest compass bearing. Allen believed that they would link up eventually with one of the forward rifle companies.

After about 30 minutes during which the two men, having negotiated swamps, ditches, and hedgerows, had both come to repent of their rashness, they came to the highway. Allen believed they had come out too far to the west, so he turned back down Route 18 in the hope of striking the missing troops; he was not yet prepared to admit that he was hopelessly lost. Both men unslung their weapons and held them cocked and ready. The moon had set, and the night was now dark and so terribly still. Allen expected at any moment to run into one of two groups, either the forward company or a German patrol.

They came to a point where a side road entered the main road from the west. Allen stopped to get his bearings, but the night was so dark that he could see no more than a foot or two. As he stepped forward to cross the side-road entrance the most immense man he had ever seen appeared from nowhere, effectively immobilizing them merely by standing there. Allen guessed him to be over 6 feet, 5 inches in height and at least 250 pounds.

This darkly looming and menacing hulk instantly convinced Allen of the futility of either resistance or flight and as he mentally began the transformation to one of "Smiling Albert's" POWs, this terrifying figure spoke: "I say, chaps, have you seen the bloody Yanks around here?"

Allen heaved a great sigh of relief and then questioned the stranger. He had a magnificent beard and moustache, was dressed in British desert battle dress complete with a "tin saucer" helmet on his head. Speaking with a clear Scots accent he introduced himself as a captain in the reconnaissance regiment; his patrol of armored cars materialized out of the darkness to the sound of a piercing whistle. They swapped information, and Allen asked him the location of the British forces. He received a typically British answer about Battipaglia: "I don't really know who has it now. The Hun had it and we had it for a bit. In fact," he continued, "we have been in and out of it four or five times today. T'is really a bit of a bloody scrap, you know."

Allen gave him directions to the regimental headquarters, for all he had to do was retrace their steps, and the huge man climbed into his scout car; despite all its armor plate even this vehicle seemed to groan in protest. No wonder he was in the reconnaissance regiment, Allen thought for at a chance meeting in the dark in no-man's-land he certainly had an immediate and paralyzing effect on anyone he bumped into in the night.

The sky began to lighten with the dawn, and Allen and Sergeant Prickett hurried on down the road to find the rifle company. The two men had not gone very far before they were challenged by an alert sentry on point. They had found the forward rifle company. They rejoined the American lines just as the first streaks of light were appearing in the sky, which in turn provided the waiting Germans with the signal to begin the attack on the Americans in the corridor.

Colonel Hutchins and his command paid the price for neglecting Persano, for they walked into a trap. Once his column had passed, enemy machine-gun and mortar crews infiltrated into the little settlement. They opened fire on the support column of the 179th and so isolated the main body. Shortly afterward German antitank and field artillery batteries also moved into Persano, and these opened fire on the American tanks and tank destroyers that were still south of the crossing at the burned bridge over the Sele.

In the meantime the lead battalion of the column clashed with an enemy outpost line just a mile short of its objective at Ponte Sele. Hutchins ordered his battalions to move into an all-around defense. Company C of the 1st Battalion was deployed to defend its rear and dug in on open ground northeast of Persano. Even before it could complete its task and prepare for battle, a battalion of panzer grenadiers spearheaded by tanks and assault guns struck from Persano and overwhelmed the company. Hutchins called for his tanks and tank destroyers to come in support. It was then apparently that he learned these were still south of the Calore.

The Thunderbirds had fought through the Sicilian campaign and considered themselves by now a veteran formation, at least in comparison with the "T" Patchers from Texas. The Thunderbirds, however, were now about to receive an object lesson or two from veterans with four years of combat and who had hitherto proved unsurpassed in armor and infantry assault. The battle groups from the 29th Panzer Grenadiers had forgotten more about war than the Americans had experienced, and what the latter were now about to learn would be acquired the hard way.

Shermans from Company C, 753rd Tank Battalion, crossed the Calore at 0645 hours under fire together with tank destroyers and the guns of Battery A, 160th Field Artillery. They were determined to hold the crossing open. Later, in response to Hutchins' appeals for assistance, they launched an attack against Persano but were repulsed with heavy losses.

By late afternoon the main body of the 179th RCT was very hard pressed. Many of the companies were without water and food, and as the casualties increased, the aid station, filled to overflowing, came under shellfire too. The two batteries of the 160th Field Artillery were down to 10 rounds a gun, which Hutchins ordered saved as a final reserve. Small-arms ammunition was now in desperately short supply, so the order to "fix bayonets" was passed down the line.

Later in the afternoon the Krüger Battle Group arrived on the scene and launched its attack south from Ponte Sele. Hutchins and his forces had been outfought tactically and were completely surrounded. Nevertheless, they dug in and held on grimly; there was no thought of capture or capitulation.

Daylight faded, and the roar of battle dropped to a whisper, then died away. Hutchins regrouped the two battalions into a tight perimeter just a few miles east of Persano. There was nothing they could do except hoard what ammunition they had and wait for the next day.

The 3rd Battalion, which had split away during the first night to advance in the shadow of Hill 424 and Altavilla as a flank guard, had crossed the Calore, but later in the day it was stopped by the German defenses. After dark it fell back to the La Cosa Creek.

The left flank advance of the 157th Combat Team had proceeded well until it came upon a German battalion that had dug in and occupied another tobacco factory. The task force or combat group, which comprised two battalions of the 157th Infantry supported by a company of Shermans from the 191st Tank Battalion, moved along a gravel road that lead northeast from Highway 18 to Eboli. This road was of crucial importance to both sides. From the highway it runs across open fields until about 700 yards north of the tobacco factory where it drops sharply to the Grataglia Plain. Here the Eboli road meets a small track, which comes from Bivio Cioffi east on Highway 18, and a second one, which cuts east through the Grataglia to a crossing point over the Sele and on to Persano. The gravel road bends northeastward from these junctions, around a hill, and then rises into the broken country and on to Eboli.

The fight for this rise and the tobacco factory was to prove of great tactical significance, for whoever held the little hill commanded the Grataglia Plain and thus the river crossing. It also controlled access to the Sele–Calore corridor on the right and the main highway beyond. Route 19 joined Battipaglia with Eboli; it passed through the upper corridor and thence to Altavilla. This was the main supply route for the Germans attacking the U.S. VI Corps.

The Shermans had moved ahead of the plodding infantry, so the Shermans were the first to hit the Germans dug in at the tobacco factory, which consisted of five large concrete buildings constructed in a circle. Letting the tank company come close, the Germans suddenly pulled aside straw stacks in the fields, and doors in the main building opened to reveal the perfect ambush. Antitank guns and machine guns opened up a devastating fire; the range was so close that they could hardly miss, and within minutes seven Shermans were in flames. The remaining tanks fell back, and regrouped on the advancing infantry.

The battle raged for the remainder of the day and on into the evening. Supporting artillery kept the panzers pinned down, but well-sited mortars and machine guns held the American infantry at bay, and the attacks lost their momentum.

For the men in the 36th Division the day by contrast was relatively quiet. Patrols had moved out beyond Altavilla in the hope that they might find the 45th Division near Ponte Sele, but they found nothing. The other two battalions of the 142nd were in position south of Altavilla and near Albanella, but except for some desultory fire they too had a quiet day.

Close to Paestum the engineers finished the airstrip, but trigger-happy American gunners from the defending anti-aircraft batteries shot down the first couple of British Spitfires that came in to land. General Walker had Colonel Wilson, who commanded the attached anti-aircraft units, in for a little talk. Wilson left ashen-faced and tight-lipped, but there were no more accidents. In the afternoon two squadrons of P-38s from the U.S. 31st Fighter Group flew in from Sicily; there were no incidents.

General Clark, who was ashore throughout most of the day, became increasingly concerned by the evidence of mounting pressure against the units of the 45th Infantry in the Sele–Calore corridor. He had also received a request from McCreery to move in more troops to close the gap in the corps boundary beyond the Sele River. At this time Dawley had very few men in reserve, but in answer to his general's appeals he sent a battalion of the 36th Engineer Regiment across the Sele. The engineers moved to the left of the 157th RCT and took up a defensive position just below Bivio Cioffi. The next morning patrols established tenuous contact with the British on the right.

The disturbing developments in the beachhead were paralleled by events offshore as the Luftwaffe launched a maximum effort against the massed Allied shipping. General Balck, the XIV Panzer Corps commander, had urged Von Vietinghoff to persuade the Luftwaffe to concentrate on the Allied warships. The German soldiers were convinced that the elimination of the devastating Allied naval gunfire was the prime requisite for success in their drive against the beachhead and through to the sea.

In the first three days of the invasion the Luftwaffe had launched more than 450 missions by fighters and fighter-bombers, while the medium Dorniers and Heinkels had flown 100 nighttime sorties. So far they had sunk four transports and seven landing craft and damaged many more. The only major warship casualty, however, the monitor H.M.S. *Erebus*, had been disabled by a mine and had left the beachhead on the evening of the first day. The cruisers and destroyers that remained, together with the other monitor, *Roberts*, were continuing to perform valiant service for the troops onshore. The effects of a naval salvo of 6-inch shells landing on a tank concentration is enhanced by the utter frustration of the enemy, for he cannot fight back against such a fire.

An equally important target for the Luftwaffe was the command ship *Ancon*. Her size, bulk, and forest of aerials made her stand out against the rest of the fleet. It didn't take much to conclude that her presence in the anchorage betrayed the location of the headquarters of the Fifth Army. The *Ancon* also served as the fighter direction ship, from which the air defense for the ships assembled in Salerno Bay was controlled. This function alone made her a valuable prize for the Luftwaffe.

General Balck's request for Luftwaffe assistance went all the way up the chain of command to the Führer's headquarters itself. Hitler ordered the squadron that had launched the attack on the Italian flagship *Roma* to turn their full attention and their radio-controlled bombs to the crowded anchorage at Salerno.

The Luftwaffe had two models of the radio-controlled bomb, a forerunner of the cruise missile. Both had fins and rocket boosters to allow corrections to the flight path. The difference between them was in speed and range. One type had a range of 8½ miles and a speed of 570 miles per hour; the second was 100 miles per hour faster, but its range was only a little over 3 miles.

Both weapons were armor-piercing, had a delayed fuse, and weighed 1,400 kilograms; they were to all intents and purposes invulnerable. Some Allied government scientists advanced the theory that as the weapons were radio-controlled, electronic impulses, such as those emitted by an electric razor, would be enough to knock them off course. Electric razors proved no defense. Neither did anti-aircraft guns or conventional fighters. The weapon was released from the mother plane at about 18,000 to 21,000 feet, well above the effective ceiling of shipborne AA and the Spitfire. Only the Lightning could intercept the parent, a Dornier 217 twin-engined bomber that had just about come to the end of its useful service. Like the venerable B-52s of today, however, a "stand-off" capability gave the aged planes a new lease of life, for it allowed them to release their weapon some distance from the target and its defenses. The bomb gave off a thin trail of smoke, which allowed the bomb aimer to guide it onto a target, and even though it had only the slightest of maneuvering capabilities, it was invincible, since its speed was too great for larger warships to avoid through evasive action.

The first warning of the menace to come from this newfangled weapon was at about 0935 hours on Saturday, September 11. A flight of enemy bombers was engaged at a height of over 20,000 feet when a smoking object was seen to fall out of the formation. Gunnery officers took it to be a crashing plane until it hit the sea with a frightful explosion just 15 feet off the starboard bow of Rear Admiral Davidson's flagship, the cruiser U.S.S. *Philadelphia*. The explosion close-tested every rivet in the 12,000-ton cruiser and caused considerable damage, though she was still operational.

Mark Clark and Admiral Hewitt both witnessed the second attack, for it is likely that the intended target was the *Ancon*. The Luftwaffe repeated a tactic from their first attempt when a flight of three FW-190s came screaming in at mast height, raking the decks with machine-gun fire while the same Dorniers circled high overhead. Some 500 yards off the *Ancon's* stern the cruiser U.S.S. *Savannah* was threading her way at 15 knots through the mass of ships to take up her station to bombard the shore.

Those on the bridge of the *Ancon* were watching the *Savannah*, a magnificent sight in the morning sunlight, when they saw a smoking bomb directly above topple over and dive steeply at terrific speed into the cruiser.

The bomb struck directly on the top of No. 3 turret, penetrated the 2-inch-thick armor plate, which is all the Brooklyn class cruisers had, and went all the way to the handling room deep in the bowels of the ship. When the bomb detonated, the force of the explosion blew part of the bottom out of the *Savannah*.

For Clark and others, the venting of the explosion was plainly visible along the port side waterline abreast of the forward turrets; it opened a seam in her side, and seawater flooded in and extinguished several boilers. The bows gradually settled until the foredeck was nearly awash while the stern came clear of the water.

A hundred men or more were killed outright, for the most part in the turrets and handling rooms. The explosion also wiped out the main damage control station and many of its party.

Discipline and seamanship saved the *Savannah*. While expert repair crews were found from the salvage tugs that clustered around the stricken cruiser, her own men were able to correct the list by pumping fuel from the fore to the aft bunkers.

At the end of a very long day the *Savannah,* under her own steam and escorted by a clutch of destroyers, left for Malta, where more thorough repairs could be completed. As she limped clear of the anchorage the ordeal was just beginning for four members of her crew. They were the operators who manned the small auxiliary radio room, a compartment located deep in the bowels of the ship and some decks below where the bomb exploded.

The compartments above, beneath, and around the radio room were flooded, and the water was shoulder deep in the "radio shack." The men there could not swim out because the door was blocked by wreckage. There could be no hope of rescue until the cruiser reached dock and her flooded compartments were pumped dry. The plight of these men was known because a single voice pipe 2½ inches thick connected them to the bridge.

The men were to remain entombed for the four days it took the *Savannah* to reach Malta. The voice pipe was used to pump fresh air into the compartment; drinking water and some liquid foods were also passed down to the trapped men.

The Luftwaffe struck again on Monday afternoon, and this time their target was the British 6-inch-gun cruiser H.M.S. *Uganda*. She maneuvered hard to avoid the missile, but it caught the ship aft, and its velocity was such that the bomb penetrated seven decks and exploded *beneath* the ship. Thirteen hundred tons of water flooded in and 16 men died, three of her main engines were put out of action, and she had a 30-foot-long split in her keel. The crippled cruiser was towed out of the battle by the U.S. salvage tug *Narragansett*, bound for Malta.

It was hardly surprising that the Luftwaffe was under orders to take out the cruisers. On Sunday night alone, the U.S.S. *Philadelphia* had fired almost 1,000 rounds of 6-inch shells on such targets as tank and troop concentrations, main road junctions, and suspected ammunition dumps. The U.S.S. *Boise* took over on Monday morning and by lunchtime had fired 600 rounds. In the British sector three light cruisers, a monitor, and destroyers performed an equally valuable service.

What is less easy to understand is why the Luftwaffe also turned their attention to the hospital ships. At dawn the British Red Cross ships *Newfoundland* and *Leinster* came under attack. They were fully illuminated, properly marked, and standing well out to sea, as laid down in the Geneva Convention.

Damage to the *Leinster* was superficial; however, the *Newfoundland* was bombed and set on fire. Salvage crews fought the blaze all that day but in the end had to concede defeat, and she was eventually scuttled.

Though the 1st Battalion of the 142nd Infantry had enjoyed a respite in and around Altavilla, their positions were none too strong. The battalion commander, Lieutenant Colonel Barron, had deployed his troops as best he could, but the scrub-covered, terraced slopes, dissected as they were by ravines and gullies, provided ample cover for those skilled in infiltration. The battalion was already thin on the ground, and Hill 424 was a weak position as long as the unnumbered hill to the south remained unoccupied; yet there were not enough men available to hold both hills.

Throughout Saturday night, men from the 2nd Battalion, 15th Panzer Grenadiers began to infiltrate through the ravines and onto Hill 424. At daybreak on Sunday morning, the Germans opened up a withering fire from so many directions that the companies became totally confused. They could not call for artillery support, since in most cases the Germans were inside the American perimeter. To make matters worse, the German artillery laid a heavy concentration on the summit of 424, where the enemy had yet to infiltrate and where there were only Americans. It also severed the communications that led to the battalion command post in Altavilla.

Barron radioed through to the regimental commander for assistance. Colonel Martin had the men available and indeed tried to beg, borrow, or steal the necessary trucks from both division and corps to rush a battalion to Altavilla, but there was none to be had at such short notice. Barron's men were on their own.

The fighting grew steadily more bitter, and the Germans drove a wedge through the defenses, splitting the battalion. Colonel Barron went out to lead a counterattack aimed at restoring the situation but was cut down by enemy fire. By midafternoon the Germans were into Altavilla itself, and the Texans in small groups fell back from the town and the neighboring hills.

One group came out of Altavilla under the command of a popular young officer named Johnny Sprague, the battalion Intelligence officer. He had been a football star at Southern Methodist University and had played in the Rose Bowl before the war. The group was pinned down by a machine gun, and try as they might, nobody could locate the enemy's position.

"Watch for it now! Locate it!" Sprague ordered. In what must rank as one of the most remarkable acts of self-sacrifice, he deliberately stood up and exposed himself to the enemy. The machine-gun burst cut Sprague down, and he was dead before he hit the ground. But the men with him had spotted the machine gun's position. Maddened by the sacrifice, they returned the fire and stormed forward and killed the enemy at bayonetpoint. Sprague was awarded a Silver Star posthumously.

General Walker detailed Colonel Martin to recapture Altavilla without delay. He gave him the 143rd Regimental Combat Team, though by then it had only one of its three battalions available. The 1st Battalion had already moved to reinforce Darby's rangers, who were fighting their own little war in Chiunzi Pass, and the 2nd Battalion was still needed in divisional reserve. To beef up the infantry element, Walker gave Martin the 3rd Battalion of the 142nd Infantry and, as a last resort, the survivors of the 1st Battalion, those who had just been defeated at Altavilla. There were perhaps 250 men left, and many of these were badly shaken by their experiences.

It took Martin the whole afternoon and evening to issue orders and get the battalions moving. In part this was because the Americans were afraid to use radio in the clear and didn't have sufficient trained code operators, and also because the division was still critically short of transportation; so the battalions had to march to their new positions. Long delays were also the result of the division's inexperience, for it takes a professionally competent and experienced team of staff officers to produce new orders suddenly and change course in midstream. Such experience can be learned only the hard way.

The loss of Altavilla to the Germans meant that the enemy could now dominate the corridor and thus compromise the positions held by the

Thunderbirds. The 179th RCT had spent Saturday night in considerable anxiety, ready to make its last stand against overwhelming odds, but come the dawn the Germans did not launch the anticipated attack. Instead, the Americans reached them first. At 0945 hours, although the road through was still raked by enemy fire, Brig. Gen. Raymond S. McLain, who commanded the division's artillery, climbed into a 6-by-6 loaded with 105mm shells and ran the gauntlet to the beleaguered force.

Clearly the Germans had no idea how close they had come to defeating the combat team, but the renewed gunfire from the artillery lines must have convinced the panzers that the Americans still had plenty of fight left in them, for the Germans quietly pulled back and out of Persano, to Eboli.

As the Germans withdrew, the route reopened, and the wounded were evacuated at once. The Shermans and tank destroyers hugging the northern bank of the Calore took the depleted 1st Battalion into Persano, where the force dug in once more. As long as the Germans were in Altavilla, there could be no further advance down the corridor. Neither was the combat team in a fit condition for any immediate resumption of the advance. The battle had resulted in 15 percent of the command being casualties.*

Across the Sele, the 157th Combat Team made a second attempt to capture the tobacco factory. The Shermans and tank destroyers, together with the field artillery, put down a blistering barrage onto the factory behind which the rifle companies stormed into the attack. After an hour of vicious combat, the Germans pulled back and left the Thunderbirds in possession of the tobacco factory. Not for long, however; within an hour the enemy had regrouped and thrown their forces into the fray once more. A full battalion of panzer grenadiers with Panzer Mark IVs in front forced the Americans out of the factory. For the rest of the day the 157th Combat Team was locked in a seesaw struggle for this vital piece of ground; but as night fell the Germans conceded and withdrew. This could only be temporary, however, for as long as the tobacco factory remained in American hands, the Germans dare not risk any move into the corridor; the crossing of the Sele west of Persano lay directly under the American guns.

Later that afternoon Clark visited Dawley at the corps command post, which was now located amid temple ruins in Paestum, and reviewed the situation. Clark was most concerned about the gap that still existed on the left between Bivio Cioffi and the British at St. Lucia. He had toured the front that morning and was convinced that the Germans must have realized there was a gap and would soon concentrate their efforts at this weak spot. Clark saw the struggle for Persano as clear evidence of the enemy's intentions; the hills above Altavilla seemed of less significance.

What also concerned Clark was that Dawley was not reading the battle the same way he did. Dawley looked at the battle in the traditional sense, and his

---

*The 179th RCT suffered 38 men killed and 121 officers and men missing. A further 363 officers and men were wounded and evacuated.

attention immediately concentrated on the high ground. In times past, possession of the high ground was the key to battle. So the corps commander was far more concerned about Altavilla, which *he* regarded as the key to the battle, together with the struggle for the tobacco factory. The latter also occupied a low knoll and commanded the approaches into the corridor. To this end, as we have seen, Dawley had already ordered General Walker to retake Altavilla at the first opportunity.

What happened next was the worst of both worlds. Clark should have countermanded the attack on Altavilla, but he did not. Perhaps his own inexperience of combat and the oft-quoted "fog of war" are in part to blame. At this stage of the battle things were happening thick and fast, crowding in on the commanders, and demanding instant decisions. So Clark, instead of resolving the differences with Dawley, concentrated his mind on the areas of the battle that reflected his own anxieties. Clark issued two sets of orders to his corps commander. First, he instructed that all units in the 45th Infantry Division were to cross the Sele and deploy in the line from Bivio Cioffi to St. Lucia, thereby covering the gap with the British. Second, he ordered Dawley to ensure that Persano and the gateway to the corridor was adequately covered. Dawley was equally determined to continue the battle for Altavilla, and this he could do, since his army commander had only disagreed, not forbidden.

The American corps, which had barely sufficient troops to defend the ground they were already holding, were thus about to assume responsibility for even more terrain and to march in three different directions to fulfill the orders.

Clark left the meeting profoundly disturbed by Dawley. By this stage he had no confidence in his corps commander and should have relieved him on the spot. The British were coping and needed little attention from Clark, who in turn could have assumed the responsibility for the tactical control of the battlefield in the American sector. Clark was much nearer the truth in his reading of the German intentions than was Dawley. The main German assault on the Americans was to come through the corridor and Persano. Had they found a gap in the line between the British and American corps, then obviously that would have been exploited as the axis of attack.

Clark's instructions and Dawley's persistence at Altavilla placed an enormous strain on an already overstretched 36th Division, for Walker would now be responsible for the defense of 22 miles of front, from the foothills around Ogliastro and Agropoli in the south to the Sele and Calore rivers. This is an exceedingly long front for a division to hold even under the most favorable circumstances. In addition, Walker had to launch an offensive operation into a mountain position at the same time.

We need also bear in mind that the division was hardly well endowed with infantry for what had already proved to be an infantry campaign. The division had landed at Salerno with nine battalions of infantry. Walker had lost one complete battalion to the rangers in Sorrento (together, of course, with the artillery and support to make it a viable combat team). The remaining battalions were all understrength, and one had been so badly mauled and demoralized that it was no longer a combat-effective battalion. In practical terms Walker had seven weak battalions to meet all the commitments against an enemy who had already shown themselves to be resourceful, brave, and professionally superior.

Walker protested to his corps commander that he could not spare the troops to expand the American sector of the beachhead, as his superiors demanded. Dawley assured him that a battalion would more than suffice to meet the needs at Persano! Dawley's reasoning was that once Altavilla was taken the Germans would not dare to advance into the corridor, with the Americans holding the high ground on both flanks. Thus a battalion in Persano would have no threat to its right, and the battalions of the 45th Infantry would be immediately across the river to its left.

Dawley showed Walker a position about 1½ *miles from Persano* that the battalion was to hold. Dawley did not even appreciate that the significant feature was the higher ground at Persano itself. Neither did Dawley tell Walker that the 45th Division had been in trouble in that very spot earlier and had come close to disaster with *two* battalions and a full combat team with support elements. Dawley maintained afterward that Troy Middleton, the 45th Division commander, had *not* informed him of the epic battle just fought by the 179th RCT. However, neither did Walker ask Dawley which troops had held the ground previously or what their fate had been. It was an obvious question to ask, yet the fog of war and the pressures on commanders experiencing for the first time a battle at this level of responsibility contributed to the errors now being made.

Blame for the tragedy that was about to befall one battalion of Texans in particular, and the failure of the corps battle plan in general, can be apportioned to all the senior commanders, though some were clearly more culpable than others.

Walker ordered Lieutenant Colonel Jones and his 2nd Battalion of the 143rd Infantry, the divisional reserve, to move from its position at the base of Mount Chirico to the Persano line. Walker did not warn Jones that he was marching into trouble, but he did promise that the artillery, which was then deploying in support of the renewed offensive at Altavilla, would cover the Persano position as well.

So the Sunday evening in the American corps once again echoed to the sound of tramping boots as Jones and his battalion set out on the 12-mile approach to Persano and as the Thunderbirds crossed the Sele to link up with the British. Colonel Martin had his battalions on the move as they prepared to launch a two-pronged attack to recover Altavilla and the high ground.

At just about the same time, another party was driving into the beachhead, from the south. They were the first arrivals from Montgomery's Eighth Army. Unfortunately, they were two carloads of war correspondents, not fighting soldiers. Alan Moorehead and his colleagues, frustrated at the slow progress in Calabria and anxious to be where the action and the news were, in Salerno, had taken off into the hills alone and largely unarmed. It took them two days of avoiding occasional patrols and negotiating ways around blown bridges, and a night in a convent en route, before they crossed into the beachhead.*

*Moorehead's own most excellent account of his adventures is to be found in his book *Eclipse* (London: Hamish Hamilton, 1947).

Chapter XXI

Black Monday

Altavilla

Von Vietinghoff scented victory for his Tenth Army. He had by now become aware of the gap between the British and American corps and assumed it had a purpose. He concluded that the Allied Fifth Army had of its own volition formed itself into two pockets as the first step toward complete evacuation of the beachhead. Over the next couple of days, the Army commander interpreted every event as further evidence to support his argument. Hence, when it was reported that another convoy had arrived in the bay, this was believed to be the additional ships necessary to withdraw the troops.

On the German side also, the arrival during the day of the 26th Panzers at the beachhead made more men available to hurl into the action and swung the balance even farther in their favor.

For the German high command, however, to allow the Allies simply to withdraw was not enough. Salerno provided them with the opportunity to inflict a humiliating defeat on the Allies. If Von Vietinghoff could destroy the Fifth Army on the beaches and prevent it from escaping, then such a lesson might further postpone what Berlin feared most, the big invasion across the English Channel.

Von Vietinghoff pressed his corps commanders to launch immediate and massive offensives against the pockets of resistance.

The Fifth Army was in trouble. Clark was very much aware of this as he toured the beachhead defenses on that brilliantly sunny Monday morning. The main problem for his forces was the one that he had in part realized all along, namely that the bickering and parsimony of the Allied high command had forced him to launch Salerno on a shoestring. The controlling factor was not the quality of his troops but their quantity. There were not enough landing ships to allow him to beat the Germans in the race to build up the forces in the area. Von Vietinghoff, with all his difficulties, could reinforce and resupply his defenders on land more quickly than could Mark Clark by sea.

The day before, Clark and his staff had said goodbye to the *Ancon* and established their headquarters ashore. Admiral Hewitt breathed a sigh of relief and sent the headquarters ship back to North Africa; she was too big a target to have in Salerno Bay for a day longer than necessary. The U.S.S. *Biscayne* now assumed her responsibilities for fighter control and direction.

The Fifth Army staff had initially chosen a large mansion, the Bellilli Palace, for their headquarters. It was more a mansion than a palace and lay secluded in a grove of pine trees just off Route 18, about a mile southwest of the juncture of the Sele and Calore rivers. The battle had passed it by, and it was relatively intact. But Clark took an instant dislike to the pink-painted château. It was too exposed and near the front line; it was too conspicuous. So he took a few of his staff officers and established a personal or advanced command post along Highway 18 and nearer to Paestum. The staff took over a large house that was surrounded by high brush and woods. The general's converted Dodge pickup was parked on the grounds. It served as his mobile home and gave him privacy and seclusion away from the busy headquarters.

The general was glad to be ashore. Besides the inconvenience of commuting to battle, he believed that his presence permanently on the beachhead would be good for the morale of the troops. Here he could see things for himself and confer with his subordinates at all times.

Clark's choice of the American corps to settle in has been a source of speculation ever since. Some observers have claimed that it was because he already had his doubts over General Dawley, but this isn't the case. Instead it was more a reflection of some of the subtleties of coalition warfare.*

Even with this new location ashore, headquarters communications were poor. There was only one good road, and that was Route 18, most of which around Battipaglia was now in the hands of the Wehrmacht. The only way Clark could commute between the corps was either by a tortuous succession of jeep tracks or, as was more often the case, by fast patrol boat.

On this Monday morning Clark stood outside the small, sparsely furnished half-ton pickup that served as his "mobile home" and contemplated the need to bring reinforcements onto the beachhead with minimum delay.

General Alexander had first informed Mark Clark on the evening of

---

*In my interview with him in Charleston, South Carolina, in August 1981, General Clark explained it this way: "With Dawley I could be brutally frank, but with McCreery I had always to be tactful and discreet." It all came down to nationality. McCreery was British, and so was Clark's superior, Alexander, and both had far more combat experience than the Fifth Army commander. General Clark always warned McCreery when he planned to visit. "If there's any reason you are busy, I won't come," he would say.

September 8 that the 82nd Airborne Division was available for Salerno after all.* During the first three days of the landings Clark and his staff considered various ways to use the division. At first he thought in terms of resurrecting his scheme to drop them at Capua to hold the bridges over the Volturno, but the failure to break out of the beachhead by the end of the second day caused him to discard such an option.

A second contingency was planned in sufficient detail to allow for a warning order to be sent to Ridgway and his division in Sicily. Clark had discussed with McCreery the possibility of using the airborne troops to clear what had become known as the "Sorrento barrier." After all, the rangers were not in the right place, German supplies and reinforcements were pouring through the Nocera defile, and Clark needed to open up the route into Naples as soon as possible. Clark asked for Ridgway to prepare an operation to land a combat team on the beaches near Torre Annunziata and Castellammare, on the northern edge of the peninsula and in the *defended Bay of Naples*. In response to these requests the 325th Glider Infantry began to embark on LSTs immediately, where they stayed until the ships eventually sailed (for Maiori) on September 15.

On September 11 Clark sent a message to Ridgway a second time. Clark wanted two airborne operations prepared. The first was to be a battalion drop on Avellino, an important German communications center inland from Salerno. The paratroops were to interdict enemy supply routes and shoot up convoys. A second drop was of a three-battalion combat team, to be dropped somewhere north of Naples, to cause mayhem in that area. On September 12 Clark asked that the operations be postponed until Monday evening, by which time he believed the British would be in a position to break through the Cava defile.

The use and misuse of airborne formations was one of the vexing questions that afflicted both the Allies and the Axis throughout the war. An airborne division was expensive. It was a division of specialists, an elite formation that was costly to recruit, train, and maintain. It seemed wrong to leave such a division on the sidelines during a battle, even if there did not seem to be a place for their special talents in the engagement. The result was that invariably they were squandered and abused and their precious talents wasted on hasty enterprises, of which those listed above are good examples. Clark was typical of those commanding generals who were really unsure of how they should use such a resource until the need became blindingly obvious.

Neither was Alexander, his Army group commander, entirely blameless. From his headquarters in Syracuse he pestered Clark for his intentions with regard to the 82nd Airborne.

---

*Mark Clark, *Calculated Risk* (London: George G. Harrap & Co., 1951); also my interview with General Clark, who claims he was first told of the 82nd Airborne Division being available on September 12. There is ample documentary evidence on both sides of the Atlantic to contradict the general.

With Battipaglia and Altavilla already in German hands and enemy pressure building at Vietri and Salerno, Clark finally decided to use the 82nd Airborne simply to reinforce his beachhead. In this he anticipated German intentions, for he called on Ridgway before the main offensive came later in the day. Clark wrote a personal letter to Ridgway saying that the fighting had indeed taken a turn for the worse and that it had now become a "touch-and-go affair." He wrote:

> Dear Matt,
>   I know it takes you thirty days to make up your mind where you'll drop that precious 82nd Division of yours, but I'm in trouble and I want you, I'm relying upon you to carry these instructions out exactly as follows. I want first a combat team to drop tonight in this drop zone on this map which is as close to the beach as we can get it for protection. I guarantee that nobody will shoot up your planes like they did in Sicily.* I will have officers briefed at every AA site and on every ship. I will guarantee that even if they come and bomb the hell out of us nothing will answer. I want the next combat team to the DZ on the following night and I want you to come with it and the next night I want the third. I know you can do this.
>
>   Wayne

By this time an Army cooperation squadron, which was used for the direction and observation of artillery fire, had a few planes operating from the rough dirt strip close to Paestum that had been completed by the engineers. One of Clark's staff officers brought Capt. Jacob R. Hamilton, a pilot, to the general's command post.

"Do you know where General Ridgway is?" Clark asked.

"Yes, sir," Hamilton said. "His headquarters is on a dirt strip at Licata in Sicily."

Clark gave him the folded message and said, "General Ridgway. Personal. His eyes only. Get this to him, son."

When Hamilton approached Licata he called up the control tower and told them he had a message for Ridgway. The tower replied that the general had just taken off in a Dakota; so the young pilot opened his throttle and gave chase. Hamilton caught up with the C-47, and flew alongside, flapping his wings to draw the pilot's attention. The Dakota turned back, and both planes landed at Licata, where Hamilton handed the note to General Ridgway.

The general read the note and then took out his own pen and wrote: "Dear Wayne, Message received, can do. Matt."

Hamilton flew back to Paestum and delivered the reply to General Clark. Clark sent staff officers to ensure that every AA gun site would be silent from 2100 hours that evening, while liaison officers were instructed to inform the navy gunners on the ships at sea.

In the meantime, other men were detailed to prepare the drop zone. The

---

*This is a reference to the disaster that overtook the airborne divisions in the invasion of Sicily when the Allied ships opened fire, shooting down 27 troop-carrying Dakotas. A second operation three nights later had a similar reception from the fleet.

site that Clark had chosen was five miles north of Agropoli in an area of flat land between the sea and the coastal highway. It measured just 1,200 yards long and 800 yards wide. Soldiers set out cans filled with sand to form the letter T. After dark these would be filled with gasoline and lit.

Ridgway earmarked the 2nd Battalion, 504th Parachute Infantry for the first mission. The only way in which the operation could be carried out in the time available was by using the staging and loading plans prepared for the Capua operation.

Ralph Jetton, a private first class in the headquarters company of the 2nd Battalion, was bodyguard to Maj. Edward Wellams, the battalion's executive officer. The men were gathered together and briefed by their commanding officer. He told them that the 36th Division was having a rough time and was in danger of losing the beachhead. Ralph Jetton had a brother in the 36th Division who, unbeknownst to Ralph, was in deep trouble in Altavilla.

Colonel Martin's plans to retake Altavilla were being confounded by the tenacity of German resistance. The 3rd Battalion, 142nd Infantry tried all day to advance along the ridge from Albanella but could make no progress against fierce resistance. However, an attack launched from the base of the hill by the 3rd Battalion, 143rd Infantry achieved some success and at last broke into the town after advancing behind a tremendous artillery barrage, though it too had suffered grievously. Martin sent Company K into Altavilla to take up defensive positions, while the remainder re-formed in readiness for the second phase of the operation, the advance on Hill 424. These preparations took longer than was expected, and the delay cost the attack its momentum. Before the Americans could move out, the Germans yet again struck first. Behind their stunning concentration of mortar and artillery fire, they launched their own counterattack. Caught in the open, the Americans suffered heavily and were gradually forced to give ground and leave Company K behind in Altavilla.

Technical sergeant Kelly won the Medal of Honor that evening. As Company K was surrounded in the town, Kelly with a small group was caught on the third floor of a building that looked out onto the main square. He fired his BAR until the barrel got so hot the shells wouldn't go through it, and then somehow he got hold of a light machine gun, which he fired until he ran out of ammunition. All that remained was a supply of 60mm mortar shells, though what they were doing on the third floor of a building in the middle of the town has never been explained. Kelly took the ammunition, which was high-explosive, and pulled the first safety pin. In normal usage the second pin is released when the shell strikes the bottom of the mortar barrel as it is projected out of the tube. Kelly didn't have a mortar barrel, so he rammed the base of the shell hard on the stone floor until the pin popped out; then he lobbed the shells out onto the Germans beneath.* Kelly later made good his own escape and got back to the American lines.

Further tragedy struck that evening when the already depleted 1st Battal-

*Kelly's claim to this unorthodox method of firing a mortar shell was carefully authenticated before the award was confirmed. The press dubbed him "Commando Kelly, the one-man army."

ion, 142nd Infantry, which had been held in reserve, was ordered forward into the fray at Altavilla. At about 1715 hours, salvoes of friendly artillery fire landed along the length of the column as it moved through a gully or ravine to the south of Altavilla. The column disintegrated as the Americans fled into the surrounding countryside in search of cover. Panic spread as they tried to outrace the bursting shells and each other, shedding arms and equipment as they ran. Some helped the slightly wounded away from the scene, and a few officers tried to stem the tide and rally their men. It was not until midnight that order could be restored and the battalion, or rather what was left, could be regrouped and re-formed. A similar fate had befallen the 8th Battalion, Royal Fusiliers when they were blasted by their own artillery.

General Walker was forward and seeing things for himself. He had received a report that German infantry had crossed the Calore just north of Altavilla in considerable strength and was infiltrating around the left flank of the 3rd Battalion, 143rd Infantry, even as it tried to re-form for another attempt on the town. Walker met with the combat team's senior commanders at their temporary headquarters in a deserted farmhouse below the ridge. There was Colonel Martin; Lt. Col. Pete Green, who commanded the 132nd Field Artillery; and the CO of the 751st Tank Battalion. While they discussed the operation, events took a turn for the worse as the German pressure increased and the left flank started to fold.

Walker had no troops in reserve. He believed that there was only one thing to do and no time to clear the orders with higher authority. Walker ordered Martin to break off the attack and fall back behind La Cosa Creek. The little stream, which roughly paralleled the coast in the divisional sector for some 8 miles, would now become the front line. Walker then went immediately to Dawley and explained the situation. The corps commander readily concurred with Walker's decisions and ordered an immediate withdrawal to the new line. There the Americans would make their last stand.

Walker and Dawley went on to a meeting with General Clark. It was about nine in the evening when Walker hurried back to his own divisional command post. There was much to be done if the line was to be reconnoitered and occupied before dawn.

Walker's orders to the division were sharp and to the point, as one would expect from such a master tactician. He divided the division's front into three sectors and placed a brigadier general in command of each sector. This was because each sector would have a mixed or all-arms task force assigned to it, which Walker clearly felt should be under the command of experienced and senior officers. The three colonels who had hitherto been in command of the regimental combat teams—Martin, Forsythe, and Werner—he now appointed as the seconds-in-command to the task forces. By all accounts it was most unusual to supersede the division's senior fighting commanders. The official histories give the same explanation as does Walker, who believed they were showing signs of fatigue and strain; and this after only five days of battle! As we shall see, after Salerno a number of officers in the division were relieved of their command.

A further explanation offered to me for this extraordinary move was that the three colonels (who were the equivalent of brigade commanders in a British division) were used to exercising direct command only over the three infantry battalions in their regiment. This explanation has little validity, however, since units of armor, artillery, tank destroyers, and engineers were under their command in battle to form the regimental combat team.

I believe the real problem was that Salerno was the division's first experience of war. The staff and subordinate commanders at all levels in the division had trained and learned their work on exercises. They now had to do it in battle, and what often looks good on paper can appear awful in reality. Lack of experience, in turn, placed an additional burden on the regimental commanding officers. Later in the European campaign they would be able to leave their staff to get on with the job, but not yet, not at Salerno, where it was all so new and confusing, so terrifying.

The United States Army has always been bureaucratically top-heavy in command. In every theater of war there were too many senior officers doing too little. The British had experienced a similar thing in the early years of the Western Desert campaign where, in the words of Winston Churchill, "never had so few been commanded by so many." When the crisis comes, the response is to pack the trouble spot with senior officers. This is what Walker did on the La Cosa line at Salerno. The moment of crisis was upon the division, and Walker did not have complete confidence in the capabilities of his regimental commanders at this stage in the battle.

The brigadier generals were "Willie" Wilbur, who had won the Medal of Honor in North Africa; "Iron Mike" O'Daniell, who had already proved himself to be a brilliant and resourceful officer; and Otto Lange, the division's deputy commander. Only the latter was found wanting, and when Walker came upon him the next morning asleep at the side of the road, he relieved him of his command and appointment.

The Corridor

The Americans had failed at Altavilla, but in the Sele–Calore corridor the situation came close to disaster that Monday afternoon. Firmly convinced that the Allies were about to evacuate the beachhead, Von Vietinghoff ordered the XIV Panzer Corps to assemble all available forces for an attack south of Eboli. The objective was to disrupt and destroy the orderly evacuation.

A battalion of the 71st Panzer Grenadier Regiment from Battle Group Krüger with a dozen Mark IV Panzers as spearhead, together with a new formation named the Kleine Limberg Battle Group,* struck the 1st Battallion of the 157th Infantry in the tobacco factory. The American battalion had

---

*The Kleine Limberg Battle Group—Hauptmann (Captain) Kleine Limberg commanded the 16th Engineers Battalion—comprised the 16th Engineer Battalion; the 2nd Battery, 16th Artillery Regiment; and a company of the 26th Reconnaissance Battalion.

not recovered from its bitter struggle for the factory on the previous day. Now the panzers punched a hole through to the command post, and the combat team lost all control and cohesion. Despite some dogged resistance, the Germans eased the Thunderbirds aside. Moving close to the Sele, they "kicked open the door" and struck deep into the corridor.

At about 1600 hours the Kleine Limberg Battle Group, by now heavily reinforced, encountered the 2nd Battalion, 143rd Infantry. This battalion had been Walker's divisional reserve at Mount Chirico, but they had moved to the Persano sector to meet Dawley's request for a battalion to fill the gap left by the 179th RCT of the 45th Infantry Division.

The 2nd Battalion, 143rd Infantry had done little to strengthen its position other than to deploy its antitank guns and hastily lay a few mines in front of the battalion's position. Why hadn't they done more? It is hard to explain other than by inexperience on the part of the officers and men, fatigue after a long and grueling march of some 12 miles, coupled with an optimistic and complacent approach to war. It was 1943, and the Allies were now used to winning. The little bit of the war this battalion had witnessed showed Germans in retreat. Colonel Jones had earlier in the day sent out some reconnaissance patrols, who had returned with the disconcerting news that contrary to their expectations, there were no friendly troops on either flank! Indeed, the nearest friendly force was their own sister 3rd Battalion, which was locked into the struggle for Altavilla some 2½ miles away. Much of the complacency was quickly dispelled as word spread that the battalion was on its own. Company officers looked to their deployments, and the men needed no urging to dig, even in that hard, rocklike soil.

Jones should now have used his initiative and his own independent power of command. The battalion was asking for trouble where it was, and he should have pulled back immediately, either to the higher ground at Persano or farther, to the river crossing. To make matters worse, Jones had deployed his battalion in poor defensive positions on low ground.

An hour later it was too late anyway. The first enemy shells fell on the position, and the outposts reported the sound of moving tanks to the front and left flank. Soon all could hear the approaching armor. Men paused to gaze anxiously in the direction of the noise before returning with renewed effort to digging. Colonel Jones' battalion was learning fast; when the infantry is in trouble it can only dig and fight, or run.

Julian Quarles, a first lieutenant and the Company F executive officer, was as concerned as anyone about their predicament. The sounds of battle, which now came from their front and the left rear, meant they had to be surrounded. In front of his company was Company G, spread thinly along the outpost line. The Germans hit them hard, and the Americans fell back through Quarles' own position and into the battalion reserve close to the command post. So far everything was going to plan, and the outpost company had done its job by the book, though perhaps it might have tried to delay the enemy a little longer. The enemy tanks and infantry were now in sight, working close together. The Germans were good, the tanks stopping to make the covering fire that allowed the infantry to advance.

At this point things started to go badly for the Americans. Immediately behind Quarles's position was the command post and the four 57mm antitank guns and heavy .50-caliber machine guns manned by the support company. Quarles looked and waited for the guns to open fire, for the Germans presented ideal targets. But nothing happened; instead, the crews ran and left the rifle companies to their own devices. The sight of demoralized men running from the battle was the saddest thing Quarles had ever seen in the Army.

The battle continued for a while longer, but bereft of support, little could be done. With the Germans swarming all over his position, Lieutenant Colonel Jones tried one last desperate ploy. He radioed back for the field artillery to fire on his own positions. The word was passed to as many of the defenders as were in touch to get down in their foxholes and brace themselves for the bombardment.

The same stratagem had worked for the hard-pressed commandos on Dragonea, but it failed for the Americans at Persano. The artillery was already fully committed to the battle for Altavilla. Neither Walker nor Colonel Forsythe of the 143rd had a contingency plan that allowed for the batteries of the 132nd Field Artillery to support both battles simultaneously; neither did they know the precise location and map coordinates for Jones and his command. Nothing happened, and in the absence of any small-arms fire the Germans took the position.*

Julian Quarles had fought the battle from a culvert. He and the company commander had killed four Germans. They had hurled grenades at the enemy, who were by then so close that Quarles took a load of shrapnel in his buttocks. The area was strewn with enemy dead. They had ducked down into the culvert to await the bombardment. The first Quarles knew it was all over was when a German soldier poked the barrel of a Schmeisser into his back. The German soldier was so angry at seeing so many of his colleagues dead that Quarles was convinced he would be shot out of hand. Quarles cursed and raged back at the German until one of the platoon commanders, Lieutenant Swanson, shut up Quarles and stepped between them.

Quarles cooled down, and the Germans herded them into a large stone barn. He noticed that all the German vehicles were painted a desert camouflage and that the men too wore sand-colored uniforms. The enemy was perfectly correct and treated the Americans with every courtesy. Some of their officers spoke a little English, and Quarles asked one why they hadn't taken their watches and other valuables. "We would be court-martialed if we took your personal possessions," he replied.

The Americans were kept in the barn overnight and then the next day

---

*The majority of the battalion were either captured or killed. Only nine officers and 325 enlisted men were able to escape.

lined up in columns and marched out of the beachhead. The Germans placed all the officers at the rear of the column, and Quarles walked with a disconsolate Colonel Jones for a while. The battalion commander's jeep drove past them with a driver and a German officer. Quarles thought for a moment that Colonel Jones would go out of his mind; he became so angry when he saw his jeep that he could hardly talk.*

Meanwhile, the German advance continued toward the sea.

Dawley telephoned General Clark and reported that the Germans had broken through the Persano front.

General Clark was astounded, as he had not been made aware of the threat that had developed in that sector during the course of the afternoon.

"What are you going to do about it?" Clark asked. "What can you do?"

"Nothing," Dawley said. "I've got no reserves. All I've got is a prayer."

The army commander was horrified to hear such abject defeatism from his corps commander.

By just after 1830 hours the German spearhead had reached the junction of the Calore and the Sele rivers. Panzer grenadiers and their tanks fanned out along the northern bank of the Calore and shot up the rear areas. There was considerable panic.

It was the worst moment on the beachhead. Through his binoculars Clark could clearly see the German tanks, and he knew that if the enemy were able to mass their troops in sufficient numbers to force a crossing of the Sele, he had nothing left to stop them from reaching the sea.

The only troops who stood between the Germans and the sea were the supporting artillery of the 45th Infantry Division. Their guns saved the day in the American sector and quite possibly the battle; for had the German advance continued through to the beaches, there would have been mayhem. The American line could then have been attacked and rolled up from the worst of all places—the crowded rear areas of B Echelon amid the piles of supplies that lined the beaches and shore area. For though the enemy would have been fully exposed to the massed gunfire of the ships offshore, the battle on land would have been fought at such close range that naval broadsides would have caused as much damage to the Allies as to the Germans.

However, the panzers did not break through, and the line held solid. Waiting for the Panzers were the massed guns of the 189th Field Artillery under Lt. Col. Hal Muldrow, ably assisted by Lt. Col. Russel Funk's 158th Field Regiment. The artillery was supported by a handful of tanks and tank destroyers, and later in the action they were joined by a battery of the 27th Armored Field Artillery Battalion.

Both battalions had their batteries deployed about 1,000 yards back from the junction of the Sele and the Calore. There were 10 yards between the guns, which had been stripped to the minimum five-man crews. The spare

---

*A few days later Julian Quarles and Captain Bane jumped from a prison train and hid out in the hills for over a month before the Allied advance reached them. They later both rejoined their old outfit.

men were sent forward to a gentle slope just south of the burned bridge to dig in and hold the line; they were armed with 1903 Springfields and .30-caliber machine guns. Directly behind them, Muldrow deployed his battery of six 37mm antitank guns. Such guns had already proved a disappointment in the European theater; the 2-pounder shell had neither the weight nor the velocity to deal with the main German battle tanks except at the closest range, where perhaps a disabling hit might be made.* However, in this situation it was all that was available.

Bellilli Palace, the Fifth Army command post, was only a few hundred yards behind the gunline. Indignant clerks, typists, stenographers, and orderlies with clean fingernails and uniforms were rousted out, given a shovel, rifle, and 50 rounds of ammunition and ordered into the line. A few remained to prepare the evacuation of the headquarters, if necessary, at 10 minutes' notice while Clark arranged to have a PT boat standing by at the beach. If needed, it was to take him and his immediate staff to the British corps, from where he intended to continue the battle.

To the right of the gunline was a large red barn. Hal Muldrow climbed onto the roof with his executive officer and directed the fire. Major Audley was on the top of the roof and shouted the instructions down to Muldrow, who had kicked in a few tiles and wedged himself midway up. He in turn shouted the instructions to his radio operator in the jeep below and thence to the gunline. It was a novel but nevertheless highly effective illustration of the chain of command. Muldrow considered his exec the real expert in gun directing and was more than happy to accept his own role in the chain; after all, if they failed, there wasn't anyplace to go but the water.

The main batteries of 155mm howitzers were not intended for the antitank role. However, the guns were being used for "red fire," which meant that the range was down to 500 yards. At that range the 95-pound projectiles made a nasty mess of any German tanks they hit.

By cutting the corners of the rule book, which had been written with safety and the avoidance of accidents in a peacetime army in mind, and skipping such procedures as pulling the lanyard before the crew was the regulation distance from the gun, the rate of fire could be increased. The gunners fired a round every 20 seconds, and they maintained this rate of fire until darkness fell and the panzers retired to Persano.†

The enemy had failed to provide sufficient artillery support for their own attack. The result was that only one American gun was knocked out in the engagement. A very popular young officer in the 189th named Torgensen, who was standing on the gun trail at the time, was killed, and others in the crew were wounded.

Even while the battle raged, just a stone's throw away, Clark called his

---

*The gun was already being replaced by the 57mm antitank piece, modeled on the well-proven British 6-pounder.

†In this phase of the battle the artillery alone fired 3,650 rounds. The armored artillery battery fired over 300 rounds.

senior commanders together for a crisis conference. It was a little after 1930 hours when Generals Dawley, Middleton, Walker, and Gruenther (the Fifth Army chief of staff) gathered around the table and discussed the situation. Walker had just returned from the Altavilla front and his own meeting with Dawley.

General Clark was worried sick that Salerno would become another Gallipoli or Dunkirk. He believed as the army commander that he had to plan for every contingency, and this had to include the possibility of an evacuation. He also knew that a commander who is completely surprised is the one to be replaced. In addition, Clark expressed his concern about the mass of supplies stockpiled on the beach. In the case of a retreat they could not be destroyed simply by putting a match to them.

The Army commander decided to adopt the approach he had been taught at the War College. Clark told his subordinate field commanders that he had ordered his staff to prepare two contingency plans. They were code named *Sealion* and *Seatrain,* and each was based on the premise of one corps acting as "host" for the other to withdraw to. Despite the urgency of the battle the irony of this particular meeting could hardly have been lost on those present, for both Middleton and Walker had been instructors at the War College when Clark was the star pupil there.

The field commanders were totally opposed to the plan. Dawley protested formally but was ignored by Clark. Both division commanders argued vehemently against the plan; Clark listened to their arguments but was undeterred.

Incredibly, no one saw fit to inform General McCreery of these decisions. There were liaison officers from the British corps at Fifth Army headquarters, but these were not invited to attend the meeting or informed of it later. In the urgency of the moment, with disaster seeming to stare the Fifth Army in the face, all thought of inter-Allied relations and the chain of command was brushed aside. There was worse to come, for the controversy over the evacuation that has raged subsequently was fueled in part by the manner in which McCreery eventually got to hear of Clark's intentions.

Before the commanders left to return to their units, Clark stressed that the contingency plan had to be kept secret. "Whatever you do," he said, "you must not mention the thought to anybody."

Walker returned to the tobacco warehouse where he put the wheels in motion to withdraw the 36th Division into a tighter perimeter along the line of La Cosa Creek.

When General Middleton returned to his own command post he issued an instruction to all his command. It was simple and to the point: "Put food and water behind the 45th," he said. "We are going to stay here."

Fighting words but a naïve move as well, for until that time the fighting soldiers hadn't even considered the idea that the whole corps might be forced to withdraw and evacuate the bridgehead. It could also be interpreted as being direct disobedience of his army commander's orders. Did Middleton intend that his division stay whatever happened? Nevertheless, the exhortation had the desired effect. It became the slogan or battle cry of the Thunderbirds in Salerno.

Later that evening, Major General Gruenther approached Admiral Hewitt to discuss Mark Clark's contingency plans. Hewitt protested in the strongest terms and at the same time pointed out an obvious practical problem: beaching a loaded landing craft and retracting it empty is quite different from beaching an empty landing craft and then retracting it when it is full, especially in the nearly tideless Tyrrhenian Sea.

Hewitt interpreted Clark's contingency plans as instructions and proceeded to mobilize his naval forces to undertake an evacuation if one part of the beachhead came under fire. The U.S.S. *Ancon,* then in Algiers, was ordered to sail immediately, load 6-inch shells at Palermo, and return to the beachhead at her best speed. In the meantime, all unloading over the American beaches was stopped.

The admiral called Commodore Oliver to a conference on board the U.S.S. *Biscayne.* Oliver left immediately in his barge for the flagship. Hewitt told Oliver of Clark's contingency plans and briefed him fully on the movement of troops in the American corps. Hewitt also asked that H.M.S. *Hilary* (Oliver's command ship) be made ready to embark General Clark and his staff should the need arise before the *Ancon* could reach the beachhead.

Commodore Oliver protested as vehemently as the others and added for good measure that he didn't agree with Walker shortening the line either, since that would simply put more of the beachhead in range of German guns. Oliver asked if General McCreery had been consulted. No one on the *Biscayne* knew the answer to that question, but it was generally assumed that he had been. It seemed too incredible to assume otherwise.

Oliver was amazed later to find when he returned to the British corps commander's headquarters outside Salerno that McCreery knew nothing of the contingency plans. It was now McCreery's turn to be angry, and he stated his intention to visit Army headquarters to protest in person. There is no record that McCreery ever made that journey, though by all accounts he was sufficiently furious at the news to have it out with Clark face to face.

It was Commodore Oliver who spread word of Clark's contingency plans beyond the beachhead. Within the hour he sent a message to Malta and his commander-in-chief, Admiral Cunningham, to enlist his support in thwarting what he was convinced to be a foolhardy if not harebrained scheme. The "genie" was out of the bottle by now with the high command in the picture.

Cunningham later received a message from Hewitt asking for help from the big guns of the Royal Navy:

> The Germans have created a salient dangerously near the beach. Military situation continuing unsatisfactory. Am planning to use all available vessels to transfer troops from southern to northern beaches, or the reverse if necessary. Unloading of merchant vessels in the southern beaches has been

stopped. We need heavy aerial and naval bombardment behind the enemy positions using battleships or other heavy naval vessels. Are such ships available?

The following evening Hewitt'a flagship decoded the reply from Admiral Cunningham:

> Count on me for all assistance you want and I will try to help you all I can. *Valiant* and *Warspite* are on their way to join you. *Nelson* and *Rodney* are available for your use.*

Such were the complications of the command situation that earlier in the day McCreery had asked General Alexander for immediate reinforcements to the X Corps. Alexander had set the wheels in motion to contact the transit camps, which were reinforcement centers in North Africa, and asked Cunningham to supply the ships. The latter readily complied; he ordered Admiral Vian and the three fast light cruisers in his squadron, *Euryalus, Scylla,* and *Charybdis,* then at Bizerte, where they were restocking after escorting the carriers covering the landings, to sail without delay to Philippeville to embark the troops.

General Alexander, in his capacity as Army group commander, sent a message to the independently minded Montgomery, who was still locked into the mountain fastness of Calabria with his Eighth Army. Previously on September 11 Alexander had sent his own chief of staff to explain the situation at Salerno personally to Montgomery. At that time the advance guard of the Eighth Army had taken Crotone, a port on the Adriatic coast just south of the Gulf of Taranto. Montgomery then designated Castrovillari, 70 miles up the peninsula , as his next objective, which he planned to reach on September 15. It was still another 75 miles to Paestum.

Now for the first time Alexander "pulled rank" on Montgomery and ordered him directly to intervene in the battle at Salerno, regardless of logistical risks.

"The situation on Fifth Army's front," he said, "is not favourable. The earlier you can threaten the forces opposite Fifth Army the better. The next few days are critical."†

Air Marshal Tedder, the air chief, offered Alexander all the air support that could possibly be mustered. At last the Strategic Air Force had been diverted from fighting its own war of bombing industrial targets deep inside the Third Reich. Now a maximum effort was to be launched in support of the troops on the beachhead.

Alexander was aware that the main requirement at Salerno was reserves of fighting troops. He believed the German counterattack had yet to reach its full strength. The Allied forces at Salerno he believed could repel the

---

*Hewitt, "The Allied Navies at Salerno: Operation Avalanche," *U.S. Naval Institute Proceedings* (1953).

†Nigel Jackson, *Alex* (London: George Weidenfeld & Nicholson, 1973), p. 217.

onslaught, but they would need the help of fresh troops to break out of the narrow beachhead and march on Naples. So he sent a message to Patton to forward additional units from his Seventh Army in Sicily (that army was now little more than a holding and training force) to increase Clark's rate of buildup. It is interesting to note that the Fifth and Seventh armies had now reversed roles.

Patton was a general in a hurry and under a cloud. His career had barely survived the famous "face-slapping incident" in the latter stages of the Sicily campaign. Patton had slapped a soldier he believed to be a coward; the doctors diagnosed shell shock, and the press demanded Patton's scalp. So he was now in his most cooperative mood, even to the British. He reached for the best unit that remained under his command. This was the U.S. 3rd Infantry Division under General Truscott; it was brought up to strength by transferring men and equipment from the 1st and 9th Infantry divisions. The latter were awaiting transportation to England and were none too pleased to be moving back into combat so soon. Truscott ordered his troops to staging areas and then boarded a warship for Salerno to confer with Mark Clark on how best to employ the division.

General Alexander diverted from Bizerte landing ships that had been due to take all the service and supply troops of the Fifth Army to Salerno, and instead sent them to Sicily to load the 3rd Infantry Division. Alexander himself planned to take a ship to Salerno on September 14.

Lt. Lew Hemmings, R.N.V.R., was also on the move that evening. Together with another LCT he had been sent south to the American sector. The beachmaster had given them instructions to report empty as quickly as possible to the headquarters ship U.S.S. *Biscayne* for further orders. It was rumored, he had said, that there was to be an evacuation of the Americans. To reach the *Biscayne* quickly meant that the LCTs had to sail inshore of the still uncleared minefield and risk the wrath of the German artillery.

Hemmings duly spotted the *Biscayne* (hers was a well-loved silhouette from the early days in the British sector) and signaled *LCT 397*'s number. "At your service," he flashed in Morse code. "W" (Wait) came the reply. This was precisely what they did do all through that night; but at least Hemmings had a grandstand seat for the ultimate act of high drama, the arrival of the 82nd Airborne Division.

The aircraft had left their base in Sicily just two minutes behind schedule at the end of a frantic day of preparation; it was a remarkable achievement. Ralph Jetton sat lost in his thoughts, like all his comrades around him. Jetton had had a bad day. He put this down to the fact that it was September 13, and this was to be his thirteenth jump. Earlier in the evening he had fallen foul of his battalion executive officer, Major Wellams. The platoon had been checking their gear and teasing Jetton about the martinet figure of Major Wellams; as his bodyguard they always jumped together.

One of the men turned to Ralph, and said, "When you go out the door tonight Dub" (this was his family nickname), "reach out and unhitch Major Wellams' static line." (This was the part of the parachute harness that was attached to the running rail in the aircraft and automatically released the parachute once the man had jumped clear.)

"I'll do that," Jetton said, laughing. "Just before he goes out the door, I'll unhitch him."

There was absolute silence in the room. Ralph turned around to see Major Wellams standing by the door.

Jetton was embarrassed; he didn't know what to say or do. Without a word Major Wellams grim-faced turned on his heel, strode out of the room, and slammed the door. Shortly afterward he sent a message down to Jetton; a sergeant delivered it.

"Jetton," the sergeant said, "the major says you'll clear the plane tonight." "Oh, my God," Jetton said.

This meant that he would now be the last man out of the plane and therefore the one most likely to overshoot the drop zone (DZ). The fact that this was a night jump considerably increased Jetton's chances of serious injury or broken limbs.

The C-47s flew low across the Tyrrhenian Sea and turned in over Capri. The pilots were nervous lest the fleet beneath them open fire and the tragedy of Sicily be repeated. It wasn't their courage that was in question, but the planes. The C-47s were straight civilian versions; they had no armor plating and, even worse, no self-sealing fuel tanks so that even a hit from small-arms fire was enough to turn one into a fireball.

Col. Reuben Tucker, the regimental commander, flew in the lead plane of the 30 Dakotas that brought in the first wave that night. It was 2356 hours, and they were now four minutes ahead of schedule. Beneath and ahead, the "T" patch marking the DZ burned brightly, and the pathfinder group, which had landed earlier, homed in the lead planes with their radar.

The men stood up and at the dispatcher's command hitched on the static lines. Jetton and the others wore the jump suits with its big pockets. Strapped to their backs every man carried two land mines in case of tank attacks, 120 rounds of ammunition for the M1 carbine, and a further 50 rounds for the .45-caliber pistol; each had a bayonet, fighting knife with its knuckle-duster handle, entrenching tool, K rations, and water bottle. An M1 carbine was held to the wrist by a short strap. Fully loaded, the average paratrooper when he stepped through the doorway weighed over 220 pounds.

As soon as the green light flashed, Jetton was anxious to be out; whatever else he mustn't overshoot the DZ, and every second counted. He shoved hard to push the line along, and then when he reached the door the worst possible thing happened: The man in front froze. A man is hard to get out of the doorway if he doesn't want to go, and this one was adamant: He was rigid with fear.

Finally in desperation Jetton stood back at the other side of the fuselage and hurled himself with all his weight. The frightened man lost his grip and with a last cry of anguish rolled out of the plane with Jetton. He was the platoon's only casualty and was later reported missing in action.

They jumped at 1,800 feet and the chute opened on its static line after the first 100 feet. The blast from wind and propellers seemed to get under his helmet, and Jetton felt as if his ears would be torn off. He was convinced the pilot had not slowed down at all.

Jetton hardly had time to look around before the ground came rushing up to meet him. At night it was impossible to judge properly, and he landed with a sickening crunch. He picked himself up, shed his chute, and ran across the rendezvous point, where a line of trucks already waited to take the men away.

Just as he was about to board the truck, Major Wellams called him over; he needed his bodyguard, and Jetton sighed with relief. They climbed into a jeep together with Captain Gorham, the battalion's S3, and his bodyguard, who sat in the back with Jetton. They were off to reconnoiter their objective.

A second flight, of 41 aircraft, reached the DZ an hour later, and this time things did go wrong. One company landed 8 miles away. Lieutenant Rocholl's men caught some. By this time the young officer was in temporary command of his company, which he had moved out of the firing line for their first rest since the battle began. He had taken them back to Penta, which lay almost directly north of Salerno on the Sanseverino road; their quarters were situated at the foot of the hills standing between them and the Allies.

Rocholl was awakened from a deep sleep by the guard violently shaking his arm and pointing to the sky. "Leutnant, Leutnant, *Fallschirmjäger* [paratroopers]!"

Rocholl saw 50 to 60 paratroopers at a height of 500 feet swinging down, while in the distance he heard the faint droning of the departing planes. It was such a bright, moonlit night that he could recognize every white fleck in the heavens.

Rocholl's crews ran to their armored cars, and the barrels of their 20mm cannon and machine guns swung skyward. Burst after short, disciplined burst cut into the descending paratroopers until the angle became too dangerous to fire. Though they were dropping all around, most of the paratroopers seemed to land in the heavily wooded slopes higher up the mountain. Rocholl deployed his armored cars along the main road and set out toward Penta with his command group to carry out a reconnaissance.

At first nothing could be seen. Though they searched some houses, they could find no trace whatsoever of the paratroopers. There only remained the last house at the edge of the village to be searched. Rocholl walked up and found the door locked. Two of his grenadiers kicked it in and then ducked as a vicious burst of automatic fire greeted their efforts. The Germans stood back and hurled three grenades into the house, followed by bursts of fire from their own automatic weapons.

The grenades exploded in rapid succession, and agonized screams rent the night air. Rocholl waited for the smoke and dust to settle and then risked shining his flashlight inside the room. There were a number of paratroopers, all wounded, who blinked in the light and hesitantly raised their arms.

Others could be heard making good their escape through the back doorway, but Rocholl considered it too difficult to chase them.*

At 0300 hours Col. Reuben Tucker reported to Fifth Army headquarters and was greeted by a delighted Gen. Mark Clark. The headquarters still had not moved though the rooms vibrated, not to the sound of the guns, but to the roar of the trucks and tanks as the Americans of the 36th Division moved into the final defenses along the La Cosa line.

The retreat into the La Cosa line involved the 36th Division generally falling back about 2 miles toward the coast. The liaison officers who worked between the regiments and divisional headquarters were constantly on the move that night, seeing that the movements of the troops on the ground corresponded with the map pins on the situation map in the division command post. Lt. Bert Carlton felt as if he hadn't been out of his jeep for days.† It was just after dark, and he had returned from a mission to locate the 143rd Infantry regimental aid post when he was called in by Col. Clayton Price Kerr, Walker's chief of staff. Kerr had been Carlton's company commander when he had first enlisted in the Texas National Guard in 1932, so they had known one another for some time.

Carlton was ordered to deliver two radio jeeps, one to General Wilbur and the other to General O'Daniell. Kerr impressed on his young subordinate that these were the last two vehicles they could round up that were equipped with large radios and that whatever else happened they must not be allowed to fall into enemy hands. With the radios went a couple of highly skilled operators and the latest set of codes. Kerr took Carlton across to the map and pointed out the route. "Now, the main road, Highway 18 beyond the bridge over the Sele, is untenable," said Kerr. "We don't know what's going on, though there is some action up there, perhaps involving stragglers from our own outfits. What you can do is cut across country toward a stone quarry" (which Kerr pointed to on the map), "and you should find a trail there. If you pass Albanella station, you've gone too far up the highway," Kerr warned. "The trail will lead you up to the La Cosa line and General Wilbur's command post on the division's left front."

Carlton saluted and went outside to get his own jeep driver, Private Putnam, before briefing his own party.

The two radio jeeps were ready. Each vehicle had a driver and an operator; a third man in each vehicle, armed with a Thompson, rode shotgun. Carlton briefed the little group of men: "You take your instructions from me and be ready to fight if we have to," he warned. "There can be no lights, so you drivers keep the vehicles fender to fender once we leave the main road."

Carlton's final words were to the two escorts: "I want you to keep a couple of grenades handy. If we hit an ambush and it looks bad, I'll give you the word to destroy the jeeps."

---

*The diary that covers the period to September 14 ends because Lieutenant Rocholl was killed. The notebook was recovered from his body.

†Carlton was the liaison officer with the 143rd Infantry, and we had last met him when he had been involved in an unfortunate incident with a captured German machine gun.

The little convoy wound its way out of the courtyard and past the tobacco barn. There were vehicles parked everywhere and the whole place was a hive of activity. Soldiers ran from the communications tents to the command post, and harassed staff officers issued a flood of orders to equally frantic clerks as the division's headquarters strove to put their commanding general's orders into effect.

In more senses than one Carlton was glad to leave the "organized confusion" of headquarters behind and take his chances in the field. The first part of the mission was accomplished with ease, for by a stroke of luck he came upon both generals together. Carlton had turned right onto Route 18 and led his convoy of three jeeps north, toward the Sele. At first the traffic was very heavy, but after a mile or so it thinned out considerably, until they had the road to themselves. It was a cool and very dark night, the moon obscured by the first heavy banks of cloud they had seen since landing in Salerno. There was a taste of rain in the air and the first chill winds of European autumn. Bert Carlton buttoned his combat jacket to his chin and for the umpteenth time checked the map by the pencil beam from his hooded flashlight. Then just as Colonel Kerr had predicted, he spotted the trail on the right of the highway that led off into the darkness and the foothills. A little farther up the highway Carlton could make out the dark, skeletal shadows that were the ruins of Albanella station. They passed the stone quarry, and a mile or two farther down the trail, when they were right at the foot of the menacing shape of Mount Chirico, the three jeeps drove into a small settlement. This is a polite way to describe the collection of primitive hovels, which huddled around a small open courtyard. The settlement was called La Maida.

The courtyard was packed with vehicles and in activity represented a division's headquarters but on a much smaller scale. Carlton squeezed the vehicles between two buildings and walked across to where an MP had indicated the regimental command post was located. There he found Captain Summers, the aide to General Wilbur, sipping hot coffee from a steaming mug. Summers explained to Carlton that both General Wilbur and General O'Daniell were in conference.

"I'll be happy to sign for both jeeps," Summers said.

"No, I can't do that," Carlton said. "I've got to have at least General O'Daniell's aide sign for one."

The last thing Carlton was prepared to do was leave one regiment with two radios and believe in anyone's honesty to pass one radio on to the other. Summers found O'Daniell's aide, and Carlton duly handed over the jeeps and their crews before driving back to division.

Private Putnam was a good driver and had been with Carlton since the last days of their training in the States, but that night Putnam missed the track. They came to a point where a number of tracks intersected the main trail. Carlton was about to order Putnam to turn the vehicle around and head back the way they had come when they heard a low-flying aircraft; by the sounds of its laboring engines, it was in trouble.

Carlton put his hand on his helmet and looked up into the night sky—he never wore the chin strap. Suddenly the air filled to the sound of a second and lighter plane, which screamed into a dive and opened up with its machine guns. By this time the first aircraft, obviously a Luftwaffe bomber, was practically overhead, and all hell broke loose. Putnam pulled the jeep off the track as the first bombs burst all around them; cannon and machine-gun shells from the diving night fighter plowed up the earth. The blast of the bombs slammed into the jeep and drove the air from Carlton's lungs. Great chunks of earth and debris rained down on them, and Carlton blacked out for a minute or two. He came to with a terrible drumming in his ears and the sounds of the aircraft way in the distance.

Putnam was slumped over the steering wheel. Carlton pulled him back and felt for wounds or blood, but there was nothing. Putnam came around. "Where're my glasses?" he mumbled.

Carlton breathed a sigh of relief. "I don't know, but we'll find them. Are you all right?" he asked.

"Where're my glasses? Got to find my glasses," Putnam insisted.

Carlton groped around the floor of the jeep until he found the spectacles. "Putnam, are you all right?" he asked.

"I think so, Lieutenant," Putnam said.

"Well, let's find out for sure. Stand up on the seat," Carlton ordered.

Putnam stood up on the seat and pitched out of the jeep head first. Carlton heaved him to his feet, reached for a canteen of water, and ordered the young soldier to rest until he felt well enough to continue the journey.

Suddenly Carlton heard the sound of something moving in front of him. He told Putnam to grab his rifle and get down in a ditch. Carlton reached for his Thompson and walked forward into the dark. It was pitch black, but he could just about pick out the shape of a vehicle a few yards ahead of him on the track. Whether it was American or German he couldn't tell. There was only one way to find out, and Carlton moved forward slowly toward the vehicle. A group of men came out of the night and clambered into the vehicle; they were no more than a dozen yards away, and all that Carlton could do was stand rock still and pray that Putnam wouldn't do something stupid. They were Germans, and Carlton could now pick out the details of the enemy half-track as it started up and drove away.

Carlton worked his way quietly back to the jeep, where Putnam was waiting anxiously. "Let's go, Putnam," Carlton ordered.

Putnam needed no second bidding but whipped the vehicle around in a masterly turn—it is surprising how quickly naked fear can clear a mind numbed by blast—and headed back the way they had come.

Carlton spotted another trail, and the jeep headed down the track until more by luck than good judgment they reached Highway 18.

There was a roadblock at the intersection, manned by about half a dozen very nervous Texans, who pointed every imaginable kind of small arms at the jeep. An MP challenged Carlton, who responded with the correct password. A colonel came out of the group and asked, "Did you just come down that track, Lieutenant?"

"Yes, sir," Carlton said.

"You'd better come with me to Army headquarters," snapped the colonel as he scrambled into the back of Carlton's jeep.

At the colonel's orders, Putnam drove hard down Highway 18 and pulled into Mark Clark's advanced command post. The staff colonel took Carlton into the house and a large ground-floor room, along one wall of which a large-scale map of the battlefront had been fixed. General Clark was standing before the map talking earnestly to a small group of officers. The colonel introduced Carlton to the general and asked him to tell the army commander where he had been. "Show me on the map what happened, Lieutenant," the general said.

Carlton swallowed nervously, more frightened now than he had been at any time during the night, and explained the incident of the enemy patrol. When he finished Carlton looked up to find that a whole group of very senior officers had gathered to listen.

Then came the questions.

"Did you see any other enemy activity along the track?"

"Could you hear if there were tanks moving in the area?"

"Which direction did the half-track take?"

Carlton answered as best he could before escaping into the night.

General Clark thanked him for a job well done, and the staff colonel took Carlton back to his jeep. The significance of his actions were, of course, beyond the young officer until the colonel explained that if the track was clear of the enemy, other than an occasional patrol, then the main attack must be coming from another direction, possibly on the far side of the Sele, where the 45th Infantry was deployed.

What Carlton and his driver did not know as they drove back to the division's command post was that their escapade had helped confirm the deployments that General Dawley had assigned to Troy Middleton's division.

Under the corps commander's order the combat teams drawn from the 157th and two battalions of the 179th Infantry had already moved into a line parallel to the Sele River. If the Germans were to attack the next day from across the river, they would advance at right angles to the American positions; this would in turn expose the enemy flanks to the defenders' fire.

There remained only the base of the Sele–Calore corridor, which still had to be the objective if the enemy were to break through to the sea. It was here on this already bloody piece of ground that Lt. Col. Hal Muldrow had deployed his artillery, together with all the spare troops that both the division and the Army headquarters could scrape together. Troy Middleton also gave Muldrow his last reserve, the 1st Battalion of the 179th Infantry.

As Black Monday drew to its fateful close, nothing else could be done but await the next day and the German offensive.

Chapter XXII

Holding the Line

Prime Minister Churchill to General Alexander, September 14, 1943:

1. I hope you are watching above all the Battle of "Avalanche," which dominates everything. None of the commanders engaged has fought a large-scale battle before. The Battle of Sulva Bay was lost because Ian Hamilton was advised by his CGS to remain at a remote central point where he would know everything. Had he been on the spot he could have saved the show. At this distance and with time-lags I cannot pretend to judge, but I feel it is my duty to set before you this experience of mine from the past.
2. *Nothing* should be denied which will nourish the decisive battle for Naples.
3. Ask for anything you want, and I will make allocation of necessary supplies, with the highest priority irrespective of every other consideration.

Even as the exhausted troops, harassed as they were by enemy shellfire, marched in the bright moonlight to the final defense line, the last acts were still being played out in Altavilla and the surrounding hills. Lieutenant Colonel Barnett, who commanded the 3rd Battalion of the 143rd, demonstrated unusual skill and extraordinary courage and determination during the withdrawal. The destruction of the 1st Battalion, 143rd Infantry near Persano had opened the left flank of the American positions at Altavilla to fresh attacks. Thus the renewed German thrust from across the Calore had cut across his line of retreat once the left flank defenses had crumbled. He made a personal reconnaissance of the possible routes of escape and organized his command into small groups, even while another party fought a tough rear-guard action and kept the Germans at arm's length. It was largely as a result of his skill that some 20 officers and 536 enlisted men eventually made it back through to the American lines.

Many were still caught up in the fighting for Altavilla, especially men in Company K. Casualties in the company had led to George Bailey being given the task of company radio operator. He had heard Barnett's call to withdraw and had relayed the order "All roses come to roses blue" to his company commander. The only problem was that both sides were now laying down an almighty barrage on the town, presumably in the belief that it was held by the other. Dead from both sides littered the rubble-strewn streets of the old town; it looked for all the world like a scene from Dante's *Inferno* as fires raged unchecked and great chunks of masonry crashed onto the ground.

There was only one way out of the town, and that was through the cavernous wine cellars beneath the houses. An old Italian had shown the colonel the way, and he had chalked a succession of numbers on the respective cellar doors.

The company command group, about a dozen men all told, broke off into groups and with a few minutes' gap between each, made their dash for freedom. The captain had lost his glasses earlier in the evening and without them couldn't see too well. He took a wrong turn and led his group right into the arms of a German patrol.

George Bailey was more fortunate. A corporal who was a full-blooded Indian from Oklahoma led his group, and once they were beyond the town his skills came into their own. He moved ahead and scouted the route. At one spot a German machine-gun team guarded a track that wound its way down through a ravine. There was no way around the obstacle, so the Indian crept forward and disposed of the enemy with his combat knife. The little group was then able to move on and eventually find a way back to their own lines. Again the Indian proved invaluable, for nobody knew the password. They were afraid that in the dark and confusion they would be mistaken for the enemy. The Indian went ahead and quietly made contact before returning to lead his party into the safety of the lines.

Some other Americans had an even luckier escape. By the early hours of Tuesday morning, the Germans had put a ring of troops around Altavilla and its hills. A sergeant with two other men had reached a fence. A voice called out in the darkness, "Hey, come on over here and climb through the fence."

The group moved over toward two men who were holding open a gap in the wire fence.

"Here, let me help you, buddy," the friendly voice said. "Hand me your rifle."

The sergeant sensed there was something wrong. He could hear a scampering in the ravine behind the fence, so he hesitated. "Come on, give us your rifle and climb through." This time the voice sounded impatient.

The sergeant instead lifted up his rifle and shot the two men down. He then scrambled through the wire and found a third, this one a man in German uniform at the head of the ravine. The enemy hesitated, and the sergeant dropped him too.

All three were Germans, and their ruse that night had netted a dozen Americans, who had all been caught in the same fashion and were being guarded by the third German in the ravine.

For others there could be no escape out of Altavilla. The wounded were left behind in the care of the battalion medical officer, Captain Kratka, and his team. Pvt. Ike Franklin believed that he had now run out of the luck that had saved him in the first hours of the landing; for he was with Kratka. They had several walking wounded and more than a dozen seriously wounded in the aid station, located in the cellar of a substantial house that fronted onto the main square.

Kratka called the six medics in the team together and told them that as capture was now a matter of time, he would need only one to stay with him and the seriously wounded. The others, he said, could make a break, provided they took the walking wounded with them.

The medics drew straws to see who would stay. Franklin's heart surged with hope. He had not pulled the short straw; perhaps he could make it out of this terrible place.

The moon had set, and it was very dark as they made their bid for freedom. Kratka split them into two equal groups and sent them on their way quietly out of the town; they helped the wounded to pick their way over the rubble and debris. The whole party was both mentally and physically exhausted. Franklin couldn't remember having had more than an hour's unbroken sleep since they had landed five days before.

The inevitable happened. The party had reached the old American positions near the foot of the hill when they ran into part of the German cordon, a standing patrol of six or seven men. Franklin grabbed the wounded man he was assisting, and together they ducked into a trench. The others were caught and rounded up by the patrol before being taken back up the hill into Altavilla.

They waited in the shellhole until the patrol had disappeared; then they scrambled out.

"Well, there're two of us the bastards didn't find," the wounded man said.

With that a powerful flashlight beam flashed across their faces, and another German stepped out of the shadows. Neither American had been in the war long enough to know that the standard German technique of night patrolling is to have one man about twenty or thirty yards behind to act as a rear guard.

"*Die Kamerad?*" the soldier asked.

"Too right," Franklin said, slowly raising his arms in the air. He was too tired to care. Their captor hurried them to the main group, and they were all taken into the church.

The bombardment had started again, and they had to shuffle from the shelter of one doorway to the next before they reached the solid sanctuary afforded by the massive walls of the ancient church.

While Franklin and the others waited to be interrogated, the Germans gave them wine and American cigarettes. Their inquisitor was a young lieutenant who spoke better English than most Americans. He looked up at Ike Franklin.

"Franklin, I., 20818428, private," Franklin said. "That's all the Geneva Convention says I got to tell you, and that's all I'm going to tell you," he concluded.

Franklin was put to work with Captain Kratka, who greeted him ruefully, and the others looking after the wounded of both sides. A German doctor and his medics were there, too. The Germans had captured the American medical supplies intact, but, though many of their own men were in desperate need, the German team would not administer any of the American plasma to them.

"You're doctors and scientists," Franklin said, "you know better than this."

"Our orders are clear," the German doctor replied. "It might be Jewish or Negro blood."

Franklin had never before encountered such bigotry.

At dawn the medics stepped out of the church and under the watchful eye of the armed guards moved around the town, the lower slopes, and finally up onto Hill 424, picking up the wounded from both sides.

When they had finished their work, all the able-bodied men were rounded up and marched off the hill and down into the valley. Close to Ponte Sele a line of captured American and commandeered Italian Army trucks awaited them. They were driven to the outskirts of Naples, where they were made to dismount and join a long column of British and other American troops to be marched through the city and on to prison camp.*

Even while Franklin was experiencing his first night of captivity, the Texans were making feverish efforts to complete the defenses of the La Cosa line before daylight and the expected German counterattack. This position, selected for what might well have become a last stand, was not naturally very strong; but then there was nothing else between there and the sea. The creek itself is no real barrier, and the hills behind, from Cappa Santa through Mount Chirico and on to Tempone di San Paolo, are neither high nor very rugged. However, though the Germans in Altavilla could see these defenses, in order to reach them they would have to cross a plain fully exposed to American firepower.

One of the key men in the construction of the line was Maj. Oran Stovall, whom Walker had assigned to command his engineers when the previous incumbent had failed. Stovall had throughout these hectic days carefully built up the engineering dump at Paestum. Mines, demolition charges, and wire

---

*After many harrowing experiences in prison and forced labor camps, Ike Franklin was eventually liberated by Soviet Army forces in East Prussia on January 29, 1945; it was his birthday.

were distributed to his companies, and they worked hard to fortify the line. Fifteen miles of double apron concertina wire was strung out in front, and minefields were laid along all possible tank approaches, especially in the center close to where the 179th was about to make its stand. The fording points across the Calore and the Sele were also sown with antipersonnel mines. Since there would be very few infantry to defend the right flank, Stovall ordered his men to blow up the remaining bridges and crater Route 18 south of Ogliastro. Road blocks were also established in that area and manned by squads of engineers.

Walker gave Stovall additional support from two companies of the 36th Engineers; they were an amphibious regiment and a first-rate unit.

Stovall roamed the lines all that night seeking out the weak spots and remedying the problems as they arose.

The weakest part of the line lay at the junction of La Cosa Creek and the Calore, where there is a stretch of low ground nearly a mile in width, sparsely timbered, with heavier growth along the banks of the Calore. It was here that Stovall directed the attentions of Captain Bellamy, who had charge of the bulldozers. These dug enormous pits in which the tank destroyers were moved into a hull down position. In such a deployment, the hull of the armored vehicle is hidden from enemy view and thus protected while the turret is free to traverse the gun as necessary onto the target.

Fire support throughout the night once again came from the Navy. The cruiser U.S.S. *Philadelphia* fired 1,000 6-inch shells on tanks, road intersections, and suspected troop concentrations. Overhead the heavy and medium bombers concentrated on Eboli and Battipaglia so that the night sky lit the horizon with a dull red glow. Every time he paused to look at the bombardment, it seemed to Stovall that the hills were on fire.

The remnants of the three infantry battalions of the 143rd Combat Team, which had been so badly mauled in the recent fighting, were withdrawn behind the new line; they needed to reorganize and rest before they could embark on further combat.

So from the Calore to Mount Chirico the line was manned by the only units available. These were the support arms such as the 2nd Battalion, 36th Engineers, a company of the 636th Tank Destroyer Battalion, a company of Shermans from the 751st Tank Battalion, and the cannon and antitank companies of the 143rd RCT. Such infantry as was available moved quickly into the line. The 2nd Battalion, 141st Infantry, which had been sent to the extreme left flank of the corps, were force-marched to garrison the southern slopes of Mount Chirico. The 1st Battalion came up from Trentinara and dug in to watch the vulnerable point south of the Sele River and east of Highway 18 at Tempone di San Paolo.

Capt. Herman Newman, the 1st Battalion's S3, had attended Walker's briefing along with his commanding officer. Walker talked, the CO listened, and Newman wrote it all down, but there wasn't very much that had to be said. The battalion was to be held in reserve ready to counterattack if necessary.

The divisional commander explained it all very simply. "Well, this is it. We can't go anywhere from here but into the sea."

Finally the 3rd Battalion moved to the extreme left flank of the corps in the swampy, mosquito-infested ground beside the engineer battalion at Bivio Cioffi.

The two battalions of paratroopers went into position from Difesa Monti in the south. They were to supply Walker with an immediate "fire brigade reserve," ready to rush to any point where the line might be threatened.

Behind the forward troops the guns were wheeled into line. Pvt. Joe Justice of Battery C, 132nd Field Artillery Battalion, didn't believe it was possible to be this tired and still awake; like most of the men, he felt and acted at times like a "walking zombie." They had fired for 24 hours, seemingly without a break, on Altavilla and had deployed out of the gun line just in time to make it back before the Germans closed the trap. Now that their guns were into the line, the battery officers came along and stripped them down to minimum crews. Each of the spare gunners was then issued with a 1903 Springfield rifle, a bandolier of ammunition, and a shovel. The guns were shielded by an olive grove, but the new infantry moved forward and dug foxholes in the rocky scrub. A sergeant came along with advice and a grenade for each man. Joe had completed his foxhole by then, but he was totally disconcerted to learn that there was nothing in front of them—he was the front line!

"Use your bayonet if you have to, son," the sergeant said.

Joe dismissed that from his thoughts; the last thing he would dare to use was a bayonet.

On the German side spirits were high as the sun rose above the horizon with the promise of another scorching hot day on the beachhead. The remaining units of the 26th Panzers had all arrived in the area intact despite the efforts of the British and American air forces to disrupt their journey from Calabria. The division left a rear guard, the equivalent of a regimental combat team, behind a trail of blown culverts and demolished bridges leading from Castravillari to their main defenses near Sapri.

Von Vietinghoff planned to use this fresh force* in place of the 16th Panzers to drive southwest from Eboli on to Salerno, where it would slice through the British defenses and link up with the Luftwaffe Panzer-Division Hermann Göring.

Though the Tenth Army commander remained optimistic and was convinced the Allies were about to evacuate, his corps commanders were nowhere near as sure. Balck of the XIV Panzer Corps reported that against the British in the Salerno area his troops found stiffening resistance everywhere. Herr of the LXXVI Panzer Corps confirmed the view; though his forces had reported the American withdrawal to the new positions at La Cosa, he was convinced it was only to a more secure line.

---

*With the rear guard in Calabria and its tank battalions south of Rome, the equivalent of a regiment was available to Von Vietinghoff.

The opinions expressed by his subordinate commanders were pessimistic but also realistic, and Von Vietinghoff would have been wise to listen. Instead he impressed upon them the need for one last effort to destroy the beachhead before Montgomery could be in a position to intervene.

The first German assault was launched against the Americans at about 0800 hours that day, and it proved a complete disaster. Ten tanks spearheaded a battalion of infantry, which attacked from the tobacco factory southward. The Germans had paid little heed to the American redeployments during the previous night, with the result that they advanced across the front of the 179th Combat Team at a distance of less than 1,000 yards. The combined American fire from two battalions each of infantry and artillery and the tanks and tank destroyers overwhelmed the German armor. Even so, the infantry tried to sustain the pressure but could really make no headway against such a cohesive defense.

A haze covered the front, and the figures of men in olive drab and gray darted in and out of it seeking cover and firing, attacking and withdrawing. Artillery observers crouched in their foxholes and yelled corrections into their field telephones to Muldrow's gunlines, and salvo after salvo blasted the ground to the front.

Gen. Mark Clark arrived at Colonel Hutchins' command post to see the German infantry suffer heavily as they tried to move forward, but the ground was devoid of cover, and the American motor and artillery fire was devastatingly effective. The noise was unbelievable.

The Germans tried once more as behind a screen of sledgehammer artillery fire the panzer grenadiers tried to recover the momentum of their attack, but again the Americans stood their ground even when, as if out of nowhere, a couple of FW-190s darted in and strafed the line.

The Germans withdrew at about 0930 hours, and it was almost as if the heart had been knocked out of them. There was a lull for about an hour, and then they came in a second time, but now it was back to the pattern of earlier tank and infantry actions probing for weak spots. They came swinging from the Grataglia, feeling their way down the west bank of the Sele River, but they failed to move the 157th Infantry. This was almost immediately followed by an assault on the 3rd Battalion of the 179th Infantry, which protected the coastal highway. The combined efforts of the Army's firepower and the 6-inch broadsides from the *Boise,* which had taken over as the "duty cruiser," proved too much. The Germans eventually pulled back and contented themselves with an artillery bombardment of the Americans, conducted at fairly long range.

The Germans made a last attempt against the Thunderbirds, and the tactics they used simply served to indicate their own sense of desperation and frustration. At about 1230 hours a half company of the enemy appeared carrying white flags in front of the 2nd Battalion. About 150 yards from the American lines the Germans dropped the flags and began to shoot, but the ruse had failed. The Americans, safe behind their defenses, opened a return fire and killed about 40 of the enemy before the remainder fled.

The pattern was broadly similar along the La Cosa line. The Germans tried a major thrust at about 0930 hours, when a company of infantry led by Panzer Mark IV Specials attacked across the Calore toward Mount Chirico. American Shermans moved out, and in a classic tank vs. tank encounter overwhelmed the enemy. The Shermans lost one of their number destroyed and two disabled, but six of the German tanks were left as burning hulks. Shortly afterward the Germans pulled back and resorted to a series of probing attacks. The guns kept up their bombardment all the day. At one stage in Battery C of the 132nd Field Artillery they were down to 10 rounds a gun. The battery commander phoned Pete Green for instructions.

"Fire the rammers if you have to," was the reply.

Lieutenant Colonel Green had always told his men that unless they were receiving machine-gun fire they were not sufficiently close to the action! The infantry loved this battalion.

Nevertheless, more ammunition arrived, and the guns kept firing on the roving tanks and half-tracks the Germans sent out to keep up harassing fire against the positions.

On the British corps front, General McCreery had made no contingency plans for a withdrawal. He had obviously dismissed Mark Clark's preparations as unworkable and, insofar as the British were concerned, unnecessary. There were a couple of anxious moments that day, but the line held firm, especially at the boundary between the 56th and 46th divisions. The headquarters element of the 23rd Armored Brigade had by now arrived on the beachhead. McCreery had given them command over an ad hoc force* of perhaps 3,000 men to watch over the extreme right flank of the corps line. They assumed this role after dusk on Tuesday.

Capt. David Appleby, the Intelligence officer with the fusilier brigade, had been across to liaise with his opposite number as soon as it was light. There was a need to discuss the minutiae of military detail that always has to be covered at the boundary of two forces, especially when they are of different nationalities. There were such considerations as arcs of fire, supporting artillery, patrol areas, and code words, to name but a few.

Appleby took a couple of cans of bully beef and was able to organize a very healthy trade in exchange for some K rations, which to the British were delicacies.

Appleby was always intrigued by the Americans, especially by the amount of equipment they carried with them. They were also remarkably informal, particularly in the relationship between an enlisted man and an officer. When he approached the 157th command post that morning he was greeted by a sentry, armed to the teeth and sitting back in a large armchair.

"In there, bud," the sentry said, jerking his thumb in the direction of a tent, in response to Appleby's request for the headquarters.

---

*Headquarters, 23rd Armored Brigade (Brig. R. H. E. Arkwright) took under command the 44th Reconnaissance Regiment, the Royal Scots Greys, the 50th Battery of the Royal Artillery, two companies of the 2/4th Hampshires, and a company of the 6th Cheshires.

The British, of course, were rather show-offish, especially in their approach to the Americans. They wore service hats rather than helmets, and Appleby wore his pistol in the current fashion, which was to undo the strap on his trousers that kept his belt in place, feed it through the trigger guard, and then do it up again. The pistol dangled loose and was highly dangerous. It must have appeared to the Americans that British officers like Appleby struck a pose of a disinterested amateur in war, one of studied nonchalance.

The Americans, it appeared to Appleby, seemed to wear every item they were issued, even in a command post; the higher the rank, the more they seemed to wear.

The Germans hammered away at the Salerno area during the morning, and the 46th Division gave General McCreery several anxious moments, for they had every unit in the lines. There were no reserves available had the Germans succeeded in breaking through the defenses. The divisions were now facing their most severe test in battle and there seemed to be no end to the ordeal in sight. Nevertheless, throughout these tense days, even when involved in this most hectic of battles, people did not show despondency. They had the greatest confidence in the guns behind and the troops around them. Perhaps this was because the ordinary young soldier was of a generation that wasn't sufficiently aware of the "big picture" to understand or appreciate the real dangers they faced.

Even while the battle still hung in the balance against the doughty infantry of the 46th Division, the Germans expanded the front and hit the line farther south. The battle group from the 26th Panzers swung west out of Eboli, skirted the ruins of Battipaglia, and ran full tilt into the units of the 56th Division, which were deployed in open ground.

Fusilier Harris with his half battalion, the survivors from the battle at Battipaglia, were still dug in at the crossroads in St. Lucia. There had been occasional German artillery barrages, but little else had come their way since the debacle in Battipaglia. Then on September 14 the artillery had a different sound to it, a sense of urgency and purpose, which to the veteran ear forewarned an attack. Across the road, the Vickers machine guns of the Cheshires had been hammering away all morning. Suddenly about 300 yards away a tank appeared from behind a large house; there were soldiers riding on its back, and a couple of half-tracks came behind.

Harris rammed a clip into his rifle and took aim, but even before he could fire there was a tremendous roar from behind. The 17-pounder antitanks were "really on the ball," and the muzzle blast nearly took their heads off. Harris and the others crouched low in their slit trenches, and the solid, armor-piercing shot slammed by just overhead. Before they could recover their composure, the guns fired a second time and hit the tank fair and square. Harris watched as the gun did its usual drunken bow, and the tank fell apart like a pack of cards. There was a great puff of smoke, and the infantry who had been riding on the tank disappeared.

The Vickers machine guns caught the half-tracks before they had had sufficient time to react. The first plowed through the greasy wreckage and hammered straight into the ditch, while the second skidded to a halt behind the building, turned around, and drove off quickly whence it had come.

That evening the 8th Battalion, Royal Fusiliers, were ordered to take over part of the line from the Hampshires. General McCreery, the corps commander, was concerned that the pressure from the attacking battle groups of the Hermann Göring Panzer Division was increasing in the Salerno area. He ordered two battalions of the 167th Infantry Brigade from the Black Cat Division (the 7th Battalion Oxfordshire and Buckinghamshire Light Infantry, and the 8th Battalion Royal Fusiliers) to move in support of the Hampshire Brigade and come under the command of the 46th Infantry Division. McCreery covered the gap left by these battalions with the ad hoc force under the headquarters of the 23rd Armored Brigade, which simply extended their part of the front line.

The Hampshires were dug in along the line of foothills near Mercatello, which was just outside of Salerno. As officer commanding the support company, it was Major Archer's task to lead the advance parties and feed them into the battalion's new position. The advance parties would then return to an agreed rendezvous, which was some distance to the rear of the new positions, to meet with the remainder of the battalion, for whom they would act as guides and take the companies into the line.

The first part of the operation went smoothly enough. Then the Germans launched a vicious counterattack just as the handover had reached mid phase, with the men of both battalions aboveground. Now began the worst night of all at Salerno for Archer; for a while at least he was convinced the enemy would break through.

The Hampshires and the Fusiliers were new to one another, and there was considerable confusion and some chaos. Eventually the Hampshires got away, and the Fusiliers, though they had taken a lot of casualties, were able to occupy the line. For some reason, the Germans did not press their advantage but stopped, as they had done so often in Salerno, just when it seemed they had the upper hand.

The incident certainly wasn't enough to concern General McCreery who, with perhaps studied nonchalance, described the corps battle as: "Nothing of interest to report during the day."[*] Herein lay one of the differences between McCreery's method of handling the battle and that of his American contemporaries to the south. Some would even go so far as to assert a difference not in personalities or styles of leadership, but in the armies themselves. A couple of battalions under McCreery's command had gotten themselves into trouble, partly through their own mistakes and also out of bad luck. It was up to the battalion commanders on the spot to resolve the problem, with the help of their brigadier and if absolutely necessary, the divisional commander. If a similar incident had happened on the American front at this time, one

*Martin Blumenson, *United States Army in World War II, The Mediterranean Theater of Operation: Salerno to Cassino* (Washington, D.C.: Office of the Chief of Military History, United States Army, 1969), p. 129.

cannot help feeling that Generals Walker, Dawley, and probably Mark Clark, too, would have become involved in the act, crowding the issue with "top brass." Whatever the merits of the different styles, McCreery did not consider the incident sufficiently important on an official level to include it in his daily dispatch. One can be sure though that the local battalion commanders at an unofficial level were made very much aware of their corps commander's concern.

A clear indication that the worst was over was that when the 180th RCT, the third and last element of the 45th Division, began to land from LSTs onto the beaches that day, Mark Clark moved them into corps reserve. There were no gaps in the line that needed to be plugged.

The momentum of the bureaucracy, which Alexander had set in motion some 24 hours earlier to find reinforcements for the British corps, was now in full spate. There was, however, one strange oversight or discrepancy that has never been explained. Alexander had sent a message to Philippeville in Algeria for reinforcements. It was from the ports in French North Africa that the British divisions had sailed for Salerno and where their bases and presumably reinforcement camps were still located. Nevertheless, at 1700 hours on September 14, Company Sergeant Major (CSM) Green of the infantry reinforcement section, No. 155 Transit Camp, which was located at Tripoli, some 450 miles from Philippeville, received a couple of signals ordering him to provide 1,500 men without delay.

Tripoli was in the rear area serving the British Eighth Army. Its transit camps were not pleasant places for a soldier to spend his days. The transit camps in the British Army served a variety of needs, but the most important was to provide reinforcements to front-line units. Consequently, new groups of troops, and men who had recovered after a battle wound, were sent to the camps until a vacancy was found for them. The camps were large, sprawling affairs with a shifting population producing the inevitable disorder and difficulties in management of men. An infantry soldier would spend the first two weeks at the camp on a compulsory course of battle hardening and fitness training before being moved across into the reinforcement area to await assignment to a unit. It was the policy of the transit camp commandant wherever possible to return men to their original units. This was especially the case for those in the 51st Highland and the 50th Tyne and Tees Infantry divisions. The scene was now set for what later became the "Salerno Mutiny."

At the subsequent courts-martial, CSM Green testified that reinforcements for these two divisions were specifically mentioned in the instructions he was given. The result was that the message spread around the tents, and when half an hour later the men paraded on the football field that adjoined the camp, there was no shortage of volunteers from the men in those divisions. The sergeant major told the men that there were three cruisers to take them back to their units. The process was code named Avalanche Draft and the men divided into three groups of 500 men, one for each cruiser. Green gave the men their instructions: "There will be a medical inspec-

OPERATIONS IN ITALY
SALERNO CAMPAIGN

Situation at Nightfall, September 14, 1943,
Following German Counterattacks of
September 12–14

0 1 1 2 3 4 5   10
Scale of Miles

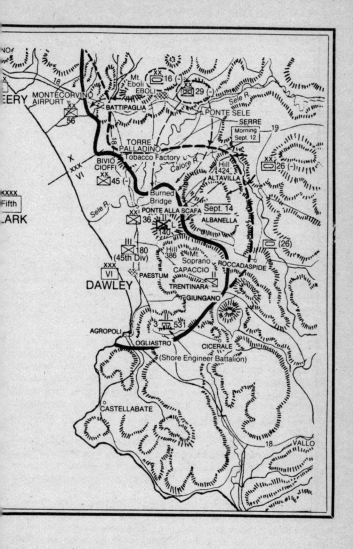

tion at 2200 hours. You will then collect your kit [personal possessions and equipment] and weapons, and sleep on the football field. Reveille will be at 0230 hours and breakfast at 0300 hours. You will fall in at 0400 hours for transport to the dock area."

When the men trooped off the field, they were more than contented with the turn of events and glad at the prospect of rejoining their own divisions. All had been in battle. Many had fought their way from the early campaigns in the Western Desert and on into Sicily, where they had been wounded. They were veterans. For the most part they were glad to be shedding the inevitable confusions and uncertainties of transit camp life for their own familiar officers and unit efficiency, for the freedom and friendliness of regimental life in the field.

In the 51st Highland Division, which marched into battle to the sound of bagpipes, strong divisional loyalty was paramount. Though the "Jocks" were intensely proud of their regiments, they had been taught that it was good soldiering to rejoin their own division, and an intense pride in it had been fostered. Indeed, at the transit camp many men still recovering from wounds tricked their way past the medical personnel and onto the draft, so eager were they to return to the division.

With the men of the 50th Division, a different system of loyalties operated. The division was named after the two great rivers of England's northeastern industrial zone, the Tyne and the Tees, for it was here among the steelworkers, miners, and shipbuilders of County Durham that it recruited. Pride in the division was there, but it was overridden by battalion and regimental loyalties and in the men of the Durham Light Infantry by a peculiar family affection for that regiment. To fight in any other regiment was unthinkable for a man from County Durham.

The men joined Avalanche Draft in the belief that they were rejoining their units fighting in Italy. At least one officer who also went with the group knew that was not the case. Capt. A. G. Lee, 1st Battalion, Yorks and Lancaster Regiment, still receiving daily dressings to his own wounds and quite unfit to fight, joined the group. He was taken aside by the commanding officer of No. 155 Transit Camp, who told him that the group was intended for Salerno and that the men should not be informed of their true destination.

Why was such an order necessary? If it was for security reasons, then it seems strange not to have informed the men that they were not returning to their units. Why did the commanding officer of the camp allow his sergeant major to perpetrate the deception? Why need the men have been deliberately deceived?

At about the time Avalanche Draft settled down to spend an uncomfortable few hours of sleep on the football field, a second wave of reinforcements from the 82nd Airborne Division arrived in Salerno. One hundred twenty Dakotas dropped 2,100 men of the 505th Parachute Infantry successfully into the DZ south of Paestum. They were moved immediately into positions on the southern flank near Agropoli. The men who had dropped the previous evening now held a position of the line southwest of Albanella in the Monte Soprano sector.

There was a more foolhardy mission to drop the 2nd Battalion, 509th Parachute Infantry far behind the German lines. Clark had resurrected the old ideas about raiders, and he selected Avellino as the target. The town lay about 20 miles north of Salerno and had certainly been acting as the logistical base for many of the German attacks on the British troops defending Salerno.

In the operation itself, everything went wrong. The 40 planes that carried the 600 men were scattered, and so were the paratroopers, over 15 miles of countryside. General Clark has always maintained that even so dispersed the paratroopers operating in small groups raided German supply convoys and disrupted their line of communications. Though, remarkably, 400 of the men were eventually to make it back to Allied lines, there is no evidence to suggest that so small and dispersed a force had any impact on the Salerno battle.

Indeed, even before the first paratroopers reached their supposed drop zone, Kesselring had his decision made for him. Hitler had ordered a gradual withdrawal north, toward Rome, and a scorched-earth policy.

So Kesselring proposed a final offensive effort against the British corps while the LXXVI Panzer Corps opposite the Americans went over to the defensive. Whatever the result of that battle, Kesselring proposed after it to defend four delaying lines. The first would be from Salerno through Potenza to Cerignola on the Adriatic coast.

That Tuesday night, as the battle gradually died down on the ground, the skies filled to the roar of engines as Wellingtons, Mitchells, and Bostons took over from the daylight raids. They blasted the main roads from Salerno to Naples and Castellammare and destroyed the rail network behind Battipaglia.

The effect of the air raids both day and night is best summed up in the 29th Panzer Grenadiers' divisional history:

> Even though we already knew from Sicily what Allied air superiority meant, the strafing we underwent at this time, and particularly on September 14, put all our previous experience in the shade. It was an achievement if one small vehicle made one short journey darting from cover to cover, and completely unscathed.

By the same token, Von Vietinghoff was to admit in his own messages that it was the concentrated and highly accurate fire support from the Allied warships that proved a major factor in the failures of the various armored counterattacks on the two critical days, September 13 and 14.

It could, of course, be argued that it was in the German interests to credit their failure to that element against which they had no answer—the warships at sea. No blame or shame could be attached to their efforts.

However, it was also the dogged resistance of the men who manned the front line of the Fifth Army that stopped the Germans at Salerno.

PART SIX

The End of the Beginning

The Fifth Army is just a young army trying hard to get along, while the Eighth Army is a battle trained veteran. We would appreciate your teaching us some of your tricks.

Mark Clark to Montgomery,
Paestum, September 24, 1943

Chapter XXIII

Pigoletti

For Lt. Lew Hemming, R.N.V.R., the night of September 14–15 was the worst at Salerno. His command, now a battered and dirty *LCT 397*, was secured alongside an ammunition ship some 4 miles out in the bay. Shelling of the anchorage by German heavy artillery was particularly bad, and the Luftwaffe were paying their nightly visit. There was a lot of smoke and noise, and the anchorage was lit by anti-aircraft tracers and parachute flares dropped by the enemy bombers. Hemming paced the bridge of the LCT and tried not to think about the consequences of a direct hit as he looked over into a hold that was beginning to fill with crates of mortar bombs and small-arms ammunition. The freighter's derrick swung out over the LCT, and a bulging cargo net crammed with yet more ammunition was lowered gently to the hold. Hemming's first lieutenant (or the "exec," as the Americans would call him) appeared on the bridge to give a progress report; he also brought a couple of mugs of steaming hot cocoa.

Royal Navy cocoa is really chocolate and is known as kye. The recipe has remained unchanged since it was first introduced into the Fleet in 1832. The beverage is made with cocoa beans from Grenada, Trinidad, and Guayaquil in fixed proportions. At a naval base in Devonport, England, the beans are roasted, crushed, mixed with sugar and arrowroot, pressed and stamped out in large, thick slabs, and issued to the Fleet. A piece of the chocolate is broken into hot water and allowed to "brew," canned sweetened milk and a small lump of butter are added, and the mixture is laced with a "tot" of rum. It has the consistency of a thick glue or resin. Kye has fortified watchkeepers in the small hours no matter the climate.

Hemming allowed the hot, sticky-sweet liquid to warm his insides and

feed new life and energy into his tired, aching body. Even as he drained the
last drops of that elixir, one of the crew came stumbling up the ladder to the
bridge. "Sir," the sailor said, trying to catch his breath, salute, and not
stumble over his words, "something's dropped into the hold." Hemming,
recognizing a voice on the edge of panic, placed his mug on the chart table
and ran down the ladders to the cargo deck. There was a bomb dangling over
the hold on what appeared to be a piece of wire.

"Good God, whats that?" Hemming asked.

The first lieutenant appeared with a flashlight, which he shone up onto
the bomb. It was, indeed, on the end of a wire, which had caught on one of the
iron stanchions that spanned the hold and carried the tarpaulin covers. By
the light of the flashlight they could see that the wire went on up and over
the freighter's superstructure. It had to be a trip wire or some type of fuse for
an antipersonnel device, but whether it was bomb, parachute mine, or shell,
Hemming neither knew nor cared. All that mattered was there was an evil
device hanging just a few feet above some stacked crates of mortar bombs.
Hemming turned to order the crew out of the hold, but they had already
gone; so he ran for the companionway that had been rigged to the freighter
and scrambled up to her main deck, where he grabbed the first seaman he
could find.

"See that wire?" Hemming said, pointing to the wire that snaked over the
ship's side and high onto the superstructure; "Stand by that wire and make
sure nobody touches it, or we will all be goners!"

It was at that moment that the captain of the freighter—it was a British
ship—together with a couple of his officers appeared. They were on their
way to the LCT to find out why the cargo was no longer being transshipped.
They seemed more anxious than most to be clear of Salerno.

"What's the trouble?" the freighter's captain demanded.

Hemming told him about the bomb.

"What are you going to do about it, mister?" the merchant captain asked.

"I don't know," Hemming said with all the honesty and frankness of
youth; he had never been so scared in all his life.

The merchant captain thought for a moment and then turned to one of his
officers. "Of course!" he exclaimed. "We've got a clown on board who will
take great pleasure in looking at that bomb."

An officer ran off to find the man in question. The latter was an old Royal
Navy seaman, with an armful of good-conduct badges and a face that
betrayed years of service on the high seas and in every dive from Shanghai to
Port Said. The war had rescued him from retirement. He was a gunner who
helped man the ancient 4.7-inch gun the freighter carried on her aft deck-
house as protection against U-boats. Apparently he liked to take shells to
pieces.

Hemming took the naval gunner into the LCT's hold, where he stared up
at the bomb under the flashlight beam. Hemming had a closer look, too, at
the bomb, which appeared to be about 2 feet long and perhaps 6 inches in
diameter. He guessed it weighed about 30 pounds.

"No problem there, sir," the gunner said. "You can give me a hand."

Hemming was about to suggest that one of his own crew would be more suitable, but there wasn't a man to be seen.

The gunner stacked boxes of grenades, clambered up to the bomb, and beckoned to Hemming to join him. The practiced ease with which the old sailor treated young and very junior lieutenants wasn't lost on Hemming either.

"Right, sir," the gunner said with an easy patience when Hemming had scrambled up beside him. "There you are. I can hold the bomb. I've got it all right. You break the wire."

The wire was made of a flexible soft steel. Gingerly Hemming held it between his hands and tried to twist it apart, but he was so nervous that he made little impression on the wire.

After a few moments of futile effort the old seaman could stand it no longer. He sucked his tongue, sighed, and said, "Here *sir,* you hold the bomb."

The gunner dumped the bomb unceremoniously into Hemming's arms and, before he could utter a protest, cracked the wire in two. The seaman scrambled down the boxes to the deck and then held up his hands to relieve Hemming of his burden.

"Right, sir, we'll throw it overboard," the gunner said.

Hemming had enough presence of mind to stop him and, instead, tied the bomb to the end of a long length of rope. Together they carried the bomb up onto the catwalk of the landing craft and then gently, very gently lowered it over the side. Once under water they were safe, for had they just thrown the bomb overboard it would have exploded on impact with the sea.

The old seaman gave Hemming a wry grin and winked as he threw him the smartest salute the young officer had seen since he had left officer training school. "Permission to return to my duty station, sir?" the old sailor said, and he was away before Hemming could think of anything to say. As if by magic the crew of *LCT 397* reappeared, and the work of loading her with the lethal cargo of bombs and shells continued.

The following morning, September 15, the destroyer H.M.S. *Offa* delivered General Alexander to the beachhead. He was accompanied by his American chief of staff, General Lemnitzer, and Air Marshal Conningham, who commanded the air support for the beachhead. The army group commander wasted no time responding to his Prime Minister Churchill's message.

General Alexander (Salerno) to Prime Minister (at sea), September 15, 1943:

> I feel sure you will be glad to know that I have already anticipated your wise advice and am now here with Fifth Army. Many thanks for your offer of help. Everything possible being done to make "Avalanche" a success. Its fate will be decided in the next few days.*

*Churchill, *The Closing Ring,* pp. 127–28, also quoted in W. G. F. Jackson, *Alexander of Tunis* (London: B. T. Batsford, 1971), p. 238.

Alexander's most recent biographers* applaud the general's steadying influence upon the Allied command ashore, and this was undoubtedly the case, for he was that sort of man. Immaculately dressed as always, his calm and unruffled demeanor could only have given confidence and strength to the nervous division and corps commanders and their harassed, weary staff. The writers also claim that he settled once and for all any question of a withdrawal. This is much harder to substantiate.

The American generals experienced the sharpest of trials and perhaps a higher degree of nervous strain than the British, if only because the latter had never considered any question of a contingency plan for a withdrawal.

General Alexander transferred from his destroyer to the flagship U.S.S. *Biscayne,* where he met with Admiral Hewitt and was brought up to date on the latest developments. The latter included the naval situation and especially the contingency plans for a withdrawal of the American corps. Alexander immediately countermanded Clark's instructions, ordered all such contingency planning to stop and the American beaches to be reopened as soon as the tactical situation in the battle allowed.

It is my contention that though Alexander did put a stop to the contingency plan, it had ceased to be a top priority in any case. The crisis had passed. Though the Germans would continue for a couple more days to probe for a weak spot in the Allied defenses, the heart had gone out of the Germans, and they no longer represented the threat of two days earlier.

The remaining assaults were launched by the diehard fanatics of the Hermann Göring Panzer Division against the British troops. The American front had some pressure but was to experience no more attacks of any real significance or threat. Instead, as we shall see, the heartache that remained for the Americans at Salerno was self-inflicted.

Reinforcements for the Fifth Army were now pouring ashore. The leading units of the 7th British Armored Division had now arrived on what was rapidly becoming a very crowded beachhead. By the following morning Clark's Fifth Army at Salerno numbered over 170,000 men. Such a force was the equivalent of seven divisions and far outnumbered the by now depleted and dispirited divisions of the German Tenth Army. Von Vietinghoff by scraping the bottom of the barrel found perhaps 20 tanks to spearhead the last attacks, while Clark had 200 British and American Shermans straining at the leash, just waiting for the infantry to secure the passes so that they could break out and strike hard for Naples and Rome!

Admiral Hewitt accompanied General Alexander and his team ashore. They landed at about 0730 hours and were met by Mark Clark, who took his visitors back to the Fifth Army command post for breakfast. Once in the villa, Clark took Alexander into his own room for a private discussion. Clark let his hair down with Alexander. Though they had known one another for less than a year, he had the greatest respect and admiration for the British officer.

---

*W. G. F. Jackson, *Alexander of Tunis*; Nigel Jackson, *Alex* (London: George Weidenfeld and Nicolson, 1973).

"Alex," Clark said, "I would like you to go now and visit VI Corps headquarters and look over Dawley. I'm worried about him." Clark went on to explain that he had had personally to place battalions in the line because Dawley seemed unable to handle the matter. "I don't want to influence you in any way," Clark concluded. "That's why I want you to see him without me along. If I had to take Dawley out of the battle, it would kill me, Alex. It would be the hardest thing I have ever had to do."

Alexander called in General Lemnitzer and explained the situation, for there was the thorny political problem of nationality and protocol involved. Together they set out by jeep for the short drive to the American Corps headquarters. Conningham stayed at Fifth Army headquarters.

General Dawley welcomed his distinguished visitors to the corps command post and conducted them into the small tent that served as the map room. It was primitive and stifling hot inside despite the still relatively early hour. Alexander asked Dawley what his future plans were for the corps. The response was embarrassing to all who witnessed the pitiful scene of a man under great strain, who with shaking hands and voice outlined in uncertain terms the future for his command.

On the return journey to Fifth Army headquarters both Alexander and Lemnitzer agreed that the most disturbing feature they had noticed was a corps staff who had lost confidence in the decisions and leadership of their commander.

Alexander and Lemnitzer joined Clark in his quarters at the command post.

"You've got a broken reed on your hands," Alexander said.

"I know it," Clark replied.

As an Army group commander, Alexander clearly had the authority to relieve Dawley—on the spot, if necessary; but he preferred in the interests of international diplomacy and harmony to do it by suggestion to Clark and Eisenhower rather than by direct action against an American general.

Later in the morning General Alexander, Clark, and Air Marshal Conningham visited the 36th Division Command post on Mount Soprano. General Walker was away, checking the La Cosa Creek defenses, so Colonel Kerr, the chief of staff, briefed the visitors. Kerr on behalf of his commanding general formally complained that the division had not been well supported by the air forces. Conningham, with his feathers ruffled, and what Kerr was later to describe to Walker as "a show of authority," promised to take care of that immediately. Walker laughed when he heard the story, and he reminded Kerr of a briefing they had both attended at Fifth Army headquarters in August when they were still in North Africa. At the end of the air forces' presentation of their commitment to the battle, George Patton, who sat next to Walker, leaned over and said in a "whisper" that all were intended to hear,

"Don't believe a damned word those British Air Force SOBs say, Fred. If you see any friendly air before the third day you will do well."

Patton had been right in his prediction until Eisenhower and Alexander had intervened to redirect the efforts of the air forces. It was so often the case that the infantry on the ground tended to judge the efforts of the air support by the number of planes they could see. What Walker, Kerr, and the others did not know was that the air forces since September 13 had struck continuously at the German communications network *to* the battle area. By September 15 the maximum effort had slackened somewhat, but nevertheless at the end of the day communications to the Tenth Army over a wide, deep arc encircling the Salerno beachhead were cut, damaged, and in some cases blocked completely. Medium and heavy bombers by the hundreds sortied from their fields in North Africa and Sicily. Fortresses, Liberators, Mitchells, and Marauders struck at road and rail routes into the area while Lightnings, Mustangs, and Kittyhawks roamed the battlefield, strafing and bombing anything German that moved.

Later Alexander and Clark drove across the Sele and the beachhead to meet with Dick McCreery and the British troops. McCreery in his calm, casual, but impressively efficient manner explained the situation and took Alexander forward into the battle area on both his divisional fronts. The contrast in the demeanor and confidence in the two corps commanders could not have been more obvious. Between visits to his divisions, McCreery took his guests down to the beach, where a picnic lunch had been arranged.

At about the same time, the big ships that Admiral Cunningham had sent from Malta dropped anchor in the bay. Even though they were well out at sea, the silhouettes of the two mighty battleships were unmistakable, and the word would quickly have spread among the troops onshore and given them fresh heart. H.M.S. *Valiant* closed in to support the British, while her 36,000-ton sister ship, H.M.S. *Warspite*, was deployed to the American corps. These battleships had a broadside each of eight 15-inch guns. The shell weighed 2,000 pounds and at maximum elevation the range was over 33,000 yards. Nevertheless, the value of the battleships at this stage was purely one of morale, for it was to take them the rest of the day to brief their gunnery officers and liaise with corps and army headquarters over troop deployments before sending their observation parties ashore.

The Americans were as obsessed as ever over Altavilla, and at 1720 hours that same day *Warspite** fired her first broadside onto the town. The U.S. cruisers *Boise* and *Philadelphia* joined in, but they had to take it quietly, for the naval ordnance stores in Sicily had loaded the last of the 6-inch shells onto *Ancon*. A destroyer had been sent by Admiral Hewitt to Malta to take shells from the crippled *Savannah*, and this shows the precarious position the Americans were in with some of their supplies.

The bombardment of Altavilla was intended to force the Germans to keep their heads down while the Americans returned to the offensive. This was the first indication for four days that the VI Corps was prepared to take the

---

*The *Warspite* didn't stay too long at the beachhead. The following afternoon the Germans launched their radio-controlled bombs en masse at the battleship. Two hit and others, near-misses, caused considerable damage. The *Warspite* followed the *Savannah* and the *Uganda* under tow to Malta.

initiative and the battle to the enemy. Just before sunset a battalion of the 179th Infantry from the 45th Division, supported by tanks and self-propelled artillery, reentered "the corridor" and cautiously advanced inland close to the Sele River. There was little opposition, and when the battalion came to stop for the night it had advanced several miles. If nothing else it helped restore morale and confidence while at the same time pushing back the Germans from the vicinity of Mark Clark's command post. The latter was an important consideration, since Alexander had decided to remain on the beachhead for the present and would stay at Fifth Army headquarters. That evening Alexander cabled Eisenhower that he was most favorably impressed by Clark's calmness and serenity under adverse circumstances, but was less favorably impressed by Dawley. He also advised that Eisenhower should come to the beachhead at the earliest opportunity.

September 15 had been a bad day for the German troops in the Tenth Army. Pounded from the air, they made desperate attempts to break through and concentrated their efforts on the by now war-weary British division. The Schmaltz Battle Group from the Luftwaffe Panzer Division Hermann Göring hammered at the Lincolns and the York and Lancasters, but though they gained some ground into the Cava defile, the doughty infantry held firm.

Farther to the south of Salerno, however, the Germans had made a strong attack, captured the village of Pigoletti, and dug in on three hills: White Cross; the Pimple; and the Crag, which was later to become known as 41 Commando Hill. It was important to recover the ground, or at least find out what the enemy intentions were likely to be, because the hills gave the Germans an excellent view of much of the British part of the beachhead.

After he had seen his high-ranking visitors back across the Sele, McCreery went straight to the commandos, who were now encamped on the outskirts of Salerno. They had been out of the line for a couple of days since the Leicesters had relieved them on Dragonea and the high ground above Vietri. They had rested and washed, safe in the belief that their part as special forces in the battle for Salerno was over. Indeed, the gossip was that they were to embark in the next 24 hours for Sicily. McCreery sought out Col. Jack Churchill, disabused him of any rumor that they were to leave his command, and explained the situation.

"I want you to do a raid up the valley to Pigoletti this evening, Jack," McCreery said. "The Germans have infiltrated onto the hills and driven the infantry in a bit. Launch a raid, get some prisoners, and see what the score is."

McCreery also outlined the role the marine commandos were to play. While Churchill and his Army commandos swept up the valley, the marines were to attack the Pimple and the Crag.

The commandos were not at all pleased to be returning to the fray. The thought of yet another bloody fire fight for the recovery of high ground that the infantry had lost struck them as yet another case of having to do the ordinary army's dirty work.

Some of the marines, too, were at the end of their tether. At moments like this the leadership qualities of young officers are tested to the limit. Cpl. Alf Branscombe watched as his troop leader called the men together.

"Well, it appears to me you've all got the 'fuck you' attitude; and if you've got the 'fuck you' attitude, I'll show you exactly what that means. Now, get fell in with your kit and weapons, and we're going back up the line."

The marines moved off quickly, fell into line, and at the word of command, with a spring in their step, marched smartly back into war.

Churchill gathered his officers together, and they discussed the operation. The biggest problem was that no one in headquarters could give them any accurate indication of enemy strength. Churchill divided his force in six columns, each the strength of one troop. The men were ordered to fan out and thus cover the whole valley. Tom Gordon-Hemming asked how they were to maintain contact among the troops, and at this point Churchill decided to make a virtue out of uncertainty.

"We'll shout to one another, Tom," Churchill said. "We'll yell 'Commando!' at the top of our voices all the way up that bloody valley."

This really was an extraordinary decision and one you will never find in military manuals on tactics. In the darkness and the confusion, the hope was that the enemy would think that a whole division was advancing, not an Army commando, which then had less than 300 men.

Churchill demoted himself to a troop leader and joined Joe Nicholl's troop. Nicholl's troop had the most difficult task, which was to advance along the base of the valley and follow the track that led up to Pigoletti. Churchill liked to be in the front. He encouraged all his officers to lead by example, by plain "bloody aggression." In the commandos the officer was up front with the scouts rather than behind the leading squad or section, as is normally the case with infantry.

The marine commandos were going to do things differently. Wilkinson attended the officers' briefing, but it was all vague to him, for he was still completely deaf after the mortar attack on Dragonea. The commandos were so short of officers that he didn't have the heart to report sick. Major Lumsden, who still was in command, decided to split his force in two for the assault on the Crag and the Pimple. They were to move out ahead of Churchill's commandos and had less distance to travel, although it was the high ground. Under these quite different tactical conditions Lumsden opted for the silent approach to get as close as they could, to be followed by a mad, headlong charge over the last bit of ground into the enemy positions.

At last light, just as the battalion of the 179th Infantry was bivouacing in the Sele corridor, the marine commandos passed through the line held by the 8th Battalion the Royal Fusiliers at Mercatello. David Appleby, who had liaised with the marines, stood outside an old farmhouse, which served as battalion headquarters, and watched them go by. The spirit of the commandos was remarkable. One of the men had an enormous silk shawl over his shoulders, with tassels hanging down to his ankles. The marine wore a pair of German officer's high boots.

The marines divided into two groups and moved up the slopes to the hills. They were to start some 10 minutes ahead of Churchill's Army commandos so they could seize the high ground that dominated the valley to Pigoletti.

It was almost as if the Germans knew that something was up, for random bursts of tracers cut across the hillside from their machine-gun nests. Alf Branscombe moved with the attack force on the Pimple; he checked the safety catch on his Thompson and plodded up the hill. Suddenly the tracers ceased, and a silence descended over the hillside. The marines stopped in their tracks, for they knew what the silence meant. The enemy had spotted or heard something and were at that moment swiveling their guns onto the target. A flare soared into the sky high overhead, and as the guns opened up, the marines dropped to the ground. The man behind Branscombe was marginally slow, and he took a burst of tracer. It cut him through the middle, and the trunk fell across Alf's legs. Branscombe pushed the gory remains away and with the others stood up to charge the position. They had the massed firepower of their automatic weapons, and, though probably outnumbered, the marines now put them to good use. The object was to scare the wits out of the enemy and keep them cowering in the trenches rather than firing their own weapons in defense.

In an attack of this nature, where the element of surprise has been lost and you know you are outnumbered, the last 600 yards count, for that is the vital ground before the enemy position. To cover the ground an attacking force has to demonstrate the old-fashioned qualities, the military virtues of courage and dash. The marines had those virtues, just as their successors were to demonstrate 40 years later in the Falklands.

The marines of 41 Commando took the Pimple and dug in. The second group took the Crag and did likewise. Their officers sent up a succession of colored flares to signal the successful completion of their mission just as Churchill led his force past the outposts manned by the Fusiliers. The Germans, they knew, were bound to counterattack.

The six troops of the Army commandos fanned out across the valley and soon the night was punctuated by loud cries of "Commando! Commando!" echoing off the hillsides.

Gordon-Hemming was up with two scouts. His batman, Private Davidson, was with him. On occasions such as these he acted as escort or bodyguard for his officer and was suitably armed with a Thompson. They were moving along the reverse slope of the Pimple and were about thirty yards ahead of the rest of the men in the troop. Gordon-Hemming and the spearhead group were close to some tall trees, which cast a deep black shadow over the moonlit ground. Suddenly the shadows moved, and the commandos eased off the safety catches of their weapons as a party of Germans ran out, arms held high in the air shouting, *"Ja! Ja! Kamerad! Kamerad!"* The four commandos lined up the frightened, leaderless, and demoralized foe—there were over 40 of them—as the rest of the troop ran up to assist. Though the prisoners outnumbered the commandos there was nothing to fear, and Gordon-Hemming detached a corporal and three men to escort them down the slope to the valley floor, where he ordered them to join up with Churchill and Joe Nicholl.

Churchill received the prisoners and placed them at the end of his column before continuing the march on up the valley; he was following the line of a goat track. An hour later the track petered out just below the village of Pigoletti; they had not encountered any more of the enemy. Churchill turned to Joe Nicholl: "I'm going to check out the village, Joe. Give me a good soldier to act as escort."

Nicholl gave him Corporal Russell, who was armed with a Thompson. Churchill whispered his instructions to Corporal Russell: "Follow me about 20 yards behind and have your Thompson ready. Don't shoot unless I yell out. I will shout if I want you to fire, but for Christ's sake, don't hit me!"

Churchill had three cardinal rules in war, which he impressed on his men. The first was to prevent your own kit from being stolen. The second was to avoid being shot by your own side. And the third was to kill the enemy. Churchill handed his bagpipes to Nicholl for safekeeping, drew his claymore, and stepped out toward the village. The faithful Russell moved behind his colonel.

There was a half moon, which gave sufficient light to pick out the shape and outline of the village. The pair reached the village, where on the right-hand side of the street—which was nothing more than a cobbled track of rough-hewn stone—the shadows of the houses provided some cover. They crossed over and crept quietly past the houses. Churchill moved with the surefooted stealth of a cat; he was in his element. He was about halfway down the street when to his astonishment he saw the telltale glow of a cigarette on the other side. Was it a German sentry or some innocent Italian? Churchill wasn't about to take chances. With all the noise the commandos had made earlier, it was a miracle the village wasn't alive with the enemy. To this day he can't understand why they weren't alert and ready. Churchill crept back up the street, joined Russell, told him of the cigarette, and whispered new instructions: "We're going back to the edge of the village, cross the street, and then come back down on the other side."

It took them ten minutes to reach the opposite side of the street, where they had to move very carefully, for now they were in the moonlight. Silently the two men slipped from one doorway to the next, taking turns to move as each covered the other.

Eventually Churchill came to an archway at the corner of the street; there was the glow of the cigarette again. This time Churchill could pick out the shapes of three men. He listened for a moment; they were no more than a couple of yards away. One seemed to be an Italian civilian who appeared to be offering the other two, who were German sentries, wine from a large jar. The sentries were taking turns drinking from the jar.

Churchill was on the point of launching himself at the trio when the Italian and one of the Germans moved away; the other sentry remained. Churchill stood rock still, waiting to see what would happen next. The sentry puffed away at the last of the cigarette; he was leaning against a wall, his rifle slung carelessly across his shoulder. The colonel was in a quandary; for there was no way he could reach him without making noise, and he didn't know where the other two men had gone.

It seemed like an age, but it couldn't have been more than a couple of minutes before the others returned. It was now or never. With his sword at the ready, Churchill launched himself out of the dark at the trio. Surprise was complete. One German dropped his rifle, the other raised his hands in the air, and the Italian with the sword at his throat stifled a sob. All three surrendered.

Churchill pushed them before him through the arch, then stopped dead in his tracks. The archway led into a small courtyard or compound where a large-caliber mortar was mounted, ammunition neatly stacked and ready to fire. The rest of the mortar crew was huddled in sleep.

"Come on, Russell, come here at once!" Churchill yelled. "Cover these fellows," ordered Churchill, pointing to the luckless trio who stood cringing against the wall still in shock; and little wonder, after an encounter with a swordsman in the dead of night.

Churchill moved among the inert forms, kicking the crew awake.

"Can anyone talk English?" he demanded.

"I talk a little English," said one man.

"All stand up with your hands against the wall."

The German repeated the instructions and his comrades—there were six of them—did as they were told. Russell checked them for weapons, and the Italian disappeared. Churchill thought it could be dangerous, but then assumed that he had had enough of a fright for one night and would stay in his house.

Churchill took the Thompson off Russell. "Go back and fetch Mr. Nicholl," he ordered. The colonel then turned to the Germans. "Stay like that," he ordered. "Nobody move. Anybody moves, he gets shot immediately. In fact," Churchill added for good measure, "if anybody moves, you all get shot!"

"Jawohl!" said the interpreter, who repeated the instructions to his comrades.

Within a few minutes Joe Nicholl and the remainder of the troop ran into the courtyard and took over the guard. Churchill with the English-speaking German, Russell, and another soldier, set off through the rest of the village. Between them the two Britons captured another three sets of double sentries without firing a shot.

There was a barn standing in one corner of the courtyard. Joe Nicholl investigated and found an aid post inside with half a dozen wounded enemy and an orderly. Three of the injured were too ill to move, so he left them with the medic.

The remainder of the troop who were not detailed to guard the compound were sent to check the houses in the village. They returned with a German officer and a sergeant. The civilians were ordered to stay inside their houses and keep the doors shut.

Churchill called for his signaler and spoke to the other troop commanders.

They all reported that they had completed their part of the operation successfully, the valley had been swept clear of the enemy, and the marines he knew were firmly ensconced on the Crag and the Pimple.

Churchill ordered the troop commanders to close down their radio and proceed to base. He then turned to Joe Nicholl to discuss the arrangements for their own return.

It is the normal custom to disarm prisoners before they are marched off the battlefield and into captivity, but not for Churchill. He had all the bolts and firing pins taken out of his prisoners' rifles and machine pistols and placed in an empty sandbag. The prisoners then slung the weapons over their shoulders, and each man was ordered to carry six mortar bombs. A couple of the commandos found a large old two-wheeled handcart, into which the three less seriously wounded prisoners were placed together with the mortar. Four prisoners were detailed to pull the cart.

Just before the commandos set off from the village, Churchill radioed base, where the corps commander was waiting for his report.

General McCreery listened to what Churchill had to say. "That's marvelous, how incredible," McCreery said. "However did you manage it?" (McCreery was never an advocate of correct radio procedure.)

"It's all right, General, we've got lots of prisoners. We're on our way back."

"Don't come back! Don't come back!" responded McCreery. "Stay there. This is too marvelous for words. Have you got good positions up there?"

"Well, we had," replied Churchill, "but we're all coming back now."

"Stop them! Stop them!" ordered General McCreery.

"I can't stop the commandos. I've got one troop I can stop and that's about 40 men under a second lieutenant. As arranged, the rest are on their way down to you, and they're off the air."

"Can you stop them anyhow?" McCreery asked.

"No, I can't," replied Churchill. "They're on the way down for a hot meal and, if I know my boys, going as fast as they can. I will leave Nicholl and his troop in Pigoletti while I come down to bring the commandos back to these positions."

Churchill discussed the new situation with Joe Nicholl and then gathered the prisoners together. He always believed in taking prisoners into his confidence. "Listen," he said to the interpreter, "there has been a change of plan. We are going to occupy your village. I will have only three men to take you down to our base, myself and two others. Is that clear? *Jawohl?*"

"*Jawohl!*" the German replied, and he told the others what Churchill had said.

"Now," continued Churchill, "we have three automatic weapons and we're going to walk behind you. If a single man runs off the path, which is easy, the rest of you will get shot. Your officer and sergeant will be at the back and get theirs first. Now, is that absolutely clear to everyone?"

"*Jawohl!*" the German said. When the latter had finished translating, Churchill ordered him to say it all again.

"Any questions?" Churchill asked.

There were none.

"Now we will go down the track. All will be friendly, and it will be quite all right. For you the war is over. One day you will all go home to your families."

Churchill and the two commandos escorted the prisoners down the valley and back to the British lines. Harry Blisset, the commandos' second-in-command, who had remained behind with the rear party, greeted them on their return. He reported the safe arrival of the other troops.

The prisoners lined up with the commandos and were given a Dixie cup of hot soup. Churchill then turned to Harry Blisset. "Send these buggers off to the nearest POW camp," he ordered.

It was by now the early hours of the morning, and Churchill had completely forgotten all about the prisoners' weapons. They were taken down to the nearest compound, where, because of the hour, the sentry at the gate simply counted them into the cage. The commando corporal who was in charge of the escort turned to the sentry: "Let these people sleep until morning when you can then get all their details. There's no need to call out your officer at this ungodly hour."

(The next morning, when the officer in charge of the POW compound arrived, he found a group of Germans sitting there with their mortar and stacked ammunition, cleaning the dew off their rifles. There was an awful row. It went all the way to the corps commander. McCreery was highly amused and got on the radio to Churchill.

"What's all this about, Jack?" McCreery asked.

"Oh, yes, I was aware they were armed, sir. I'm afraid I never got around to taking their weapons off them. Harry Blisset has probably got the bolts."

"Well, next time take the arms off them before they go into the compound. You frightened the life out of the rear-area staff!")

Meanwhile, Churchill gathered together the remainder of the commandos, quickly briefed his troop leaders, and rushed with them back up to the village of Pigoletti. It was a race against time, but they arrived just before dawn.

It had been a long couple of hours for Joe Nicholl, but he had not wasted time. The young officer knew that the Germans had to respond to this commando move and were bound to counterattack with the dawn. If the enemy used tanks the commandos would be in trouble, for the only anti-armor weapons they had were a few PIATs; they didn't even have mines. So Nicholl set his men digging holes in the ground in front of the village and then covering the holes with mounds of earth to give the appearance of a minefield, which he then covered with some carefully sited Bren light machine guns in the hope it would fool the enemy.

Churchill quickly deployed the extra troops through the village and onto the terraced slopes to link up with the marines on the Pimple and the Crag. The commandos dug in among the vines and together formed a horseshoe-shaped defense position with the village as a strongpoint in the center. The colonel radioed back to base from his command post and arranged artillery covering fire. There was nothing to do but await the inevitable fury of the German counterattack.

Dawn came and with it the Germans. Stung to anger by the insolence of the commandos, the enemy stormed the Pimple, where the outnumbered marines were soon overwhelmed and forced to fall back and re-form across the valley onto the Crag.

Fighting around Pigoletti was furious, but Churchill and his men resisted the first attack, though casualties on both sides were appalling. A second assault was launched later in the morning, and this time the enemy was able to attack from the high ground of the Pimple as well as from the front. Wellington's No. 2 Troop on the left flank took the brunt of this assault.

Churchill, who was about 300 yards away, could see that things looked bad, so he radioed No. 2 Troop.

"Get Captain the Duke of Wellington," he ordered the young signaler who manned the radio.

"He can't come, sir," the soldier said.

"Why not? Is he wounded?" Churchill asked.

"No, he's not wounded, but none of us can move. We're pinned down, sir," was the reply.

"What's the position there?" Churchill asked.

"It's very bad, sir, the attack is heavy. I think we might be overrun."

"Well call out to the duke and say the colonel says if things are bad the troop had better fall back on Pigoletti."

About 20 minutes later the men of No. 2 Troop came stumbling into Pigoletti carrying their wounded with them. Wellington reported to the command post.

"Thank goodness you are here, Morny," Churchill said. "I gather you had a rather ghastly time."

"Oh, no, Colonel, it wasn't too bad."

"Well, I thought you were about to be overrun," an indignant Churchill said.

"No, Colonel, I had an order from you to fall back," Wellington said. Wellington thought for a moment and then said, "I'll go back up if you like, sir."

"Can you really do that?"

"Oh, yes. The Germans are not too far away, but we should be able to get back into the position."

Wellington gathered his troop, and they stormed out of Pigoletti and up the hill. The remainder of the force gave them as much covering fire as they could, but the Germans had beaten them to the vacated ground. The Duke of Wellington led a furious charge, the sheer impetus of which carried them into the trenches and desperate hand-to-hand combat with the enemy. The casualties were heavy and included the duke, who fell at the head of his troop. Later, when there was a brief respite in the battle, the men recovered his body. The Duke of Wellington lay next to a German officer; it appeared they had killed one another.

Churchill was told of the death of Wellington, and he radioed the information back to Brigadier Laycock, who led the commando brigade. There was little time to spare for remorse because the Germans struck again, and Churchill had to concentrate all his attention on repelling the repeated onslaughts of the enemy.

Alan Moorehead and his fellow correspondents, having now recovered from their spirited dash through the mountains of Calabria, clambered up into Dragonea and were in time to witness what was to be the final act in the German offensive. They watched as German soldiers and vehicles prepared to evacuate Cava. Just 500 yards away, peasant women with bundles on their heads and men with laden donkeys passed through the German lines and down the road that led into Salerno, ignoring the British outposts as they headed toward the marketplace. Thursday is market day in Salerno. Moorehead watched this with utter fascination. He had seen the same thing in Tunisia but not on anything like such a scale. He could only assume they did this out of habit because those were the only things to cling to in the cataclysm of war; they went on with their lives even when their homes were falling to pieces. An escorting soldier from the Lincolns pointed to a figure on the opposite hillside. A man and his horse were plowing a strip of field, even while the mortar shells fell around him in the freshly turned earth.

The Eighth Army, which Moorehead and the other correspondents were officially accredited to, was at that moment just 50 miles from Dawley's corps headquarters at Paestum. Montgomery's advance battalions were contesting the roadblocks defended by the German rearguard from the 26th Panzers at Lagonegro. General Von Vietinghoff ordered the rear guard to break off contact and move northward beyond the Salerno front without delay. Kesselring endorsed Von Vietinghoff's decision and ordered a general withdrawal behind the Volturno River to begin no later than September 18.

Even as the first battle groups of the Tenth Army began to move behind their rear guards, British reinforcements were arriving on the beachhead in increasing numbers.

Lew Hemming had just about finished unloading all the ammunition from *LCT 397* after the excitement of the bomb. It had taken a beach party of soldiers and the crew many hours of backbreaking toil to empty those holds of the stacked crates of ammunition.

The LCT was empty when along came the beachmaster. "Look!" he said. "There's a cruiser coming up. She's the *Scylla*."

The Dido class anti-aircraft cruiser hove into view, closely followed by her sister ships *Euraylus* and *Charybdis*.

"She's got some troops on board we want to get in quickly," the Beachmaster said. Can you go out and meet her and bring them in?"

The beachmaster hurried away to organize additional landing craft to take the troops from the other two cruisers.

The troops on board the three cruisers were the group from the reinforcement camp in North Africa. They were angry and very discontented. While at sea they had been informed that they were bound for Salerno, not

Sicily, where their divisions were. This announcement was greeted by emotions that varied from puzzlement to dismay, anger, and even incredulity. Not all the men had heard the news, and some were still convinced they were to join their own units. The cruisers had been rife with rumors ever since the announcements. Tales such as "The 50th Division is at Salerno," or "The Highlanders are fighting with the Eighth Army, and we will rejoin our units when they reach Salerno" spread around the crowded mess decks. Others were convinced that they had been "shanghaied" by the authorities and were unlikely to see their old units again.

Neither did it help to have 500 soldiers, with their kit bags and weapons, crammed into a cruiser that displaced less than 6,500 tons. The soldiers were dumped into every empty space, and some had had to spend the voyage on the upper decks. Discipline under such shipboard conditions was lax, but the officers and sergeants in the groups did little or nothing to settle doubt and uncertainty among the men. Indeed, some officers gave reassurance to the men, sympathized with their plight, and suggested that if all 1,500 stood firm, the authorities would have to send them back to their own units. Some soldiers, especially those in the Durhams, discussed their chances for an "honorable desertion" in the belief they would be praised if they rejoined their units illegally.

H.M.S. *Scylla* stood about 4 miles offshore. Her engines were closed down, and she lay with her bows into the wind. The upper decks were black with troops. Lew Hemming maneuvered *LCT 397* alongside, not the easiest thing to do, and made fast while the gangway was rigged and the first troops, sullen and silent, clambered into the holds of the landing craft. Another boat stood off waiting to take the rest.

A young officer came down from the cruiser and joined Hemming on his bridge. "We sailed at full speed right from Tripoli," he confided. "We've been told the battle is bad, and there have been a lot of casualties." Hemming explained that, on the contrary, he thought the situation had eased considerably in the past couple of days.

Hemming took about half the group and then headed in to the beach in the 46th Division sector. The group scrambled ashore and a beach party directed the men toward some fields immediately behind the sand dunes. There to a considerable extent they were left to fend for themselves. No one seemed to be in charge, uncertainty grew, and rumors spread like wildfire. Two rumors in particular seemed to be alarmingly credible. A detail of clerks and cooks had eventually set up some tents to feed and administer the group. From them the men learned that they were indeed to reinforce the 46th and 56th Infantry divisions. The second rumor was an angry story spread that the appropriate reinforcements for the 46th Division had been left behind in Tripoli. To many of the men assembled in the fields, this appeared all the more credible, for the frightening laxity in "authority" that it illustrated showed in the behavior of that same "authority" that was now ignoring them at Salerno.

Night descended over the battlefield, and the group, disgruntled and in an ugly mood, settled down to sleep where they were and as best they could. The noise of battle sounded in the foothills where Churchill and his commandos still hung on grimly. If Von Vietinghoff had decided to withdraw, nobody had told those members of his army who were still attacking Pigoletti.

It was to prove a long and costly night for the embattled commandos. At one time in the small hours Joe Nicholl ran down to the house that served as Churchill's command post. The mortar barrage and machine-gun fire was particularly loud and lethal. The young officer saw an exhausted Churchill pouring over his maps by the flickering light of a couple of candles. Suddenly Churchill cursed, threw down his pencil, stood up, and walked outside, bagpipes in his hand.

Oblivious to enemy shot and shell, Churchill walked up and down the street playing the bagpipes. Though the commandos frequently cursed their colonel and his pipes, it was just the sort of thing that kept them going in crisis hours. It made the blood course through tired bodies and tightened their resolve. The emotional appeal of the bagpipes in moments like these is inescapable. God alone knows what that sound did to the Germans.

Farther down the valley, the Fusiliers in their trenches heard the pipes. It was an eerie sound: The valley echoed to the fire of Spandaus and bursting shells, but above it all came the swirl of the pipes played by an expert. Those who could, recognized the haunting strains of the lament, "Will ye no come back again?"

Chapter XXIV

Once More to Altavilla

For the Americans in the VI Corps that Thursday, September 16, proved to be a relatively quiet day along the La Cosa line, with the enemy sending small probing attacks and fighting patrols seeking the weak points; but there were none.

Nevertheless, Clark was still concerned about Dawley. General Ridgway, the commanding general of the 82nd Airborne Division, arrived that morning, but the two regiments from this division were under Walker's command; so there was little for Ridgway to do. Ridgway was a very old friend of Mark Clark; they had been classmates at West Point. The Army commander now took the very unusual step of appointing Ridgway deputy corps commander. Together they went to see Dawley.

"Mike," said Clark, "I know this has been awful hard because you have had one hell of a mission here with one division, and you have been up against one hell of an enemy. I'm going to put Matt Ridgway up here to help you because you can't be all places at once."

Clark did not recall Dawley objecting to the appointment, and that too was pretty revealing. Any corps commander worth his salt would have questioned such a unique step, which could only be interpreted as a vote of no confidence, and it is inconceivable that Dawley could not have recognized that his days as a corps commander in the Fifth Army were numbered.

In his evening message Clark informed Eisenhower that Dawley "should not be continued in his present job. He appears to go to pieces in emergencies."

As deputy corps commander, Ridgway was able to watch over the arrangements as the Americans prepared to launch an offensive that it was hoped would signal the return of the initiative to the Fifth Army at Salerno. On the evening of September 16 Walker, still trying to take Altavilla, ordered two battalions of Col. Reuben Tucker's 504th Parachute Infantry to attack that high and bloody ground on the corps right flank. Just before dusk the paratroopers moved across their start line near Albanella and headed for the ill-famed Hill 424, which was to be their initial objective.

Unfortunately, an alert enemy spotted the movement of the paratroopers, and by the time Reuben Tucker's men had reached the lower slopes of Hill 424, they were under intense mortar and artillery fire. They worked their way up the slopes, taking casualties almost every step of the way. The Allied Navy and field artillery plastered Altavilla and the slopes beyond, which probably had the adverse effect of preventing the Germans from conducting their own orderly withdrawal. In the face of such heavy fire the enemy had little option but to battle it out with the American paratroopers.

Pvt. Ralph Jetton, still acting as a bodyguard, spent an uncomfortable first night on the slopes below Altavilla. The men moved in single file along a goat track, which contoured up the hillside at a crazy angle. There was considerable confusion. The battalion had lost its 81mm mortar platoon. Its presence on the lower terraces giving close support would have been a godsend. Somehow (nobody in Jetton's hearing was to give a satisfactory reason) in the fog of war the platoon had been left behind at Albanella; so the battalion had to make do with the smaller 60 mm mortars.

It was to take the paratroopers another 24 hours of blood, sweat, and toil before they were able to clear Altavilla and climb the last few feet onto Hill 424. The sight that greeted them turned their stomachs. Hill 424 was littered with dead "T" Patchers. It was the most terrible sight that young Jetton had ever seen. His brother was in the division, and at first he turned the bodies over, half afraid but unable to look to see if his brother lay among the dead. The bodies had been lying there for some days in the hot sunlight. They had turned black and swelled up into grotesque shapes as the gases inside expanded until the carcases burst through the uniforms. The sweet, cloying smell of death, that unforgettable smell, pervaded everything. The paratroopers could smell it on their clothes and taste it in their food; there was no escape. Identification of the dead was impossible, for even the dog tags had been engulfed by the grossly swollen throats. Jetton dug his trench among the dead and prayed his brother wasn't there.

Clearly the Germans weren't ready for the Americans to occupy Altavilla; maybe they were remnants of the rear guard from the 26th Panzers who still had to complete their escape from Calabria. At any rate, the paratroopers had hardly dug deeply enough into the hard earth to give themselves the shallowest of shell scrapes before the Germans counterattacked. A Panzer Mark IV tank followed by a couple of assault guns came trundling up the road that led from Ponte Sele and the valley below. The armor brushed aside the paratroopers in the outpost line and moved toward Altavilla; behind them gray-clad German infantry fanned out and charged the main defenses. The

Americans rained 60mm mortar shells down onto the enemy. This was all they had until the radio link back to Walker's command post brought succor in the shape of a barrage from the field artillery. This was enough to dent the armor's resolve and send the infantry scuttling back down the hill slopes. One of the assault guns, which was open-topped, received a direct hit and disintegrated into a bloody fireball. The tank and the other assault gun beat a hasty retreat down the track to Ponte Sele.

For the first time in a long while the Americans had the advantage of the high ground in the hills above Altavilla, and this they put to excellent use as the Germans tried repeatedly during the day to recapture the position. After a while the enemy counterattacks lost some of their drive, and then suddenly German soldiers were surrendering in droves.

Jetton kept close to Major Wellams, but when the battle was over Jetton was sent to guard the prisoners. Jetton was impressed by the Germans. They seemed good troops, young, stouthearted, and strong; not in the least bit intimidated by their captors.

One of the Germans spoke excellent English. "We ought to be friends," he said to Jetton. "We ought to be fighting the British and the Russians."

Jetton turned to his buddy, a little redheaded Jewish boy from the Bronx named "Cosh" Lemnitz. "What do you think of that dumb remark, Cosh?" Jetton asked his friend.

The German heard the word "Cosh" and spat at Lemnitz' feet.

Cosh reached for his trench knife and went for the German. "You lousy Kraut bastard!" Cosh yelled.

Jetton had to wrestle Cosh to the ground, pry the knife from his hand, and sit on him until he had cooled off a little.

Later that night the prisoners were taken back down the hill and escorted to the cage, which Sheriff Puck and his policemen from the 36th Division had established on the beach. Jetton had returned to his position on the hill, where he sat on the edge of his foxhole looking out over the plain and enjoying the cool night air. A lieutenant came up the path over the rise and as he moved toward Jetton the latter recognized the 36th Division's shoulder patch on his combat jacket.

"What outfit you out of, Lieutenant?" Jetton inquired.

"The 141st Infantry," he replied.

"What battalion?" Jetton asked.

"The 3rd Battalion, soldier," the officer said. "What's it to you?"

"Do you know a fella named Jetton in your outfit?"

"Sure do," the officer said.

"Is he all right?"

"Well," the lieutenant said, "he was a few minutes ago. He's sitting down the track waiting with the rest of the company to come to relieve you!"

Jetton gave a whoop of delight, jumped out of his hole, and ran down over the hill. It was pitch black, and he could hardly see. All that he could make out were the shadows and shapes of men lying against the hillside waiting to come up the path.

Jetton moved along the path, calling his brother's name, but quietly, for although the Germans had pulled back, one couldn't be too careful.

"Jetton! Jetton!" he called in a loud whisper. (His brother never used a Christian name; everybody since childhood had called him Jetton.) "Jetton!" he called again.

"Yeah, what the hell do you want?" said the voice of a man who clearly thought he was about to get sent on a particularly nasty patrol or some other unpleasantness.

"It's me, it's Dub," Ralph said, using his family nickname.

"You little son-of-a-bitch," his brother said.

They hugged one another, and others in his brother's section gathered around, for many came from the Jettons' hometown in Texas.

The Texans moved on up the hill and dug in beside the weary paratroopers. The two brothers shared a foxhole and talked what was left of the night away.

General Eisenhower visited the beachhead on September 17 for the first time. General Lemnitzer, the army group's chief of staff, went out in the patrol boat to meet Eisenhower's destroyer. Lemnitzer used this opportunity to brief his superior on the situation at VI Corps and the problems that confronted Mark Clark.

Eisenhower listened for a while and then burst out angrily. "Why doesn't he relieve Dawley?" he asked.

Mark Clark was waiting at the shore for the party to arrive. He asked Eisenhower to do the same as Alexander and visit Dawley, so Lemnitzer conducted Eisenhower to the VI Corps command post, where they were given a briefing. Dawley appeared even more nervous than the day before.

Later Mark Clark met with General Eisenhower and Admiral Hewitt, who was also in the party at Walker's command post. The divisional commander briefed his visitors on the battle situation.

At the end of Walker's presentation Eisenhower rounded on Dawley. "How did you ever get your troops into such a mess? he asked.

It was Walker's turn to be amazed. Instead of explaining that there really wasn't any mess but that he had retained a firm tactical control of the battle, exercised through his divisional commanders, Dawley mumbled some reply and then appeared lost for words.

The party left the 36th Division command post to drive north to see Gen. Troy Middleton at his command post close to the Sele before going on to meet with the British. Eisenhower shared a jeep with Clark and they discussed Dawley. "Wayne, you had better take him out," Eisenhower said.

"Well, Ike, I've come to that conclusion, and I want to put Ridgway in command."

"It's your baby, Wayne," Eisenhower said. "We'll hear what Washington has to say."

Later that same evening Eisenhower sent a cable to Gen. George C. Marshall, the U.S. Army chief of staff, in Washington:

Dawley is a splendid character, earnest, faithful, and well informed; but he cannot exercise high battle command when the going is rough. He grows extremely nervous and indecisive.

At about the same time that Eisenhower was communicating with Washington, General Walker received the following letter, which he immediately sent on to the regiments under his command.

HEADQUARTERS FIFTH ARMY

Dear General Dawley:

As your Army Commander, I want to congratulate every officer and enlisted man in the Fifth Army on the accomplishment of their mission on landing on the western coat of Italy. All the more splendid is your achievement when it is realized that it was accomplished against determined German resistance at the beaches. Every foot of our advance has been contested.

We have arrived at our critical objective; our beachhead is secure. Additional troops are landing every day, and we are here to stay. Not one foot of ground will be given up.

General Montgomery's battle-proven Eighth English Army, our partner in the task of clearing the German forces out of Italy, is advancing from the south and in a matter of hours its presence will be felt by the enemy. Side by side with this Eighth Army, the Fifth Army will advance to occupy Naples, Rome, and other cities to the north and to free Italy from German domination.

I am highly gratified by the efficient manner in which the U.S. VI Corps and the British X Corps have worked side by side in mutual support, each being proud to serve by the side of the other. Their performance has justified the confidence placed in them by the people of the United Nations. They know that we shall drive on relentlessly until our job is done.

I desire that the contents of this letter be communicated to all ranks of your command.

Sincerely yours,
Mark W. Clark,
Lieutenant General, U.S.A.,
Commanding.

1st Ind.
Headquarters, VI Corps
To: Commanders, all units and organizations.

The receipt of this letter is a matter of intense satisfaction to me. To you who have made such a commendation possible belongs the credit. Carry on. We are on the way.

E. J. Dawley,
Major General, U.S. Army
Commanding.*

---

*Fred Walker, *Texas to Rome* (Dallas, Tex.: Taylor Publishing Company, 1969).

At 0130 hours on Friday the Royal Marines of 41 Commando moved off the Crag and up to the start line. They were about to assault the Pimple and recapture the hill from the enemy who had thrown them off it the night before.

The marines had been in the very thick of battle for six days at Salerno; they had not had sufficient sleep for over a week; they had been under incessant artillery fire, even in their so-called rest area; and they had lost more than 40 percent of their strength in battle casualties. Churchill and his Army commandos still clung to Pigoletti, but if the marines could capture the Pimple it would take a lot of pressure from the village. The thickly wooded slopes of the Pimple lay just 300 yards north of the point where the marines grouped for the assault.

At 0200 hours the planned artillery barrage from the massed guns of the 46th Infantry Division opened up, and for 11 minutes hundreds of shells rained down, not on the German slit trenches, but on the marines standing in the open and waiting for the advance.

Other men, too, had been in action, for over a week. They too had suffered from loss of sleep, stress, and nervous exhaustion. One of these men, an officer on the divisional staff, had blundered and given the gunners the map coordinates for the start line rather than the marines' objective.

Major Edwards, who had assumed command of the marines since Colonel Lumsden was wounded early in the battle at Vietri, was grievously wounded. There were many other casualties and the survivors fell back, though in good order, to their original positions on the Crag. Churchill and his commandos were on their own a little while longer.

Even though the commandos were still locked into a bloody battle, the end of the beginning was September 18. Allied Intelligence reported a general German withdrawal, and Dawley urged his divisional commanders to assume the offensive. However, it was to take the best part of that day to unravel the confusion of units along the La Cosa defense lines. Walker planned to launch a major attack that night.

Meanwhile, reconnaissance patrols moved forward and found that the enemy had melted away. Before dusk, patrols from the 45th Infantry had moved right through the corridor and at day's end came to rest at Ponte Sele. A patrol from the 36th Infantry came down out of the hills above Altavilla, and a reconnaissance troop of armored cars from the British 56th Division patrolled from Battipaglia. The Allied Fifth Army had at last secured their D-Day objectives, 10 days behind schedule.

The troops in the front line, battlewise and now veteran, did not have to be told that the crisis was passing. They could sense it in the lifting barrage; shells began to fall farther and farther inland. There were new faces and fresh, clean uniforms on the beachhead as the reinforcements flooded in to take up the advance for the breakout. On the British side, the 23rd Armored Brigade, spearhead of the famous 7th Armored Division, the Desert Rats, landed, while Truscott's 3rd Infantry came ashore at Paestum. Trucks and tanks stood nose to tail blocking all exits out of the beachhead.

On the afternoon of Saturday, September 18, a liaison party from the 5th British Infantry arrived from the Eighth Army at Walker's command post. As the emissaries from Montgomery, now only 40 miles away, they were to finalize the details for the formal linkup with the Eighth Army. This would be at Vallo the following morning.

Vince Lockhart remembers them as being dusty and dirty. He was nevertheless impressed by how quiet and reserved they were. If they had been Americans he thought they would have been going around beating people on the back and saying, "Okay, fellas, we're here!" Instead their attitude was one of "another day's job done."

Later Lockhart talked with Joe Gill, a platoon sergeant from Kenyon, Texas. Gill turned to Lockhart and asked, "Captain, you know why we succeeded at Salerno?"

"Well, I have my own ideas Joe, but what are yours?"

"We just thought that was the way war was and we didn't know any better. If we had known any better," Gill continued, "we might not have made it."

Epilogue

On the same day that Montgomery's liaison officers arrived at Salerno, the Germans claimed their victory. Von Vietinghoff praised his troops and reported to Berlin that the Tenth Army had taken 5,000 prisoners as well as inflicting massive casualties on the Allies.* "Success has been ours," he said. "Once again German soldiers have proved their superiority over the enemy."†

Hitler must have thought so too. He promoted Von Vietinghoff to *Generaloberst* (colonel general) and gave him temporary command of Army Group B in northern Italy in place of Rommel, who was ill again, this time with suspected appendicitis.

Kesselring was also well pleased with the outcome at Salerno, for after all, German strategy was based on a limited withdrawal. He had never thought in terms of contingency planning to destroy the Fifth Army on the beaches,

---

*The official histories give the following figures for casualties at Salerno to September 18:

British	Germans	Americans
2,734 wounded	2,002 wounded	835 wounded
725 killed	840 killed	225 killed
1,800 missing	630 missing	589 missing
5,259 total	3,472 total	1,649 total

†Tenth Army War Diary, as quoted in Martin Blumenson, *United States Army in World War II, The Mediterranean Theater of Operation: Salerno to Cassino* (Washington, D.C.: Office of the Chief of Military History, United States Army, 1969), p. 137.

though he had tried hard enough when the opportunity was presented through Allied mistakes and miscalculations. The German forces were to deny the Allies Naples for another three weeks. It wasn't until October 5 that the first troops entered the city. Mark Clark had moved substantial reinforcements, including elements of the 82nd Airborne and the Royal Scots Greys, to Chiunzi Pass to bolster the rangers. American paratroopers and rangers rode the tanks down into the plain at Nocera and then battled their way into a ruined and deserted city. The day Naples fell and Mark Clark entered the city in triumph was his wife's birthday.

The Germans had also prevented the Allies from achieving any real advantage from the Italian surrender, and this Eisenhower had intended to be his trump card! He had expected to achieve a quick and complete victory from the Italians changing sides; instead the Fifth Army had paid a heavy price for counting on the Italians. It was indeed the Germans who gained the more tangible benefits from Italy's surrender. They were well rid of a troublesome, expensive, and doubtful ally.

The generals had miscalculated, their planning was faulty, and their assumptions were hopelessly optimistic. When the enemy attacked it was the soldiers who resisted stubbornly and in the end saved their commanders from the predicament their own failures had produced. Salerno was a soldier's battle in every sense of the word.

By the end of the battle for Salerno the Germans showed they were a formidable and resourceful foe. Once again the Germans, as they had in Sicily and were to continue to do for the next eighteen months until their last stand on the Po River, extricated their forces from trouble and dictated the pace of the battle. Perhaps Mark Clark had come closer to downfall than we realize at Salerno. The fair-minded and phlegmatic Alexander's comments in the War Diary of the Fifteenth Army Group for September 25 said it all: "The Germans may claim with some justification to have won, if not a victory at least an important success over us."[*]

One of the major miscalculations on the Allied side was the anticipation that Eighth Army would reach Salerno to link up with Mark Clark and the Fifth Army much earlier than it did. From the very beginning of Operation Avalanche, Clark had counted on the Eighth Army. He wrote in his diary on September 6 while en route to Salerno: "Baytown is proceeding with little or no resistance from the Italians, and presumably they are ready to help us."[†]

At the time and for a long while since, the popular myth has persisted that the Eighth Army rescued the embattled and desperate Fifth at Salerno. The Montgomery public-relations band wagon and the news coverage by the BBC was in large measure responsible for such exaggerated claims. It is clear, however, that except in the very broadest of senses the Eighth Army did little to affect the outcome at Salerno.

Montgomery's own chief of staff, General de Guingand, has provided a

*Blumenson, *Salerno to Cassino.*
†Mark Clark to author, August 1981.

most accurate assessment of his master's role at Salerno: "Some would like to think, I did at the time, that we helped if not saved the situation at Salerno. But now I doubt whether we influenced matters to any great extent. General Clark had everything under control before Eighth Army appeared on the scene."*

Could the Eighth Army have done more to help at Salerno? General Montgomery at the time, as we have seen, made much of the problems he encountered, and they were certainly real enough. It is easy to be critical of the slow progress made by Montgomery, but we do need to take account of the distance involved over difficult terrain and the poor roads that confronted an Eighth Army inadequately equipped and supplied. We need also to remember that Montgomery had two forces to "rescue," for the British 1st Airborne Division, which had landed at Taranto and advanced as far as Apulia, could not be left without support for long. This meant that Montgomery had to split his forces and advance on a northwest axis to Salerno and a northeast axis toward Taranto.

The Eighth Army marched and fought over 200 miles in 13 days against a tough and clever enemy who had terrain and conditions on his side. Even so, I must conclude that Montgomery could have released a battalion or two to march cross-country and reach Salerno by September 12 or 13. Had they followed the route used by Moorehead and the correspondents, this force could have arrived in time to contribute to the battle. Their early arrival could in turn have convinced the Germans to break off contact sooner. Even more importantly, the landings of the Eighth Army from across the Strait of Messina undoubtedly could have taken place three or four days earlier than September 4, had it not been for Montgomery's insistence on a full-scale prelude to the amphibious operation. It was time-consuming to deploy the massed artillery that his caution and ego demanded.

There were still some weeks of bitter fighting before the Allies could eventually break completely free of their shallow beachhead. The Tenth Army was determined that their own withdrawal was to be an orderly affair in which they were to inflict heavy casualties on the advancing Allies and at the same time withdraw the bulk of their forces and equipment. The Tenth Army established a number of rear-guard lines.

The first stretched from Salerno to Cerignola, with the former as the pivot. The Lincolns led the assault on it through the Cava defile and found it hard going. Douglas Scott, as second-in-command of 272nd Field Company, Royal Engineers, was in the company command post. It was a little corner cafe in a square at the edge of Vietri. The commanding officer, Ian Keland, was away on reconnaissance when a message was received from the 46th Division. They wanted a house and grounds checked for booby trap and mines. The large, rather prominent house in its own grounds was set high into the southeastern slopes above the defile at Cava. The division intended

---

*De Guingand, *Operation Victory*, p. 312.

to use it as a command post. Scott gathered together a few men, a mine detector, and Muncy, his ever-attendant batman, and set off in a couple of jeeps across the valley and up the precipitous hill track to the house.

There were occasional mortar bombs and shells coming over, and there was the crackle of rifle and machine-gun fire from just a few hundred yards away, where the infantry was still slugging it out. They parked the jeeps at the entrance to the driveway of the house and prepared to move forward; the man with the mine detector went first, sweeping the way clear with a machine that looked for all the world like a great vacuum cleaner.

A shot rang out, and Douglas Scott fell to the ground. He had been shot in the head, and the bullet penetrated the temple directly above his left eye. Had he been wearing his steel helmet, the bullet might have been deflected; but his service hat offered no protection, and he was now a bloody mess. Dazed but conscious, Scott lay in the gravel; he could feel the eyeball down on his left cheek. Thereafter, Scott drifted out of and into consciousness. He remembers coming to in a cellar, lying on a mattress. The room was cool and dimly lit by a few candles and what little natural light managed to filter through. A mixture of smells invaded his nostrils, musty scents of long-stored foods overpowered by the pungent stench of massed humanity, disease, and death. Alongside was a haggard old nun, and from what Scott could see in the poor light and with his one good eye, she was in a bad way, her frail old body lacerated and ripped by what Scott could only assume to be shell fragments. There was another old nun, an equally frail creature bending over her, and she had a large bottle of dark brown fluid. The nun turned to Scott and came forward to dab the liquid on his face. Scott was convinced it was iodine, which he remembered was fine for childhood cuts but on his eye, which still lay on his cheek, and in its empty socket!

"My God, for God's sake, no!" Scott begged.

Muncy suddenly appeared—Scott had never been so glad to see his batman in all his military service—and restrained the nun, calmly oblivious to her tirade and gestures of protest.

Scott lost consciousness again, and when he next came to he was in a casualty station. There was a large bandage swathed around his head and left eye, which at least no longer rested on his cheek. Scott could only hope that it was back in its socket and not removed altogether. He tried to concentrate his mind on a life in the future with only one eye, but he felt drowsy and warm and drugged. There was no sign of Muncy.

There followed a long and harrowing journey in an Army ambulance. The Britiush Army ambulance of the day was a most dreadful affair. Everything fell off the top deck to start with, including the patient, if he wasn't careful or strapped to his stretcher. The lurching, swaying ride caused nausea, and most men ended their journey in a worse condition than when they started out. The ambulance was also lethal: It took only one tracer round through the camouflage-paint-encrusted canvas sides to turn it into a firebomb.

Scott's nightmare journey ended on the airfield at Montecorvino. It was the early morning of September 19, and somewhere he had lost 24 hours. A couple of stretcher bearers carried his litter from the ambulance over the artificial planking that had been laid to stiffen up and support the grass field.

"That's been laid by the 56th Division sappers," he thought. "They haven't done a bad job by the feel of things."

There were shells falling around them, and the stretcher bearers scurried forward, anxious to be rid of their charge.

"Oh, God," Scott thought. "Will it never stop, even now?"

An old C-47 Dakota with South African Air Force markings came into view. Scott was dumped unceremoniously aboard, and the flight crew moved his stretcher clear of the doorway. There were no racks for the stretchers, and the cargo floor of the plane was loaded with stretcher cases until there was no more room. Scott watched a youthful pilot close the double freight door and climb over the stretchers to the flight deck. There were no medical orderlies.

The flight did not last very long, and Scott guessed they had landed in Sicily. Once the plane came to a stop, the doors were thrown open, and a number of doctors climbed inside the hot, fetid cabin. The doctors moved among the stretcher cases. Occasionally there would be a shaking of heads and a blanket lifted over the head of a still form. Eventually Scott was loaded into yet another ambulance for an equally uncomfortable albeit less dangerous journey to the hospital.*

September 19 was the last day the commandos spent in Pigoletti. They were relieved by a battalion of the Queen's Regiment, which had landed with the reinforcements from the 7th British Armored Division, the Desert Rats of El Alamein fame.

Jack Churchill recognized one of the reinforcements, a man named William Brown. They had been together as officer cadets in the same class at Sandhurst and had been commissioned into the Manchesters together. Brown was a heavy drinker who fell on evil days in the prewar army and had had to resign his commission. He then joined the Queen's as a private and was now a sergeant.

"Hello, Jack! How nice to see you," Brown said. "I didn't know we were taking over from you!"

"William," Churchill said. "This is simply splendid. Now I know that Pigoletti is in safe hands."

The commandos marched back down the valley and into the rear areas, where food, a hot bath, and plenty of rest awaited them before they embarked for Sicily.

The beachhead still was a dangerous place to be. It wasn't until September 26 that Salerno finally was out of range of enemy gunfire, the harbor party was ordered in, and the port was pronounced open by Admiral Hewitt. Two merchant ships berthed there that day. Even then some of the British beaches still were under fire, and there were casualties. One was Capt. David

---

*Douglas Scott was evacuated to a general hospital in Alexandria, where after a major operation he regained the sight of his left eye and eventually made a full recovery. After a time convalescing in a training unit, he returned to front-line duty in time to land in Greece in 1944.

Appleby of the Fusiliers, the Intelligence officers with the 167th Infantry Brigade.

The brigade headquarters was located in an olive grove about half a mile beyond St. Lucia. Appleby had just returned from visiting the units that had moved into Battipaglia. He got out of his jeep to speak with the brigadier, who was there with his driver. The three started to walk along one of the tracks that led through the vineyard and into a woods behind which the brigade's artillery still was deployed. The Germans had been shelling this gunline for a couple of days, but the soldiers had become attuned to the passage of the shells, and with a sixth sense a veteran acquires, knew when to take cover.

Suddenly the Germans fired a barrage of air bursts over the vineyard. The passage of such shells is impossible to predict, and it was a favorite ploy to catch troops in the open and unaware. One shell burst directly overhead; the round came so quickly that Appleby didn't even hear it go "bang." He felt a thump, his feet were knocked from under him, and he sat down on the path. In a daze, he looked up and saw his right leg on the other side of the path. It was then he realized he was wounded. Remarkably the leg, which had been severed cleanly below the knee, didn't bleed at all; the blast of the shell had effectively cauterized the wound. Appleby sat there and pressed his hands onto the stump; there was no pain, though he knew that would come all too soon.

Corporal Mould, the brigadier's driver, was grievously wounded in the chest and died shortly afterward. The brigadier had a flesh wound in the ankle.

Men came running from the brigade command post and attended to the prostrate Mould. The brigadier lifted Appleby into a jeep and got hold of another officer to hold Appleby in the seat while the brigadier drove quickly to the nearest aid post.

The jeep came to a halt outside a regimental aid post in a shower of dust and dirt, and the brigadier yelled for an orderly. Appleby was now in shock. He remembered the large red cross outside a tent and thought that was something he was going to see an awful lot of in the future. A medical orderly came out with a small field dressing, which was totally inadequate. Eventually the medics got things organized, and the last thing David Appleby remembers before he lost consciousness was being lifted gently onto a stretcher.

Later he was evacuated to a hospital ship. His batman met him at the beach with his personal kit before they took him by landing craft to the hospital ship in the bay.

There were other casualties at Salerno, but of a different nature. Matters were coming to a head with the new group from North Africa.

The men had spent four days in various fields at the beachhead. During this time noncommissioned officers came to organize the men into groups as reinforcements for the different units. Some had marched off reluctantly to their new battalions, but others had refused categorically to go either to the

46th or the 56th Infantry divisions. Perhaps the whole sorry business could have been prevented had a few strong-willed sergeants gripped the malcontents and marched them off to be disciplined. Instead the sergeants left the decision to the men's good sense, which simply hardened the resolve of those who believed in the justice of their cause. Many were convinced they were behaving in a soldierly fashion and were determined to be returned to their own fighting units, come what may. In the absence of firm authority and command, various beliefs and rumors became common currency. "Stand firm and you'll get backed up." Others believed the story that "If you go to the 46th Division now, you'll never get back to your own unit. There's safety in numbers."

Officers from the X Corps transit camp and some senior sergeants visited those who remained in the fields and asked them if they were willing to join the infantry units in the corps. The men saw this as a sign of doubt on the part of the authorities and thus a weakness that could be turned to their own advantage if they remained firm.

Eventually on September 20 the men were moved to another field, farther inland. An order was given to move to the 46th Infantry Division, and the majority obeyed this first direct order they had been given. Some 300 men out of the original group of 1,500 refused the order.

General McCreery arrived and addressed the men. He explained that a grave mistake had been made but promised that as soon as conditions permitted the men would be given every opportunity to return to their own battalions. In the meantime he asked them to make the best of things and join their new units. By this time authority was seen as clumsy and malicious, unjust and incompetent. McCreery may have been a general, but he was not "their general" and they doubted his word.*

McCreery left the scene, and the men were formally paraded. A staff officer stood in front of the assembled ranks. "Parade! Fall out on the road, pick up your kit, and move off to the 46th Division area," he ordered.

Many, though still undecided, yielded to the express command and moved reluctantly to obey the order. However, 192 men instead stood rigidly at attention. Some were convinced that authority would still be proved wrong and that their own divisional officers would fight the issue. Other men, perhaps the majority of those who remained, stood firm because they did not understand what was happening or because their friends stood firm.

Another officer appeared on the scene. He read out passages from King's Regulations and the Mutiny Act. The men were horrified; never in their wildest moment did they believe their actions would be seen as mutiny. Squads of military police descended upon the shaken men, and they were disarmed on the spot and marched away to a compound next to a German POW cage on the beach. The Germans jeered at them and called them

---

*McCreery was as good as his word. Sgt. Oliver Hardy remembers the reinforcements who came to the Lincolns being assembled in early October after the fall of Naples and offered the chance to return to their old units. Very few, he remembers, took up the offer.

cowards and deserters. The disgrace of the veterans from the 51st Highland Division and the 50th Tyne and Tees Division was complete. Degraded and humiliated, they awaited their fate.*

The last casualty at Salerno was General Dawley.

One evening after supper at the 36th Division command post below Mount Soprano, General Walker sent his son to find Sheriff Puck. "Sheriff," said the general, "I have been summoned to the Fifth Army CP. Please have my jeep sent around. I want another officer to accompany Charlie here and myself."

"Why don't you come along, Sheriff?" Charlie asked.

"I think I will."

Sheriff Puck didn't at this time sense that anything was amiss. Puck traveled in the lead jeep and left Charlie Walker to travel with his father. The convoy went straight to the main command post in the Bellilli Palace outside Paestum. General Dawley and his jeep, led by the usual escorting military police vehicle, drove into the compound ahead of them. Sheriff Puck drove through the guard gates and past the messing tents that had been set up for the staff in front of the building.

The two generals entered the building together. Puck didn't see any sign of Mark Clark and assumed that he was waiting inside. The drivers parked the jeeps at the side of the building while Sheriff joined Charlie Walker and they strolled along the graveled driveway. They sensed that something was amiss, and neither wanted to be far from Walker, father and commanding general.

The meeting didn't last long. After about ten minutes the two generals came out of the building together. Dawley saluted General Walker. "Well, Fred," Dawley said, "I'll be seeing you."

"Goodbye, Mike," Walker replied.

As soon as Walker appeared, Puck signaled the two jeeps from the compound. The vehicles pulled up alongside, but Walker took hold of the two officers and steered them away from the front of the building where Dawley was climbing into his jeep. Walker reached into a side pocket in his light, zipper-fronted rainproof field jacket, pulled out the stub of a large cigar, and accepted a light from his son. The general exhaled, and the evening air filled with the rich aroma of the Havana cigar.

"Let's wait for a coupla minutes, boys," Walker said. "I don't want to drive through the dust raised by *Colonel* Dawley's jeep."

Later, when they were back at the division's command post, Walker strolled around the area with Sheriff Puck. "I don't mind admitting, Sheriff,"

---

*Eventually the men were shipped back to North Africa where in October that year they were court martialled in Constantine. The charge was mutiny. The men were still convinced of the justice of their cause, and their behavior was exemplary. They were found guilty. Private soldiers were sentenced to seven years penal servitude, the corporals received ten years, and the sergeants were sentenced to be shot. The sentences were then suspended on condition that the men would join new units. They had no choice.

he said, "that for about five minutes inside that goddamn château I didn't know whether it was going to be Col. Fred Walker or Col. Mike Dawley."

For Walker's Texans the initiation was over. They had been through their ordeal by fire and completed the transition from a National Guard outfit to a veteran division. In that process it had had to pay a high price, not just in battle casualties but also in the attrition rate among the division's senior staff officers and subordinate field commanders. As a result of the battle, the assistant divisional commander, the artillery commander, and four of the senior staff officers were relieved. The attrition rate among the nine battalion commanders was the highest of all. Six were relieved, two captured, and one transferred to the staff.

Neither did Gen. Mark Clark have it all his own way. Washington did not agree to the appointment of Ridgway as corps commander. On September 20 Major General John Porter Lucas arrived at Salerno. He had served as Eisenhower's personal deputy in 1943 and later commanded the II Corps in Sicily. Lucas was another nominee of General McNair and commanded the VI Corps until he, too, was relieved—at Anzio.

Appendix A: The Germans at Salerno

Kesselring's Headquarters (OBSUED)
near Rome Controlled Other Units
(Available as Reserves to the Tenth Army)

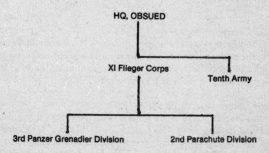

The Tenth Army Order of Battle, September 8, 1943

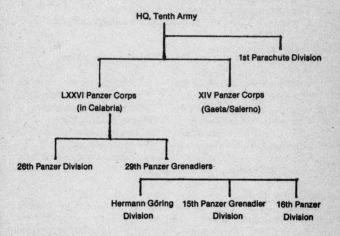

The 16th Panzer Division Order of Battle

2nd Panzer Regiment

This had an establishment of three battalions, but its 1st Battalion was at this time reequipping in Germany with Panzer Mark V's. At Salerno there was a battalion of Panzer Mark IV's (66 tanks) and a battalion with 75mm self-propelled assault guns (42 tanks).

64th Panzer Grenadier Regiment

This comprised two infantry battalions, one mounted in half-tracks, and a support company.

79th Panzer Grenadier Regiment

Two infantry battalions and a support company. (Each infantry battalion consisted of three rifle companies and a heavy company. The heavy company was comprised of an antitank platoon, a pioneer platoon, and an air defense platoon equipped with multibarreled 20mm guns.)

16th Panzer Reconnaissance Battalion

The reconnaissance battalion of a panzer division is the cavalry of old and can provide the fighting vanguard of the division. With its "squadrons" or companies of light and heavy armored cars and its own field artillery, the battalion has a considerable striking force. The battalion was comprised of:

Two reconnaissance companies
Two infantry companies mounted in half-tracks
One heavy company similar to that of the infantry battalion

16th Artillery Regiment

This was comprised of four battalions of artillery, as follows:

One battalion of three batteries	105mm gun (towed)
One battalion of two batteries	105mm gun (self-propelled)
one battery	150mm gun (self-propelled)
One battalion of one battery	105mm gun (towed)
two batteries	150mm gun (towed)
One battalion of two batteries	88mm anti-aircraft
one battery	multibarreled 20mm air defense

(there were four guns to each battery)

16th Pioneer Battalion

German *Pioniere* were the equivalent of the British or American engineers. The pioneer is a general servant of the army—he is everywhere and does every job. Like every other soldier, he is a trained infantryman because he has to advance in close contact with the infantry. He is particularly skilled in bridge building, mine laying, building concrete dugouts and blockhouses, and minefield clearance.

16th Signals Battalion
Tank Complement

On September 8 the division could muster fit for battle 87 Panzer Mark IV tanks, 7 Panzer Mark III's—some were armed with the 57mm long-barreled gun, others had flame throwers—and 12 Panzer Mark II's.

The 16th Panzer Division at Salerno, September 8, 1943

The division was deployed in four battle groups (each named after its commander). They were roughly 6 miles apart and 3 to 6 miles inland. Looking seaward, the deployment was as follows:

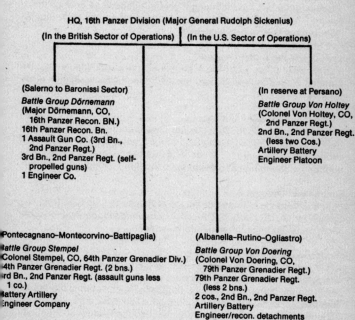

HQ, 16th Panzer Division (Major General Rudolph Sickenius)

(In the British Sector of Operations) (In the U.S. Sector of Operations)

(Salerno to Baronissi Sector)

Battle Group Dörnemann
(Major Dörnemann, CO,
  16th Panzer Recon. BN.)
16th Panzer Recon. Bn.
1 Assault Gun Co. (3rd Bn.,
  2nd Panzer Regt.)
3rd Bn., 2nd Panzer Regt. (self-
  propelled guns)
1 Engineer Co.

(In reserve at Persano)

Battle Group Von Holtey
(Colonel Von Holtey, CO,
  2nd Panzer Regt.)
2nd Bn., 2nd Panzer Regt.
  (less two Cos.)
Artillery Battery
Engineer Platoon

(Pontecagnano–Montecorvino–Battipaglia)

Battle Group Stempel
(Colonel Stempel, CO, 64th Panzer Grenadier Div.)
64th Panzer Grenadier Regt. (2 bns.)
3rd Bn., 2nd Panzer Regt. (assault guns less
  1 co.)
Battery Artillery
Engineer Company

(Albanella–Rutino–Ogliastro)

Battle Group Von Doering
(Colonel Von Doering, CO,
  79th Panzer Grenadier Regt.)
79th Panzer Grenadier Regt.
  (less 2 bns.)
2 cos., 2nd Bn., 2nd Panzer Regt.
Artillery Battery
Engineer/recon. detachments

The Other German Divisions at Salerno

The Panzer Grenadiers

In 1939 the Wehrmacht used motorized infantry divisions in the Polish campaign. Though the infantry were carried in ordinary army trucks, they nevertheless proved their worth. Even then it was realized that they would need strengthening to perform their intended role.

After March 1943 these divisions were reorganized, upgraded to semi-armored status, and named panzer grenadiers. These divisions contained two regiments of infantry, a battalion of tanks or self-propelled guns, and a battalion of antitank self-propelled guns (jagpanzers). The panzer grenadiers were not infantry. The original grenadier in military history was a soldier who threw a grenade. He had to fight in advance of his regiment of infantry, and as such his unit was a force of elite or shock troops. The panzer grenadiers in 1943 were such elite shock troops and were the fire brigade of Germany's defenses, trained in the counterattack role. They were rarely up to strength, never had their full complement of vehicles, and were invariably equipped with a motley collection of captured trucks and scout cars. At Salerno there were two such divisions.

15th Panzer Grenadier Division

This division was formed in May 1943 from the remnants of the 15th Panzer Division that had escaped from Tunisia. It was also known as the Siziliendivision.

29th Panzer Grenadier Division

This was originally the 29th Infantry Division, which was first raised in 1937. It fought in Poland, France, and on the Russian Front until destroyed in Stalingrad in January 1943. In March of that year the survivors were joined with the 345th Infantry Division to form the 29th Panzer Grenadiers.

26th Panzer Division

The division was formed in France in the autumn of 1942 from the elements of the 23rd Infantry Division. It remained in France under training until June 1943, when it was transferred to Italy.

Panzer Division Hermann Göring

The origins of this strange division can be traced back to the Nazis' assumption of power in 1933 and the creation of a special police unit to stamp out any resistance to National Socialism. Hitler entrusted this task to Hermann Göring, and the formation was called Landespolizeigruppe Wecke (after its first commander, Polizeimajor Wecke of the Prussian State Police). Later that year the unit was retitled Landespolizeigruppe General Göring (who was state minister of Prussia). In April 1935 it became Regiment General Göring but still part of the Landespolizei.

In March 1935 Hitler introduced conscription, and in October of that year the regiment was incorporated into the Luftwaffe. From its ranks volunteers formed the first parachute training battalion (*Fallschirmschützen-Bataillon*) as a cadre for the future German paratroops (*Fallschirmtruppe*).

From this time on this regiment, later to become a division, displayed the highest morale and fighting spirit through to the closing days of World War II. For the most part its recruits were volunteers who were most carefully selected; they were required to meet the most exacting physical and political standards. It was Göring's pet, and thus its members enjoyed the finest barracks and the very best of everything as long as the good times lasted.

At the outbreak of war the regiment provided part of the flak defense for Greater Berlin, while a specialist unit acted as Göring's bodyguard. The regiment's first combat experience came in the French campaign in May and June 1940, when its flak battalions operated with the panzers and motorized units. After the cease-fire the regiment reassembled to provide the air defense for Paris before returning to Berlin. In 1941 the regiment fought in the Balkans and on the Russian Front before once more returning to Germany for reequipping, and then garrison duty in France.

In 1942 the Hermann Göring Division became a sort of "private army" with different tasks to perform. There was a regiment that escorted Göring and Hitler (*Führer-Begleit-Regiment*) and another that provided the anti-aircraft defense for the Führer's headquarters (*Führer-Flak-Abteilung*). There was a large administrative headquarters in Berlin with a band, while in France a brand-new panzer division, Panzer Division Hermann Göring, was created. Even this division had more flak regiments than other field divisions, and there was a considerable influx of trained panzer personnel to replace the inexperienced Luftwaffe officers and men. The Hermann Göring Panzer Division recruited up to 20,000 men a year to meet all its commitments.

Early in 1943 the Hermann Göring Panzer Division was ordered to move to Italy, and its headquarters was located at Santa Maria near Caserta, about 15 miles north of Naples. There it gathered its various regiments as they completed their training, which by now included two battalions of its own paratroopers. The latter, Fallschirmjäger-Regiment Hermann Göring, was sent straight to Tunisia, where it fought with the 10th Panzer Division. Many other units from the Hermann Göring Panzer Division followed later as they completed their training, including panzer grenadier and artillery regiments and the first panzer regiments.

Only a handful returned to Italy. The bulk of the division capitulated on May 12, 1943, in southern Tunisia. To replace the shattered division, new recruits were assembled from all corners of the Third Reich and transferred to the training camps around Naples as well as to others in Holland and the division's old administrative headquarters near Berlin. Within a month or two, the troops in Italy were deployed into Sicily to combat Operation Husky and the Allied landings. The division, under its commander, Generalleutnant Conrath, counterattacked at Gela and very nearly scored a decisive success against the landing forces there. Subsequently the division played its part in the defensive battles and retreat toward Messina and crossed to the mainland bloodied but intact and with most of its equipment, by August 17, 1943.

Technically the division remained part of the Luftwaffe because Göring remained its "honorary colonel," but many of its personnel were Wehrmacht while in spirit and political convention it was Waffen SS.

The 1st Parachute Division

As we have seen above, the first parachutist unit in the German Army was recruited in 1935. It was a Luftwaffe formation and when employed on airborne operations came under Luftwaffe operational control. The division fought in France and the Low Countries, Crete, and the Russian Front before being recalled to France in 1943. By this time Hitler realized that the Allies were training a large airborne force, and he ordered a similar expansion on his own to provide defense or counter. When the Allies invaded Sicily, the 1st Parachute Division was flown in as reinforcements, and some men were dropped onto Catania airfield to save time. The division contained three parachute rifle regiments (each of three battalions), an artillery regiment, an antitank battalion, and a reconnaissance battalion, together with engineer and signal units. The division was an elite formation used as a highly effective fire brigade force; their main weakness was the absence of heavy weapons.

Appendix B: The Allies at Salerno

Mediterranean Theater of Operations, August 30, 1943

Eisenhower (Supreme Allied Commander, Mediterranean)

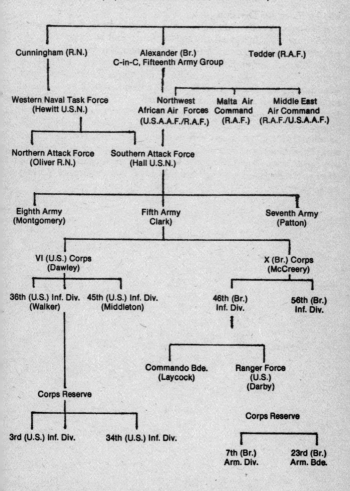

Appendix C: The U.S. Army at Salerno*

The Staff of a Divisional Headquarters

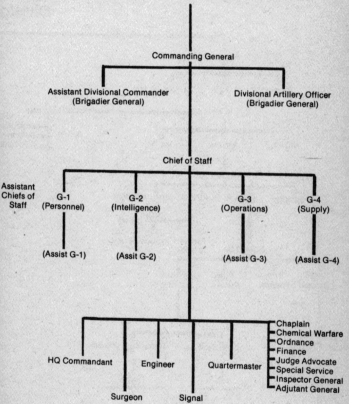

*Details taken from George Forty, *U.S. Army Handbook, 1939–1945* (London: Ian Allan, 1979).

Organization of a U.S. Infantry Division
Total Strength, All Ranks: 14,523 men

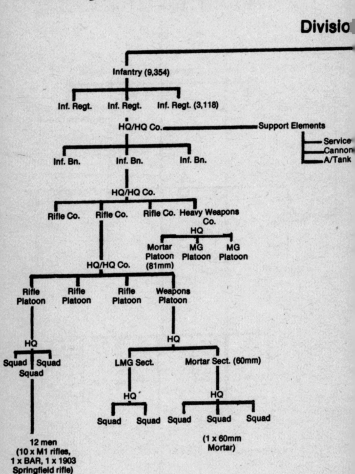

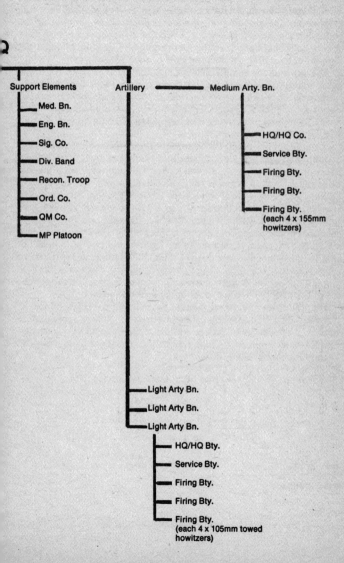

Q

Support Elements
- Med. Bn.
- Eng. Bn.
- Sig. Co.
- Div. Band
- Recon. Troop
- Ord. Co.
- QM Co.
- MP Platoon

Artillery ————— Medium Arty. Bn.
- HQ/HQ Co.
- Service Bty.
- Firing Bty.
- Firing Bty.
- Firing Bty. (each 4 x 155mm howitzers)

- Light Arty Bn.
- Light Arty Bn.
- Light Arty Bn.
  - HQ/HQ Bty.
  - Service Bty.
  - Firing Bty.
  - Firing Bty.
  - Firing Bty. (each 4 x 105mm towed howitzers)

U.S. Infantry Division Organization and Equipment*

The organization of the wartime U.S. infantry division was the brainchild of the commander of Army ground forces, Gen. Lesley J. McNair. He cut the cumbersome "square" division, with four regiments in two brigades, which had survived from World War I, to a "triangular" organization, with three regiments, which was more suited to open warfare. This organization was adopted in June 1941 and modified in 1942 and 1943.

At every level the new division was based on a triangular structure. The three regiments each controlled three battalions, each with three companies of three platoons each, and three squads to a platoon. Each headquarters also controlled additional support weapons, ranging from the company's 60mm mortars and .3-inch machine guns to the regimental cannon company with 75mm or 105mm howitzers.

In support of the infantry were two light artillery battalions, each with 18 105mm howitzers and a medium artillery battalion with 12 155mm howitzers. Each division also possessed a reconnaissance squadron of mechanized cavalry and an engineer battalion with construction plant and light bridging equipment. There was a large medical battalion. American divisions were not responsible for supplying their battalions; this was done from army-level dumps. Each division, therefore, had only one quartermaster company, with trucks to carry reserve supplies or one infantry battalion. The ordnance company was responsible for some vehicle repairs, although as much work as possible was done by units themselves, and really serious repairs by army workshops. The signal company was responsible for divisional headquarters' communications, and the division was completed by the military police platoon and the headquarters company.

The total manpower of the division varied between 14,000 and 15,000. Just over 5,000 of these were front-line infantrymen. In battle, divisions were reinforced by other units, such as tank battalions and engineers, and commanded three regimental combat teams—all-arms groupings based on infantry regimental headquarters.

*Details from Heron Books part work series on the Second World War.

Appendix D: The British

The British Infantry Division in 1943

The infantry division was the largest permanent tactical unit, with a paper strength that varied from 15,000 to 18,000 men. Above the division (as with the U.S. Army) were the higher formations of corps, army, and army group.

The infantry division was organized into three brigades (roughly the equivalent of a U.S. Army regiment). Each brigade contained three battalions of four rifle companies, and the rifle company was subdivided into platoons and sections (the latter the equivalent of a squad in the U.S. Army).

In the battalion there was a headquarters company with six platoons, separately responsible for anti-aircraft defense, mortars, signals, pioneers, administration, and intelligence.

The artillery component of a division comprised three brigades totaling 72 guns. There were, in addition, an antitank regiment with the 17-pounder antitank guns and an anti-aircraft regiment with Bofors 40mm and 20mm quick-firing guns.

The British infantry divisions that fought at Salerno were organized as follows:

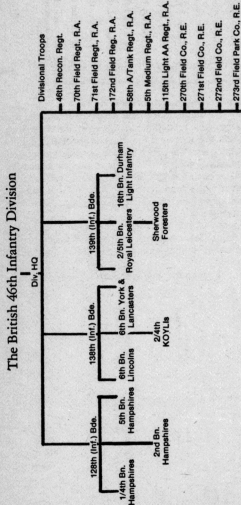

The British 46th Infantry Division

Div. HQ

128th (Inf.) Bde.
1/4th Bn. Hampshires
5th Bn. Hampshires
2nd Bn. Hampshires

138th (Inf.) Bde.
6th Bn. Lincolns
6th Bn. York & Lancasters
2/4th KOYLIs

139th (Inf.) Bde.
2/5th Bn. Royal Leicesters
16th Bn. Durham Light Infantry
Sherwood Foresters

Divisional Troops
46th Recon. Regt.
70th Field Regt., R.A.
71st Field Regt., R.A.
172nd Field Reg., R.A.
58th A/Tank Regt., R.A.
5th Medium Regt., R.A.
115th Light AA Regt., R.A.
270th Field Co., R.E.
271st Field Co., R.E.
272nd Field Co., R.E.
273rd Field Park Co., R.E.
2nd Bn., Northumberland Fusiliers (heavy-weapons support)

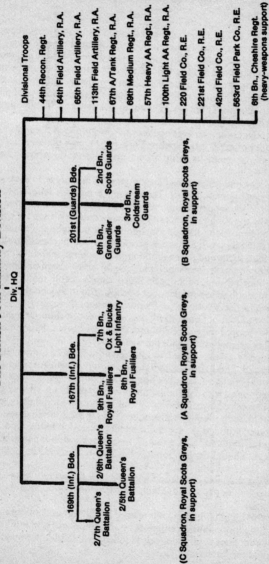

The British 56th Infantry Division

Div. HQ

169th (Inf.) Bde.
2/7th Queen's Battalion
2/6th Queen's Battalion
2/5th Queen's Battalion
(C Squadron, Royal Scots Greys, in support)

167th (Inf.) Bde.
7th Bn., Ox & Bucks Light Infantry
9th Bn., Royal Fusiliers
8th Bn., Royal Fusiliers
(A Squadron, Royal Scots Greys, in support)

201st (Guards) Bde.
6th Bn., Grenadier Guards
2nd Bn., Scots Guards
3rd Bn., Coldstream Guards
(B Squadron, Royal Scots Greys, in support)

Divisional Troops
44th Recon. Regt.
64th Field Artillery, R.A.
65th Field Artillery, R.A.
113th Field Artillery, R.A.
67th A/Tank Regt., R.A.
69th Medium Regt., R.A.
57th Heavy AA Regt., R.A.
100th Light AA Regt., R.A.
220 Field Co., R.E.
221st Field Co., R.E.
42nd Field Co., R.E.
563rd Field Park Co., R.E.
6th Bn., Cheshire Regt. (heavy-weapons support)

The Regiments Explained

Introduction

The modern British Army can trace its origins back to the midseventeeth century and the restoration of the monarchy in 1660 after the death of Oliver Cromwell and the Republic. Except for a period during World War I, World War II, and a decade or so after 1945, the British Army has always been an all-volunteer regular force organized on the regimental system. A soldier who served in the infantry or the cavalry joined a regiment and stayed there throughout his military service. He lived in a closely knit "family" group, which was the regiment.

The regiment promotes tremendous pride and *esprit de corps* that has been the envy of many other armies. The soldier knows the history of his regiment and can recite its battle honors and the great moments from its past.

The fighting regiments of the British Army, the infantry and the cavalry, have a long and glorious history. The first regiments were raised after the restoration of the monarchy and were named after the colonel who was appointed by the King to recruit and command them. This system caused administrative problems because sometimes there would be more than one colonel with the same name. Another problem was that the colonel might be killed during a battle and a new officer appointed to command; this could happen perhaps two or three times in a single day, and it caused considerable confusion. Nevertheless, by the beginning of the eighteenth century, when the Duke of Marlborough commanded a British army in Europe, there were some 39 regiments of infantry (or foot, as they were then called).

In 1751 the Duke of Cumberland, the commander-in-chief, changed the system. He dropped the colonels' names and instead gave each regiment a number that roughly corresponded to their "seniority."

Cumberland's system survived for 130 years until in 1881 a further reform was introduced. The Army was reorganized with the regiments that were really about a battalion in strength, being paired into a single new regiment and then associated with a particular county or part of Britain. (A very good example is explained in detail below with the Oxfordshire and Buckinghamshire Light Infantry.) A new regiment, with its 1st and 2nd battalions, was also associated with the militia and volunteers of its local area. Since the Army was still a volunteer force, this allowed the regiments to recruit in the local district. The cavalry regiments were later reorganized in a similar fashion.

In 1908 the volunteer battalions were reorganized into a new force called the territorial Army (they were roughly similar to the National Guard in the United States).

After World War I, the Army was reduced in size, and as a consequence a number of regiments, both infantry and cavalry, were amalgamated. Those regiments that came from the South of Ireland were disbanded upon the emergence of the Republic of Eire.

During the interwar years, the cavalry regiments gave up their horses and were mechanized and reequipped either with armored cars or, later, tanks. Even so, they retained their original "horse organizations" of troops and squadrons.

The various battalions of infantry and the regiments of cavalry were organized into the higher formations of brigades (which roughly corresponded to the U.S. Army's regiment) and then placed into divisions. Sometimes the division would draw all its component units from the same geographical area of Britain. Others would contain a mixture of British and Indian Army battalions and brigades.

Let us now look at the regiments and battalions that fought at Salerno.

56th (City of London) Infantry Division

The division went to war in 1939 under its old name of the 1st City of London Division. This was later renumbered to the 56th Division, though it still retained its London links. It was popularly known as the "Black Cats" after the black cat emblem the men wore as a shoulder patch; this symbolized Dick Whittington's black cat.

167th Infantry Brigade

8th Battalion, Royal Fusiliers
9th Battalion, Royal Fusiliers

This brigade had two territorial battalions (the 8th and 9th battalions) of Royal Fusiliers. The Royal Fusiliers were originally the 7th of Foot and have always been London's own regiment. The regiment was first recruited in 1685 from the soldiers who guarded the Tower of London. They formed part of the ordnance regiment that escorted the artillery of the day. Their officers were assigned to the new regiment from other more fashionable regiments and were given the nickname "The Elegant Extracts." In 1689 the regiment took the title of the Royal Fusiliers and to this day still have their headquarters in the Tower of London.

The Oxfordshire and Buckinghamshire Light Infantry

This regiment was popularly known as the "Ox and Bucks," although its officers would never use such a name. It takes its name from the amalgamation in 1881 of the 43rd Monmouthshire Light Infantry and the 52nd Oxfordshire Light Infantry. Both regiments fought in the Spanish Peninsula during the Napoleonic Wars under Sir John Moore. Both were light infantry regiments, which meant they were armed with a rifle rather than a musket, and were used as an advance guard, or rear guard in case of a retreat. Like the other regiments of light infantry they march at 140 to 160 paces a minute as opposed to the 120 paces of the line infantry.

The 7th Battalion was a territorial Army battalion.

169th Infantry Brigade

2/5th Battalion, Queen's Royal Regiment (West Surrey)

2/6th Battalion, Queen's Royal Regiment (West Surrey)
2/7th Battalion, Queen's Royal Regiment (West Surrey)

The Queen's formed the 2nd Regiment of Foot and is the oldest English infantry regiment. It was first raised in 1661 in London to garrison and defend Tangiers, which Charles II had received as part of the dowry provided by his wife, Catherine of Braganza, hence the name Queen's. The regiment served for 18 years in Tangiers, where it became known as the Tangerines; the nickname remained, as it rhymes with the cockney slang for "Queen's." The title "Royal" was conferred after the Battle of Tongres in 1685, when the regiment held its position for 28 hours against an enemy force numbering 40,000 men.

The battalions that fought at Salerno were territorial Army battalions at the outbreak of war in 1939. Some territorial battalions were doubled so that the 5th Battalion became the 1/5th and the 2/5th battalions.

201st Guards Brigade
6th Battalion, Grenadier Guards
3rd Battalion, Coldstream Guards
2nd Battalion, Scots Guards

Among the first regiments to be raised in 1660 were those who were associated with the royal household and acted as the King's personal guards. These elite forces included the regiment of the Foot Guards and the Household Cavalry. Every tourist who visits Britain knows of the guards seen in red uniforms guarding the Tower of London, Buckingham Palace, and other royal residences. Few realize that these men are also fighting soldiers whose units have a long history of valor on the battlefield.

The guards were not numbered along with the infantry of the line but have their own seniority or precedence. This is reflected in their uniforms and the groupings of the buttons on their tunics. (The Grenadier Guards have single buttons; the Coldstream Guards, in pairs; the Scots Guards, in threes; the Irish Guards, in fours; and the Welsh Guards, in fives).

The Grenadier Guards were first raised when in exile in 1656 and were called His Majesty's Regiment of Guards (Wentworth's Regiment, after their first colonel). With the restoration of the monarchy in 1660 they became the King's Royal Regiment of Guards and later the 1st Regiment of Foot Guards.

The regiment became the Grenadier Guards in 1815 after their defeat of the French Grenadier Guards at Waterloo.

In the nineteenth century the regiment was known as the "Coalheavers" because their officers would hire the men out as civilian laborers to carry coal. Their other nickname is the "Sandbaggers," earned at the Battle of Inkerman during the Crimean War, when they fought a bloody battle with the Russians at the Sandbag Battery and won four Victoria Crosses in a single day.

The Coldstream Guards take their name from a little town about 50 miles south of Edinburgh. In 1660 the regiment was in the Parliamentary or Republic Army and formed part of the force, under the command of General

Monck, that marched south to London to restore Charles II to the throne. It was first known as Colonel Fenwick's Regiment of Foot when it was raised in 1650, and later it became General George Monck's Regiment of Foot. It was the only regiment in the Parliamentary Army not to be disbanded after the restoration of the monarchy. Though the Coldstream Guards are the 2nd Regiment of Foot Guards after the Grenadiers, they resolutely refuse to recognize this. They are known as the "Lilywhites" in the Army after the white band on their forage cap.

The Scots Guards were raised as the 3rd Regiment of Foot Guards but can trace their history back to a time earlier than the other Guards. In 1639 the Duke of Argyll raised Argyll's Regiment, which fought in the British Civil War. By this time it was known as the Scotch Guards, though no one can explain why it was spelled in this fashion.

The regiment reappeared after the restoration of the monarchy in 1660, when it was called at various times the 3rd Foot Guards or the Scots Fusilier Guards. In 1877 the regiment finally became known as the Scots Guards. Strangely, the regiment has no nickname other than "the Jocks," which is used for most Scottish regiments.

Royal Scots Greys (2nd Dragoons)

The Royal Scots Greys was the last cavalry regiment to become mechanized. In 1943, equipped with the Sherman tank, the regiment formed part of the 56th City of London Division.

The Royal Regiment of Scots Dragoons was raised in 1678 and in the 200 years that followed was known in turn as the Royal North British Dragoons, the Grey Dragoons, and the Scots Regiment of White Horses. In 1877 the name was changed to the 2nd Dragoons (Royal Scots Greys) and in 1920 to the Royal Scots Greys (2nd Dragoons). The regiment was always mounted on gray or white horses.

Earlier in their history the regiment earned the grudging admiration of Napoleon, who referred to them as "*ces terribles chevaux gris.*" At Waterloo, shouting their battle cry, "Scotland Forever!" they charged the French infantry and captured the French regimental eagle standards. Thereafter they wore the imperial eagle as their regimental badge and became known in the Army as the "Birdcatchers." Their officers have always had a reputation for liking champagne, and this gave rise to their other nickname, the "Bubbly Jocks."

46th (North Midlands) Infantry Division, 128th Infantry Brigade

1/4th Battalion, the Hampshire Regiment
2nd Battalion, the Hampshire Regiment
5th Battalion, the Hampshire Regiment

The three brigades of the division, together with many of their supporting troops, have traditionally come from the North Midlands of England. However, in 1943 at Salerno it had lost one brigade, and this was replaced by three battalions drawn from the Hampshire Regiment.

The Hampshire Regiment was first raised in 1702 as the 37th Regiment of Foot, Meredith's Regiment, and later became the North Hampshire Regiment. The 37th is one of the six British infantry regiments that fought at the Battle of Minden on August 1, 1759. The battle is commemorated to this day by the regiment wearing a rose on the anniversary of the battle. The regiment amalgamated in 1881 with the 67th of Foot, the South Hampshires. The latter had been raised in the West Indies and fought later with great gallantry in India, in memory of which it wore the tiger as the regimental badge. The regiment is known as the Hampshire Tigers.

138th Infantry Brigade
6th Battalion, the Lincolnshire Regiment
2/4th Battalion, King's Own Yorkshire Light Infantry
6th Battalion, York and Lancaster Regiment

The Lincolnshire Regiment was first raised in 1685 as the 10th Regiment of Foot. One of its earliest nicknames was earned in the American Revolutionary War. Along with the 62nd of Foot (The Wiltshire Regiment), it became known as the "Springers" because of the speed and mobility with which these regiments chased the "rebels."

The Lincolns are also known as the "Poachers," an allusion to the famous old ballad or folk song "The Lincolnshire Poacher," which is also the regimental march. In the local area the regiment is also called the "Yellow Bellies." There is no definitive explanation except that it has nothing to do with its prowess on the field of battle. One explanation is that the regimental colors were once the red cross of St. George on a yellow background.

In Lincolnshire a "yellow belly" is a man of the fens, and the name comes from the eels that live in the bogs and fen ditches. There is also a local frog known as a "yellow belly." A further explanation is that Lincolnshire is famous for its potatoes, which have a yellow tinge and form the staple diet of the local inhabitants.

The 6th Battalion was a territorial Army unit, which drew most of its recruits from Grantham and the surrounding towns.

King's Own Yorkshire Light Infantry

This regiment was formed in 1881 with the amalgamation of the 51st (2nd Yorkshire, West Riding, the King's Own Light Infantry) Regiment and the 105th (Madras Light Infantry), which became, respectively, the 1st and 2nd battalions of the new regiment.

The 51st fought at Minden and was a light infantry regiment with the same characteristics as the Oxfordshire and Buckinghamshire Light Infantry. The regiment was first raised in 1756 and from the outset was always associated with Yorkshire. The regiment served as part of the Light Division under Sir John Moore in his famous retreat to Corunna, when it served as the rear guard.

The 105th (Madras Light Infantry) Regiment was a British regiment in the private army in the pay of the East India Company. Increasingly after the

Indian Mutiny these regiments were disbanded; most saw service under the British Crown in the Indian Army. Some in 1861, such as the 105th (Madras Light Infantry), became part of the British Army. The regiment came to England for the first time in 1874.

York and Lancaster Regiment

The 65th (2nd Yorkshire, North Riding) Regiment of Foot was first raised in 1756 and sent immediately on active service to the West Indies. There are few regiments in the Army that have spent so many years in overseas service. The 65th was sent to South Africa in 1801, where it stayed for over twenty years. Later a similar period was spent in Australia and New Zealand.

In 1881 the regiment amalgamated with the 84th (York and Lancaster) Regiment of Foot, which had first been raised in 1793 in York. The 84th saw service in India, where the bulk of the regiment was massacred in Cawnpore during the Indian Mutiny.

After amalgamation, the regimental badge was a fierce-looking tiger surmounted by the Union rose. This gave rise to its nickname "The Cat and Cabbage." It was also known as the "Twin Roses" from the War of the Roses and more disparagingly as "The Young and Lovelies" from the letters Y and L.

139th Infantry Brigade
2/5th Battalion, the Royal Leicestershire Regiment
5th Battalion, the Sherwood Foresters
16th Battalion, the Durham Light Infantry

Royal Leicestershire Regiment

Originally the 17th Regiment of Foot, the Royal Leicestershire Regiment was raised in 1688 and later fought with Marlborough and in the conquest of Canada. From 1804 to 1823 the regiment served with great distinction in India, and the tiger was adopted as their badge. The regiment became known as the "Tigers" or sometimes the "Lilywhites" from the white facings on their scarlet uniforms.

Sherwood Foresters (Nottinghamshire and Derbyshire Regiment)

The Sherwood Foresters came into being in 1881, when the 45th and 95th regiments of Foot were amalgamated. The regiment started its new life with the nickname that became its official title in 1902.

The Sherwood Foresters must rank as one of the more romantic titles in British regimental history, and the cap badge of the Stag and Oak Leaves reflects the forest districts of the two counties of Nottinghamshire and Derbyshire. The uniform has a green facing that is called Lincoln green.

The 45th Regiment of Foot was raised in 1741 and later served without a break throughout the whole campaign in the Spanish Peninsula, 1808–14.

At the Battle of Talavera the regiment gained its nickname of the "Old Stubborns" because of its splendid bravery.

The 95th Regiment was recruited from Derbyshire and at first had a checkered history. It was raised at the time of war and then disbanded when its services were no longer required. In the nineteenth century it served with great distinction in the Crimea and later in India.

Durham Light Infantry

The 68th of Foot was raised in 1756 by General John Lambton for service in the Seven Years' War and later served as light infantry in the Spanish Peninsula. The 2nd Battalion came from India, where it had been part of the East India Company as the 2nd Bombay European Regiment.

The Durhams, though relatively new in Army terms, has a well-earned reputation for always being at the center of hard-fought actions, hence its nickname "Faithful Durhams."

Appendix E: The Special Forces

The British Commandos

The British Army and Royal Marine Commandos in 1943 together with the battalions of U.S. Rangers were all of broadly similar structure and organization. The chart below shows No. 2 Army Commando in August 1943.*

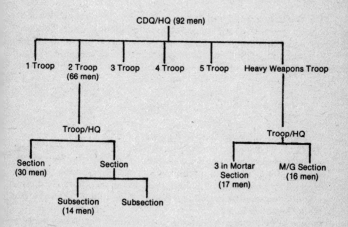

The Commando Idea

The first British special forces were formed into independent companies and first used as raiding forces in German-occupied Norway in May 1940. After the fall of France the idea of raiding groups took shape in the minds of the high command. The troops were organized into commandos in memory of the Boer farmers in the South African War who through their skill and mobility defeated ten times their number of British troops in the war between 1899 and 1902.

*The data are based on James Ladd's excellent book *Commandos and Rangers of World War II*, published in 1978 by Book Club Associates by arrangement with Macdonald & Jane's.

No. 2 Army Commando

First raised in 1940 as a parachute unit, it was later retrained for amphibious warfare. The commandos took part in a raid on Vaagsö in Norway and then in August 1942 formed the principal fighting force on the famous raid at St. Nazaire, where it was to all intents and purposes destroyed.

This commando unit was re-formed under Lt. Col. Jack Churchill, M.C., and in 1943 arrived in the Mediterranean.

41st (Royal Marine) Commando

This commando unit was raised in the autumn of 1942 and landed in Sicily. In structure and organization it was broadly similar to an Army commando unit.

The Special Boat Section (SBS)

The Special Boat Section was comprised of special teams of highly trained troops charged with general reconnaissance and sabotage raids. They used the two-man Folbot canoe. The unit was first created in the summer of 1940.

A section comprised 47 men and contained four operating groups each of seven canoeists.

U.S. Rangers

1st Ranger Battalion and Darby's Rangers

When the United States entered World War II in 1941, President Roosevelt was determined to have commandolike formations in the United States Army and Marine Corps. In this he was undoubtedly influenced by Prime Minister Winston Churchill. The Rangers took their name from the force of the same name raised by Maj. Robert Rogers to fight the American Indians in the mid-eighteenth century.

In May 1942 an order was posted throughout the U.S. forces then stationed in Northern Ireland "for volunteers not adverse to dangerous action." Two thousand men answered that call, and from them five hundred were selected to join the first Ranger Course at the Commando School in Scotland. The 1st Ranger Battalion was formed on June 19, 1942.

The battalion, under Col. Bill Darby, fought in North Africa, where it was split in April 1943 to provide the cadres for the 3rd and 4th battalions. Other volunteers were recruited from U.S. forces in North Africa, and all three battalions landed in Sicily as special forces for Operation Husky.

These three battalions were roughly similar. Each had a complement of 419 (all ranks). A battalion was divided into six companies. A company had two platoons each of about 30 riflemen and a support section.

The U.S. 82nd Airborne Division

The 82nd was raised in March 1942 as the initial airborne division in the United States Army. The success of German parachute troops in the early campaigns of World War II proved a major incentive and stimulant for the Americans to create their own force. In June 1941 the United States Army created the 501st Parachute Battalion as an experimental force. By the time the Allies landed in Normandy three years later, the U.S. Army had five divisions of airborne troops.

The airborne division was an infantry division in miniature. It had a total strength of 8,505 men divided into three regiments. The 82nd Airborne had two regiments of parachute infantry and one glider infantry regiment. There were 1,985 men in a parachute infantry regiment (compared to 3,333 in a regiment of an infantry division), while the gliderborne infantry had 1,605 men to a regiment.

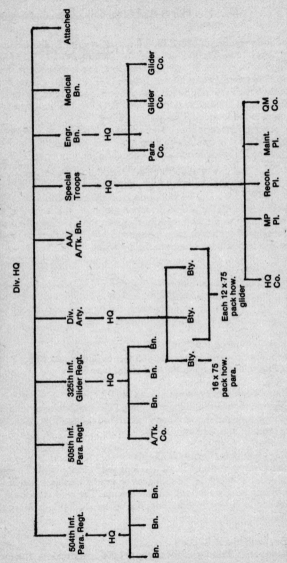

U.S. 82nd Airborne Division (1943)

Appendix F: Landing Craft

The Royal Navy

Landing Ship Tank (LST) Boxer Class

These were specially built British ships, with a displacement of nearly 6,000 tons. Their funnel was built on the starboard side, which gave them a very distinct and odd shape, but it allowed them to have a clear tank deck through to the stern. There were two decks, providing space for 25 tanks on the lower deck and 30 trucks on the top. A couple of hundred troops could also be carried. Despite their capacity, they were not a success. The complicated design did not lend itself to mass production, while their deeper draft meant that they could not beach in shallow water.

Landing Craft Tank (LCT)

The Landing Craft Tank Mark II displaced 460 tons fully loaded and could carry seven tanks. The Mark III craft displaced 640 tons and could take 11 tanks, but it was slower. Both versions carried a crew of 12 and had a defensive armament of two 2-pounder guns.

Landing Craft Infantry (Small) (LCI [S])

These were much smaller craft, 105 feet in length and with a 22-foot beam; they could carry up to 100 fully armed troops.

Landing Craft Vehicle (Personnel) (LCV [P])

A high-sided craft measuring 36½ feet by 11 feet, built to carry vehicles or troops from a mother ship to shore. The craft had a square bow that lowered onto a beach to form a ramp.

Landing Craft Gun (Large) (LCG [L])

These were converted LCTs, 192 feet long and 31 feet in beam. They were armed with two 4-inch or 4.7-inch guns of ancient vintage, together with some lighter weapons for anti-aircraft defense. The crew comprised two officers and 10 ratings, together with one officer and 22 Royal Marines to man the guns.

Landing Craft Tank (Rocket)

This was an LCT converted to carry up to 1,000 5-inch rockets. These were fitted in launch tubes on a superimposed deck. They were introduced to meet the requirement for devastating fire to hit the beach in the path of the first wave of assaulting infantry to demoralize the enemy or at least to make them keep their heads down while the troops landed. Conventional gunfire from supporting warships had to be stopped before the assault waves hit the beach to avoid causing casualties among the assault troops. The rocket craft were developed to fill this gap.

U.S. Navy

Many of the British craft were built in American yards to British Admiralty requirements, so the U.S. Navy in some instances by 1943 had broadly similar amphibious warfare craft to those used by the Royal Navy. The U.S. Navy, in turn, gave its requirements to the shipyards, and many of these designs were also adopted by the Royal Navy. As the war progressed there was a considerable proliferation of design and adaptation to even more functions, too numerous to mention here. The following, however, were at Salerno.

Landing Ship Tanks (LST)

By the war's end a total of 1,152 ships of this class had been constructed in American yards. They were built originally to a British specification for a craft capable of carrying tanks across the Atlantic from the United States to the beaches. The British craft were called Mark I, and the Mark II served in the U.S. Navy. In both navies they were more popularly known as Large Slow Targets; herein lay their weakness, for at a top speed of 9 knots they were dreadfully slow. For an amphibious—that is, beaching—operation, they displaced 2,366 tons fully loaded and could carry 20 tanks on the main deck. Lighter vehicles such as trucks and towed guns were stored on the weather deck. The early ships had an elevator to the tank deck, but later ships had a ramp, which allowed for a much faster rate of unloading via the bow doors and ramp.

Landing Craft Infantry (Large) (LCI [L])

The Landing Craft Infantry (Large) also started life as a British Admiralty requirement. Like the craft discussed above, it became the basis for numerous specialized amphibious warfare craft. The craft had a capacity of 300 troops, which disembarked from gangways rather than elaborate bow doors. The craft displaced 385 tons with a full load, carried a crew of 24 men, and had a top speed of 15 knots.

Landing Craft Personnel (Ramped) (LCP [R]);
Landing Craft Vehicle/Personnel (LCVP)

These were shipborne landing craft designed to operate from a mother ship and negotiate surf and beach. Again, there were numerous versions. The earlier versions were made of wood and could carry only troops. After

1942 a more sophisticated craft appeared, with an armored ramp and the capability to carry vehicles up to a light tank. So the standard landing craft (LCVP) appeared. The early work and designs were carried out by the Eureka (Higgins) Company of New Orleans, hence their nickname "Higgins boats." By the end of the war more than 22,000 of these craft were built. They could carry 3 tons of vehicles or 36 fully armed troops and had a three-man crew.

Bibliography

Bailey, D. C. *Engineers in the Italian Campaign: 1943–45.* London: Printing & Stationery Services, C.M.F., 1945.

Barker, A. J. *Waffen SS at War.* London: Ian Allan, 1982.

Blore, Trevor. *Commissioned Barges: The Story of the Landing Craft.* London: Hutchinson & Co., 1946.

Blumenson, Martin. *The Mediterranean Theater of Operation: Salerno to Cassino.* United States Army in World War II. Washington, D.C.: Office of the Chief of Military History, United States Army, 1969.

Butler, Rupert. *Hand of Steel.* London: Severn House Publishers Ltd., 1981.

Clark, Mark. *Calculated Risk.* London: George G. Harrap & Co., 1951.

Dorling, Taprell (Taffrail). *Western Mediterranean, 1942–1945.* London: Hodder & Stoughton, 1947.

Forty, George. *Fifth Army at War.* London: Ian Allan, 1980.

Hummer, John F. *An Infantryman's Journal.* Manassas, VA.: Ranger Associates, 1981.

Jackson. W. G. F. *The Battle for Italy.* London: William Clowes & Sons, 1965.

Lewin, Ronald. *Ultra Goes to War: The Secret Story.* London: Book Club Associates, by arrangement with Hutchinson & Co., 1978.

Liddell Hart, B. H. *History of the Second World War.* London: Cassell & Co., 1970.

Lindsay, Martin, and Johnston, M.E. *History of the 7th Armoured Division: June 1943–July 1945.* London: Printing & Stationery Service, British Army of the Rhine, 1945.

Lund, Paul, and Ludlam, Harry. *The War of the Landing Craft.* Slough, England: W. Foulsham & Co., 1976.

Molony, C. J. C., Flynn, F. C., Davies, H. L., and Gleave, T. P. *The Mediterranean and Middle East.* London: H. M. Stationery Office, 1973.

Nelson, Guy. *Thunderbird: A History of the 45th Infantry Division.* Oklahoma: Oklahoma Publishing Co., 1969.

Neville, Ralph. *Survey by Starlight.* London: Hodder & Stoughton, 1949.

Wagner, Robert L. *The Texas Army: A History of the 36th Division in the Italian Campaign.* Austin, TX: Robert L. Wagner, 1972.

Werthen, Wolfgang. *Geschichte der 16. Panzer-Division.* Bad Nauheim: Verlag Hans-Henning Podzum, 1958.

Index